The Finest in Fantasy from
JIM C. HINES:

*Coming soon from DAW

REVISIONARY

MAGIC EX LIBRIS:
BOOK FOUR

JIM C. HINES

DAW BOOKS, INC.

DONALD A. WOLLHEIM, FOUNDER

375 Hudson Street, New York, NY 10014

ELIZABETH R. WOLLHEIM
SHEILA E. GILBERT
PUBLISHERS

www.dawbooks.com

First paperback printing, February 2017
1 2 3 4 5 6 7 8 9

DAW TRADEMARK REGISTERED
U.S. PAT. AND TM. OFF. AND FOREIGN COUNTRIES
—MARCA REGISTRADA
HECHO EN U.S.A.

PRINTED IN THE U.S.A.

To Amy. I couldn't do this without your love, patience, and support.

Author's Note

Attention! When your name is called, please stand to receive your acknowledgment and gratitude. I've got a lot of people to thank, and there's a story to get to, so let's keep things moving.

- Sheila Gilbert—for editorial services above and beyond the call of duty, and for helping to make this and every other book I've written for DAW better.
- Joshua Bilmes and the JABberwocky crew—for meritorious agenting and helping me make a career from this writing thing.
- Gene Mollica—for bringing Isaac and Lena (and Smudge!) together on an amazing cover.
- Amy, Skylar, and Jamie—for surviving one of the most hazardous environments known to humanity: the home of a writer struggling to make a deadline. Thank you so much for putting up with me.
- Myke Cole—for teaching me how to break into

a Coast Guard ship. (Wait, that doesn't sound quite right . . .)
- Alistair Kimble and Diana Rowland—for offering help and advice with various law enforcement details.
- Kelly McCullough—in recognition of his repeated missions as Volunteer Beta Reader, First Class.
- Gabrielle Harbowy—for expertise and assistance in helping me (hopefully) not screw up my portrayal of Rabbi Miller and his synagogue.
- All my readers and fans—thank you more than I can say for your continued support. It means the world.

Before you start reading the story, I wanted to expand on that last bullet point. Three weeks after I turned this manuscript in to my editor, I walked out the door at my day job for good in order to focus on writing and my family.

I've dreamed about writing full-time for half my life. For a long time, I never believed it would happen. Thanks to the support of my wife and kids, as well as the enthusiasm of my readers, I have never been happier to be proven wrong.

I can't wait to begin this new chapter in my life, and I look forward to sharing new stories with you all for many years to come.

Jim C. Hines
August 2015

HEARING
OF THE
JOINT COMMITTEE ON MAGICAL SECURITY
BEFORE THE
U.S. HOUSE OF REPRESENTATIVES
AND THE
U.S. SENATE

CHAIRMAN: ALEXANDER KEELER

U.S. HOUSE OF REPRESENTATIVES,
COMMITTEE ON MAGICAL SECURITY

DEREK VAUGHN, LOUISIANA   SUSAN BROWN, FLORIDA
TAMMY HOEVE, MICHIGAN   ELIZABETH GARCIA, OKLAHOMA
TIMOTHY HOFFMAN, OHIO   JOHN SENN, NEVADA
ANTHONY HAYS, COLORADO

U.S. SENATE,
COMMITTEE ON MAGICAL SECURITY

ALEXANDER KEELER, ILLINOIS   MARY PAT CLARKE, MARYLAND
KENNETH TINDILL,   KENT CHILDRESS, OREGON
   RHODE ISLAND

TESTIMONY AND QUESTIONING OF WITNESS NUMBER 18: ISAAC VAINIO

The CHAIRMAN: This hearing will come to order.

It's my privilege and honor to welcome the members of the Joint Committee on Magical Security, as well as the witnesses who have been called to testify as we help to shape the future of this great nation during this time of worldwide turmoil and conflict.

Mister Vainio, thank you for taking time from your work with New Millennium to join us today.

Mr. VAINIO: Your invitation made it clear I didn't have a choice.

The CHAIRMAN: Do you affirm that the testimony you will give before this committee is the truth, the whole truth, and nothing but the truth?

Mr. VAINIO: Aren't I supposed to be sworn in on a Bible?

The CHAIRMAN: For security reasons, no books will be permitted in the chamber during your testimony.

Mr. VAINIO: Don't worry, I'm not about to try libriomancy with a Bible, or any other religious text. Gutenberg might have been able to handle that kind of intensity and belief, but—oh, sorry. Yes, I do so affirm.

The CHAIRMAN: Thank you. You may be seated. Mr. Vainio, would you please—what is that?

Mr. VAINIO: His name is Smudge. He's a fire-spider. He's perfectly safe as long as he's in his cage. Don't go poking your fingers in there, though. He's my service animal. My lawyer advised me this was permitted under disability law.

Mr. CHILDRESS: You have a service spider?

Mr. VAINIO: He senses danger. Like Spider-Man. Having him around helps me with some . . . anxiety issues. It's been a traumatic few years. I have a letter from my therapist if you'd like to see it.

The CHAIRMAN: That won't be necessary. For the record, please state your history and current role with the organization known as the Porters.

Mr. VAINIO: I've been a member of the Porters—intermittently—for about seven years, working to protect the world from magical threats. I've been a cataloguer, field agent, and researcher. Ten months back, I helped to found the New Millennium project in Nevada, where I currently work as Director of Research and Development.

The CHAIRMAN: Ten months. That would be shortly after you announced the existence of magic to the world.

Mr. VAINIO: Correct.

The CHAIRMAN: You constructed New Millennium in the United States. You yourself are an American citizen, born and raised in Michigan. Are you loyal to this country, Isaac?

Mr. VAINIO: How do you mean?

The CHAIRMAN: There are hundreds of you libriomancers scattered throughout the world, and thousands of other creatures. Vampires and merfolk and werewolves and bigfoots and Heaven knows what else. What assurances does this committee have that you won't turn against the United States of America? How do we prevent people like you from selling your abilities to the highest bidder?

Mr. VAINIO: Maybe you could start by not treating us all like potential criminals and terrorists.

Chapter 1

"You didn't think this would be easy, did you?"

"I knew there'd be conflict. Fear. And yah, violence too."

"You're mincing words. The world is headed for war."

"Humanity has been at war for more than ninety percent of recorded history."

"Not like this. What you've seen over this past year is only the beginning. The warm-up act, if you will."

"Says you. Not even magic can see the future."

"Not magic. Experience. I watched humanity for centuries. They fear you. Humanity works to control what it fears, and to destroy what it can't control."

"You're a pessimist. Also an asshole."

"Neither of those facts changes the truth. Your actions helped bring the world to this precipice."

"And yours didn't?"

"They did, but let's be pragmatic, shall we? Of the two of us, only one is in a position to affect current events."

"One of the advantages of not being dead, eh?"

YOU'D THINK MY TIME in the field fighting everything from possessed libriomancers to magically animated metal monstrosities to a thousand-year-old dead necromancer would have prepared me for an afternoon testifying before a pack of Washington politicians, but by the time I emerged, I longed for the simplicity of a rabid were-jaguar whose motivation was straightforward, foamy-jawed murder.

I ignored the reporters waiting in the hallway and made my way toward a wooden bench where Lena Greenwood sat whispering with Nicola Pallas and Nidhi Shah.

"Well?" asked Nicola.

"I understand now why a group of vultures is called a committee. I didn't turn any of them into roaches, if that's what you're asking." Though in several cases, it would have been an improvement. "Why drag us out here when they've already decided we're the biggest threat to world peace since the atom bomb?"

"To show that they can." Nidhi had been a psychiatrist for Die Zwelf Portenære, the magical—and until recently, secret—organization better known as the Porters, for as long as I'd known her. Of the four of us, she was the only one with no inherent magical abilities of her own. She got paid to keep the rest of us magic-users sane. Her job was far more challenging than my own.

She'd dressed conservatively for her testimony earlier today, in a simple black jacket and matching trousers, with a subdued blue shirt and a minimum of her usual jewelry. "And a few minds haven't yet clamped shut. Senator Clarke supports the Porters and our work. Representatives Hays and Hoffman have spoken out against the overreactions from Homeland Security and the FBI, and Secretary McGinley at DHS has said he'd be willing to sit down with representatives from different inhuman communities."

"Our job now is to demonstrate to the world that we're not a threat." A pair of white earbuds hung around Nicola's neck like a pair of anorexic pet snakes humming a faint jazz tune. She reached into her jacket pocket, and the music died a moment later. "Be thankful it isn't worse. The Chinese Central Military Commission charged Shin-Tsu Chang with treason last month."

Shin-Tsu Chang and Nicola Pallas were two of the six Council Masters who had taken over the Porters after the death of Johannes Gutenberg last year. I didn't know Nicola's Chinese counterpart well, but I'd read and respected most of his magical research from the past two decades. "Is he safe?"

"For now," said Nicola.

Lena took my hand as we walked down the hall. "Try to think positive. If they do decide to throw us all into internment camps, you could stop stressing about that IRS audit."

"What's the IRS going to do, take my house?" I snorted. My home had burned to the ground last year, and I'd been commuting between a little apartment in Michigan's Upper Peninsula and my quarters at New Millennium ever since.

"As of this morning, they're also suing the Porters for centuries of back taxes," said Nicola. "One of our lawyers will be in touch with you about your options."

"Just let me know how much pirate gold to pull out of *Treasure Island* to get them off my back."

"It's not that simple. Governments around the world are cracking down on magically created wealth. The Senate proposed legislation adding a minimum twenty-year sentence for magical counterfeiting. They're worried about inflation and consumer confidence."

"Maybe they should be worried about getting the riots under control," I said. "Not to mention beatings, lynchings, and, oh yeah, the fact that half the world is using magic as an excuse to rekindle old wars or start new ones."

"And the rest are preparing for the spillover," Lena commented. "Near the end of my testimony, Senator Tindill asked what it would take for me to enlist in the Marines. Russia instituted a mandatory draft for inhumans eight months ago."

"Along with seventeen other nations we know of." I shook my head. "Did Tindill explain how you're supposed to enlist if they refuse to recognize you as a citizen?"

Lena was my ... *girlfriend* wasn't strong enough, but the law wouldn't allow us to be husband and wife, on account of her not being human. Lover and partner were the two words that came closest, and also accommodated Nidhi as Lena's other romantic companion. We'd built our own little three-person family over the past few years, though the process hadn't always been smooth. What relationship was?

Lena had stopped hiding her dryad nature after the revelation of magic. Today that meant a crown of budding leaves growing directly from the skin of her brow and poking from beneath her thick hair. It gave her a playful, otherworldly air.

Short, plump, and dark-skinned, with endless energy and a gorgeous smile, Lena was one of only three nonhumans who had been allowed to testify. I wondered how fast they'd have crossed her off the witness list if they'd truly understood what she could do, but she didn't come across as the kind of person who could knock out a minotaur with one punch.

Whereas the rest of us had dressed up for the hearings, Lena wore old jeans and a black leather motorcycle jacket over a tight-fitting T-shirt of Groot and Treebeard.

The caption beneath the two walking trees read, GOT WOOD?

We stopped in the lobby to give Nicola time to compose herself. As frustrating as today had been for me, these hearings and the publicity had been harder on her. As the only member of the Porter Council residing in the U.S., she'd been under more scrutiny than any of us.

New strands of silver threaded through her black hair. Her eyes were shadowed, and from the way her jacket hung on her taut shoulders, she'd lost weight. Overuse of magic could do that, but so could good old-fashioned stress. She fidgeted with a pair of silver rings on her left hand as she looked through the glass doors at the waiting crowd.

"You know, when I was younger, I *wanted* to be famous," I said, taking in the number of microphones and cameras waiting outside to pounce. "I wanted to be an astronaut, the first man on Mars. Or a scientist who discovered time travel and lived in a mansion guarded by robot sharks. Or Batman."

"Your glasses would clash with the cape and cowl," said Lena. "Besides, I'm not sure you could pull off the spandex look. I like the tie, though." She leaned closer to read the silver type printed on the black silk. "Is that new?"

"I only owned one tie, and it had burn spots." I glared at Smudge, who was resting at the bottom of a small rectangular cage clipped to my belt. A layer of fiberglass shielded me from the fire-spider's heat, though if anything set him off, there was a decent chance he'd ignite the bottom of my suit coat.

I'd ordered this particular tie online. It was custom-made with the word OOOK printed in small, diagonal stripes, a tribute to Terry Pratchett and his orangutan librarian from the Discworld books. I loosened the knot and unbuttoned my collar. "Remind me to assign someone from my team to look into time travel. I want to take a trip to the seventeenth century."

"I'll bite," said Lena. "Why?"

"The necktie supposedly originated with King Louis XIV. Thanks to him, millions of us have to walk around with a literal noose around our necks. If I go back and kill Louis, I'll never have to wear these things again."

"I'm ready." Nicola wrapped her earbuds around a small MP3 player and tucked them away in an inside pocket. "Thank you."

I squared my shoulders, feeling vulnerable and exposed without my traditional assortment of books. Today's unpleasantness wasn't over yet. What I wouldn't have given for just one paperback and the chance to pull an invisibility cloak from its pages.

Lena flexed her hands. Tiny buds sprouted from her knuckles and fingers, a pattern of green dots that made me think of henna tattoos. "Remember, the press can smell fear."

I pulled a box of orange Tic Tacs from my pants pocket, popped one into my mouth, and gave another to Smudge to keep him occupied. "All right. Let's go be famous."

Young Isaac had dreamed of fame.

Young Isaac was an idiot.

The shouts hit us like ten-foot waves as we stepped through the doors. Wooden barriers edged the sidewalk. Eight uniformed D.C. police officers worked to keep the crowds back, guarding the narrow path to our waiting SUV.

The first person to spit at me was an older gentleman

to my left, wearing a charming SALEM HAD THE RIGHT IDEA T-shirt.

Part of me wanted to point out that, according to Porter records, none of the people executed in seventeenth century Salem were actual witches or magic-users. Another part simply wanted to turn him into a pickled egg.

The four of us fell into a diamond formation with Lena at the head, while Nidhi and I walked a step behind to either side, helping to create a buffer for Nicola.

A reporter shoved a microphone over the barriers. "What are the Porters doing about magic-using rebels and mercenaries destabilizing Africa?"

"I've got this one." I raised my voice. "Africa is a continent. A big one. You'll have to be more specific. Are you talking about the libriomancer helping the government fight Boko Haram in Nigeria? The rumors about rebels in Mali using blood magic? Or do you mean the three adze who've been acting as vigilantes, most recently in the Ivory Coast?"

The adze in question had become known as the Diamond Fireflies after disrupting a diamond mining operation in Sierra Leone and freeing twenty-six child slaves. The vampire-like trio had also brutally murdered three overseers before transforming back into their firefly forms to escape.

I kept walking before the reporter could respond.

"Ms. Pallas, why are the Porters unwilling to defend this country?" asked another reporter.

"The Porters are a worldwide organization, founded in Germany. We have more members from India and China than we do from the U.S." Nicola's voice cut through the shouts like a shark through water, a trick of her bardic magic. "The Porters will continue to work with the international community to protect this world from magical threats. We will *not* support legislation to allow the selective drafting of magically gifted individuals, or any other efforts to militarize our people and our work."

The anger wasn't all directed at us. I spotted one small group holding signs that said JUSTICE FOR MARCUS VISSER. Visser was a young werewolf from Maine who'd been shot and killed in early September by a pair of hunters, neither of whom had been charged with any crime.

"Isaac, will you autograph my library card?" A young woman shoved a laminated card and silver Sharpie at me. I scribbled my name and returned it. A camera flash went off directly in my face.

I tried to smile, remembering the photo *USA Today* had run of me in mid-sentence with my mouth open and eyes half-shut. I'd looked like a stoned Muppet. How the hell had I gone from a small-town Michigan librarian to having to worry about paparazzi in a single year?

"Isaac, please heal our son!"

I stopped walking. A small gap opened to my right. Reporters jockeyed for a better angle.

The plea had come from a couple with a boy no more than two years old, asleep in a stroller. The parents looked to be in their mid-to-late twenties, roughly the same age as me, but in that moment I felt decades older.

"Isaac . . ." Nicola pitched her voice only for me, but that single soft-spoken word carried both warning and a history of arguments stretching back almost a year. Arguments I had generally lost.

"What's wrong with him?" I asked, unable to stop myself.

"His name's Caleb," said the father. He had both hands on the wooden barrier. Two police officers moved closer, ready to intervene. "He has hypoplastic left heart syndrome. We've been waiting six months for a heart transplant."

"We saw a story about you on television," the mother added. "The Discovery Channel one. How your team had cured cancer and diabetes in rats, regrown missing limbs, and healed broken bones. When we heard you were gonna be here, we thought . . ."

She bit her lip and fell silent. The crowd grew still, waiting for my response. Several of the police officers were listening as well. I thought I read sympathy in the eyes of one. Fear in another. A third touched the handcuffs on his belt, a not-so-subtle warning.

"I'm sorry," I whispered, hating myself for how mechanical it sounded. "We're only beginning human trials this month, under strict supervision from the National Institutes of Health."

They'd come hoping I'd heal their son's heart, and instead it was like I'd reached into their chests and squeezed the life from theirs. The mother's eyes filled with tears. The father put a hand on the stroller as if to keep from falling.

I could do what they asked. I could cure an entire ward of children of every disease known to humanity. A battered copy of *The Lion, The Witch, and the Wardrobe* waited in the SUV, along with my other books. I could open the pages and pull the power of Lucy's healing cordial into the world. A single drop, and their son would be healthy.

At which point they would be taken into federal custody, their son quarantined, and I would be arrested for violating hastily passed and ill-informed laws against using magic to "physically or mentally influence, alter, or otherwise interfere with another person."

Most states had eventually added Good Samaritan clauses, allowing exceptions for emergencies that posed "immediate threat to life and limb," but those didn't apply here. I could use magic to push someone out of the path of oncoming traffic, but thanks to the fearmongering and ignorance of people like Senator Alexander Keeler, I couldn't help a child suffering from a potentially deadly heart defect.

If they'd come to me in private, that would be one thing. But not here. Not with so many cameras, so many people, so much raw emotion waiting for a spark.

The moment they publicly asked for my help, they guaranteed I couldn't give it. I'd bet anything that within the week, a doctor from the NIH would be stopping by their home, not to help, but to confirm their son was still critically ill. To make sure I hadn't helped him by using "untested and unproven magical techniques that have not been fully evaluated for safety and long-term side effects."

People had gone to jail over this fight. Libriomancers as well as doctors who'd been forced to watch patients die when the simplest magic could have saved them.

I was tempted to do the same. Save Caleb, and to hell with the consequences. Only those consequences wouldn't stop with me. My arrest would derail every research project under my supervision, including medical research. It would also provide more ammunition to people who saw us as rebellious outsiders, people who would take any excuse to dissolve the Porters and seize full control of New Millennium.

"I'm sorry," I said again. I pulled a business card from the inner pocket of my suit jacket. "Call this number. A woman named Kiyoko Itô handles all incoming calls. Tell her you spoke with me. I'll try to get Caleb into the next round of medical trials at New Millennium."

"Medical trials?" the father snapped. He pressed up against the barrier, his fists clenched. Lena shifted her balance, ready to take him down if needed. "You know how many damn medical trials we've been through in the past two years?"

I could guess. My niece had suffered through multiple surgeries and procedures for years, following an accident that took her leg. I'd seen how slow and tortuous the American medical system could be. I'd been fighting for the past year for the right to help her, and others like her.

The mother took my card. Tension tightened her face. Both of them were fighting tears.

Nidhi pressed past me. "Did someone tell you to come here and ask Isaac for help?" She kept her voice low enough most of the mics wouldn't pick it up.

The father nodded. "Yeah, that's right."

Someone had set this family up, using their pain and desperation to stage footage of a libriomancer heartlessly refusing to help a dying child.

Before Nidhi could press for information, another man shoved to the front of the crowd and shouted, "A year ago, you said magic was a gift! When you gonna share that gift with the rest of us?"

"What's New Millennium really doing behind those walls?" yelled another. "They get fat off of our taxes, then let us die!"

New Millennium had no federal or state funding, but this wasn't the time to point that out.

"We should go," said Nidhi. "Now."

Heat from the cage at my hip added to Nidhi's warning.

Lena took my hand and pulled me toward the car. Whatever else people might have said, whatever the crowd shouted after us, it all turned to gray noise.

We were halfway to our next meeting when my phone went off. Not the smartphone in my pocket; this was a private line, known to only a dozen people, three of whom were sitting in the SUV with me.

I clenched my jaw to activate the connection. "This is Isaac."

The communicator in my lower right molar would pick up subvocalizations almost as clearly as speech. But speaking out loud let the others know I was on a call. Also, I'd been told I sounded drunk when I subvocalized.

"She escaped again!"

I closed my eyes and gently thumped my head against the headrest. "Vince, it's been a long day. Wherever Kerling has gone, she always comes back eventually."

"She took half my bologna sandwich, scattered trash over my desk, stole my favorite pen, and left a feather on my printer. I think the feather was deliberate."

"I'm two thousand miles away, Vince. I can't help you find your missing crow."

Beside me, Lena chuckled.

"I wired the door of her cage yesterday afternoon. If she opened the latch from the inside, it should have set off an alarm."

Vince Hambrecht was an infectious storm of energy and enthusiasm, the first of three libriomancers I'd brought onto my research team at New Millennium. His indignation at being outsmarted by a crow was tempered by his obvious delight in their ongoing game. "Maybe you should have had Talulah or Charles double-check your setup."

"Everything was working just fine. The cameras went dead for three hours last night, right when she got out. That can't be coincidence, Isaac. And what about the time she stole the Escape key from my keyboard? She was taunting me."

At nineteen, Vince was the youngest researcher on site. He'd discovered his abilities a year and a half ago, and was still in that overenthusiastic phase where he was likely to blow himself up along with everyone within a hundred-foot radius if you didn't keep a close eye on him.

Some people would say we never really outgrew that phase.

The Porters had found him working part-time at the Toronto zoo to put himself through grad school. He'd begun college at the age of fourteen, finished his undergrad at seventeen, and had just completed his veterinary coursework when Nicola recommended I bring him onto my team at New Millennium.

He'd read *The Story of Doctor Dolittle* more than forty times, trying to gain the power to speak with animals. Failing that, he'd used various other books to try to get similar abilities. Last month, it was drinking dragon blood from Mercedes Lackey's *Tales of the Five Hundred Kingdoms* books.

Magic didn't make the animals particularly intelligent conversationalists, but for Vince, an endless litany of "Feed me!" and "Mine!" and "I'm horny!" never seemed to get old.

"I told you, I've checked Kerling twice. There's no trace of magic, aside from the healing and rejuvenation you did for her. I still think it's Talulah messing with you. Heaven save me from libriomancers with too much time on their hands. How's the rest of the menagerie doing?"

His voice went soft. *"Mortimer died yesterday afternoon."*

"I'm sorry, Vince. He was one of the rats, right?"

"He came in three months ago with a missing tail and infected teeth. Once we healed him, he bit you on the palm."

"Yah, I remember."

"Doctor Dickinson took the body. As far as I can tell, Mortimer died of old age, not anything we did. But those NIH ghouls insist on cutting him up for study. They'd

*better give the remains back this time. That rat deserves a
proper burial."*

"Email me a copy of Mortimer's file and your report,
and let me know if the NIH finds anything unusual."

"Will do, Boss."

"Don't call me that."

"Sorry." He hesitated, then blurted, *"While I've got
you on the line, could we talk about Project Crichton?"*

"We are *not* making baby dinosaurs, and that's final.
The last thing we need is a bunch of juvenile velociraptors eating one of our federal babysitters."

"They wouldn't get loose, Boss."

"Says the man who can't keep a little crow secure.
Have you even read *Jurassic Park*?" Our SUV pulled
into a parking lot on 8th Street. "I've got to go. Remind
me when I get back, and we can try putting a tracking
spell on Kerling."

Lena was smirking when I hung up. "Vince versus the
crow again? What is this, round eight?"

"At least." I climbed out of the SUV and grabbed my
old duster from the back, not caring how badly the battered leather jacket clashed with my suit and tie. The reassuring weight of the books in their various customized
pockets was more important than any fashion faux pas.

"When are you planning to tell him you uplifted Kerling's intelligence?" Lena asked.

"When it stops being funny."

"You shouldn't interfere with New Millennium research projects," said Nicola.

"I'm not. I've been keeping detailed notes on Kerling's progress. And Vince's." I raised my hands as if to
ward off an assault. "The particular magic I used on Kerling could have all kinds of implications for healing brain
damage and mental incapacity, not to mention boosting
intelligence in general. It's a legit project, I promise."

Lena smiled. "You light up when you talk about that place. It's a shame you couldn't get them to build it in the U.P."

Michigan's Upper Peninsula would have been an ideal location, with plenty of open land away from populated areas. We also had a healthy werewolf pack, and I'd hoped we could hire some of them for security and other positions. I'd gone to Lansing to push the potential job creation and publicity benefits, but Governor Sullivan was firmly in the anti-magic camp, as was much of the state legislature. I'd hardly left the capitol building before they were passing bills prohibiting magical research in Michigan.

"There's so much we could learn, so much to do. Medicine, engineering, archaeology, astronomy . . . I'm close to getting a meeting with NASA about a permanent magical portal to the moon!"

She laughed and kissed me. "Almost makes the politics worth it."

The politics were the second worst part of my job, right below having to leave Lena for weeks at a time. She'd been out to visit, but Lena was a dryad. Her oak tree was still rooted in Michigan, as was her other lover. She carried part of that tree within herself, allowing her greater freedom, but she still had to return home at least once a week.

"Before you go to the moon, how about one of those portals between Vegas and Copper River, hm?"

"It's at the top of my To Do List," I promised.

She laughed again—I loved that sound—and took my hand as we walked into the restaurant. Tension knotted my muscles like Christmas lights after a year in storage, but being with Lena helped. She had a gift for finding joy and beauty, and for helping others to remember those things.

The Square Pie Pizzeria was one of the more upscale

D.C. restaurants, complete with candles and white table-cloths and wait staff in black bow ties. More importantly, they provided privacy and damn good pizza. Lena, Nidhi, and I had come here at least once on each of our too-frequent trips. Nicola had reserved a small, private room near the back.

Representative Derek Vaughn looked to have arrived only moments before. He finished removing his jacket, then waited politely while the rest of us took our seats. Once the waiter jotted down our drink orders and left, shutting the door behind him, Vaughn leaned over to kiss Nicola hello.

"Hell of a day." Weariness dulled his vote-winning smile. "I thought that hearing would never end." Thanks to his New Orleans accent, it came out *Ah thought dat hearin' would nevuh end.*

As I understood it, he and Nicola had met after a committee hearing in early August. A few weeks later, he'd taken her to one of the best jazz bars in D.C. It was love at first song. How he and Nicola had kept their relationship a secret from the media and the Joint Magical Committee these past two months was a whole other kind of magic.

I unclipped Smudge's cage and set it on the table between Vaughn and myself. Smudge perked up and poked his forelegs through the bar. He knew this place, and had developed an appetite for anchovies.

"What do you think?" Nicola asked, without preamble.

Vaughn sipped his water before answering. He was an intelligent, quick-witted man who'd started out as a public defender. His ruffled graying hair and gentle blue eyes, framed by laugh lines and silver-rimmed glasses, tended to make people underestimate him. "Hard to say. Homeland Security is pushing hard to get more of you

Porters on the payroll. People are scared, Nic. They want guarantees that some voodoo curse won't turn New York City into a graveyard, or a vampire won't mind-rape the president into launching nukes at his own country."

"Voodoo is a religion, not a school of magic," I pointed out. Though technically, enough authors had written about voodoo dolls to make them a viable tool for libriomancers to pull out of books.

"I know that, boy." Vaughn took another drink. "Point is, they think you're holding back. A lot of folks want all of you Porters rounded up, along with the vampires, werewolves, and the rest. Dryads, too, I'm afraid."

Lena smiled. "They're welcome to try."

"I haven't seen things this tense since the Cold War," he went on. "Folks think World War III is coming, and when it arrives, it's gonna fly in on broomsticks, waving wands and massacring muggles."

"The world's doing the best it can to make it happen," I snapped. "North Korea is mandating everyone read one government-approved novel each month, trying to build up a library of magical weapons. Here in the States, Senator Keeler wants us to help him turn hundreds of soldiers into vampires. China detonated a fucking nuke trying to get to the Students of Bi Sheng."

Vaughn's eyes narrowed. "How do you know that?"

"Because I have friends there." The Students of Bi Sheng were a small group of survivors from five hundred years ago, practitioners of an alternate form of libriomancy. They'd fought a magical war once before, and were determined to stay out of world events. There were days I'd been tempted to join them.

"Best not mention that to the committee," said Vaughn. "Last I checked, the Porters weren't exactly innocent in this whole mess. Look at all those casualties from your battle in Copper River. What about the victims of rogue weres and vamps and all the rest? Like that fellow you told me about, the one in the U.P. who fed on Boy Scouts?"

"He hasn't touched a child since the day I put a bomb in his skull. I'm not saying we ignore killers, but—"

"Did you hear what you just said, Isaac?" Derek let out a long, slow breath that smelled faintly of pipe smoke. "You put a bomb in that fellow's head. You Porters were judges and executioners, and people know it. Fact is, you *are* dangerous."

"Of course we're dangerous. So are you. So is every paranoid, trigger-happy idiot ordering vampire-hunting kits off eBay or melting antique candlesticks to make silver bullets. You know what's more dangerous? Entire nations doing the same damn thing." I raised a hand before he could argue. "You're right, the Porters screwed up sometimes. I screwed up. I also saved a lot of lives, and we could save a hell of a lot more if people would just let us. There are kids dying out there, Derek. People who need our help. We can't fix everything, but we can do so much better than we are right now, and all anyone wants to do is talk about preemptive magical strikes and how many people they can kill with the next libriomantic superweapon."

"What do you suggest?" he asked. "Should we abandon national defense, let you run off to produce your magical rainbows and unicorns, and wait for some genie from the Middle East to wish the American people into turnips?"

"That's not how genies work, you ignorant—"

"Isaac." Nidhi spoke quietly, making me realize how loud I was getting.

I sat back, pulled off my glasses, and rubbed my eyes. "I'm sorry. I know you're trying to navigate this mess the best you can, but it's not enough."

"You think I don't know that? You get to go home to Vegas to play in your lab. I have to jump back into that snake pit every day." He sounded as tired as I felt. "How's Lex doing?"

Vaughn had an excellent memory for people, and never failed to ask about my niece. "She's excited. Nervous, too, but mostly impatient to be done. I'll be flying back to Vegas later tonight so I can be there for her procedure."

"We need more success stories like hers," said Vaughn. "Show the world how magic restored a little girl's leg."

"We could have showed the world a year ago," I pointed out.

"Isaac, you know this has to be done by the book. If there's the slightest possibility of things going wrong, you could do more harm than good."

"Tell that to Lex and her parents."

Before he could answer, Nicola's cellphone buzzed on the table, playing the opening bars of a Harry Connick Jr. song.

"Excuse me." She picked up the phone and turned away.

Vaughn's phone went off a moment later. My hands clenched. I hoped it was coincidence, but I wasn't surprised when my own communicator chimed to signal an incoming call.

"This is Isaac. What happened?"

"It's Talulah. New Millennium is on lockdown. Have you seen the news?"

"Not yet." I looked around the table. Nicola was a statue, sitting with deliberate stillness as she listened. Vaughn's face had gone red, and he was swearing under his breath.

"They're reporting multiple attacks by inhuman terrorists."

"How many, and where?" I asked.

"At least four." Talulah hesitated. *"Including one in Lansing. Michigan's governor is in critical condition. Similar attacks were launched simultaneously in California, Oklahoma, and New York."*

I felt like I'd swallowed a twenty-ounce bottle of battery acid. I stood and grabbed Smudge's cage, clipping it to my belt with an aluminum carabineer.

Nicola covered her phone. "Go. Help the wounded, and assist the police."

"Isaac," said Vaughn. "Make yourself visible."

I grimaced. In other words, play nice for the cameras and put on a good public relations face for the Porters. I hated this part of my job, but he was right. Especially if these attacks had been carried out by nonhumans.

"How long will it take you to get to Michigan?" asked Nicola.

"Five minutes." I donned my jacket and hurried toward the door, Lena and Nidhi close behind.

No matter how quickly we arrived, no matter how much we helped, part of me was starting to believe it would never be enough.

From: donotreply@porterbot.net
To: ivainio@newmillennium.org
Subject: Catalog Reservations

Hello Isaac,

This is an automated reminder from the Porter Databots.

We noticed you have an unusually large number of titles reserved in the Porter catalog. While we appreciate your diligence in helping to minimize overuse and magical charring, we wonder if maybe you've forgotten to release some of those 184 books back into circulation for use by other Porter researchers and field agents.

The ten books that have been reserved the longest are listed below. Please log into the Porter catalog to see the full list and release any books you're no longer using.

If you have a legitimate ongoing need for these books, please contact Porter librarian Zsuzsanna Varga.

Thanks!

Titles Checked out by Isaac Vainio, User #M3714:

1. Lewis, C. S. *The Lion, The Witch, and the Wardrobe*.

2. L'Engle, Madeline. *A Wrinkle in Time*.

3. Pierce, Tamora. *In the Hand of the Goddess*.

4. Carroll, Lewis. *Through the Looking Glass*.

5. Goodkind, Terry. *Debt of Bones*.

6. Gabaldon, Diana. *Outlander*.

7. Homer. *The Odyssey*.

8. Gaiman, Neil. *Neverwhere*.

9. Donaldson, Stephen. *The Mirror of Her Dreams*.

10. Valente, Catherynne. *Palimpsest*.

Click here to log into our catalog and review the full list

Chapter 2

"I thought you'd made plans for all this."

"There have always been contingency plans for the revelation of magic, as well as for my own death."

"What happened? Did you forget to share those plans with anyone else?"

"To paraphrase Von Moltke, no plan survives beyond the first encounter with the enemy. I left the Porters with certain goals and strategies. Proper disposal of my body, for one. Delegation of power to a small group, no more than six. The importance of international neutrality. The safety and security of our own people. Most importantly, a focus on the long term that should help us all survive the short-term chaos and upheaval."

"Define 'short-term.' "

"Historically speaking? Years. Decades, most likely."

"How many people are going to lose their lives as a result of that chaos?"

"As you've said, magic can't predict the future."

"It can damn well guess."

"By my estimate, given human nature? Millions."

THE SERVICE THE PORTERS WERE USING for transportation and security in D.C. wasn't scheduled to pick us up for at least another hour, so Lena hailed us a cab while I took a copy of Neil Gaiman's *Neverwhere* from my jacket.

"Where to?" asked the driver, an older woman in a yellow headscarf with the gruff voice of a longtime smoker.

I scooted into the back and handed her a ten. "Just keep it parked here for a minute, eh?"

"You waiting for someone?"

"Not exactly."

Lena sat down beside me. "Shortcut?"

"I hope so." *Neverwhere* was one of the books I'd been rereading as part of my own research. I might not be able to create a stable portal from Vegas to the U.P. yet, but I was getting closer, and I'd learned a few tricks in the process.

I'd also accidentally sent a pair of lab rats to either Alpha Centauri or possibly a wardrobe in London. I doubted Vince would ever forgive me for that one.

I turned to a page marked with a blue Post-it note. I could recite the scene from memory, but it was simpler to touch the book directly, to reread and submerge myself in the story. Every page had its own texture, as unique as a fingerprint. I could feel the individual letters and the ink pressed into the paper, like a blind man reading embossed print in the days before Braille.

Gaiman had created a character named Door. I'd experimented with her magic back at the lab. This would be my first time using it in the field.

My fingertips sank through the paper, touching the

world so many of Gaiman's readers had visualized and dreamed about. While that world was fictional, the belief and imagination of his readers was quite real. That was where the story's true magic came from, with the physical book serving as a magnet and anchor for that cumulative belief.

The driver twisted around. "What are you doing back there?"

"We'll be on our way in a moment," said Nidhi.

Libriomancy in its most common form allowed us to grasp an object from a story and pull it into the world, transforming belief and potential magical energy into physical reality. Assuming said object would fit through the pages.

If that was 101-level libriomancy, what I'd been working on for the past year was post-graduate work.

My vision blurred, like I'd been reading too long in poor light. My mother used to tell me I'd ruin my eyes that way. As it turned out, she hadn't been entirely wrong.

I yanked off my glasses and slipped them into my shirt pocket. The spots of shadow floating around the edges of my vision grew worse, but the book's text sharpened. The damage to my eyes was a result of magical charring, and behaved similarly to early cataracts. Glasses helped me to compensate, but paradoxically made it harder for me to truly see magic.

I'd tried to heal the damage, but the scars weren't physical. Magic simply flowed around the charring, like a stream past rocks.

I reached deeper into the book. My hand touched Door's back. Rather, the composite imagination of Door's back. I wasn't truly touching the outline of her shoulder blades, or feeling the faint beating of her heart. I was touching readers' belief. Belief in the character, and belief in her particular ability.

"Our driver's getting twitchy," Lena commented.

"I'm almost done." From here, I could have plucked an object from Door's hand and created it in my own. Instead of pulling anything physical from the page, I grasped Door's ability and drew it into my body. Lines of text crept up my skin. In essence, I was making myself an extension of the book.

This kind of libriomancy carried two significant risks. For one thing, the magic came from a fictional universe. Any portal I created would want to connect to that non-existent universe. If I screwed up, we'd be lucky to find ourselves lost in the sewers of London. If we were un-lucky, the magic would try to send us into Gaiman's fic-tionalized London.

Since that world didn't exist, it would just kill us in-stead.

Then there was the danger of letting a book get into your head. As the story flowed through my blood, I be-gan to hear the characters calling me. When I looked around, it was as though the fictional world had been overlaid with this one. I saw our driver staring at my truncated arm, watched her mouth move, but I heard the murmurs of the London crowd, saw tunnels and subway lines passing through the cab, smelled the damp fog . . .

"Isaac?" Lena touched my neck, helping ground me in the real world.

I placed my other hand on the inside of the cab's door and pushed the story through me, into the metal and plastic of the car. The words were like a windstorm trying to escape, trying to create a gateway back to their book.

I forced them instead to a place I knew well enough to anchor my thoughts against the fragments of *Never-where* swirling around me like a maelstrom. "It's like herding cats across a river."

"I can call Nicola if you need help," said Nidhi.

"No, I've got it. Probably." I pushed the last of the text into place and opened the door. When I climbed out, I emerged from the back of a pizza delivery car parked on the side of a very different road.

Had Gutenberg been alive, I'm sure he would have cast this spell without a second thought, putting us down on the front steps of the capitol building. Given another five hundred years of practice, I liked to think I'd have done the same.

"What the hell are you doing?" The shout came from a young woman across the road, carrying an empty red delivery bag. "Get out of my car!"

"Sorry!" I stumbled away from the car, shoved *Neverwhere* into my jacket pocket, and checked on Smudge. He didn't look happy, but he wasn't about to set anything on fire either, which meant the driver probably wasn't going to pull a gun and shoot me just yet. I glanced around. I'd put us down in East Lansing, on the campus of Michigan State University. "Technically, we weren't in your car. We just—"

"What do you mean 'we'?" She hurried across the road and pushed past me to check the back seat, which was empty. She tossed the delivery bag into the back, aimed her cellphone at my face, and snapped a picture before dialing what I assumed was the police. "What did you take, asshole?"

"Nothing," said Lena as she emerged from the car.

The poor woman jumped so hard she dropped her phone. Lena caught it before it hit the pavement.

I flexed my hand. The fingertips were a bit numb, but I saw no sign of charring. I checked the magnetic sign on the top of the car. "Georgio's, eh? I used to eat there all the time when I was an undergrad." I pulled out my wallet and handed her a twenty. "I'm sorry we scared you. Consider this part of your tip for the night?"

She stared at me, then at the car, where Nidhi now appeared to be climbing out of nothingness. "That's . . . that's magic."

"Pretty cool, isn't it? If I had more time, I'd tell you how it worked."

"He would," Lena said. "Even if you asked him to stop."

I pointed to the three-story brick building across the street. "That's Mason-Abbot Hall, which puts us on the northeast corner of campus, about ten miles from Lansing." I turned back to the delivery driver. "How'd you like to make a bigger tip?"

"If traffic doesn't pick up soon, I'm going to fly the rest of the way," I muttered.

"You can do that?" Our impromptu driver's name was Callie, a second-year communications major who had agreed to drive us into Lansing only after getting a selfie with Lena, and another with Smudge.

"I can. The FAA gets cranky about it, though."

Callie swerved into another lane, then slammed the brakes. "Shit. Sorry. I knew they'd closed 496, but it looks like they've blocked off Saginaw, too. I'll get you as close as I can. Is it true this was a terrorist attack?"

"We don't know yet," said Nidhi.

Lena was studying her hands. "I should get rid of these," she said, touching the buds on her knuckles. "It's probably safer for everyone if I pass for human."

I wanted to argue, to tell her to be herself. I looked at Nidhi and saw the same conflict in her eyes. If the attackers weren't human, advertising Lena's nature could make her the target of angry crowds or overzealous law enforcement. Neither of us spoke as the green buds slowly absorbed back into Lena's skin.

Callie broke the silence. "There was a campus march for Marcus Visser last week. A real werewolf came to speak. It was pretty intense. The cops showed up at the end. Six people got pepper sprayed." She turned north and snuck a block closer before hitting another line of stalled traffic. "I think this is as close as I can get you."

"It's close enough." I handed her another forty bucks and climbed out of the car. I could see the capitol dome a short distance away, past bumper-to-bumper traffic. "Thank you."

She rolled down her window. "Hey, that libriomancy stuff. Can anyone learn it? I was thinking of changing majors."

"Sorry. It doesn't work that way."

The noise hit hard: horns blaring uselessly in the streets, sirens wailing, shouts and chants in the distance. I heard dogs barking as well, but I couldn't tell if they were pets howling at the noise or police dogs trying to track the perpetrators.

Then there were the people making their way toward the capitol. Many had similar expressions of shock, confusion, and grief. Others had skipped past grief to rage. Even if I hadn't known where I was going, the flow would have carried us to the site of the attack.

A uniformed police officer stood in the intersection up ahead, diverting traffic. Another officer on horseback trotted up the opposite side of the road. Two helicopters circled overhead. From what I could see, one was a news chopper, while its louder big brother looked military.

Lena took the lead, being the best equipped to deal with physical confrontations. Nidhi and I followed close behind, letting Lena serve as our icebreaker. I split my attention between Smudge and the crowd, watching for potential magical threats. Smudge seemed more interested in the bugs swarming about the street lamps.

Yellow barricades blocked the streets at Ottawa and Capitol. Beyond those barriers, ambulances and police cars lined the roads. The news vans had parked farther off. It looked like every camera crew in the state was pressed up against the yellow tape surrounding the capitol building, along with reporters from some of the national outlets.

The tension after the hearing in D.C. had been bad, but at least that had been in daylight, with a short, clear path to our escape.

The emotion here was colder and less stable. Officers in riot gear were doing their best to keep things under control. I found myself holding my breath, like I was afraid of setting off an explosion. Sweat trickled and tickled down my back.

All reporters were being kept back with the rest of the crowd. Some called out to officers and detectives for statements, while others interviewed random bystanders. I eavesdropped long enough to overhear one reporter say something about werewolves and an unknown number of casualties. I turned up the collar of my duster and approached the nearest uniformed officer, keeping my hands in full view.

"Sir, you need to stay back." This was a man clearly practiced in using his voice as a tool to keep people in line, and his tone suggested he was equally prepared to use other tools if his words failed to do the trick.

I glanced back to make sure none of the reporters were paying attention. The last thing I wanted was to get mobbed by news crews looking for a sound bite. "My name is Isaac Vainio. I'm a libriomancer, one of the directors for New Millennium and a member of the Porters. We can help."

He looked the three of us over. "Nobody gets across that line. Especially magic-using types."

I understood his paranoia, even as frustration tightened already-tense muscles in my neck and jaw. For all
he knew, we were here to finish the job the werewolves
had begun.

I looked past him to the two ambulances parked on
the sidewalk. Their crews were checking over a small
group of people with blood on their clothes. A short distance beyond was a white FBI truck, possibly a command vehicle. I counted three other vans, another FBI
truck, and six state and Lansing police cars.

I glanced at his badge. "I know your people and the
EMTs are doing everything they can, Officer Blackwell.
But if it's true werewolves did this, then their victims
could have been infected, and we have a very limited
window to help them. I'm the only person within a hundred miles who can guarantee those people remain human."

He jerked his chin at Nidhi and Lena. "They're libriomancers too?"

"I'm Doctor Shah," said Nidhi. "I've been with the
Porters for more than fifteen years." She touched Lena's
arm. "Ms. Greenwood is my assistant."

"Depending on what species of werewolf did this, the
survivors could be a danger to your officers," I pressed.
"I've consulted with the State Police in the past. They
can vouch for me."

"Don't move." He stepped back and spoke to someone on his shoulder-mounted radio, never taking his attention off us. I couldn't make out the response, but a
moment later he raised the police tape and beckoned us
through. He patted each of us down, a process that took
much longer with me, given the number of books tucked
into my duster pockets. By the time he finished, two
more people had joined us.

"Identification." The speaker was a middle-aged

woman in a state police uniform and vest, with the kind of focus and determination that made me think she could work this case for thirty-six hours straight on nothing but coffee and attitude.

Her companion was an older man with the face of a graying bulldog and an FBI badge clipped to his belt. Between the street lamps and various floodlights, I was able to make out that his name was Steinkamp, and he was a Special Agent from the Magical Crimes Unit in the Detroit Field Office.

Nidhi and I produced our driver's licenses. The police officer inspected them both, handed them back, and looked expectantly at Lena.

"I don't have one." Lena held out one hand and grew a single green bud from the palm of her hand. "Michigan's DMV refuses to grant a license or state ID to non-humans."

"She stays here," said Steinkamp. "We've had too many people contaminating the scene as it is."

"It's all right," Lena said, before Nidhi or I could argue.

"Sign here." The officer, whose badge read ROWLAND, passed me a clipboard. I jotted down my name, title, organization, and the date and time, then handed it to Nidhi to do the same. "You touch *nothing* unless absolutely necessary. Blackwell's going to be your police escort. You obey his instructions at all times, got it?"

I nodded, trying not to let my impatience show. "How did the werewolves get inside?"

Steinkamp scowled. "There was a fucking Boy Scout tour scheduled for six o'clock. Normally tours end at four, but the scout leader has a friend in the legislature. The werewolves waltzed right in with them."

"Are the kids all right?" asked Nidhi.

"Define all right," said Rowland. "They're terrified

enough they'll be pissing their beds for a month, but physically they're fine."

"Four people have been taken to Sparrow Hospital," said Steinkamp. "The rest of the wounded are being checked over by the EMTs. We've got agents interviewing witnesses across the street, several of whom have minor cuts and scrapes."

"I can call Nicola and ask her to send a Porter to the hospital," said Nidhi.

"The Evidence Response Team is inside with the coroner," Steinkamp continued in a softer voice. "They haven't taken the bodies away. Is there anything you can do . . ."

"Raising the dead has been tried before. It wasn't pretty."

Rowland clucked her tongue. "I guess there are limits to magic after all."

"You have no idea."

Agent Steinkamp was staring at me like I was a book he couldn't quite read. "You're the guy who wrote that letter a year ago. I've seen your file."

"You have a file on me?" I should have been annoyed, but it was actually kind of cool. I'd have to submit a Freedom of Information Act when I got home to see if I could get a copy.

"Mister Vainio, have you ever heard of an organization called Vanguard?"

I shook my head and glanced at Nidhi, who did the same.

He handed me a business card. "Give me a call if that changes, all right?"

"Enough chatter," said Rowland. "Get moving. Blackwell, make sure they sign out with me before they leave."

Blackwell walked us toward the ambulances. The vehicles provided some degree of privacy, but plenty of gawkers strained to see what was happening. One of the EMTs moved to intercept us.

"They're here to help," said Blackwell. "He's one of those book wizards."

I moved toward a woman with a blanket around her shoulders. Her knee and thigh were bandaged, and blood matted her scalp, but none of her injuries looked severe. I tugged a small, mostly empty crystal vial from a heavily padded pocket inside my jacket. "My name's Isaac. Have you ever read *The Lion, The Witch, and The Wardrobe*?"

She nodded. "My niece loves those movies."

"This is from the book. It's the healing cordial Lucy was given by Father Christmas. A single drop will heal you inside and out."

"You can't use magic on her," said the EMT.

"Except in life-or-death situations," I snapped. "This woman was mauled by a werewolf. Do you have anything in your ambulance that will stave off lycanthropy?"

The woman's face went pale. Nidhi shot me a *think-before-you-speak* look, then took the woman's hand and began talking in a low, calm voice. "You're going to be fine. What's your name?"

"Margaret. Margaret Edwards."

I peered over the top of my glasses, searching for magical residue in her bloodstream. She was clean. No trace of lycanthropy or other magical infection, but I saw no need to mention that until after I healed her injuries. I'd be damned if I was going to let anyone else suffer tonight if I could help it. "Do me a favor, Margaret, and stick out your tongue?"

She did so, and I used a dropper to transfer a tiny bead of Lucy's potion onto her tongue. She swallowed, pain or shock preventing her from asking questions. Within seconds, her body started to relax. She poked cautiously at her knee. "That's it? I'm . . . better?"

"One hundred percent human," I said. "Not a trace of werewolf in you."

She tentatively tested her bandaged leg. "Thank you."

The EMT looked from me to Margaret and back. "I'm convinced. Bring that bottle and come with me."

Next up was a young man on a stretcher, covered in blood-soaked bandages and shallow bite marks. The medic working on him shouted, "I can't get the bites to clot up."

I stepped past another man who lay shivering beneath several blankets. His sleeves were torn and his face bloody, but he appeared otherwise undamaged. "You'll want to get that one in handcuffs until I can get to him."

"Why?" asked Blackwell.

"Trust me." I stopped beside the medic and removed my glasses. My brain automatically began cataloging the different species of werewolf that might have inflicted this kind of damage, studying the height and angle of the bites, the size of the jaws, the depth of the claw marks . . .

I could only make out scraps of magical text: remnants of the werewolf's curse swimming through the injuries, preventing the body from healing itself. I reached for the worst of the bites, a deep wound on the forearm. "How many werewolves were there?"

"I'm not sure. I didn't know what was happening until one of the kids screamed. I saw a woman fall, and then something hit me from the side."

Someone shoved a pair of gloves at me. I ignored them and focused on the text, letting the rest of the world blur away.

"This is going to feel weird." I pressed my fingers into the wound like it was a book.

He cried out, more in shock than pain. I wasn't physically reaching into muscle and bone, any more than I tore the paper pages when I performed libriomancy. I felt Nidhi step in beside me, heard her whispering to the EMT and the patient both.

Heat spread up my arm. I pulled the words and their magic into my own flesh, then dissolved them into nothingness.

"Did the werewolves say anything?" I asked, my voice low.

He shook his head.

"You're going to be fine." I grabbed the healing cordial and gave him a drop to cure the physical wounds. "If you were hoping for cool scars to show off after your fight with the werewolves, I'm afraid I've got bad news."

"What do you mean, bad news?" He stared at his now-undamaged arm and wiped the blood away. *"Oh!"*

I was already moving back to the fellow on the ground. He was going to be harder to save. This had to be another of the chaperones for the Boy Scout tour. He was dressed too casually to be a government employee, in old jeans and an oversized pink hoodie. His scalp was a mess of matted blood and hair, but the skin was smooth and undamaged. Officer Blackwell had cuffed his hands behind his back.

"What's happening to me?" Tears cut through the blood on the man's face.

"Lycanthropy—werewolfism—is contagious." I sat in front of him, out of arm's reach. I didn't think he could snap those cuffs, but I wasn't positive. A low ripple of flame passed over Smudge. I shoved my coat back to keep it clear of his cage. "Some people catch it by accident after reading a book. It's rare, but someone with magical talent who doesn't know what they're doing can reach into the book and draw the infection into themselves without realizing it. That's how most strains of lycanthropy and vampirism came into existence. More often, it's spread by bites."

"You mean like rabies?" He held up his arms. "The doctor said the blood wasn't mine. She couldn't find any puncture wounds. She said I was just in shock."

"You probably are." I studied the infection as I talked. The text had made its way through his body, binding to blood and bones. It was one thing to counter a surface-level infection, to pull scraps of magic from an open wound. Once that magic bound itself to the victim, most strains were impossible to cure. Including this one, from the look of it.

"I was chaperoning my son's field trip." His voice cracked. "I haven't seen Jaiden since the attack."

"The children are all fine," said Nidhi. "The attackers weren't interested in hurting them."

"I've explained that to him three times," murmured one of the medics. "He keeps forgetting."

Medical training, both for nonhuman patients and for supernatural injuries, was another area where New Millennium should have been doing more. I understood the need for caution with trials and research, but the average medical professional knew next to nothing about magic. How could they be expected to do their jobs in a situation like this?

"You'll be back with Jaiden soon," I said. "What's your name?"

"Will. Are you a doctor?"

"Better. I'm a librarian." The magic was strongest near his throat. I touched my fingertips to the skin of his neck. His pulse was far too rapid. I tried reaching for the text as I'd done with the other victim. When I touched the magic, he jerked and stiffened like I'd jolted him with an electric shock. Both the EMT and Officer Blackwell moved in to catch him by the arms.

"What did you do?" snapped the EMT.

"Just getting a sense of what did this." The text of his curse was different from what I'd read on the previous patient. That confirmed at least two werewolves, then. "What did the werewolves look like?"

"You're supposed to be healing them, not interrogating them," snapped Blackwell.

"If I have a better idea what kind of werewolf did this, it'll be a lot easier to heal him."

"Tall and lean," said Will. "Like a man, but with a wolf's face, covered in black fur. I thought he was wearing a mask at first, like this was a gag or something. He was wearing sweatpants and a Red Wings jersey. Oh, and blue Crocs."

"Loose-fitting clothes. He'd planned on changing forms." Not all werewolves could change at will. The fact that this one had an intermediate, more-or-less humanoid form narrowed things down as well.

I grabbed a *Star Trek* novel from my jacket. "Do you read science fiction, Will?"

He shook his head.

"That's too bad. Because this is going to be *really* cool."

His eyes went round as my fingers disappeared into the book.

"What else can you tell us about the attack?" I asked.

"I heard they killed two guards," Will said numbly. "Someone said the governor and attorney general were both in the building. There was so much screaming . . ."

Governor Sullivan and Attorney General Duncan were strong proponents for anti-magic legislation. If this attack was about them, it meant someone had known they'd be here this evening. Either by hacking into their schedules, or because someone on the inside passed the information along. Possibly the same someone who'd arranged this after-hours tour for the Boy Scouts?

I focused on the book, drawing the magic of a particular scene into myself and once again walking the line between fiction and reality as I worked to bend the story's magic to my particular needs.

A few years back, I'd have said what I was hoping to do was impossible, but recent crises and conflicts had shown how little we truly knew about the rules and limitations of libriomancy, and of magic in general. If things continued at this pace, we could be looking at a magical revolution in more than one sense of the word.

"Is there anything more we should know?" I asked.

"Last warning, Mister Vainio," said Blackwell. "Just do your job and let us do ours."

Will shook his head. "I'm sorry."

"Don't worry about it." I gave him a reassuring smile and touched his chest, leaving a vaguely hand-shaped collection of golden sparks.

"What's happening to him? Did you set him on fire?" Officer Blackwell shoved me to one side and reached toward Will.

"Keep your hands back if you don't want to lose them," I snapped.

Will's entire torso was glittering now. Light passed through him, growing brighter. A high-pitched hum filled the air. Will screamed.

"You're all right," I shouted. "You're *not* on fire, and you're going to be fine."

Blackwell reached for my arm. "Whatever you're doing—"

Nidhi moved between us. "Would you interrupt a doctor in the middle of surgery?"

"Will isn't in pain. He's just scared." I kept one hand

outstretched, channeling the book's magic. "Probably because a cop just told him he was on fire."

The screams began to fade. So did Will himself. Seconds later, he vanished completely.

Blackwell stepped back and drew his sidearm. "Isaac Vainio, stand up and place your hands on your head."

"If I do that, he dies." The humming sound returned, bringing with it the golden outline of my patient. I heard shouts and people running toward us, but I couldn't look around to see what was happening. I hoped nobody shot me before I finished. It would be great if they didn't shoot me after, either.

The light and sparks died, and Will sat before us once again. He was completely whole and completely baffled.

"What happened?" He looked around, then down at himself. His clothes were intact. The handcuffs were gone. "Did my blood sugar drop? I checked it after lunch, but I can't remember—"

"That's probably for the best," I said. "My name's Isaac. You're all right. Your son Jaiden is waiting for you. I'm sure one of these people would be happy to take you to him."

Blackwell seized my jacket collar and hauled me to my feet. Sweat dotted his face as he swung me around. He jammed the barrel of his gun into my ribs like he was trying to stab me. "What the hell did you do? Why doesn't he remember anything?"

The walls wavered around me. Between healing Will and Blackwell's manhandling, I felt like I'd just stumbled off the world's worst carnival ride.

"I'm guessing this is your first close experience with magic?" Nidhi said calmly. "It can be disconcerting."

"Stand down, Blackwell!" Officer Rowland stood about eight feet away, along with several other police officers and two FBI agents, most of whom had drawn their own guns.

"It's an old *Star Trek* trick," I said slowly, trying not to move. "In the book, one of the crew was infected with an alien virus. They use the transporter beam's pattern buffer to restore her to an earlier state, before the infection. It's a complete deus ex machina, but—"

"You waved your hand, and he fucking disintegrated!"

"I what?" asked Will. "I'm sorry, who are these people? What's going on?"

The EMT who'd been checking Will rose. "Isaac just saved this man's life, Officer."

Will blinked. "You did?"

"It was pretty cool, yah. Also, for what it's worth, your body is like an hour younger now." Smudge was pacing in his cage. Smoke rose from his back, and his attention was fixed on Blackwell.

"Officer Blackwell." Nidhi's voice was sharper, more authoritative, with an emphasis on *officer*. Stressing his role and responsibilities. "Isaac is no threat. Helping those people took a great deal out of him. Look how his hands are trembling. He'd probably fall and break his nose if you weren't holding him upright. In the meantime, there are other people who need help."

She was exaggerating, but not as much as I would have liked. Pulling a potion or ray-gun out of a book was one thing. Shaping raw magic and belief had a bigger price tag.

Blackwell glanced toward my hip. "That thing in the cage. What the fuck is it?"

Great. Not only was he freaking out about magic, he was probably arachnophobic, too. "His name's Smudge. He's harmless. Mostly harmless. He probably just wants some candy. I can—"

"Don't move! Keep your hands where I can see them!"

"Daniel Blackwell, drop your weapon and back away *now*!" Rowland raised her own gun. "Nobody wants to do this, Dan. Think about Lisa."

"But he—Did you really cure him?" Blackwell stared past me toward Will. "Or did you kill him and replace him with . . . with whatever *that* is?"

It was a fair question, one science fiction had struggled with pretty much since the first story about teleportation. And there was no way in hell I was going to get into that discussion with Officer Twitchy.

"My first experience with magic was a sixteen-year-old client," Nidhi said, her attention fully on Blackwell. "He'd been complaining about hearing voices. None of the medications I prescribed had helped. I was afraid I'd have to have him committed. It turned out he was magically gifted, but nobody realized it. He'd turned to reading to escape the stress of high school. He was so desperate to escape the real world, he connected with fictional ones. The romance novels he'd been going through had convinced him he was the son of a Scottish lord. It's called Type Two Partial Libriomantic Possession. His accent was terrible."

Blackwell appeared to be listening. "What happened?"

"The Porters interrupted a session as he was trying to seduce me. They eventually taught him how to get the delusions under control, and to use his magic. They *helped* him. Without the Porters, he could have hurt someone, or else he would have ended up medicated and locked up somewhere. Instead, he's now grown up and married with three kids. They live in Copenhagen. He sends me a Christmas card every year."

Standard Porter procedure at the time would have been to adjust Nidhi's memories of the encounter in order to conceal the existence of magic. She must have impressed them a great deal if they'd offered her a job instead.

"The idea that magic was real terrified me," she continued. "It took away my understanding of the world. I had to question everything I'd learned, everything I believed. Nothing felt real anymore."

Blackwell was nodding. I just did my best not to move. I hated feeling helpless, but if I was the one triggering his panic, anything I said or did would likely make things worse.

"I don't know how the police handle scenes like this, day after day, without breaking down." Nidhi pointed to the wounded, and to the capitol building behind us. "I'm running on nothing but adrenaline right now. I'll probably fall apart tonight when I get home and this is all over."

"You never really get used to it," Blackwell admitted.

Nidhi nodded. "You've seen the ugly side of magic in there. You also saw magic save a life. Focus on that. We're on the same side."

Slowly, he lowered his gun. Rowland moved in quickly to take it from him. Two others caught Blackwell's arms and escorted him away from me.

"Are you all right?" asked Agent Steinkamp.

I sagged. "It's not the first time someone's wanted to kill me."

"It's surprising how often it happens," Nidhi added.

"Thanks." I squeezed her shoulder. She nodded once.

"Nice work, Doctor Shah," said Rowland. "I'm sorry about Blackwell. He's a good cop, and a good man. I've never seen him lose it like that."

Smudge looked to be calming down, which meant I was no longer in immediate danger of being shot. "Does anyone else need magical treatment?"

"Several others should be checked for infection, including the witnesses we're questioning across the street." Steinkamp glanced over his shoulder. "Before that, there's something else I'd like you to look at."

"Sure," I said wearily. "Just answer me one question?"

"Shoot." He grimaced. "Sorry, bad choice of words."

"We arrived about a half hour after the news broke," I said. "If I'm remembering right, the nearest FBI field office is in Detroit, about an hour away with clear traffic, eh?"

"That's right," he said cautiously.

"So how is it the FBI got here before we did?"

STATEMENT BY DEPARTMENT OF HOMELAND SECURITY SECRETARY LAWRENCE MCGINLEY ON THE ATTACKS IN CALIFORNIA, NEW YORK, OREGON, AND MICHIGAN

For Immediate Release
DHS Press Office Contact: 202-282-8010

Tonight, the United States and the world witnessed a series of cowardly and unspeakable attacks that resulted in the loss of at least fourteen lives. Our hearts and prayers go out to the victims and their families.

The Department of Homeland Security and the FBI are working with state and local law enforcement to bring those responsible to justice, and to prevent future incidents.

We encourage the American people to remain calm and vigilant. "If You See Something, Say Something."

For the past year, we have worked to improve our security measures, seen and unseen, in preparation for magical attacks. We will continue that work, using the lessons learned tonight, to make our country safer.

These murderers used their power to sow fear. They will find only resolve. They sought to spread violence. They will see justice.

This is a time of tension and change. Whatever magic our enemies might bring to bear against us, they will succeed only in bringing us together. No magic in the world can break our strength and unity as a nation.

Chapter 3

"The world has never been kind to people like us. I told my Porters their priority was to protect the world from magic, and to protect magic from the world. I made it my priority to protect the Porters."

"Were you protecting me when you tried to take my magic and my memories?"

"Yes."

"Next time, don't."

"Next time?"

"You know what I mean."

"I kept you alive. I preserved your mind and your sanity, more or less."

"You took a part of me."

"Which you eventually reclaimed. Many never have that chance. Ask those who fell at the hands of Archbishop Adolph von Nassau."

"Von Nassau. He started the Baden-Palatine War."

"The act of pulling your murdered friends and colleagues from a magical inferno changes you forever. History will tell you it was a war over the Archbishop's *throne, but it was far more. Von Nassau hoped to destroy me and my discoveries. I underestimated his resolve, and I failed to act."*

"I'm sorry."

"You're beginning to discover your power and potential. That is when you and those around you are most vulnerable. The world is larger than ever before. You can't help everyone, Isaac. They won't let you. Where will you focus your energies? Will you hesitate, or will you act?"

***

"**D**ID YOU LEARN ANYTHING about who did this?" asked Agent Steinkamp.

"We're only here to help the injured," said Nidhi.

"Don't bullshit me, Doctor."

"I treated bites from at least two different werewolves." I searched the crowd for Lena. "You haven't answered my question."

He led us toward the capitol building. We stopped at the front entrance, where another FBI agent handed us paper-thin, elastic-rimmed shoe covers and rubber gloves.

"You're sure about this?" asked Rowland.

"I've worked with Porters before," said Steinkamp. "I've got clearance to bring them on as temporary independent contractors. Washington wants this solved yesterday."

I looked back and forth between them. "Who's in charge here, the police or the FBI?"

"Technically?" Steinkamp cocked a thumb at Rowland. "State Police, until we establish this was an act of magical terrorism."

"You asked about a group called Vanguard," I said.

"That's right, I did." His expression was neutral. "Let's go."

He led us inside past armed guards, up the steps and to the rotunda. The capitol was almost as crowded and busy as the grounds surrounding it. Everywhere I looked, men and women were taking photographs. Others pulled fingerprints. They appeared to be concentrating their efforts in a few specific locations, including the doorway to the governor's office. Blood dripped down one of the wooden columns to our right.

"This way." Steinkamp led us to the body of a young man.

I was no medical examiner, but even I could tell he hadn't been killed by werewolves. I counted six bloody gunshots, most to the torso. "He wasn't human." I peered over the tops of my glasses. "You think this is one of the killers."

He and Rowland looked at one another, but neither spoke.

I crouched beside the body. "Back to my earlier question. The FBI was on site, set up, and working within a half hour or so of the attack. Either you used magic to get from Detroit to Lansing impossibly fast, or else you were already here, or at least on the way, when it happened."

"You're right." Steinkamp scowled at the dead werewolf. "We were driving down to arrest this guy."

"If you knew what he was going to do—" I started.

"We didn't. We've been watching him as part of a human smuggling operation. Inhuman smuggling, to be precise." He shook his head in disgust. "Homeland Security picked up whispers that they were on to us, and he was getting ready to go wild."

"But he decided to try to assassinate Governor Sullivan first?" Nidhi paced around me, examining the body. "That doesn't make sense."

Rowland glanced around, as if to make sure nobody else was listening. "He didn't *try* to kill the governor."

Damn. That was the first official confirmation I'd heard. "What about the Attorney General?"

"Both men were dead when we arrived," said Steinkamp. "We'll be announcing it to the press shortly. In the meantime, what can you tell me about our killer?"

I pulled off my glasses and tucked them into my shirt pocket. "He's Lykanthropos Stroudus. From *The Golem's Eye*. The Porters can email you the full info on his species. I'm pretty sure he came here because someone had been messing with his thoughts."

"Explain," snapped Rowland.

I dropped to all fours, getting as close to the body as I could without touching the drying blood. I moved one hand over the face, like a child reaching for the special effects at a 3D movie. "A lot of magic fades with death. *The Golem's Eye* is strongest, and easy to read. But I can see another text overlaid with the first."

"Can you read it?" asked Steinkamp.

"It's too degraded."

Nidhi turned her attention from the body to me, her brows crinkling together. I avoided eye contact.

"Are there werewolf species who can control thoughts like that?" asked Rowland. "An alpha wolf or something, ordering the others to help?"

"I don't think a were did this." I sat back. "There are books I can use to look into the past and hopefully give you a better idea exactly what happened. The spells manipulate real light, so you'd be able to photograph the attackers and broadcast their faces throughout the state."

"Magical evidence isn't admissible in court, and you know it." Rowland scowled as she listened to a report from one of her officers via radio. "Defense attorneys would argue it was all illusion, that you could condemn anyone you liked."

"More importantly, we've got plenty of security footage for that," added Steinkamp. "We'll be running facial recognition against FBI and DHS databases."

"Besides," said Nidhi, "you're done with magic for the day."

Rowland looked up. "What's that mean? Do you libriomancers run out of gas after a certain number of spells?"

"Sort of." Given the physical damage I'd done to my eyes last year, Nicola Pallas had ordered me to limit the amount of magic I did in any twenty-four hour period. Recreating Will had put me close to that limit. I massaged the tingling numbness from my hands. Close to that limit, or maybe a little beyond it.

"How do you plan to stop the other weres?" I asked. "Stroudus are tough, but they can obviously be killed by normal bullets. That won't work on most species. Pepper spray will be effective on some. Heightened olfactory senses make them more sensitive. Don't bother with a Taser. In most cases, that'll just piss 'em off."

"You have something that will take them down?" asked a passing CSI. "I didn't sign up for this shit. The academy didn't teach us how to deal with ghouls and goblins."

"Oh, goblins are easy," I said. "They're cowards. They'll run away if you so much as look at them cross-eyed."

He looked from me to Rowland, probably trying to tell whether I was joking. She waved him away. "The feds have agents who've been trained on this sort of perp. They'll be helping us bring the others in. Is there anything else you can tell us about this one?"

"*The Golem's Eye* came out in 2004, which means he

might have been a werewolf for more than a decade, but he wasn't born that way." Whoever this had been, he didn't look like a kidnapper or murderer. He reminded me of my high school gym teacher, complete with bushy brown mustache, broad shoulders, and tight-laced high-tops.

"When you take the body out, make sure he's covered," said Nidhi. "You'll want to contact his family as soon as possible to arrange for his burial, once you're done examining him."

"We know the procedure," Steinkamp said.

Werewolves were touchy about proper respect for the dead. "I can ask around up north, see if anyone knows our killer."

"We've got this under control," he said. "We'll be interviewing his friends and neighbors, as well as local werewolves."

"You think they'll talk to the police or the FBI?" asked Nidhi. "Pack loyalties are as strong as any family bond."

"But they'd talk to you?" Rowland sounded skeptical.

"Most werewolves would tell me to go piss into a fan, but I've got a couple of friends outside Copper River. Give me this guy's name, and I can find out if there's been any gossip."

He and Rowland looked at one another.

"Sandy Boyle." Steinkamp grabbed my arm. "Anything you find out, you call me, got it?"

I gave him a halfhearted salute.

"Before we take you over to check the other witnesses," he continued, "would you mind looking at the victims? We want to be sure they won't come back as mons—as whatever killed them."

"You're thinking of vampires, not werewolves. With werewolves, once you're dead, that's it."

"Are you one hundred percent certain, Mr. Vainio?"

I thought briefly about other rules of magic I'd been one hundred percent certain about, and how many of those rules had ended up bent or broken. I extended a hand toward the door. "After you."

Both the governor and the attorney general were thoroughly dead, and no magic was going to change that fact. So were the three other bodies I examined.

Rowland handed me off to a woman from the Lansing Police Department, who took me to check the other witnesses. LPD had a station right across North Capitol Avenue, which was where the FBI and police were completing their interviews.

I treated three more people, using Lucy's Narnian potion to heal the wounds beneath their bandages. Thankfully, only one of the three had been infected with lycanthropy, and it hadn't taken hold yet, so the potion was able to eradicate that from his system as well.

By the time we emerged, the streets were mostly clear. The mayor had declared an emergency curfew, and police were working to break up the few remaining groups. All that remained were reporters and law enforcement.

Lena waited for us outside of the station. "The politicians aren't wasting any time. Senator Keeler gave a speech a half hour ago, calling for tighter regulation of inhumans and magic-users."

"Of course he did," I said wearily.

"He also wants increased border security, and an extension of the zero-immigration policy on inhumans. He said Homeland Security would be investigating the possibility that these attacks were orchestrated by America's enemies."

Lena had rented a green Chevy Cavalier while Nidhi and I were inside with the other witnesses. I climbed into the back seat and called Helen DeYoung's cellphone. *"Helen? It's Isaac."*

"You all right, Isaac? You sound—"

"Drunk, I know. It's a glitch in the phone implant. Have you and Jeff heard what happened in Lansing?"

Helen and Jeff used to live in Tamarack, one town over from Copper River. They'd abandoned their house and retreated into the wild after Governor Sullivan signed the order condemning the old mining town. Nothing remained now but empty roads and bulldozed lots.

In some ways, the move had done them good. Helen said they were in better physical shape these days, and their diets had improved. So had their sex lives, which they both insisted on chatting about in impressive detail. Werewolves were notoriously open about sex. They could talk about their escapades like a Red Wings fan going on about game six of the 2008 Stanley Cup Finals. But at this point, I think they talked about it mostly to make me squirm.

Their pack tried to stay within range of the cell towers, and Jeff insisted on running into town for his weekly beer runs, but they weren't always in touch with world events.

"We got a call earlier tonight. What the hell happened down there?"

I filled them in while Lena maneuvered through the blocked-off streets of downtown Lansing, crawling toward 496. *"Do you or Jeff know a fellow named Sandy Boyle? Stroudus werewolf. I'm told he was involved with trafficking inhumans."*

"Doesn't ring a bell. Hold on." Her voice went muffled. *"Jeff? You know anyone named Sandy Boyle?"*

"Who's asking?" Jeff yelled. *"If it's that pug-faced ass-*

hole from the collection agency, tell him I'm not ratting anyone out. They think they can harass us about back taxes on property they stole—"

"Calm your fur before you give yourself another heart attack. It's Isaac."

I heard Jeff snatch the phone from his wife. *"Isaac! Is this about that mess in Lansing?"*

"Yah. We don't know much about who was behind it, but at least two of them were werewolves."

"Aw, shit. Listen, I don't know any Sandy Boyle, but the packs are fragmented these days. Most of us are laying low. Some of the young pups have been grumbling about fighting back against the humans. The older wolves are keeping 'em in line so far, but that ain't gonna last forever. They've been turning more of your lot, too. Plenty of humans want the strength and sexiness of being a werewolf. Truth be told, some of us think it's a good idea to boost our numbers for whatever comes next."

Sandy Boyle could have been a relatively new convert, headstrong and caught up in the flush of power. *"What about a group called Vanguard?"*

"Where'd you hear that name?" he asked cautiously.

"A fellow from the FBI mentioned it."

His voice dropped a full octave, not quite a growl. *"You're working for the feds now?"*

"You know better, Jeff."

"Helen and I, we've learned not to take things for granted these days." Jeff sighed. *"Early this year, we got a call from a fellow who said he was with Vanguard. He gave us the heads-up to get out of Tamarack. Offered to help us relocate somewhere safe."*

"So you've worked with them?"

"Nah. We don't need no outsiders to help us find a home. But it's thanks to them we had time to gather up our belongings and vacate before the National Guard

showed up with guns and bulldozers. Otherwise, things would've gotten a lot uglier."

"Thanks, Jeff. Now what's this Helen was saying about a heart attack?"

"Helen talks too much. She—ow! Dammit, I'm on the phone! I'm fine, but I'm not a pup anymore. The first week of running around and howling at the moon damn near did me in."

"Why the hell didn't you call me?" I knew why. Jeff's pride was going to get him killed one of these days.

"Doc called it a minor incident. As long as I lay off the burgers and ribs from Emma's Diner and stick with meat I catch myself, I should be fine."

"You're not fine, you stubborn son of a bitch," Helen shouted. *"And if you skip your pills one more time, I'll grab you by the scruff of the neck and shove them down your throat!"*

I smothered a laugh. *"Jeff, if you have any more trouble, so much as a damn twinge, you call me, got it? Otherwise I'll come up there right now and microchip you like a runaway Chihuahua so I can keep tabs on you."*

"Chihuahua. Now that's good eating."

"Jeff . . ."

"Yah, fine, whatever. 'Sides, I thought you weren't allowed to do your healing mojo on folks."

"Not on humans. What are you going to do, turn me over to the cops?"

"Bastards won't be happy until they've thrown us all in kennels. You watch your ass, Isaac."

"You do the same."

He chuckled. *"I'd rather watch Helen's. You ever romped naked in the woods? You and Lena ought to try it one of these days. Just check for ticks when you're done."*

"I'm serious, Jeff. The governor and attorney general

*are both dead. Whatever heat you've been dealing with up
there is about to get a lot worse."*

"*Good to know, thanks. I'll call you if I hear anything.*"

"*Thanks.*" I hung up. "Jeff and Helen don't know the
late Mr. Boyle."

"Have you checked.in with Nicola yet?" asked Nidhi.

"I'm sure she's dealing with enough right now. I can
follow up with her tomorrow."

Lena and Nidhi glanced at one another.

"When we make it to the highway—" I began.

"Head toward Detroit," Lena said. "Got it."

"How'd you know that?"

It was Nidhi who answered. "You told the police and
the FBI Sandy Boyle's thoughts had been manipulated,
but I could tell you knew more than you were saying. I
thought maybe it was another Porter who'd done it and
you were trying to protect them, but if so, you would
have called Nicola first."

"That narrows it down to the handful of inhumans on
your friends list who can mess with people's minds,"
Lena continued smoothly. "Deb DeGeorge is the closest,
and she's definitely not above a stunt like this. With her
being an ex-libriomancer and former friend, you'd want
to investigate personally rather than handing her over to
the authorities. Is she still living over on Benson?"

"I think so, yah." So much for my dramatic announce-
ment.

"Try to relax, would you?" Lena said without looking
back. "I can feel your tension from here. I like being attuned to my lovers, but you're making my neck tighten
up."

"Sorry." I rubbed my eyes and leaned back in the seat.
Between the hearing, the attack in Lansing, and the
amount of magic I'd burned through, I was spent. Sleep
would help, but magic tended to leave you hyper and

insomniac. It also destroyed the appetite. Not a healthy combination. I grabbed a protein bar from my jacket and forced myself to start eating.

"It's not just you."

Nidhi snorted. "It's been a rough night for everyone. My job has given me plenty of practice at feeling powerless. That doesn't mean I like it."

"Tonight could send everything we've been working toward for the past year straight to hell," I said. Whatever Gutenberg's flaws, and there had been plenty, at least when he'd been running things, I hadn't spent all my time jumping through red tape and worrying about political bullshit. "New Millennium was supposed to show the world what magic could do. Instead, the government is pissed because we won't make them weapons, and the rest of the world is freaked out because they think we're making weapons. Do you realize we could have had a working space elevator two months ago?"

Sometimes I wondered if libriomancers like Weronika Bulat had the right idea. Weronika was one of more than twenty people who'd quit the Porters and gone rogue. She spent her time traveling from hospital to hospital in Poland and healing the most critical patients. She was saving lives, and many considered her a national hero. At the same time, the ease with which she evaded hospital security only fed fears of what we could do.

The song on the radio came to an end. None of us spoke as a somber DJ announced that Governor Sullivan and Attorney General Duncan had been murdered by werewolves. He went on to remind listeners that Lansing, East Lansing, and surrounding suburbs were under curfew. "We're getting reports that a group of Michigan State students have gathered in an impromptu protest demanding stronger regulation of magic. They've rallied near the site of the campus library, which was destroyed several years ago in what's now understood to be an internal Porter conflict. Another group is counterprotesting across the street. Campus police are threatening to deploy tear gas to forestall a riot."

I thought about Callie, the pizza delivery girl who'd gotten us to Lansing, and wondered if she was part of the counterprotest. "We're not the ones who demolished the library."

"They're not protesting because of the library," said Nidhi. "They're protesting because they're angry and afraid."

"They're not the only ones." There had to be a better way, one that didn't lead to fear and violence and war. But damn if I could find it.

DETROIT SALT MINE

From Michipedia, the free encyclopedia of Michigan facts and history

Note: This article may not meet Michipedia standards for neutrality. Please see the Discussion Page for further information.

The Detroit Salt Mine was established in 1910 beneath the city of Detroit, Michigan. The mine soon produced 8000 tons of rock salt each month from the salt beds more than 1000 feet below the surface.

The mine was believed to cover approximately 1500 acres underground. Customers included leather tanneries and food suppliers. Today, the Detroit Salt Mine primarily sells rock salt for deicing roads.

Last year, it was discovered that the Detroit Salt and Manufacturing Company had dug an additional mine two miles away. This second mine was operational from 1909 to 1916 before being shut down and eventually erased from the public record.

This hive of tunnels and caves deep beneath the surface was an ideal nesting place for a community of vampires. They occupied the second mine for almost 100 years, hidden from the world and the potentially deadly rays of the sun, and emerging at night to hunt and feed.[Citation Needed]

Detroit Edison estimates the electricity siphoned from their grid to power the vampire nest cost the people of Detroit at least $926 million.[Citation Needed] The vampires also tapped into gas, water, and sewage services.

Earlier this year, a vampire murdered 13-year-old Jennifer Wilson.[Citation Needed] The people of Detroit responded with riots, demanding the authorities hunt and destroy the vampires and their home. Forces from the National Guard and the Army Corps of Engineers eventually discovered the second mine and used explosives to collapse the tunnels.

No one knows how many vampires lived beneath the city of Detroit. Estimates range from a few hundred to more than twenty thousand. A letter to the *Detroit Free Press* written by someone claiming to be a vampire condemned the destruction of their home and blamed Michigan governor John Sullivan for the murder of a thousand vampires who died when the tunnels collapsed.

Sullivan responded that every effort had been made to warn the vampires of the coming demolition, including radio and television broadcasts, and leaflets dropped into the mine. He said he regretted the loss of life, but stopped short of apologizing, saying his priority was the safety and security of the people of Michigan, and likening the vampire community to a hornet's nest in a basement.

Chapter 4

"New libriomancers are all the same. So optimistic. So caught up in awe and wonder, eager to learn what they can do."

"Some of us never outgrow that stage."

"I'm sorry, who did you think I was referring to when I mentioned new libriomancers?"

"I've been doing this stuff for more than a decade."

"Talk to me when you've finished your first century. If you survive. I'm not criticizing you, you know. The passion and excitement of people like yourself have advanced our knowledge of magic tremendously over the years. But it's equally important to discover your limits, and to accept there will be things you can't do. To recognize that some problems can't be fixed by magic. Some can't be fixed at all."

"Or maybe you just haven't looked hard enough for a solution."

I TRIED TO stretch out in the back seat to catch a nap during the drive. I failed. After a night like tonight, I usually needed to pop at least two Melatonin capsules to get my brain to scttle enough to let me sleep, but if I did that, I'd be too drowsy when we reached Deb's house. Instead, I pulled out my smartphone to check my work email.

First up was a report from Charles Brice on the side effects of his new bionic eye. The man was going to kill himself one of these days. Fortunately, his latest "upgrade" had caused only minor migraines and occasional double vision, an afterimage that appeared to come from the book he'd used to create the eye.

I signed off on the report and brought up the next message, an order for the following month's supply of animal feed. Reading through Vince's meticulous line-item breakdown was almost as good as the Melatonin.

Unfortunately, the very next message burnt the fatigue from my thoughts. I jabbed the screen and dialed Charles.

"Tell Potts the answer is no," I said as soon as he answered.

"I see you got my email."

"To paraphrase my friend Helen, New Millennium is not DHS's bitch. We're not building weapons, we're not giving them surveillance tech, and I'm sure as hell not letting them use the Gateway Project as a replacement for drone strikes."

"I don't like the idea either, but Gateway *would* be more precise," he said. "It could reduce civilian casualties and eliminate a lot of bad people."

"Charles, do you know how many high-ranking government officials consider *us* to be bad people?"

"Hey, I'm just playing devil's advocate."

"Since when did the devil need your help?"

"What's that supposed to mean?"

Nidhi twisted around and touched my knee. I bit back my retort. Charles had a gift for getting under my skin. I took a series of slow breaths. "Nothing. It's been a long night. I'm probably not going to be back tomorrow morning."

"I thought your niece was getting her leg fixed in the morning."

"She is." I closed my eyes.

"No wonder you're worked up. What do you want me to tell Potts?"

Russell Potts was one of two civilians on New Millennium's four-person Board of Directors. Fortunately, the other board members—Nicola Pallas and Thérèse St. Pierre from the Porters, along with Doctor Heather Neuman from the National Institutes of Health—had consistently voted down his efforts to turn our work toward offensive military magic. "What I *want* you to tell him . . ." I shook my head. "I'll set up a meeting to talk with him next week."

"He doesn't like waiting."

"Good. Make it two weeks." I hung up the phone. "I've decided to relocate to the moon to pursue a career as an astrohermit. Either of you interested in a job as Director of Research?"

"You couldn't afford me," said Lena.

"Besides, Smudge would hate the moon," added Nidhi.

"He might enjoy the decreased gravity. Can't you see him jumping around my moonbase, spinning like a little flaming pinwheel?"

"What could possibly go wrong?" asked Lena.

I sighed and shoved my phone back into my pocket. The rest of my messages could wait. At the rate I was going, I'd give myself a stroke before we reached Detroit.

When all else failed, there had always been one guaranteed way to calm my thoughts. I hooked a clip-on reading lamp to the collar of my jacket, grabbed one of my newest acquisitions—Nnedi Okorafor's *Zahrah the Windseeker*—and started reading.

The recession a few years back, combined with the decline of the auto industry, had hit Detroit hard. The city had just begun to turn things around when word got out it was also home to the largest nest of vampires in the Midwest.

That was back in late June. A week later, a thirteen-year-old girl turned up dead, her throat slashed. There was no proof a vampire was responsible, but it didn't matter. Her death led to mobs of self-styled vampire hunters roaming the streets. At least two vampires ended up dead, along with five "suspected vampires" who turned out to be humans in the wrong place and time.

It wasn't until the vampires began fighting back that the National Guard was called in. They used ground-penetrating sonar and satellite images to pinpoint the nest's location, deep within a forgotten salt mine.

For eight days, they poured fire and explosives into the mine. By the end of July, not a single vampire remained in the nest. Some escaped and fled to join nests in other parts of the country. Others refused to abandon their home town.

Parts of Detroit were once again beginning to recover. Deb DeGeorge lived in one of the areas that wasn't.

We passed abandoned houses and vacant lots as we got farther from the highway, making our way toward the northeast part of the city. Cars lined the streets and plugged narrow driveways like corks.

Deb lived at the corner of Benson and Concord in a narrow two-story brick building with broken windows and a gutter jutting down over the front porch like a compound fracture.

We parked on the opposite side of the road, just past a street lamp. I saw no lights inside the house, but that meant nothing. Deb could see perfectly well in the dark. It was one of several changes she'd gone through when she traded her humanity for a longer life as a creature from a book called *Renfield*, by Samantha Wallace.

I scooped Smudge off the ledge beneath the rear window where he'd been sleeping and eased him into his cage. He twitched awake and began to pace, giving off the faint scent of burnt dust. He wasn't on fire, but he was nervous about something.

I kept meaning to attach a thermometer to the outside of his cage. Smoke and flame were vivid enough, but more sensitive readings might help me notice sooner when he was upset, especially if I could jury-rig the thermometer to an audible alert of some sort. Talulah back at the lab could probably set it up to talk to my smartphone via Bluetooth.

"My turn to sit things out," Nidhi said. Of the three of us, she was the least able to protect herself against something like Deb, and she knew it. "Watch yourself, Isaac. You pushed your limits in Lansing. Call me as soon as the house is secure."

Lena kissed her, then climbed out and fetched a thick oak cane from beneath her seat. The cane's twisted design reminded me a little of the caduceus with its twin snakes spiraled around one another. She gripped the end with both hands and pulled.

The wood softened like green willow branches, untwisting and thickening into a pair of wooden bokken. The curved swords continued to shift in her hands, taking on edges as sharp as steel.

I double-checked Smudge and my books. Hopefully I wouldn't need them. I pushed the door shut as quietly as I could. "Shall we?"

"Never let it be said that dates with you are normal." She swatted my backside with the flat of one sword.

"I wouldn't want my lady to get bored."

The front lawn was mowed, which surprised me a little. I couldn't imagine Deb pushing a mower back and forth every week. Though she was certainly capable of manipulating one of her neighbors into doing it for her.

Weeds grew through cracks in her driveway. An old tire hung like a blackened wreath over the fire hydrant by the curb. Bars covered the first floor windows, and curtains blocked our view of the inside. The porch light was broken.

I squinted to read a paper sign taped to the screen door: SOLICITORS WILL BE EATEN. Given that Renfields fed on bugs and birds, I was pretty sure it was a joke. I opened the screen door and knocked. When nobody answered, I tried the knob. "Locked."

Lena touched the doorframe. The wood warped and twisted, and the door popped inward. "Did you bring a flashlight?"

I clipped my reading lamp to my jacket and switched it on.

The house was a wreck. Rotting brown carpet covered floorboards that creaked and sank with each step. Peeling wallpaper revealed crumbling plaster and visible studs. The air smelled like mildew and animal piss.

Red flame rippled over Smudge's back.

"Deb? It's Isaac." I pulled my jacket tighter. If she had a working furnace, she hadn't bothered to turn it on. "It's been a hellaciously long day."

Lena raised one sword and approached the staircase. She touched the rail, then one of the steps. "The wood's old, but sturdy. It'll hold our weight."

Her skin roughened as she climbed the steps. The wood living within her flesh usually grew alongside her bones. It made for fascinating X-rays. But she could manipulate that wood into a kind of subdermal armor when she wanted to, growing plates of hardened oak over muscle and organs.

She could grow the armor externally as well, along with sharp wooden spurs from her knuckles and joints, but for the moment she retained a more-or-less human appearance.

"I'm not in the mood for games, Deb," I called out. "This doesn't have to get ugly."

"Breaking into my house, issuing threats and demands?" The voice came from upstairs to the left. "The Porters never change, do they?"

"Can you see her or her magic?" whispered Lena.

"I don't have X-ray vision." Though if I dug up a Superman novelization, maybe Roger Stern's *The Death and Life of Superman* . . . I mentally added that to my never-ending list of potential research projects.

Footsteps creaked overhead, on the opposite side of the house from Deb's voice.

"I'm sorry," I called. "Did you have company?"

"Oh, you know. The life of a MILF."

"MILF?"

"Monster I'd like to—"

"Right." There was an image I didn't need.

I checked Smudge, then signaled for Lena to go ahead. She moved forward and flipped a light switch at the top of the stairs. A lone incandescent bulb lit up overhead. I tucked my reading lamp away and followed.

If anything, the second story of Deb's home was in worse condition than the first. The doors had all been removed from their frames, exposing a truly foul bathroom suffering from water damaged ceilings and decorated in a mildew and rust stain motif. To the left was a bedroom with an old twin mattress on the floor and a swarm of carpenter ants attacking what looked like leftover Chinese food.

The only room that showed signs of civilization was a small library on the other end of the hall. Deb might have let everything else go, but she continued to care for her books. The lone window in the library was undamaged and covered with a sheet of insulating plastic for additional protection. A small dehumidifier hummed by the wall.

There was no sign of Deb or her guest.

"Renfields can't change form or go invisible," I whispered. "She's here somewhere."

"Check the library for an attic door," said Lena. "I'll look in the bedroom."

The dust on the shelves and books suggested Deb hadn't been in here lately, which was a shame. She'd once told me the best part of her transformation was the near-immortality that came with it, giving her more time to catch up on her reading.

I skimmed the titles: mostly history and biography, with a smaller section of vampire-related fiction. With a sigh, I pulled myself away to search the walls and ceiling. "No attic access in here."

Something scampered past the window. I ripped the plastic away, opened the window, and peered out to see a bulky figure—too tall to be Deb—jump to the ground. Judging from the way he'd scrambled down the wall, he was probably a vampire. It would have been easy enough for him to transform to mist and sneak out through a vent.

"I've got a runner," I called. "It's not Deb."

"Found it." On the other end of the hall, through the empty doorways, I saw Lena rummaging through a closet. "There's a door in the back—"

Two men lunged out. One grabbed Lena around the waist like a linebacker and pushed her across the bedroom, slamming her against the wall hard enough to crack the plaster. The other grappled for her weapons. Lena brought her knee into the first attacker's chin. When that didn't work, she braced herself and struck again. Though the strike was identical, the sound and the result were very different. An oak spur punched through the man's chin with a popping sound. He staggered back, screaming and clutching his bloody jaw.

"Quite the House of Inamoratos you've got here." I was halfway to the bedroom when the front door smashed inward. Two more men moved toward the bottom of the stairs. Deb must have sent them out and around to flank us. Both appeared human and looked to be in their early twenties. I could see the vampiric magic in their veins from here.

I moved to the top step and folded my arms. "Listen, I'm having a bad day. I'd prefer not to take it out on you, but—"

They charged up the stairs.

"Love, do you mind?" I called.

"Do it."

I reached out to touch Lena's magic. Her power came from an old book called *Nymphs of Neptune*. I'd read it several times to better understand her and her origins. That familiarity made it relatively simple to read the story within her and pull a particular passage into myself. I channeled that power into the staircase.

The wood surged to life, remembering the touch of sun and soil. Branches sprouted to entangle the lead vampire's foot. He went down hard enough to do something crunchy to his knee. While he screamed in pain, his friend struggled to climb past.

I redirected my borrowed magic. When contestant number two was almost within reach, the steps simply collapsed beneath his weight, sending him crashing down into what sounded like a storage cabinet or cupboard of some sort.

The first vampire was dissolving into mist to escape the branches. I released my hold on Lena's magic, returning her power. Not that she needed it at the moment. Both of her attackers lay bloody and groaning on the floor.

"Last warning," I called out, studying the mist-vamp's power and preparing to strip it from him.

"That's enough." Deb DeGeorge emerged from the attic door in the closet. She held a silver revolver in one hand. "Drop the swords, Lena."

Deb appeared ... unwell. Her short, graying hair was a dusty mess. Her face was gaunt, and she looked like three-day-old death. Smelled like it, too. The stench suffused the entire hallway.

A wasp flew from the open attic door behind her. I flinched instinctively.

Deb snatched it out of the air, crushed it between thumb and forefinger, and bit off the end. After spitting what I assume was the stinger onto the floor, she popped the rest into her mouth. The gun never wavered. "The swords. Don't make me shoot you, Lena. Or Isaac."

"Shoot him and you'll die slowly." Lena stabbed the swords into the floor. "Ever had a really nasty splinter? Imagine them growing through every inch of your skin." She flexed her hands. Her knuckles made a distinctly wooden popping sound. "Shoot me, and you'll just piss me off."

I studied her battered minions. "The one with the perforated chin looks like a Renfield. You turned him?"

"Consensually. I have the notarized paperwork to prove it."

Which would be worth absolutely nothing in any court. "You were expecting us," I guessed.

She shrugged. "I figured someone would try to round me up sooner or later. Isn't that how these things work? First they came for the vampires, et cetera."

Each time I encountered Deb DeGeorge, I saw more of the monster and less of the person she'd been. Her humanity wasn't entirely gone. The sleeveless black dress and knee-high studded leather boots were pure Deb. But not much remained of my one-time friend.

"Sandy Boyle," I said.

"Never heard of her." Despite being armed, Deb took a step back as I advanced.

"Cut the bullshit, Deb. I examined the body. I saw your magic worming through the meat of his brain. This is the part where you tell us everything you know, and we take your cooperation into consideration when deciding what to do with you."

"Or what, you'll beat the truth out of me? Hon, I'm the one with the gun. I'd rather not use it, but if you keep trying to play alpha librarian, I'll put a bullet through your knee. Same goes if you make one move toward those books of yours in your trench coat there."

"It's a duster, not a trench coat." I studied her weapon. The barrel was relatively short, no more than two inches, but at this range it would be hard for her to miss. "Six-shooter, eh? What's it take, .44 caliber? .45?"

I didn't wait for her response. Just as I'd done with Lena, I pulled Smudge's story and power into myself and hurled it forth, into the bottom chamber of Deb's revolver.

The bullet discharged. Normally, the force would have propelled the bullet out of the case, down the barrel, and through my flesh ... but that bullet hadn't been aligned with the barrel, meaning all that energy had to find another way to escape.

Fire flared from the cylinder. A sliver of hot steel embedded itself in the wall beside me. The gun clattered to the floor.

"Son of a fuck!" Deb jumped back, clutching her hand. The gun's cylinder looked like a cracked walnut. "What the hell was that?"

"That was the last of my patience." I pulled an M&M from a bag in my pocket and slipped it to Smudge as I returned his fire. He didn't like it when people messed with his magic. Having been on the receiving end of something similar from Gutenberg, I didn't blame him in the slightest. He scarfed down the M&M and demanded two more before he forgave me and settled down.

I looked around to make sure none of her minions had started moving again. "Last chance, Deb."

Deb sat down on the edge of the mattress and nudged the leftover Chinese food, sending the ants into a frenzy. She licked her thumb, pressed it down, and brought a group of injured, squirming ants to her mouth. "Trust me, hon. You're on the wrong side of this one."

"Are you suggesting the right side is the one embracing terrorism and assassination? Do you realize how much harder you've made things for all of us? They're going to use tonight as an excuse to come down even harder."

"Oh, Isaac. You really need to step out of the sci-fi section and brush up on your history. You think they needed an excuse?"

"So tonight was what?" asked Lena. "A preemptive strike?"

Deb's laugh was dry, bitter, and more than a little disturbing. "Tonight was retaliatory."

I stepped sideways, where it was easier to keep an eye on Deb and her pet vamps. "This is about the Detroit nest."

"This is about survival. About being gunned down in the streets. Driven from our homes. What are the Porters and your precious New Millennium doing about *that*, Isaac?"

"We're *trying* to show the world we can exist without killing each other."

"I forgot what you're like." She smiled bitterly, displaying a dying ant squirming between her front teeth. "I bet you hate every minute of your trips to D.C. and your time in front of the cameras. You'd rather be locked away in your ivory tower, shut away from the real world."

I spoke softly and quietly, fighting to keep my anger under control. "The blood on my sleeves looks pretty fucking real to me, Deb. So were the bodies I saw tonight."

"What happened in Lansing was part of several coordinated attacks," said Lena. "Who are you working with?"

"How many vampires do you have working at New Millennium?" Deb asked.

"Seven," I said.

"Let me guess. They're all in security?"

"Six are security, yes. The seventh prefers janitorial work. She works nights, and it's nice having someone who can command insects and rodents to evacuate a building."

"While everyone with any real power is human. Typical Porter setup. For all your talk about remaking the world, did you ever consider who you're remaking it *for*? Because it sure as hell isn't us. And don't pull that 'But my best friend is a dryad' bullshit. Your pet nymph doesn't prove shit."

"Pet nymph?" Lena repeated softly. The room fell silent, save for the creak of wood as she flexed her hands.

Deb snorted. "I read your file, back when I was like him. I read your book. You're just a happy little sex slave."

Lena lifted Deb by the throat. A spike of oak grew from the palm of her other hand. "Are you *trying* to make us kill you?" She hesitated, then tossed Deb away. "My god, that's exactly what you're doing, isn't it."

I studied Deb, and the anger drained out of me. I recognized the numbness in her voice, the despair and hopelessness in her eyes. "Lena's grown beyond her book. We could help you do the same."

Deb rubbed her throat and worked her jaw from side to side. "Beyond her book, hm? How'd you pull that off?"

That spark of curiosity was the most I'd seen of the old Deb since we'd arrived.

"You first," I said. "Who planned those attacks?"

"Hell if I know."

I pulled a book from my jacket. "I could make you tell me."

"The fact that you haven't is why you're losing." Deb rubbed her eyes. The skin appeared strangely loose, like old, ill-fitting latex. "You're the only one playing by the rules."

"Who hired you to manipulate those werewolves?" asked Lena.

"Don't know that either. Everything was done by phone. I had three conversations totaling less than five minutes, all with the same woman. She never gave me her name."

I swapped books, taking out *The Goblin Wood*, a middle-grade fantasy. Shadows vignetted my vision, and characters whispered of war and refugees. I squinted to read a scene with an enchanted bell. I didn't need to create the actual bell; simply making the connection should be enough. "Lena, would you mind telling a lie for me?"

"Bacon-crust pizza was a brilliant invention."

From within the magically active book, a bell rang, signaling a lie. I glanced at Lena. "Really? I thought that was your kind of culinary innovation."

"Too greasy," she said. "They're trying too hard."

I turned back to Deb. "You messed with their heads and helped them commit murder, and you didn't bother to ask who you were working for?"

Deb spread her arms, a gesture that encompassed her crumbling home. "Do I look like I can afford to turn down paying work?"

"No evasions. Do you know who they or you were working for?"

"No."

The book remained silent. "Senator Alexander Keeler," I said, taking a shot in the dark. "He was one of the first out of the gate with a press conference following the attacks, and he'd have the connections to get his hands on Governor Sullivan's schedule. Is he involved?"

"Could be. He's a bigot and a jackass. Hey, do you mind?" Deb gestured to the groaning man with the bloody chin. She dropped to one knee. Her magic swept over the line of ants, who turned to march toward him. He scooped them into his mouth like a half-starved man at a Vegas buffet. "His whining was getting on my nerves, and he needs to feed to fix himself back up. Like I was saying, I don't know anything."

I watched her Renfield servant. Healing himself was one thing, but if he took one step toward me or Lena, I was going to end him. For the moment, he seemed fully occupied with devouring bugs. "Sandy Boyle and his two friends—there's no way you'd pass up the chance to pick their brains. You can start by giving me their names. Then you'll tell me everything else you learned from them, including whatever you know about Vanguard."

"Vanguard's as much a terrorist organization as the Girl Scouts. They're a wannabe underground railroad that got started after the feds burned us out of the salt mines. They keep tabs on things and try to give people like me a head start when it's time to run."

"Maybe they got tired of playing defense," I suggested. "Keep talking."

Deb lifted a corner of the mattress. Lena raised her bokken, but Deb just cringed and froze.

"Go ahead," I said.

Cockroaches scurried out as she pulled an old spiral-bound notebook free. "You've got a hacker on your team, yes?"

"Talulah Polk, yes." My team's names were public record. I wasn't telling her anything she couldn't have found from Google.

Deb tore off a piece of paper, slid a well-chewed pen from the spiral binding, and started writing. "Here are the names of Sandy's friends. You're right, I tried to loosen their tongues a bit. They didn't know much more than I do, but one of them said he was originally supposed to hit a different target, a Coast Guard ship off the east coast. The *USCGC Kagan*. Have your hacker look into the *Kagan*. Find out what would have made her a target, and what changed."

"Are you part of Vanguard?" I asked.

"Yes."

"Are you aware of any other plans to assassinate or harm anyone?"

"No."

I waited, but the book didn't react.

"What are you going to do with me?" Deb asked.

I should hand her over to the FBI, along with the names of the other two werewolves. Deb had facilitated two assassinations tonight.

"I know what you're thinking," she said. "If you turn me in, they'll either dissect me or use me."

Once again, the book remained silent. Deb believed what she was saying. "What exactly do you think I should do? You amped up the hate and rage of three murderers. You're as responsible as they are. You don't get to walk away from that."

"Then kill me."

Looking at the emptiness in her eyes, hearing the flatness in her words, it was as if a part of her *wanted* me to do exactly that. "What happened to you, Deb?"

"Keep your damn pity to yourself." She snorted and turned away. "You won't hurt me. Because you're still playing their game, by their rules."

I turned away. "Lena, could you keep an eye on her while I check the rest of the house?"

"Knock yourself out," Deb muttered.

The panel at the back of the closet was about three feet high. I shoved aside old dresses and shirts, switched on my reading lamp, and crept into the attic.

Two seconds later, I launched myself out again. I tripped over my heels, and my lamp went skittering across the room. I scooted past Deb, rolling and slapping at my jacket. Two wasps flew up and away, while a third stung my wrist.

Deb leaned down to pluck that one away. "Be careful," she said as she chewed. "That's my snack bar you almost fell through."

"Your *snack bar*?" The wasps were an inch and a half

long. They'd built their nest between the rafters. There had to be twenty square feet of wasp nest in that attic, so thick it was like another layer of insulation. "You could have warned me, you little shit-weasel!"

She was laughing now. "Relax, Isaac. If I really wanted to piss you off, I'd command them to swarm. At which point you'd get all pouty, steal my magic, and turn them against me. Honestly, you're no fun at all these days."

"Shit-weasel?" Lena repeated. She was trying not to laugh, but wasn't doing a great job of it.

"Shut up." I got to my feet and shuddered. "I hate wasps. I should let Smudge burn this place to the ground."

"Where would you like to search next?" Deb asked innocently.

I glared death. "Do you have anything else in this house that's illegal, dangerous, or could help me find the people behind tonight's attack?"

"Nope." *The Goblin Wood* remained silent. Deb caught another wasp and crushed it in her hand. "You know, you could have asked that up front and saved yourself the humiliation."

I refused to dignify that with an answer. Not that I had much dignity left. Instead, I swapped books again, grabbing my thin paperback copy of Philip K. Dick's *Flow My Tears, The Policeman Said*. It was an older book, and that made it harder to use, but it retained enough power for my purposes. I extended one finger into the page, touching a sheaf of crinkled paper within the scene. In the story, each sheet had been impregnated with a microdot transmitter.

I pulled one of those papers free and transferred its magic into Deb's skin. Like copying and pasting a bit of code, as Talulah would say. "I think we're done here."

I looked over at Lena, who nodded in agreement and said, "Deb can stay with me."

"I'm your prisoner now?" asked Deb. "How are the bugs at your place?"

"You can share Smudge's cricket stash."

"Be careful, hon." Deb grabbed an old black coat from the closet and tossed it on. "This isn't one of your field missions for the Porters. This is war. If you don't figure that out soon, it's gonna kill you."

The CHAIRMAN: How were subjects selected for human medical trials at New Millennium?

Mr. VAINIO: We asked for volunteers with life-threatening medical conditions that couldn't be cured by mundane means. From that pool, a team of Porters and NIH doctors selected candidates who—

The CHAIRMAN: Why don't we skip ahead to the favoritism and nepotism?

Mrs. CLARKE: I believe Mr. Keeler is referring to the inclusion of Alexis Vainio in your medical trials. Your niece, yes? You have to admit that's not normal practice.

Mr. VAINIO: Lex is my niece. She's also an ideal candidate, with severe injuries and complications from an automobile accident when she was younger. She lost a leg, suffered brain damage, and continues to experience chronic pain. I suggested they apply for the trials, but I wasn't involved in the selection process, nor did I have any influence on the decision to include Lex.

The CHAIRMAN: You expect us to believe that, out of a pool of hundreds or thousands of desperate volunteers, this selection committee just happened to pick your niece?

Mr. VAUGHN: Isaac, is it possible Lex was deliberately included in the trials as a way to reassure the public? To say, "We're so certain magic is safe and helpful, we'll use it on our own family members."

Mr. VAINIO: Maybe. You'd have to ask the selection team.

The CHAIRMAN: If magic is as safe as you'd like us to believe, why didn't you help your niece at the time of the accident? Why force her to suffer all these years?

Mr. VAINIO: The Porters . . .

The CHAIRMAN: I'm sorry, could you please speak up?

Mr. VAINIO: The Porters—Gutenberg, really—felt that it was more important to preserve the secrecy of magic. Lex's accident was public knowledge. I wanted to help her, but any miraculous recovery would have raised too many questions.

Mrs. BROWN: Why did Johannes Gutenberg want to keep magic a secret?

Mr. VAINIO: He was afraid of what people like you would try to do with it.

Chapter 5

"How do I know I can trust you?"

"Trust is a choice. Actually, trust is more of a desperate, hopeful guess based on limited information. I wouldn't trust me if I were you."

"What's your game? You've always had control issues, especially when it comes to the Porters. Are you trying to run things through me? To turn me into another you?"

"Heavens, no. I'm done with that circus. I'm happy to let someone else wrangle the monkeys and shovel out the elephant cages. And let's face it, you do spend a lot of time stepping in shit. Metaphorically speaking."

"That doesn't sound like the Gutenberg I knew."

"Think, Isaac. I'm not that Gutenberg. I'm who he wanted people to remember. An idealized version, if you will. I was never intended to be your personal chatbot."

"I can send your book back to Nicola, if you'd prefer."

"Not at all. I rather enjoy this pseudolife, though it would be nice to do more than sleep between our conversations, or to find others to converse with. Which reminds me, have you spoken with Juan recently?"

"Nobody's seen or heard from him since last year."

"No surprise. Juan Ponce de Leon, ever the survivor. He once hibernated for twelve years to escape the Anglo-Spanish War. If you do reach him, please send him my . . . my regards."

"I will, but you're evading the question. Either you are the Gutenberg I knew, in which case you have your own agenda. Or else you're this idealized version, in which case I don't know you."

"You must be cautious. Not your strong suit, I understand. But the world is at a turning point. So are you. It's what you've been struggling with for months, for years, really. It's why you keep reaching out to me. You hope I'll help you find the right answer."

"Answers are easy. What's the question?"

"Don't worry. You'll see it when you're ready."

"What if I don't?"

"I suspect you'll probably get yourself killed."

NIDHI AND LENA dropped me off at the Detroit airport at three in the morning. The next available flight to Las Vegas wasn't until noon, meaning the only way I could possibly get back to New Millennium before my niece's procedure was to use magic.

Given how twitchy I was, and the amount of magic I'd used in the past twenty-four hours, teleportation was out of the question. Some sort of superspeed would be marginally safer, but I was still far more likely to smear myself across a mountainside than I was to reach Vegas in one piece.

Even the tiny bit of illusion I'd used to sneak Smudge past airport security had exacerbated the ashy smears in my vision. My eyes kept shivering with the excess energy, making the whole world jump and skip like a scratched DVD.

I called the New Millennium main line and left a message with Kiyoko letting her know I'd be getting in later than expected. I thought about calling my brother next, but it was past midnight in Vegas, and I didn't want to disturb them.

Or maybe I just didn't want to hear his disappointment when I told him I wouldn't be there for them. Again.

I hiked the full length of the terminal three times, trying to burn off the manic energy. I passed a number of people napping, stretched out across chairs. There was no way I'd be able to do the same, but maybe if I kept moving long enough, I could calm my nerves enough that I wouldn't spend the entire flight bouncing and jostling my seatmate.

I finally wore myself out enough to sit and rest. I bought a newspaper and caught up on the details of yesterday's other attacks. In each case, at least one public figure who'd been outspoken against inhumans had been killed. The attack in New York had been the worst. A pair of lake trolls had killed more than twenty-three people before being gunned down.

Whoever was behind this, they subscribed to a philosophy of equal-opportunity terrorism. Trolls in New York, werewolves in Michigan, wild chupacabras in Oklahoma, and nagas in California. I wondered if Nicola knew anything about the chupacabras. She raised chupacabra hybrids, and loved the ugly things as much or more than most people.

Three of the chupacabras in Oklahoma had escaped, as had every one of the four nagas. Had they all been mentally pushed into becoming assassins, like the Lansing werewolves?

I composed a short email on my phone, letting Nicola know about the werewolf and the traces of mental manipulation I'd seen. I hesitated, but finally added another paragraph explaining that I'd traced that manipulation to Deb, and we had her under guard. As soon as I got back to New Millennium, I intended to follow up on a lead she'd shared.

It couldn't have been five minutes after I clicked send before the phone in my jaw went off.

"When I told you to assist with the aftermath in Lansing, I didn't mean for you to withhold evidence from the FBI and harbor an accessory to assassination and terrorism."

"Hi, Nicola. What are you doing up this late?"

"Damage control. Which will be completely pointless when word gets out about what you've done. Why, Isaac?"

She was singing under her breath, something she tended to do when she was angry or upset. But at least she was giving me the chance to explain. *"Because I can do a better job of finding whoever orchestrated these attacks than the police or FBI, and we both know it."*

"And because she used to be your friend."

I didn't deny it. *"What's more important, making nice and playing by their rules, or stopping the people behind this and saving lives?"*

"Then why tell me at all? Why put me in a position where I'm forced either to turn you in or to join your conspiracy?"

One nice thing about talking to Nicola: she didn't mind silence. She was content to wait while I pondered that question and dug at my own motivations. *"Because you have a different perspective on things, and I trust you to rein me in if I go too far."*

"I notice you didn't give me the chance to rein you in before you confronted Ms. DeGeorge."

"Yah, well, I tend to get caught up in the moment."

"You don't say."

"Give me time to piece this together. Someone did a lot of work to coordinate these attacks. They had to build each team, and at least here in Michigan, they had to hire a third party to brainwash that team into finishing the job. There's a bigger pattern here. We can't see it yet. Too many missing pieces. Too many questions. Why limit each team to a single type of inhuman? Why arrange the attack for a time when the FBI was en route? That reminds me, do you know the response time at the other attacks?"

"The state police were already on site in Oklahoma," said Nicola. *"Someone had called in a bomb threat. In California, the attack took place less than ten miles from an FBI field office."*

"They wanted the authorities to arrive quickly. Were any of the attackers captured alive?"

"None that I'm aware of."

"All right, I only have one more question for now. Do you trust mundane authorities to handle this?"

It was Nicola's turn to think in silence. I drummed my fingers against the chair until she finally said, *"Keep me informed. You understand that if this goes badly, the Porters won't be able to protect you? McGinley at DHS is determined to make an example out of anyone involved."*

"Understood. Thanks, Nicola."

"I hope everything goes well with your niece."

"Thank you," I said, more warmly this time.

"I'm sorry you missed your flight out of D.C. I know you wanted to be there."

"I needed to be in Lansing." I sighed and checked the information screen mounted on the wall. I needed to be in Vegas, too. I trusted the New Millennium medical team, but I was the one who'd assured Lex and her parents that it wouldn't hurt, and that everything would be okay.

Toby had never forgiven me for letting Lex suffer all these years. What would they think when I wasn't there for her in the morning?

I managed a forty-five minute nap on the flight before jolting awake when the plane touched down in Vegas. I sat up and rubbed the drool from my cheek, texted Lena to let her know I'd arrived, and gathered my carry-on bag of books. The rest of my luggage was back at the hotel in D.C.

I picked up an overpriced coffee from one of the half-dozen airport Starbucks and hiked my way to long-term parking where my pickup truck awaited. I made the slow drive east through the city on mental autopilot. It was almost two o'clock when I finally left the worst of Vegas traffic behind, and another half hour to reach my destination beyond the city limits.

The New Millennium Complex looked like a cross between a medieval fortress and a space station. Seamless stone walls surrounded roughly fifteen acres of land. Four gleaming, glass-walled towers rose from within those walls, as majestic as anything you could find on the strip. Though the New Millennium towers lacked the garish colors and lights of the casinos.

The entire population of Copper River, Michigan, could have fit inside our compound, and you'd still have room for our former neighbors from Tamarack.

The Porters had purchased the land ten months ago through a series of deals and negotiations with Las Vegas and the state of Nevada. The amount of paperwork involved made the Wheel of Time series look like flash fiction, and there were at least five separate legal battles currently in play about everything from zoning requirements to air rights.

Coming here from Michigan felt like traveling to another planet, a hot, arid world where the spectrum of visible light had boycotted the color green. Patches of dark scrub along the side of the road came close, but for the most part, the landscape was all browns and tans and yellows. The first time Lena visited, she'd remarked that the lack of trees made the land feel like a graveyard.

There were no protesters at the front gates today, but it was obvious they'd been here recently. The desert plants and flowers by the entrance were trampled into the dirt. I kept suggesting we replace them with cacti. New graffiti denounced us as witches and demons and Satanists, which always amused me. I'd heard the same accusations about role-playing games when I was a teenager.

Visible security measures included cameras and electrified wire along the top of the wall and guards at the large, arched gate. Other protection was embedded within the stone. The wards looked like braids of barely legible text forming a black fence inside the wall, with a thinner framework stretched overhead: an invisible dome designed to block out aerial cameras and worse.

I pulled up to the small booth at the gate. A metal sign warned: YOUR THOUGHTS MAY BE TELEPATHICALLY SCREENED FOR HOSTILE INTENTIONS. Several paragraphs of fine-print legal jargon followed.

Technically, it was more of an empathic screening than a telepathic one. We were more interested in hatred and rage, unusual levels of fear and anxiety, that sort of thing. I hated the mental intrusion, but the Director of Security had insisted. After they caught three different would-be attackers in the first month, including one with a trunk full of fertilizer-based explosive, I stopped protesting.

I rolled down my window and handed my ID to a

middle-aged woman in a turquoise New Millennium polo shirt. "Good afternoon, Marion."

Marion was Sanguinarius Meyerii, from the *Twilight* series. Her particular species of vampire was better known as sparklers. Marion had been a diehard fan of the books, no pun intended. Last year, after learning magic and vampires were real, she'd snuck across the border and paid a Mexican vampire nest to convert her.

She was damn lucky she hadn't gotten herself killed. Sparkler venom was nasty, dangerous stuff.

Her life as a vampire hadn't worked out as well as she'd hoped. Skin that glittered in the sun wasn't easy to hide, and she soon lost her job as a middle school English teacher. She'd ended up working at a junkyard near Reno. When New Millennium announced we'd be hiring humans and nonhumans alike, Marion was first in line with her resume.

She was a pleasant enough woman who'd taken it upon herself to organize a weekly BINGO game among the staff. She was also strong enough to flip my truck one-handed if she decided I didn't belong here.

Marion glanced at a second vampire behind her. My head throbbed softly as he checked my emotions.

She returned my badge. "Welcome back, Mr. Vainio. How was Washington?"

"One more day and I'd have turned a U.S. senator into an earthworm and fed him to Smudge."

Marion smiled and peeked in at Smudge. "Aside from the fire-spider, do you have anything magical with you?"

"Half a vial of healing potion. Catalog number CSL1950-8."

She typed a quick note on the computer. "Weren't they fixing your niece's leg this morning?"

I wondered if her partner could sense my frustration. "That's right."

"Well, you tell that little angel I said hello!"

The gate slid open a moment later. I pulled through and followed the winding blacktop to the left. In the week I'd been away, they had erected a second security booth inside the wall. Another armed guard, a human this time, nodded at me as I passed.

Most of the grounds were landscaped with orange and gray stone. Cacti and palm trees bordered walking paths between the four towers and various smaller buildings. Silver and black road signs guided visitors to housing, a small food court and general store, supply warehouses, and of course the ten-story towers spread out at the corners of a rough square: Medical, Admin, Research, and Library.

The Johannes Gutenberg Memorial Library Tower was the real treasure. The building housed the contents of six former Porter archives along with an additional twenty thousand titles, including some from Gutenberg's private collection. Given the choice, I would have happily abandoned my studio apartment in the eastern housing building to live full-time in Gutenberg Tower.

Instead, I drove past the library to the small parking lot behind the eastern residential building. I didn't spend much time here, and couldn't bring myself to think of the empty apartment as home. It felt like a larger version of the place I'd had during grad school, only without the Escher prints or the Renaissance festival swords hanging on the walls. Once inside, I started up the coffee machine, turned the television on for Smudge, and headed for the shower.

Between the cold water and the hot coffee, I got my brain jump-started enough to sit down and log on to my computer. I ignored several interview requests from the media and used my access as Research Director to pull up Alexis Vainio's medical folder.

The patient summary described the results of the accident in clinical terms, but I could never read it without hearing my father's voice. He had been the one to call me that night. I'd just gotten back from dinner, and it was raining outside, a hard-core Michigan storm with raindrops big enough to bruise.

I remembered him spitting profanity like bullets, as if he could ward off the grief with anger. *"God damned drunk ran the fucking stop sign. Angie and Lex are both in the hospital. Your brother's with them. Your mom and I are driving down tonight. The doctors say Angie should be all right. They don't . . . they don't fucking know if Lex . . ."*

It was the only time I could recall hearing him cry.

I'd flown down as soon as I could. I stayed with them, brought Toby food at the hospital, took care of the house and their pet lizard, and did everything I could to help . . . except to use magic.

Magic would have triggered a visit from Gutenberg and his automatons. The accident was public knowledge, as were the injuries Lex had suffered. If I healed her, there was no way to explain her sudden and miraculous recovery. My magic would have put myself and the Porters at risk of exposure, and Gutenberg was enough of a bastard to do whatever it took to preserve his secrets.

I could restore my niece's amputated leg, and Gutenberg would simply remove it again. There was nothing I could do.

At least, that was what I told myself.

I closed my eyes, remembering the letter Toby had written last year after learning what I was.

Do you know what it's like trying to explain to your five-year-old daughter that if we don't let the doctors cut off her leg, the infection will kill her? Or to know that even the amputation might not save her?

She's had four surgeries to try to repair the damage from the crash. To pin her pelvis back together. To ease the pressure on her brain. Depending on the results of her next MRI, we may have to go back for number five before the end of the summer.

I never said how much it meant to us that you flew out here after the accident. That you watched Lexi's brother and brought us badly cooked meals and did everything you could to help.

Only you didn't, did you? You didn't do everything.

Maybe you had good reasons. Maybe your precious secret was more important than your niece. Well, the secret's out now, and Lexi deserves better. She deserves the chance to be a kid ...

I pushed the memories aside and skimmed Lex's record. The background was fourteen pages long, detailing multiple surgeries, medications, and chronic pain. Pain I could have spared her.

New Millennium had spent months on tests, working under the direction of NIH doctors to ensure that all non-magical options had been exhausted. There were memorandums of agreement with Toby's insurance company, piles of waivers and disclaimers, and even a court challenge to Toby and Angie's fitness as parents. That bullshit had come closer than anything else to making me openly break the laws against magical assault and battery.

I clicked through to the most recent entry, dated today at 8:38 a.m.

A longer report would come later. For now, I wiped my eyes and focused on the photograph of Lex standing in front of a hospital bed. Each of her parents held one of her hands, holding her steady as she tested her balance.

She wore a hospital gown, and her feet were bare. Her

new leg was several shades paler than the other. It was skinnier, too. She'd be in rehab and physical therapy for weeks to come. Months, probably.

I checked the doctor's notes. Lex had spent the next hour getting X-rays, MRIs, and other scans of her new leg. They'd also completed a long list of tests on her brain. The physical damage had disappeared, but we would continue to monitor her for seizures and other side effects for at least a year.

A two-tone whistle filled the apartment. I'd programmed the door chime with the boatswain's whistle sound from the original *Star Trek*. I cleared the computer screen, wiped my face, and headed for the door.

Russell Potts, the Department of Homeland Security's representative on the New Millennium Board of Directors, shoved a trade paperback into my hands. "Right now, every man, woman, and child in North Korea is reading this book. Do you know why?"

I glanced at the cover, which showed an idealized painting of North Korea's supreme leader. There was no title, not that I could have read it anyway. Nor did I need to. I did my best to sound bored. "Because it describes various weapons the North Korean military could use to guarantee the supremacy of their nation, including a kind of supersoldier serum, long-range assassination drones with cloaking technology, and an implantable spy chip for monitoring their own people and anyone else they feel like snooping on. One of our libriomancers intercepted a South Korean spy, a gwisin, who filled us in. How do you think your boss at DHS found out about it?"

Potts was a tall, narrow-faced man with a thick brown mustache who always wore suits and ties, even in the desert heat. He pursed his lips, clearly reevaluating what he'd been intending to say. "A gwisin?"

"A kind of ghost."

"What is your team doing about it?"

"Charles is monitoring their progress. North Korea has a population of twenty-five million. Not all those people are literate, of course. He's estimating an upper limit of ten million who are actually reading the novel as ordered. We're trying to chart how quickly they can empower a book for libriomancy, and comparing it to the data for other novels. Charles believes since the population knows this book was deliberately crafted not for story, but for the weaponization of magic, that this will reduce the effectiveness of reader belief. It's also just flat-out bad prose, but that could be problems with the translation, or our cultural filters affecting how—"

"That's it? You're standing around watching while North Korea builds magical superweapons?"

"You want me to fly to North Korea and tell them to stop reading? I'm a librarian, Mister Potts. I don't believe in banning books."

"Do you believe in letting a madman terrorize the international community?" He started to say more, then caught himself. He pressed his lips together and looked me up and down. "You're baiting me."

"A little." I made a show of checking the time on the wall clock behind me. "I'll fill you in next week. Right now, I'm late for another meeting."

"With your niece, I know." He folded his arms and waited, knowing perfectly well I wouldn't use magic to evict him from my doorway. I could try to physically shove him aside, but Potts had spent fifteen years in the Army, and he'd played college football before that. I'd have better luck climbing out a window and flying away, and from the smirk on his face, he knew it.

"First of all, North Korea can't do anything without a libriomancer," I said. "The Porters number around five hundred people, very few of whom would be interested in helping North Korea develop a superweapon. Given their population, the odds of them having an undiscovered libriomancer on hand are slim."

"Would you risk this planet for 'slim'?"

I ignored him and kept talking. "Second, like I said before, we're tracking their progress. The moment the book approaches any real magical potential, I intend to lock it."

He ran a thumb over his mustache while he studied me. "That's the equivalent of wiping the hard drive, right? I thought Gutenberg was the only one who knew how to do that."

"Close enough, and yes. He was." I shrugged. "He's been teaching me. Ponce de Leon might be able to do it, too, I'm not sure. I'll ask if I ever talk to him again."

Potts' face had been growing gradually redder throughout our conversation, and that last comment started him on the path to purple. He glared at me, like he was trying to discern whether or not I was playing with him. Which I was . . . but I was also telling the truth. "We were informed that Johannes Gutenberg was dead."

"That's right." I returned the book, then folded my arms and waited for his response.

"I see." He took a slow breath. "I expect you to keep me informed of North Korea's progress. I'm holding you personally responsible for making sure that book is locked before it becomes a danger. You might prefer to hide away with your books and your animals and your magic portals, but there are a lot of very bad people beyond these walls. People who see magic as an opportunity to kill you, me, and everyone else in this country. Maybe they're not as impressive as rogue libriomancers and ghosts and whatever else you've fought, but we cannot underestimate them. You might think yourself invincible, but what about everyone else? Think of your niece. You brought her here to heal her with magic, but all it takes is one radicalized magic-user, one creature with a grudge, and she's another corpse. Just like the ones in Lansing."

I stepped away to grab Smudge and return him to his cage. It was either that or punch a high-level DHS official in the mouth, and there was no way that would have ended well. I slung a bookbag over my shoulder and turned back to face him. "They'll have to get past me, first."

From: cbrice@newmillennium.org
To: npallas@newmillennium.org
Cc: tpolk@newmillennium.org; vhambrecht@newmillennium.org
Subject: Speaking Tour

Ms. Pallas,

You may not be aware, but several weeks ago I requested New Millennium send me and my wife on a speaking tour to promote our work. Mr. Vainio denied this request.

I've been a libriomancer and a member of the Porters for longer than Isaac Vainio has been alive. As you know, I am also a bestselling and award-winning author. I've been a featured speaker and guest of honor at countless conventions. I was part of a science advisory panel for President Clinton.

In the old days, the Porters held storytellers in high esteem. Maybe that's changed. Maybe the new council wants us to keep our heads down and follow orders like good little drones.

Setting aside false modesty, New Millennium needs the positive publicity I can provide. I'm sure Isaac is doing the best he can, but this is just one more instance of his inexperience and lack of judgment as a manager. I suppose it's normal for someone his age to become enamored of the spotlight, and to try to keep the attention to himself. But allowing a fresh-faced libriomancer barely out of college to go to Washington D.C. to speak on behalf of New Millennium? Ye gods and little fishes, what was the council thinking?

I've attached a proposed tour schedule that would begin next month. I look forward to your prompt response.

Best,
Charles

—
Charles L. Brice, Science Fiction Author
http://www.clbrice.net
Coming Next Month: *Dark Wanderer*, the newest book in the bestselling *Dark Star Chronicles*. Available for pre-order at Amazon and other retailers.

From: vhambrecht@newmillennium.org
To: tpolk@newmillennium.org
Subject: Re: Speaking Tour
Wow. What a tool!
-V

Chapter 6

"History says you broke a contract to be married."

"History is the world's most egotistical gossip."

"You worked so hard to preserve yourself, but you never mention anything about family. Were you protecting their privacy, or is it that you never had time?"

"Revolutionizing literature and magic leaves little time for anything more. Particularly for those of us who are so different. I'm practically another species. I had dalliances over the years, naturally, but none that survived more than a few weeks or months."

"What about Ponce de Leon?"

"Every relationship is unique. Juan and I were colleagues first, then rivals. But as time passed, and we watched our friends and family grow old and die . . . our priorities shifted. Humanity struggles with change, and we were so very human back then. We each provided an anchor, a stable fixture in the other's life. We needed one another far more than either of us would ever admit."

"You kicked him out of the Porters. You banished him."

*"Lovers clash. Relationships evolve. I have no doubt
we would have found one another again in time, as we
started to do ..."*

*"Did you ever consider leaving the Porters to be with
him?"*

"Oh, yes. Many times."

"What stopped you?"

"Responsibility. Fear. Love."

*"Love stopped you from running off with Ponce de
Leon?"*

*"I've had two great loves in my lifetime, Isaac. Juan
Ponce de Leon is one. The Porters—magic—is the other.
Perhaps you'll have better luck than I did when it comes
to balancing those relationships."*

WE HAD PLANNED the New Millennium
complex with an eye toward long-term growth.
Thanks to legal hurdles and red tape that mul-
tiplied like tribbles at a buffet, the majority of our facilities remained vacant. Of the ten floors in the Metrodora
Medical Tower, seven were sealed off and gathering dust
while we waited for the day we could bring in more patients and healers.

Lex and her parents were in room 318 in the pediatric
wing. Silhouettes of children, all painted in primary colors on the walls, played beneath large rainbows and
cheerful white clouds. Shooting stars marked different
trails along the floor: blue stars led to the main desk,
green to the elevator and stairs, purple to the snack machine and play area, and so on.

I offered nods and greetings to several nurses, each of
whom glanced at my badge before letting me pass. I
found myself dragging my feet as I approached room

318. I'd faced any number of monsters and murderers in recent years, but in each of those battles, I'd known how to fight.

With Toby, I didn't know how to *end* the fight. Truth be told, there would always be a part of me that believed my big brother was invincible, and that if I said the wrong thing, he'd put me in a headlock, bloody my nose, and shut me in the closet. Or shave off one of my eyebrows while I was sleeping, like he did after I accidentally scratched his car.

The door to Lex's room was shut. The whiteboard outside noted that she'd eaten lunch and was scheduled for physical therapy at three thirty. I glanced at Smudge as if he could tell me what to expect, but Smudge was better at sensing threats to life and limb than he was the anger and bitterness of family.

I heard several voices inside: doctors and libriomancers taking turn asking Lex questions. She answered each one calmly and methodically, with her parents occasionally jumping in to offer additional details about her medical history.

I straightened my shoulders and knocked.

"Be right there," Toby called. I heard slippers shuffling over the tile floor, and then the door swung inward.

Toby Vainio was taller, broader, and stronger than me. On the other hand, I still had all my hair.

His thinning blond fuzz was shaved to half an inch in length, a habit he'd kept up for close to a decade, ever since joining the National Guard. It made it easy to see the jagged scar above his left ear from falling through a rotten dock board when we were kids. He wore an old Detroit Lions T-shirt and loose sweatpants.

"Isaac." We stared at one another for several awkward seconds. He stepped into the hall and pulled the door shut behind him.

"I'm sorry, Toby. I wanted to be here. I had to go to Lansing last night, and then—"

"We heard about the attacks." He leaned his back against the door and folded his arms. "Was that all?"

"No, it's not all," I snapped. "I wanted to see how Lex was doing."

"Lex is fine. We all are."

"You know, maybe instead of being all pissed off at me, you could try being happy for your daughter."

"Turns out I can do both."

"Well, aren't you the efficient little multitasker."

"Mom and Dad called this morning before the procedure. And afterward. They've been watching Nick and getting him to school every day so we could be here with his little sister. They all video chatted with Lex last night. They'd have been here if New Millennium allowed it. They sent flowers. Angie's dad mailed a new pair of roller blades. He's called four times this week."

"I said I'm sorry."

"I get it, Isaac. I do. I'm not even that angry."

"Really? Because you do a great impression."

He snorted. "Yah, okay. I'm angry. But I'll get over it. I keep having to remind myself this is who you are. You're off doing important libriomancer shit and trying to save the world, and that's always going to be your priority."

"Would you rather I *didn't* try to save the world? You think I wanted to be in the middle of a magical crossfire last year in Copper River? Of all the ways I like to spend my free time, fighting dead magical megalomaniacs is really far down on the list."

"What is it you want, Isaac?" he asked wearily.

"I want to say hi to my niece. To see how she's doing." Years of habitual secrecy made me hesitate before adding, "I also want to read what they did to her."

"Read what? You mean her records?" He snorted. "I didn't think you Porters cared about privacy laws. You were keeping medical information about my family for years. Why bother asking permission now?"

"I didn't know the Porters had a file on you." Though I should have. The Porters had recruited me before I finished high school. Of course they'd have investigated my family as well. "You're right. I have access to all of the research files, including Lex's."

His face went stony. "You're looking for something that's not in her files."

"I'm not looking for anything specific. I just want to be sure, to read *her*. To see the magic they used to heal her."

"You can do that? I thought libriomancers just pulled stuff out of books."

"They—we do. But there are outliers. I know a girl who learned to do libriomancy with ebooks. Gutenberg carried stories around in a sword. As for me . . ." How to explain everything I'd learned, all the ways I'd changed in recent years?

A pair of doctors emerged from the room. I waited until they'd gone, then said, "Call it trial-by-fire. I've had to learn new tricks to survive some of what's come my way."

For the first time, I saw something more than frost and anger in his eyes. "What do you mean? What happened to you?"

Despite public hearings, investigations, and countless interviews, there were plenty of details I'd never shared. Details I tried not to think about. My instinct was to deflect the question, but that would only lead to another round of verbal fencing with poisoned blades. "Which time? Do you want to hear how I got stabbed, then merged my body with a five-hundred-year-old wood-

and-metal automaton built by Johannes Gutenberg?
That was a fun day. I got to visit the moon."

He stared at me. "Bullshit."

"When I was done, I plummeted through Earth's at-
mosphere. Nearly burnt myself to a cinder in the process.
Then last year, I deliberately triggered a trap created a
thousand years ago by Pope Sylvester II that ripped my
mind from my body and locked it away."

"Why the hell would you do that?"

"Because the woman inside that trap had taken a
friend of mine, burned down my house, and murdered
thirty-seven people in Copper River, and I was damn
well going to stop her." He'd grown up in that house, too,
and we'd both known most of those thirty-seven people
who died. The only difference was that I'd always known
why they died.

My heart thudded against my ribs, and my throat
tightened. Memories surged through my mind: collapsed
buildings and broken bodies, the smell of smoke, screams
of fear and pain. I clenched a fist and looked away.

"What happened to her?" he asked. "The woman who
took your friend?"

"She tried to escape." I swallowed. "I stopped her."

Neither of us spoke for a while. "That healing magic
you Porters can do. How many times have you had to use
that on yourself?"

I didn't answer. Which was an answer in itself.

"Jesus, Isaac."

"It's not all bad." I stared at one of the painted stars
on the floor. "I spent a lot more time cataloging and re-
searching than I did in the field. I've gotten to hang out
with magic-users who were born centuries ago, and seen
things everyone insisted were impossible. I've been to
space twice. I even tried a Pan Galactic Gargle Blaster."

"From *Hitchhiker's Guide*? How was it?"

"Not a clue. I remember taking the drink, and I remember waking up two days later. In Ontario. Wearing a nineteenth century Mountie uniform. Everything else is a bit of a blur."

"None of this makes me want to lct you anywhere near my daughter." His chuckle was short-lived. "There's more you're not telling me."

I sat down with my back against the wall. He followed suit a moment later. "It's something Alexander Keeler said during the hearing in D.C."

"Keeler's the guy who wants to license and regulate magic, right? The one with the face of a hairless cat with epic constipation?"

"Oh, great. Now I'll never be able to look at him without seeing that image." I nodded to a passing nurse. "They're not wrong to be cautious. New Millennium could change things. *Really* change things, I mean. Magic can't fix everything, but it could make the world so much better. It could also do unimaginable damage. That's one of the reasons we've had to move so slowly."

"What kind of damage?" Toby glanced over his shoulder at Lex's door.

"Nothing that could hurt Lex." I hesitated. "But her being here doesn't make sense. You know the Porters and New Millennium are fighting hard for public support, right? We can't afford any kind of taint or scandal. So why sign off on bringing the Director of Research's niece into the medical study?" Whatever I might think of Senator Keeler and his committee, the man had a point about favoritism and the potential bias to our research.

"I figured it was because most people didn't feel safe enough to volunteer."

I shook my head. "We can cure cancer, Toby. Plenty of people are desperate enough to try anything, even magic."

Toby wasn't stupid. I could see him sifting through the implications. "Could be someone did it so you'd owe them. They want to call in a favor down the line."

"Maybe."

"Or they want to use her against you somehow. Isaac, I swear to God, if you've put Lex in danger—"

"Let me look her over. I'll be able to tell whether anyone has used additional magic on her. Or you and Angie." I peered at him over my glasses. "You're clean."

"What kind of additional magic?"

I looked away. "When I was working as a field agent, I once installed a magical bomb in a vampire's skull to keep him from preying on humans."

"Jesus H. Christ." His hands started to shake. "If they did something like that to Lex, can you fix it?"

"Yes. It's probably nothing, Toby. I just need to be sure."

"What if it's not nothing? What if someone tries to use us for leverage?"

"Then I'll make them wish they hadn't."

"Look at you, getting all badass." His words trailed off. "Damn. You're serious, aren't you?"

I shrugged and stood up. "Shall we?"

"All right. But if you lie or hold back anything that could hurt Lex, I'll kick your skinny ass." He got to his feet. "And then I'll tell Mom."

Lex sat in a wheelchair, wearing a purple princess nightgown. A trio of New Millennium medical staff examined her leg, while her mother hovered next to the chair.

Lex's brown hair partially hid a circular white patch the size of a quarter stuck to the side of her neck. A single LED on the edge of the patch glowed green, indicating that her vitals were within normal range.

The monitor patch was one of my accomplishments . . . sort of. It had come from an article in *Medical Science Today* about the future of diagnostic medicine. The author had described her vision for the next generation of medical monitoring tools, from a disposable monitoring patch with a wireless transmitter to a diagnostic capsule capable of providing a full-body scan from the inside. I'd contacted her the next day with a contract allowing us to use libriomancy to create those tools, and granting us the rights to use them in our work at New Millennium. Within a week of the magazine's publication, we'd created twenty-four sets.

"Uncle Isaac!" Lex beamed and waved.

"Hi kiddo," I said. "Long time no see. How are you feeling?"

"We're fine," her mother answered. Angie tended to be a quiet woman, always listening and assessing. Right now, she looked like she was assessing the best way to dispose of my body if I said or did anything to harm her daughter. "New Millennium has taken very good care of us."

"It's amazing." That was Jennifer Simpkin, an orthopedic surgeon from Reno who'd been working and consulting for us part-time. She returned her reflex hammer to the pocket of her lab coat and stood to shake my hand. "The new leg is as healthy as the original. Healthier, in some respects. There's no scarring where it joins the older skin and tissue. Blood flow, reflexes, everything is flawless."

A younger woman I didn't recognize glanced up, spotted Smudge, and jumped to position herself between Lex and me. "Sir, you can't bring a spider in here."

"Would it help if I told you he was self-sterilizing?"

"It's all right," said Dr. Simpkin. "Lex has no open wounds or sutures to worry about, and most hunting spiders are better than some people about grooming and cleanliness." She typed something into her tablet computer. "I've been validating the readouts from the diagnostic patch, and they've been accurate within about two percent. If New Millennium can mass produce them, the applications are mind-blowing. Continual glucose tracking for diabetics, monitoring infants overnight to prevent SIDS—have you tested to see if they can distinguish fetal life signs from those of the mother?"

Her enthusiasm made me smile. *This* was why I'd fought so hard to help create this place, for the possibilities and the hope and the wonder. "I don't actually know. Email me a reminder to add it to the research agenda at next week's meeting? As for mass production, that's trickier. There's a limit to how many times a book can be used for libriomancy. They develop magical charring, like burning out a filter. Magazines are even more short-lived. But we're looking into other ways of duplicating them." I sat down on the side of the bed. "Do you mind if I give Lex a quick magical once-over?"

"Will it hurt?" Lex asked. There was none of the stuttering that had marked her speech since the accident.

"Nope." I swallowed a knot in my throat, dropped to one knee, and unclipped Smudge's cage. "You remember Smudge, don't you?"

"Your pet tarantula? Cool!"

Most people cringed at the sight of a four-inch spider, but I remembered Lex's interest in all things creepy crawly, from worms and lizards to snakes and her short-lived pet cricket Jimmy. I lowered my voice to a conspiratorial level. "I couldn't tell you before, but he's not exactly a tarantula." I grabbed a plastic bag of gummi worms from my pocket. "Do you want to feed him?"

She looked to her parents for permission, then took one of the gummi worms. I grabbed a narrow table from beside the bed and rolled it over by the wheelchair, then set the cage so the fiberglass-lined side was down.

Lex stretched the worm until it broke, popped half into her mouth, and poked the rest through the bars of the cage. Smudge snatched it up in his forelegs.

"Watch this." Tiny triangles of red flame flowed down Smudge's legs. The worm softened and began to melt.

Her mouth formed an O. "Smudge is *magic*?"

"He's a fire-spider. He can create his own flames when he's afraid or angry, or when he wants to cook his meals. He once set my laundry on fire because he was mad at me."

Lex leaned in to watch as Smudge slurped up red and green semi-liquefied gummy worm.

Her parents pressed closer. Dr. Simpkin and the other medical staff crowded behind me. I felt like an exhibit.

I studied Lex's feet. One was moderately dirty, the toenails rough and torn. The other was clean and lacking in any callouses, with short, perfect nails. "Ready for the first test? I'm betting the doctors forgot to do this one."

Lex steeled herself. At nine years old, she had endured more procedures and labwork and injections than most people five times her age, but that didn't make them any less unpleasant.

I tickled her toes. She squealed and jerked back hard. Angie caught the wheelchair's handles to keep it from tipping over.

"Tickle reflex appears to be working," I said in my most official voice. "But we should probably check the other foot for comparison."

"No," she said, laughing.

"All right, fine. But don't complain to me if you end up tickle-impaired!" I winked. "How did your first round of physical therapy go this morning?"

"It's *boring*." She made a face like she'd bitten something rotten. "I mean, walking up and down three steps was cool the first time, but they want me do it a *million* more times!"

"Physically, she's perfect," added Dr. Simpkin. "But her brain has to relearn so much about balance and movement. It's going to take time and practice."

"What about . . ." I searched for a tactful phrase to describe the mental impairment she'd suffered.

Lex saved me the trouble. "No more brain farts!"

"That's what we called it when she struggled to remember words or had balance problems," said Toby. "When she had a full-blown seizure, that was brain vomit."

Seizures had been one of the many ongoing effects of Lex's damaged brain. Medication had suppressed most of them, but for the past year, she'd been averaging one seizure every couple of months. I'd never witnessed her full-blown brain-vomit. I'm not sure what I would have done if I had.

"The MRI and CAT scans we took before lunch appear normal," added Dr. Simpkin. "We've got specialists reviewing the results, and we'll be running a lot more tests, but it looks very encouraging."

I could have healed Lex years ago. We could have done this for thousands of other kids by now. I thought about the family who'd spoken to me after the hearing in D.C. and the long list of critically ill and injured people on our research trial waiting lists.

"Uncle Isaac?"

"Sorry." I removed my glasses and set them on her meal tray. The rest of the room blurred, but the text of the magic in Lex's body sharpened.

"Why don't you just fix your eyes with magic?" asked Toby.

"For the same reason healing magic doesn't change a vampire back into human. The damage isn't a physical thing. It's magically written into the essence of who and what you are." I leaned closer, trying to read the fading magic in Lex's body. The text was faint, and I didn't see any active spells. "Did the libriomancer explain that this was a one-shot thing? That means the next time you scrape your knee, it'll have to heal the old-fashioned way. So be careful."

"I know." Lex sounded so annoyed and put-upon by the reminder I couldn't help but smile.

I read several lines, enough to identify the source of the spell. "They used a book called *Our Lady of the Islands*. The protagonist develops the ability to heal with a touch. What exactly did it look like when they healed Lex?"

"Dr. Parisi did the actual healing," said Dr. Simpkin. "She called it a controlled partial manifestation."

"It was like the book was a window and the lady inside the book reached out and shook hands with Doctor Alyce!" Lex added. "She put the book-lady's hand on my forehead, then on my knee."

"Makes sense." With the NIH and everyone else looking for the slightest excuse to shut us down, we'd been going with the least intrusive measures possible. Alyce Parisi was a good libriomancer and an equally good doctor. She wouldn't have done anything that risked harm to her patient.

Despite its effectiveness, I wasn't entirely comfortable with the technique. Living manifestations of fictional characters were too unpredictable, especially intelligent characters. They couldn't handle the transition to the real world. Lena was one of the only exceptions I'd encountered, and her existence and sanity had come with a cost. Even Smudge had struggled when I accidentally drew him from his familiar goblin tunnels into my high school library.

Partial manifestations—a single hand or arm reaching from the pages—were certainly safer. We'd used them in the past to take blood samples and such. But exactly how much of the character did we create in the process? Did the mind achieve any kind of momentary sentience? Was there a flicker of awareness, of existence spread between the real world and the magical potential of the text?

I stood and slid my glasses back onto my face. "Lex is great. It's exactly what we'd hoped for."

"That's a good thing." Toby's hesitation turned it into as much a question as a statement.

"Yah, of course." I was being paranoid. Whatever chaos was happening throughout the world, she was safe here.

"Is there anything magic can't do, Uncle Isaac?"

"Plenty." I forced a smile. "But wouldn't it be boring if we could do *anything*?"

From her frown, she wasn't convinced.

"Want to see something I *can* do?" I clenched my jaw, glanced at the phone, and subvocally dialed their direct extension. When the phone rang, I smiled at Lex. "It's for you."

She picked up the phone. "Hello?"

"Hi, Lex!"

Her face lit up. "Uncle Isaac? How are you doing that?"

"I told you. It's magic!"

She climbed out of her chair. Her parents both swooped in to catch her if she fell, but she shooed them away. She grabbed my arm for balance and stood on tiptoes to study my mouth "Do it again."

"You mean, do it again, please?"

She laughed and touched my throat near the jawbone. "Your lips aren't moving, but this is. Do you have a phone in your *mouth*?"

I hung up and laughed. "You're too clever for me. My team built it. They had to combine magical tech from three different books into a practical communicator with the ability to tap into existing wireless and satellite, at which point I pulled the essence of those technologies—" I could see her eyes glazing over. "Yes, it's a magic phone in my mouth. I'm going to leave the number with you and your parents. You can call me any time you need. If anything happens, this is the quickest way to get in touch, and it's completely secure."

I emphasized that last sentence, and Toby nodded slightly in response.

"Can I be a libriomancer when I grow up?" asked Lex.

Hoo boy. "I don't know. We don't really understand why some people can do magic and others can't."

Her shoulders sagged.

"But if that's what you want, the best thing you can do is read. Libriomancy is all about reading and loving books. Find the stories you love, and don't ever let anyone tell you you're wrong for loving them. If you want, I can send you some of my favorites to read. As long as it's all right with your parents."

She nodded solemnly. "I promise I'll read them all."

I made a face. "Don't do that unless you love them all. There are too many books in the world to waste time slogging through the ones you hate." I waited while she eased herself back into her chair, then grabbed Smudge's cage. "I should get out of the way and let Dr. Simpkin finish up. Thanks for letting me interrupt. It's great to see you again, Lex. Maybe when you're a little stronger, I could introduce you to Kerling and the rest of the animals over at research."

She nodded again, beaming.

Toby followed me into the hall. "Should I be worried?"

"I'm going to review all of Lex's paperwork and double-check who selected her, but I don't think so. I'm probably overthinking things. New Millennium has good security, magical and mundane. Much better than the capitol in Lansing."

"No kidding. The woman in charge of security—what's her name? Palmer? She spent most of our first day reviewing security procedures with us. This place is locked down tighter than the White House."

"Babs Palmer, yah."

He paused. "You don't like her."

"She and I butted heads a few times. She ended up trying to kill a friend of mine. I mean, that friend was trying to kill her too, but still . . . Then I had to stop Babs from creating an army and seizing control of the Porters. So no, she's not on my Nice List."

"Are you serious?" He stepped closer and lowered his voice. "How the hell did she end up running things here?"

"A lot of things were up in the air after Gutenberg died. Whatever I might think of Babs, she's very, very good at what she does. Nicola Pallas and the rest of the Porter Council spent a long time telepathically checking her intentions before sending her to New Millennium. She believes in what we're doing here, and she wants to see it grow."

"Do you trust her?"

"I trust Nicola. I wouldn't have let you come here if I didn't believe it was safe. But if I hear the slightest whisper that your family could be in danger, I'll get you out."

"Thanks." He put a hand on the door. With his back to me, he added, "Be careful out there, eh?"

I thought about the potential clue Deb had given me, and about the blood and bodies in Lansing. With Lex and her parents safe, it was time to find some answers. "Not really part of my skillset, but I'll do my best."

INTERPOL'S MOST WANTED MAGICAL CRIMINALS

1. Name: Juan Ponce de Leon
   Nationality: Spanish
   Date of Birth: 1474
   Height: Unknown
   Hair: Unknown
   Eyes: Unknown

   Charges: Murder, enslavement, theft, and other war crimes.

Ponce de Leon is believed to be a sorcerer. The International Criminal Court has issued a warrant for his arrest based on crimes committed by him and soldiers under his command in the early sixteenth century.

2. Name: Yvan Marchais
   Nationality: French
   Date of Birth: 16/06/1984
   Height: 1.59 meter
   Hair: Brown
   Eyes: Brown
   Charges: Murder, attempted murder, kidnapping, extortion.

Marchais is a mercenary and religious extremist, and is believed to be a vampire. He is wanted in connection with three large-scale massacres in eastern Europe.

3. Name: Samoud al-Rahman
   Nationality: Afghani
   Date of Birth: 02/10/1991
   Height: 1.45 meter
   Hair: Black

| Eyes: | Red |
| Charges: | Murder, terrorism, arms trafficking, treason. |

Al-Rahman is the son of an Afghani warlord. The people believe him to be part demon. He's been implicated in more than four thousand murders and executions.

4.
Name:	Lucy Bell
Nationality:	U.S.A.
Date of Birth:	28/04/2001
Height:	1.38 meter
Hair:	Blonde
Eyes:	Hazel
Charges:	Drug trafficking, blackmail, extortion, sale of prohibited magical material.

Bell ran away from her parents in 2011. In recent years, she has been linked to gang-related drug dealing in the southern United States. She is believed to be using libriomancy to create new, powerful, and deadly drugs.

IF YOU HAVE ANY INFORMATION ON THE WHEREABOUTS OF THESE INDIVIDUALS, PLEASE CONTACT YOUR LOCAL OR NATIONAL POLICE, OR INTERPOL.

Chapter 7

"For someone who claimed to want nothing more than to be a researcher, you certainly spend a great deal of time in the field."

"It's hard to concentrate on research when the world's going to hell."

"Yet somehow, billions of people go about their lives every day, resisting the urge to track down terrorists and conspiracies."

"You think I should stay in my lab? Let someone else worry about whoever orchestrated those attacks?"

"Not at all. I simply think you should stop lying to yourself about who you are."

BABS PALMER'S OFFICE was on the fourth floor of the Reginald Scot Administrative Tower, along with offices for the NIH liaison and representatives from the FBI, Department of Homeland Security, and our human resources team.

In addition to working for the Porters, Babs had been a practicing lawyer until a year ago, when the State Bar of Texas discovered her "supplemental employment." More than half her cases were now being appealed and retried on the grounds that she could have used magic to influence judge and jury. Which, knowing Babs, wasn't a completely implausible idea.

Her receptionist, a young Japanese woman named Kiyoko Itô, guarded the path to Babs' office like Cerberus protecting the gates of hell. Kiyoko also acted as the main receptionist for New Millennium during business hours, and coordinated the occasional birthday party for employees.

She looked up as I entered the small outer office. "How c-can I help you, Mister V-Vainio?"

"I need to talk to Doctor Palmer."

She cocked her head to one side. Probably sending a message to Babs via her computer link.

I had no idea where Babs had found Kiyoko, but she was no libriomancer. Kiyoko was tall, slender, and looked to be in her late twenties. Her head was shaved, presumably to allow a better connection with the series of small electrodes stuck to her scalp. Thin gold wires linked the electrodes like a circlet before trailing down beneath the back of her black suit jacket.

As far as I could determine, there was nothing magical about those electrodes. They simply relayed the electrical impulses from Kiyoko's brain through our network to one of the shielded computer servers. That was where the magic happened, translating her thoughts into commands that allowed Kiyoko to mentally manage her system without keyboard or mouse.

Her stuttering was part of a larger neurological problem that also affected her balance. I'd offered to try to get her into our medical trials, but she refused each time, saying others needed our help more than she did. She got around well enough, using forearm crutches for stability.

A black pearl pendant protected her from magical influence or assault. Babs wore a similar necklace, describing it as a necessary security precaution. The pearls came from a tank of oysters in the basement of the Rosalind Franklin Research Tower. One of Babs' first acts as Director of Security had been to arrange the publication of a fantasy novel called *Sea Change*, specifically for a passage describing the magically resistant oysters.

"Doctor P-Palmer has a meeting scheduled in fifteen minutes," said Kiyoko. "Could you c-come back this afternoon at two-thirty?"

"It's important. I won't be long."

She paused again, then glanced at the flat-screen monitor on her desk. "Five minutes. Please leave your spider outside."

I saluted and set Smudge's cage on one of the chairs to the side. The door to Babs' office unlocked with an audible click as I reached for the knob. I stepped inside and shut the door behind me.

Babs Palmer looked more like a gym teacher than a lawyer or libriomancer. She was thick and muscular, with tattoos of a tiger and a dragon on her forearms. The colorful tattoos concealed magically inked text, similar in some respects to the forehead tattoo Nidhi wore to protect her thoughts, but Babs' ink was far more powerful. Rings decorated her fingers. Several of those were magic as well, but I couldn't read any of it, thanks to the black pearl hanging from a thick silver chain around her neck.

"How can you stand to wear that thing?" I asked. "Cutting yourself off from magic for days at a time? I'd go mad."

"What do you want, Vainio?" Babs looked tired. Her

tanned skin had developed new lines at the eyes, like cracks spreading through concrete. Books and papers covered her desk, which was as large as my first car. One open folder held a map of Asia and official-looking documents in Chinese. Another looked like a building plan of some sort.

A map of New Millennium dominated the wall to my left. Dots of differently colored ink moved slowly over the paper. I studied it more closely. "Did you finally figure out how to make that Marauder's Map work in the real world?"

The map from *Harry Potter and the Prisoner of Azkaban* was one of the first projects my team had worked on, but we'd never been able to calibrate it.

"We went a different route." She rearranged the files, stacking things in several haphazard piles. "You're down to four minutes."

"I was in Lansing yesterday."

"I know. I got Nicola's report."

I sat in the chair opposite her desk. "I want to put my team to work helping to root out whoever orchestrated that attack. I've got one lead already."

She sighed and leaned back, finally giving me her full attention. "What does that have to do with me?"

"Honestly? I may not like you, but you're good at your job. I could use your help." I cocked a thumb at the map on the wall. "Some of the things you've worked out for New Millennium's security could be adapted to help us track—"

"I have enough of my own responsibilities without taking on yours. You're our Research Director. If you want to push for this, do it. But don't be surprised when the board shoots it down. The slightest whiff of magic is enough to taint even airtight court cases."

"I'm not talking about building a legal case. I'm

talking about saving lives. This is the kind of thing we started New Millennium to do. Either one of us could have stopped those werewolves if we'd been there. We should be working to prevent or resolve future attacks, like Gutenberg used to do with his automatons."

Her eyes tightened, and she started fiddling with one of her rings. "Don't tell me you want to rebuild the automatons."

"Hell, no." True, Gutenberg's constructs would have made short work of most magical terrorists, with spells worked into their metal-block armor to allow them to travel at the speed of a sunbeam, create fire and brimstone, warp magical attacks, and generally bring the pain to whoever Gutenberg sent them after. They also required the enslavement of a human soul, which was one of the reasons I'd destroyed the damn things.

"I'm sorry, Isaac. I have too much on my desk already."

I didn't answer right away. She was trying to brush me off. That much was standard procedure between us. But she lacked her usual confidence. I wished Nidhi was here to observe her reaction. "Whoever orchestrated yesterday's attacks, we both know they'll try again."

"You're our lead researcher, and your work is here," she said firmly, but her hands trembled as she spoke. She pulled them into her lap where the desk blocked my view.

"Think of the PR," I said. "If New Millennium helps bring a bunch of terrorists to justice—"

"Leave it alone, Isaac." Each word was clipped and tight.

What the hell was going on? I'd seen Babs angry. She could be as loud and bombastic as a grizzly. This was different. She was almost *pleading*.

She glanced at her watch, and the cold mask fell back

into place. "If you want to help with PR, work with medical to make sure their patients are camera-ready, and get your team prepared to show off their flashiest projects. We're planning a press conference in two weeks. The more oohs and aahs you can bring, the better."

I lowered my voice and asked something I never would have imagined saying to Babs Palmer. "Are you all right?"

She stiffened. "I have a meeting to get to, and I believe your five minutes are up."

"Right." I stood. "Thanks for your time."

I left her office without another word. Kiyoko smiled at me as I passed her desk. I nodded absently and grabbed Smudge.

I'd told my brother that Nicola and the rest of the Porter Council had vetted Babs Palmer before appointing her to this position. I hadn't been lying when I said I trusted Nicola and her judgment.

But Nicola wasn't perfect, and while our security measures scanned for hostile intent, Babs had helped to create those measures. She was the most qualified person I knew to bypass them.

"This is exactly why I can't just concentrate on my research and leave the fieldwork to somebody else," I muttered to no one in particular.

I stopped on the way out to pick up my newest batch of hate mail.

Most of the nastiness we received came by email. It was easier to send threats and bile via the keyboard than to write it all out by hand, and for most of these people, their laziness was second only to their poor spelling.

I took the handwritten ones more seriously. These

people were *invested* in their hate. They took the time to scrawl page after page of graphic, grammatically tortured prose describing the evils I and New Millennium represented, and the horrific fates we would all suffer for our sins.

All physical mail was screened by security before delivery. We made sure law enforcement received copies. Those letters were also scanned and saved on our servers as evidence in case anyone tried to carry through on their threats.

I'd begun posting the most creative, interesting, or bizarre letter I got each month in a place of honor outside my door, where all could marvel at the people with far too much time on their hands. Last time, it had been a gentleman who was angry about our use of animals in magical research. He apparently thought our PETA protesters were too laid-back and easygoing, and suggested my team should be skinned alive, our hides tanned into leather, our meat processed into McNuggets, and our bones ground into gelatin to be fed to little children in Easter jellybeans.

It was the jellybean bit that earned him a spot by my door. That and the crude drawing he'd included of the Easter Bunny skipping along, carrying what I assume was supposed to be my bloody head, but looked more like a hairy pumpkin in oversized glasses.

The nice thing about people like Jellybean Man was that I knew exactly where I stood. There was no subtlety, no subterfuge or second-guessing. It was a refreshing change from talking to politicians.

I waved my ID at the scanner in front of the main doors to the Franklin Research Tower. A musty odor greeted me as I walked past the guard at the front desk. Patricia Bordenkircher was the only zombie on site. She'd been infected from a zombie romance novel, a subgenre I never would have imagined being popular enough for libriomancy.

As long as she fed regularly—and we had an ongoing contract with a butcher from Vegas, along with a week's supply of cow brains in an industrial freezer—she appeared as human as the rest of us. She was significantly stronger, with a powerful sense of smell, and teeth strong enough to crush bone. She looked up from her knitting as I passed.

"How's the grandkid?" I asked.

Patty beamed and held up her half-completed blanket. "Bobbi's turning one in November. She's been babbling up a storm. She's a talker, that one. Just like her daddy."

I smiled and headed through another set of doors into a large, open space that smelled of hay, fur, and animal droppings. We'd converted most of the ground floor into a kennel for everything from rats to rabbits to monkeys, even a Galapagos turtle with a cracked shell who'd been shipped in two weeks ago from the Toronto zoo. And, of course, Vince's favorite crow, Kerling.

Smudge smoked as we passed the rat cages. He didn't mind the other animals, but I suspected the rats were close enough to his size for him to see them as potential competitors. Or maybe potential meals, though I couldn't remember the last time he'd hunted anything bigger than a grasshopper. I really needed to get him out more while I was here. Parts of the desert were barren enough for him to roam and hunt without setting the land ablaze, and he needed the exercise.

I found Vince Hambrecht at a stainless steel table, next to a mobile desk with three computer monitors. He and an NIH doctor named Jeremy Dishaw were examining a six-foot-long boa constrictor. "Hi, Boss! How was D.C.?"

"Eventful." Where Dr. Dishaw wore a shirt, tie, and lab coat, Vince was dressed in his favorite blue robe over a too-tight T-shirt. Knee-length shorts and Birkenstock sandals completed the image. The robe was part of his ongoing effort to cultivate a magical fashion style. An effort which had so far failed to take off. His attempt to grow a "wizardly" beard had been equally unsuccessful, resulting in thin, scraggly patches along his cheekbones and chin.

I looked past them at the snake. "How's he—she?—doing?"

"He," said Vince. "His name's Olaf. He likes warm hugs. He came in with IBD eight days ago. That's inclusion body disease. It's like AIDS for snakes. He's good as new, now. But Doctor Dipshit here wants to reinfect him to see if our cure created immunity."

Dishaw glared at Vince. "You've proven you can cure the virus, so there should be no long-term risk to the animal, even if it's still susceptible to IBD. We need to know how magic affects the immune system, both in the short and long term."

"He also wants to feed Olaf some of our rats."

Dishaw flushed. "You've done zero work to see how consuming magic will affect the food chain. What if it works like mercury poisoning, where the harm ends up concentrated in the apex predators?"

"That wasn't in the original research plan," I said mildly.

"Well, it should have been." Dishaw gave the snake a fond pat on the head. "Don't get me wrong, Isaac. What you're doing here is amazing. But we've got to be certain it's safe. A single unforeseen magical mutation could have serious consequences for the entire world."

It sounded reasonable. It always did. "All our rats are part of other research projects. They're not expendable.

If you want to submit a modified proposal, I'll be happy to take a look."

"Bam!" Vince crowed. "Rats: 1. Doctor Dishaw: 0."

"Knock it off," I said. "He's got a point about checking Olaf's long-term immunity. If you want to make your case against reinfection, write it up and have it on my desk by the end of the week."

Vince sagged. "Damn, Boss. See, this is why everyone likes it better when you're away on your road trips."

"Don't call me boss. Also, staff meeting upstairs in the Wheeler room in thirty minutes."

"That's cold, Boss. What did we do to deserve that?"

"Keep it up, and I'll make you sit through a Power-Point presentation."

He raised his hands in surrender. "Cruel and unusual punishment."

I headed for the stairs and made my way to my office on the second floor. I doubted I'd ever get used to being the kind of guy who had his own office, or called staff meetings.

My office was nowhere near as impressive as Babs', but that was how I liked it. Bookshelves lined the walls on either side. A large window behind my desk opened onto the New Millennium grounds, giving me a view of the warehouse and southern wall. I sat down and switched on the computer.

Our network ran on a customized operating system, a modified version of the Porters' old network. I'd worked with Talulah to build an additional layer into the user interface for our team, a bit of magical blue text that appeared to float in front of the monitor. I pressed my fingers to the text and concentrated on the programs I needed.

The screen came to life, opening up my email, calendar, and a spreadsheet of current and closed research projects. I sent a note to Charles and Talulah about the meeting, then grabbed a LEGO *DeLorean* Lena had given me for Christmas and fiddled with the doors as I skimmed the latest updates.

Charles was still griping about wanting to do a book tour on New Millennium's dime. He also wanted to upgrade his hearing, and had narrowed the possibilities down to four books. I skimmed his notes, but my mind was elsewhere. I ended up reading the same paragraph on selective frequency echolocation three times before giving up.

I cleared the screen and ran a search for the *USCGC Kagan* instead, then sat back to read.

The *Kagan* was a Coast Guard cutter, commissioned in 1989 and currently based off the U.S. East Coast. It was a hundred and ten feet long, with a crew of eighteen and a top speed of more than thirty knots. Armament included two fifty-caliber machine guns and one twenty-five millimeter chain gun.

There was nothing about its current mission, nor could I find any public details about the commander or crew. The ship hadn't been in the news recently. None of the articles or information gave any hint why Deb's pet terrorists might have been interested in hitting the *Kagan*, or why they'd changed their minds.

I was still poring over what I could find of the ship's history when the computer made the whooshing sound of the TARDIS engines from *Doctor Who*, letting me know I was about to be late for my own staff meeting. I grabbed a book from my pocket, performed a quick spell, and hurried off.

The Wheeler room was one of the smaller conference rooms, with a narrow table and a dozen chairs, along with a whiteboard that doubled as a projector screen. An old-fashioned crystal ball mounted to the center of the table served as the equivalent of both speakerphone and video monitor, though I always had trouble keeping it attuned to our world. I could never eliminate the static and random images from the book we'd used to produce the crystals, and every once in a while a green-skinned warlock would pop up to threaten us all with doom and destruction until we recalibrated him out of existence.

Vince was leaning back in his chair, his feet crossed on the edge of the table. Talulah sat on the opposite side, flipping through a gaming magazine.

‹Welcome back,› said Talulah. She'd given herself a limited form of mind-speech shortly after joining up with New Millennium. I could see the text of her telepathic magic when she spoke, like ink hidden between layers of onion paper.

‹Thanks,› I said. Talulah was one of four people at New Millennium with a criminal record. Hers was a minor vandalism charge from when she was a teenager. Although, given her skill with technology, she could have easily erased more serious crimes from her records and none of us would know.

Talulah had grown up on a Choctaw reservation in Oklahoma. Her family had steered her toward gaming as a way to keep her out of trouble. It had worked a bit too well. In addition to competing in statewide and national gaming tournaments, she had her own YouTube channel, and had developed a following as a video game guru in the years before she was outed as a libriomancer.

There was an ongoing and vicious debate online as to whether her game run-throughs were magically assisted, but she swore she never used her powers while gaming. I'd been among the skeptics until I watched her beat the original *Super Mario Brothers* in under five minutes.

‹Did you make any progress on those gaming manuals?›

‹I think it's a lost cause. Nobody reads the manuals these days. Everything's online. And the manuals have

some of the same limits as comic books: too many pic-
tures, not enough active reading. It's a shame. I wanted to
see what a 1UP mushroom would do in the real world.›
 ‹*Better than the fire-flower you were working on.*›
 ‹*Says the man with the flaming spider.*›
I double-checked Smudge, but he was resting peacefully in his cage. ‹*Where are you at with the IAS Project?*›
 ‹*Ready for a trial run. We're just waiting for FCC ap-*
proval.›

Natural disasters were one of Talulah's obsessions. In
addition to working to predict and detect them more
quickly, she'd been developing a tool to give people as
much advance warning as possible. Her proposed International Alert System was intended to broadcast to television, radio, cellphone, even things like hearing aids. An
extra five minutes' notice could save thousands of lives.

Before I could respond, Charles Brice strode into the
room and took a seat at the far end of the table. "How
long's this gonna take, Isaac?"

When I'd first heard that a Nebula award-winning science fiction author would be joining my research team,
I'd been ecstatic. That feeling lasted until approximately
thirty seconds after meeting him in person.

Most libriomancers had an arrogant streak. Playing
fast and loose with the laws of the universe had that effect. But Charles took it to an entirely new level.

Part of his problem was that he'd worked as a Porter
researcher for twenty years, and wasn't thrilled about
having to report to an upstart half his age. I was pretty
sure he thought he should have been put in charge of
research at New Millennium. The fact that I had to su-
pervise and sign off on his research was weird to me too,
but he took it as a personal affront, and never passed up
the chance to catch me in a mistake or undermine me in
front of the team.

His wife and frequent co-author Jodi was far more pleasant. She had no magic of her own, but had been living on site with Charles for the past four months. The last I'd heard, she was close to finishing up a solo project about libriomancers fighting off a colony of mutant vampires from Venus.

Charles studied me through his mechanical eye, a black-glass-and-chrome bionic replacement with telescopic, X-ray, and infrared modes, as well as a laser capable of cutting through one-inch steel in twenty seconds. With magic out in the open, he'd begun harvesting body modifications from various science fiction novels. His eternal complaint—one of them, at least—was his inability to access tech from his own books.

The risk of stories infecting your mind and thoughts was exponentially higher when the libriomancer was also the author. Gutenberg was the only person I knew who had successfully performed libriomancy with his own work, and even then, the attempt ultimately killed him.

Charles drummed the metal fingers of his left hand on the desk. He'd also given himself the ability to sense magnetic fields, a sense of smell as powerful as that of a turkey vulture, and upgraded adrenal glands. "Well?" he said. "Are you going to tell us what this is about?"

I took off my jacket and set it over the crystal ball. "Talulah, we'll need privacy, please. Magical and mundane."

She cocked her head, but popped open her briefcase and brought out one of her books. She skimmed the pages and created a device that looked like a thick smartphone. "That will jam any listening devices." A second book produced a small dagger, which she placed next to the jammer. "And that should disrupt magical spying."

I opened Smudge's cage and lifted him free. "I have a new research project for this team, one that takes precedence over your current work."

Charles was the first to react, rising to his feet and placing both hands on the table. "That's bullshit."

"I've got a cat coming in tomorrow with FIV," added Vince. "You expect me to just let him die?"

"I expect you to multitask. Talulah, I need you to find out everything you can about the *USCGC Kagan*. Crew details, mission logs, and a breakdown of its activities for the past year."

‹*What's going on, Mister Vainio?*›

‹*I don't know yet,*› I answered. ‹*Maybe nothing. I don't want to prejudice your research with rumors.*›

"Coast Guard?" asked Vince. "Are we doing military research now?"

Smudge crawled up my arm and settled onto my shoulder, cool and calm. "You're helping me with a puzzle. The less you know, the easier it will be for you to plead ignorance if this goes badly."

Charles huffed up like I'd slapped him in the face and pissed on his three-hundred dollar shoes. "If there ever comes a day when I deliberately embrace ignorance, I'll have lived one day too long."

Vince jerked his chin at Charles. "What he said."

‹*I agree.*›

"Isaac was in Lansing," said Vince. "Odds are this has something to do with the attack."

Talulah nodded. "New Millennium has measures in place to protect our privacy. If he's asking for additional shielding, it means he doesn't trust those measures."

"You think there's a mole in New Millennium," guessed Charles. "Do you believe we're at risk of a similar attack here?"

"If that was the case, he'd have gone straight to Dr.

Palmer." Talulah shook her head. "You think she might be in on this?"

"I don't know." This kind of insight and intelligence was exactly why I'd wanted these three for my team, no matter how annoying some of them could be.

"If you're so paranoid, why trust us?" asked Charles.

"I'm taking a chance," I admitted. "But I've worked with you for close to a year now. I've seen your passion for your work, and for the things New Millennium could do. I don't intend to let anyone corrupt or destroy what we're doing here, and I don't believe you would, either. I think I can trust you. Am I wrong?"

I looked at each of them until they answered out loud. The copy of *The Goblin Wood* I'd tucked into my pocket remained silent. They were telling the truth.

"Are any of you familiar with a group called Vanguard?" They looked at one another, shaking their heads. "They've been warning inhumans about police and government raids, helping to relocate them, and so on. The FBI believes they're connected to these attacks. I don't know if they're directly involved, or if someone's just recruiting extremists from the Vanguard pool."

"I'll ask around," said Charles. "I have a lot of friends in the inhuman community. I've gone to them for research with my books."

I looked across the table at Talulah. "Earlier today, I spoke with Babs about investigating these attacks. She got scared."

"Scared?" Vince repeated. "Babs Palmer?"

"Scared of *you*?" Charles added, sounding equally incredulous.

I pushed my annoyance aside. "Not of me. Scared for me, maybe. Scared of what will happen if we dig into this." I paused. "I can't and won't order any of you to do this. If you want out—"

"You've worked with Dr. Palmer," said Talulah. "Do you believe she could have been involved with those attacks?"

"I believe she's ambitious, arrogant, and potentially dangerous," I said slowly. "I don't think she'd help murder innocent people, but that's not good enough. She's one of the top people at New Millennium, and she's in charge of security. If whoever's behind this decides to target us next . . ."

Talulah's brow was furrowed, and she kept chewing her lip. "I'll do some digging."

"All of the primary targets were people who'd spoken out *against* magic," said Vince. "Coming after a group like New Millennium would be a complete one-eighty."

"It could be about theft," Talulah said. "Do you know how much people are paying for black market magic these days?"

"I'll run an inventory check here in Research," Vince offered. "Make sure none of our projects have gotten up and walked away."

I stood up and looked at them each in turn. "If you find anything, tell me. That's all. Do not talk to anyone else about this, and do not pull any lone-wolf spy crap. If you do, I'll use you as my next test subject for the Gateway Project. If you're lucky, I'll send you somewhere on this planet."

Security Council Votes Not to Impose Sanctions Against the United States

After expressing deep concerns regarding the magical research being conducted at the New Millennium center in Las Vegas, Nevada, the Russian Federation joined Jordan and Malaysia in calling for economic sanctions against the United States of America. The resolution was voted down 10-3, with China and Nigeria abstaining.

The representative of the Russian Federation said this resolution was an expression of international concerns over America's alliance with the organization known as the Porters. They demanded regular U.N. inspections and the immediate cessation of all military research, despite the fact that New Millennium denies performing any sort of military work.

Today's vote followed six months of angry negotiations. Proposals to build additional New Millennium centers in other member nations have been met with anger and threats.

The representative from France likened this time in history to the beginning of the nuclear age. "We have one opportunity to prevent a magical arms race, an escalation that could bring about a second Cold War. This is a time for unity."

Following the vote, the representative from China reaffirmed his belief that all nations have the right to the benefits and advantages of magic.

The Security Council will be voting later this month on a resolution to establish an International Magical Regulatory Agency, similar in structure to the International Atomic Energy Agency.

Chapter 8

"*Change is a difficult, often violent process, both for individuals and for whole species. The more rapid the change, the uglier the conflict.*"

"*I can't accept that violence is inevitable.*"

"*Look at the breakthroughs you've discovered in your libriomancy. How many of those discoveries were born from conflict and violence and desperation?*"

"*I don't want to talk about it.*"

"*Technology advances more swiftly in times of war. Violence and change aren't separate concepts, Isaac. All too often, they're different facets of the same thing.*"

"*Has anyone ever told you how damn depressing you can be?*"

"*Yes.*"

THE NEXT MORNING found me walking across the grounds just before sunrise. Blue-tinged solar-powered lamps illuminated the sidewalks.

A small brown lizard scampered away from me. Smudge crouched in his cage, as if preparing to pounce. I couldn't tell if he meant to attack or play.

Looking around, I imagined New Millennium as it had been during construction. I remembered the bulldozers, the beds of concrete and rebar, the skeletal girders stretching skyward, built with magic and machinery both.

I wasn't the only one up and about. To my right, behind the eastern residential building, three young children played on brand-new, brightly colored climbing equipment. The swing set and sandbox had been part of the original construction, but the monkey bars, dinosaur-themed slides, merry-go-round, and climbing wall had gone up just last month. The parents watched from a wooden bench. I waved and kept walking.

I'd seen every phase of development and construction. I'd flown to Vegas to argue the benefits of magic to the mayor and his staff. I'd hovered over our architect's shoulder until she grew frustrated enough to banish me from her office. I was here for the groundbreaking, and I was here for the ribbon-cutting ceremony.

I was tempted to turn myself invisible and break into Babs' office, but Babs was in charge of security for a reason, and if I got caught, she was in a position to have me kicked out of New Millennium altogether.

I passed the greenhouse, where a variety of magically enhanced plants grew under strict quarantine. I had lunch twice a month with Elvira Pop Caal, the Guatemalan libriomancer in charge of agriculture, to compare hate mail. The people who got upset about genetically modified crops had nothing on the folks who thought magic seeds were going to destroy the planet. According to Elvira, a few years of crossbreeding and research should be enough to create stable strains of rice and wheat and other foods that might someday feed the world.

Assuming the world didn't wreck itself in the meantime.

Habit brought me back to Franklin Tower. I walked through the doors on autopilot, still lost in thought. Most of the animals were awake and scurrying about, eager to be fed. I nodded to one of Vince's assistants and headed for the elevator. I waved my badge in front of the scanner, stepped in, and punched the button for the fifth floor. I might have better luck if I lost myself in work and let my subconscious worry about terrorists and Babs Palmer for a while.

Once the elevator doors slid open, I headed down the hall and unlocked Large Project Room number three, which had come to be known as Isaac's Playroom. I flipped on the lights, illuminating an open area the size of a basketball court. I'd started the Gateway Project in my office one afternoon when I was avoiding paperwork, but it had grown like Lena's garden, expanding to take up whatever space I could get.

High speed cameras stood on tripods like slumbering robots. A plastic wading pool sat in front of one. Another pointed to a simple chalk circle on the tile floor.

Books were everywhere. A set of whiteboards listed every title I'd brought over from the library. Many were crossed out, while others were annotated with Post-it notes.

Last year in Copper River, I'd watched a sorceress named Meridiana use libriomancy to turn a body of water into a portal to the moon. It hadn't ended well for her, but the idea had stayed with me.

Magical gateways were such a common element of speculative fiction that they had their own unofficial subgenre: portal fantasies. You couldn't pull the magical wardrobe out of C. S. Lewis' Narnia books, of course. The size of the book limited what you could create, and a wardrobe that took you to a fictional world would almost certainly kill you. But Meridiana had successfully combined the magic of multiple works in a way that allowed her to anchor a stable portal to another real-world location.

I'd glimpsed her magic, the way the text of the different stories twined together, but as I'd been in the middle of a small magical war at the time, I hadn't gotten to study it as closely as I wanted.

That didn't matter. I knew the one thing that truly mattered. I knew it could be done.

The wading pool was part of my initial attempt to duplicate her original portal, but without opening up a rift to the cold vacuum of the moon. The patched section of floor was the result of that attempt, which had simply disintegrated everything in a five-foot diameter circle.

A black shape perched atop the smartboard on the wall to my left. "Good morning, Kerling."

The crow ruffled her feathers.

I switched on the board, which could act as a television screen, whiteboard, remote network terminal, and more. After logging in with my New Millennium ID, I pulled up a map of the United States and tagged the locations of the attacks from earlier this week. Michigan, California, Oklahoma, and New York. There was also the aborted plan to hit the *Kagan*, but without knowing where on the East Coast she was stationed, I had no way of adding that to the map.

If future attacks followed the same pattern, they would target prominent anti-magic politicians, which narrowed things down to pretty much anywhere in the United States. Assuming they continued to limit their focus to one country.

I cleared the screen and pulled up the last Porter census map of inhuman populations within the U.S. The clustered dots, each color representing a different species, suggested a weak potential correlation. The killers in Lansing had been werewolves, and Michigan had one of the larger werewolf packs in the country. New York had a disproportionate number of trolls. There was a group of nagas living in the California desert, and Oklahoma was known for its chupacabras. Each attack had been carried out by a single species, one more-or-less native to the area.

Was that cause or effect? Vanguard or whoever was behind this could have simply recruited whoever was convenient, but a truly random sampling would have resulted in mixed-species groups. The exclusion of vampires seemed odd as well. They were one of the most widespread inhuman groups, and many vampire species would have done a far better job at killing and terrorizing their targets.

I rubbed my eyes and turned away. Glaring at the screen wouldn't force it to produce the answers I wanted.

Instead, I skimmed my list of potential Gateway Project books, reviewing the combinations I'd tried so far. Anything more than five texts together was too much for me to control or manipulate. The few times I'd tried, the magic had promptly fizzled, and I ended up with the twenty-four-hour migraine from hell.

I picked up *Through the Looking Glass* and *The Mirror of Her Dreams*. The mirror theme of the two books should help them work together, and might add stability to the portal. Eventually, I added Diana Gabaldon's *Outlander*. I'd read it two weeks ago for part of my research. It was incredibly popular, with some very passionate readers. The belief and power in this paperback should provide a good boost to the overall magic. *Outlander*'s portal used standing stones instead of a mirror, but I could work with that.

"A mirror mounted within some kind of standing stones," I muttered, pacing a tight circle. I debated adding Catherynne Valente's *Palimpsest* to the mix, but the last time I'd used that book, I ended up with a tattooed map of Las Vegas covering my skin. It had taken a week to get rid of the thing.

My original timeline would have had us using Gateway to transport supplies to the International Space Station by the end of the year. It shouldn't have taken more than an additional six months to adapt the Gateway Project for space exploration, assuming I could figure out some sort of magical valve to keep the vacuum on the other side from sucking all the air out of the room . . . or we could just build the portal in an airlock. If I figured out how to miniaturize the portal, there were surgical applications as well. Not to mention routine trade and travel.

I retrieved a compact mirror and a pouch full of gravel from a table full of miscellaneous supplies— Talulah called it the Junk Desk—and spent the next half hour using a glue gun to affix pieces of gravel to the edge of the mirror. It was hardly the stones of Gabaldon's *Outlander*, but it would do in a pinch.

I switched on the cameras and sat down on the floor. I opened each of the books and set paperweights on the edges to hold them in place. One at a time, I touched the books' magic, drawing that belief into myself, then pushing it into the mirror.

"Gateway Project, experiment number one eighty-three. Carroll, Donaldson, and Gabaldon."

I set a travel magazine in the center of the triangle formed by the three books. I turned to a story about street food in Hanoi, drawing fragments of description into the glass. If this worked, the smells of bun rieu cua thit nuong and hien luon xao should fill the room.

"Isaac?"

I jumped hard enough I almost dropped the mirror. None of the stories about implanted communicators warned how damned startling they could be. Once my breathing slowed, I got up and switched off the camera. "What's up, Vince?"

"I finished that inventory check. I didn't find anything suspicious."

"All right, thanks."

"There's more. I was up last night thinking. If someone's infiltrated New Millennium, maybe it's not about stealing our work. Maybe it's subtler than that. What if they're guiding our research instead?"

"How do you mean?"

"I built a database of all the proposals and projects we've worked on, then went through to categorize and score the delays. For the most part, it was pretty random. We've all had our work put on hold. There were more roadblocks in the beginning, and a spike when the NIH moved in, but I figure that's normal. For the past three months, about fifty percent of the roadblocks came from NIH, with another thirty percent from DHS, and the rest split between the Porter Council, the New Millennium board, and other governmental groups. Plus a few projects you personally shot down."

"I'm not hearing anything earth-shattering here, Vince."

"The thing is, you can't just graph the number of delays, right? You've got to include other factors in your analysis. I played around with a bunch of other variables, including potential public risk. You'd expect the most dangerous projects to have the biggest hurdles. Nobody wants this to turn into Chernobyl."

I used a small screwdriver and needle-nose pliers to

remove the pin from the compact's hinge. With proper targeting, you could open a portal to Washington D.C. and assassinate the president from two thousand miles away. DHS should have been all over that from day one. Instead, they'd essentially rubber-stamped it. *"Let me guess. DHS has been pushing some of those dangerous projects, the ones with potential military applications."*

"That's part of it. No shock there, right? We know Potts is a bloodthirsty bastard. But the graphs weren't lining up right, not until I added a second variable. For lack of a better term, I went back and scored everything based on their altruistic applications."

I'd known we were being pressured to produce potential weapons, but I wouldn't have thought to look at our purely philanthropic work. *"What did you find?"*

"They're not just pushing for potential weapons. It looks like someone's actively stalling our most altruistic projects."

Of course our government babysitters wanted magical guns and ammo. But why try to delay our most helpful projects, things that could benefit the whole world? *"Were those delays coming from any particular person or office?"*

"I can't give you a statistically conclusive answer to that one yet, Boss. Correlation isn't causation, and some of my scoring was subjective."

All the hoops NIH had made us jump through, all of their delays before they'd allow us to heal Lex and a handful of others. I thought back to my conversation with Nicola and Representative Vaughn at the pizzeria in D.C. *"It's about PR."*

"Say what?"

"Public relations. Someone's shooting down the work that would make people more sympathetic and support- ive of New Millennium, and of magic in general." I

couldn't help remembering how quickly Senator Keeler had capitalized on the attacks, gathering support for harsher legislation against magic and inhumans. The man certainly understood the importance of PR and how to manipulate it.

"I'm not seeing anything coming directly from Dr. Palmer or her team, though. She pretty much stays out of our business, except when there are potential security implications."

"Thanks, Vince. How certain are you that this isn't coincidence or random chance?"

"Looking at the numbers, there's less than a one percent chance of it being normal statistical noise."

"All right. Try to dig deeper into who did or didn't sign off on every project for the past six months. Don't stop with the name on the reports. Check who they report to, all the way up the chain of command."

Vince's melodramatic groan filled my head. *"Great. Because the only thing more exciting than spreadsheets and statistical analysis is org charts."*

"If you need a break, you might want to double-check your security cameras down in the kennels. I'm told Kerling snuck out again."

"Dammit! I'm going to superglue a tracking chip to that crow's head!"

I hung up and tilted the mirror in my hand until I spotted Kerling perched behind me. "What do you think?"

Kerling scratched under her wing with her beak.

"How did you get in here through a locked door, anyway?"

She cawed softly, partially spreading her wings.

"Right." I set the mirror on the table. In addition to using the Gateway Project for long-range assassinations, there were potential privacy concerns as well. You could create a small portal and use it as a virtual peephole, or eavesdrop on conversations half a world away.

I considered trying to open a portal into Babs' office, but I wouldn't be able to get a fix on her as long as she wore that magic-damping pearl.

Maybe Babs wasn't the one I should focus on. Back when I was fresh out of college, my father had pulled me aside to share job-hunting advice. I hadn't paid as much attention as I probably should have, since I'd known I had a position waiting with the Porters, but I remembered most of it, including his comment that the second most important person at any company was the boss. The most important was the boss' secretary.

Kiyoko knew Babs Palmer's schedule. She likely knew Babs' contacts and projects as well. She'd be aware of any unplanned phone calls or confidential meetings. She might even have access to Babs' email and files, though Babs was smart enough to keep anything incriminating locked away.

I turned to the smartboard and pulled up the New Millennium personnel directory. It would be safer to chat with Kiyoko when she was away from her desk and unplugged from whatever magical interface she had glued to her scalp.

I couldn't find a residential listing for Kiyoko Itô. Most of us who were directly involved in research or other magic lived on site, but more than half our people commuted from Vegas or its suburbs. I switched files and checked the parking lot reservations. She wasn't listed there, either.

I sat back in my chair. The simplest explanation was that she carpooled with someone, or maybe she lived close enough to walk or bike to work. I tried plugging "Kiyoko Itô" into Google. I got the usual Google noise, but nothing relating to Babs' receptionist.

Her personnel file described her as having dual citizenship in Japan and the U.S. There was no work history, no resume or copy of her job application, and no emergency contact listed. What kind of woman had Babs hired?

‹Isaac?› Talulah Polk peeked through my door.

I shut down the board. ‹Speak, friend, and enter.›

She blinked. ‹Huh?›

‹It's from The Fellowship of the Ring. Never mind. What's up?›

She shut the door behind her and handed me a file. I brought it to the closest table and sat down to review her notes. She'd found the same basic information I had regarding the history, armaments, and crew of the *USCGC Kagan*. I picked up a map of the Atlantic coast. Red lines, each one marked with a date and time, crisscrossed the ocean.

‹These are her missions?›

‹Training runs, mostly. Officially, they've been practicing search and rescue.›

I grabbed a highlighter and traced one of the search patterns, an expanding square centered on a point about fifteen miles east of Georgia. Another mission had followed a sector-based pattern, the lines forming what looked like an enormous pinwheel.

‹I checked the news reports and some of Homeland Security's files. Nothing's been reported missing or lost in that area.›

If Deb was right about this ship being a potential terrorist target, then there had to be more than training missions. I put a red X in the center of one of the search patterns. ‹The earliest mission was here.›

‹They've had a lot of crew turnover, too. Seven new personnel, including four officers.›

‹What happened here?› I pointed to the most recent mission, another expanding square pattern.

‹What do you mean?›

‹If you unfold the patterns, all of the pinwheels and spirals and squares are pretty similar in length. They spent roughly the same amount of time on each mission, up until this last one.› I compared the routes and did some quick math. ‹It looks like they called it quits about twenty-five percent sooner.›

‹If these were real search missions, maybe they found what they were looking for.›

I flipped through the rest of her notes. ‹The Kagan has been docked for the past three days. It says they're prepping for their next launch tomorrow night.›

‹That's right.›

I highlighted the end point of that last mission. ‹Talulah, where do the Kagan's orders originate?›

‹They came out of the Coast Guard Seventh District office in Miami, but I couldn't tell you who issued them.›

‹Charles served in the navy, didn't he? Could you please tell him I need to talk to him?›

She gazed past me, then nodded. ‹Done. What's so important about that spot?›

‹It's directly on the migratory path of one of the largest siren colonies in the Atlantic.›

The CHAIRMAN: As a field agent for the Porters, what rules were you bound by, if any?

Mr. VAINIO: No resurrecting the dead. No pulling living creatures from books. No—

The CHAIRMAN: What about the rules regarding relationships with nonhuman creatures?

Mr. VAINIO: I'm not aware of any such rules.

The CHAIRMAN: You're in a romantic relationship with both Lena Greenwood and Nidhi Shah, are you not?

Mr. VAINIO: Nope.

The CHAIRMAN: Sir, please remember you took an oath to answer truthfully, regardless of—

Mr. VAINIO: I've been romantically involved with Lena for about a year and a half. Lena is also in a relationship with Doctor Shah. I hope you didn't make me fly out here just to gossip about my sex life.

Mr. VAUGHN: Is there a point to these questions, Senator Keeler?

The CHAIRMAN: Simply to demonstrate the moral and ethical gulf between most Americans and gentlemen like Mister Vainio. He engages in sexual congress with a creature who isn't even human. Who, according to our understanding, is half tree? Is this the kind of thing you want to legitimize?

Mr. VAUGHN: We're here to talk about magic, not to finger-wag like my grandma over what consenting adults do in their own homes. Mister Vainio, have you had the chance to look over the recently proposed legislation?

Mr. VAINIO: You're referring to the Regulations on American Magical Protection and Response Tactics

Act? Yes, I've read Mister Keeler's bill of wrongs. All nine hundred thirty-six pages.

Mr. VAUGHN: Would you mind sharing your thoughts on that act?

Mr. VAINIO: I think you're out of your goddamned minds. Bad enough you've got the FBI spying on us. Tapping our phones, flying drones over our homes, interrogating our friends and family and neighbors. Now you want the authority to imprison us on a whim? To hold us without trial? Is the chairman so ignorant of U.S. history? We tried this in World War II. Locked up more than a hundred thousand men, women, and children whose only crime was having Japanese ancestry.

Mr. CHILDRESS: The RAMPART Act is hardly comparable to that sad chapter in our history, which you'd know if you'd truly read it.

Mr. VAINIO: Pages six thirty-four through six forty-one. Sections 184 A and B specifically state, "Whereas intelligent nonhuman entities, including but not restricted to vampires, werewolves, merfolk, sirens, nymphs, dryads, and cryptids, have been living in the United States under false pretenses, such creatures are not presumed to have the rights or obligations of citizenship. Furthermore, whereas such beings pose a potential danger to the security of this nation and its people, authority is hereby granted to both the Department of Homeland Security and the Federal Bureau of Investigation's Magical Crimes Division, under the supervision of the Department of Defense, to hold without charge anyone suspected—"

Mr. VAUGHN: I think we get the point, thank you. I trust that was enough to jog my esteemed colleague's memory?

Mr. CHILDRESS: I . . . yes, thank you. But that refers

to nonhuman creatures, not individuals such as your-self.

Mr. VAINIO: I can see you scrolling through your tablet to check the text of the bill. You want section 184 D, which throws people like me under the bus as potential terrorists. You'd give DHS and FBI the right to arrest and hold us indefinitely, without trial or charges. Please let me know if you need me to explain any more of your proposed legislation to you.

Chapter 9

"Nobody fears magic more than kings and priests."

"We don't have many kings in the twenty-first century."

"If you believe that, you're a fool, Isaac Vainio. In my day, before the spread of libriomancy, sorcerers were few. If you hoped to survive and prosper, you had to choose your alliances well. Loyalty to the church or monarchy could protect you. It could also cost you your life."

"We have the same kind of loyalties back home, only with hockey teams."

"I created the Porters in part to build a community with its own strength, but that strength relied in part on secrecy. We disappeared from view, erased ourselves from history. We were not beholden to anyone."

"We're doing our best to keep it that way. Or are you suggesting the Porters align themselves with a particular church or government?"

"Don't be daft, boy. I'm trying to help you understand the fragility of your position. To continue your hockey reference, if you're not one of the teams, you're probably the puck."

I WAITED close to an hour in the luggage claim area of the Savannah Hilton Head International Airport in Georgia. Lena's flight had been delayed because of a thunderstorm in Detroit. She arrived just before sunset, with Deb DeGeorge in tow.

Though it had only been a few days, Lena kissed me like I'd been away an entire year. I returned the embrace with enthusiasm, sliding my fingers into the waistband of her jeans and pulling her tighter. I pretty much forgot we were in a public area until Deb cleared her throat.

Lena broke away, then hugged me again. "That one was from Nidhi. So when are you going to finish Gateway so I can see you without having to fly halfway across the country?"

"I'm working on it." I patted one of the pockets in my carry-on backpack where I'd packed the mirror I'd been working on. "We don't have much time. I've got a car waiting outside."

"Anyone know you're here?" asked Deb.

"Only my team back in Vegas. I pulled a bit of magic from Frank Herbert to make sure we don't show up on anyone's crystal ball, either." In the books, a millennia-long breeding program led to the creation of humans who were invisible to psychic detection. I'd discovered those passages could be used to hide me from most forms of magical scrying.

I didn't say another word until we'd gotten into the rented sedan and were pulling out of the airport parking lot. "At ten p.m., the *Kagan* and two other Coast Guard vessels will be setting out for a siren colony fifteen miles from the coast. How much did you and Vanguard know about this?"

"Nobody tells me anything," said Deb. "I knew the *Kagan* was a potential target, and then it wasn't. That's it."

"Have you told Nicola?" asked Lena.

"Not yet." I trusted Nicola, but I also knew she'd talk to the rest of the Porter Council. If Babs was compromised in some way, who was to say she was the only one? "I said I was taking the weekend off to spend time with Lena in Michigan."

Deb chuckled. "You're finally catching on."

"You can't trust anyone these days, eh?" I didn't give her time to answer. "You sent Sandy Boyle to his death back in Lansing. How do I know you won't do the same to us?"

"I didn't expect him to die," Deb said sullenly. "I don't give a rat's shit about you. I'm not here for the Porters or for Vanguard. But I'm not gonna let the military sail in and do to the sirens what they did to the vamps in Detroit. Whatever conspiracy we're dealing with, it's targeting people like me. I need your help to bring them down. As long as we're going after the same assholes, I've got your back."

"Fair enough. Hey, while we're talking, do you still think it was worth it becoming a Renfield?"

She hesitated. "Sure. Why do you ask?"

A muffled bell rang from within my jacket.

"What was that?"

I deactivated the lie-detecting magic of the book and ignored her question. "I've been trying to think of a way to warn the sirens."

"Warn them to do what?" Deb snorted in disgust. "You want them to run away while their homes are destroyed? Hope their children and their elders are healthy enough to travel and hide? Wait until the next ship finds their new nesting place and finishes them off?"

"Better than being caught unprepared," I snapped. Unfortunately, sirens preferred privacy and isolation. They kept to the deeper areas of the ocean, and it wasn't like they had cellphones. "You said Vanguard originally intended to hit the *Kagan* as part of their joint attacks the other night, but they changed their mind. Why?"

"Not enough manpower?" suggested Lena.

"I doubt it," said Deb. "Believe me, there's no shortage of volunteers willing to fight back against the people who want to lock us in cages."

"How did they find out about the *Kagan* and her mission in the first place?" I asked. Deb didn't answer. "Maybe they were waiting for confirmation that she was going after the sirens."

"Or they wanted a bigger audience," said Lena. "The Michigan state capitol attracted a good-sized crowd and plenty of media attention. You can't get that same mob coverage by attacking a single ship fifteen miles from land."

P.R. again. My gut tightened, a sensation that usually preceded being punched or shot at. "Vanguard hasn't officially claimed responsibility, right? All they accomplished by murdering a handful of anti-magic politicians was to turn public sentiment more strongly *against* people like us."

"If Vanguard wants to look like the good guys, they can't just attack a Coast Guard ship. People can sympathize with wanting to kill politicians, but murdering our military?" Lena was flexing her fingers one at a time. Each made a series of quick wooden snapping sounds.

"You have to make the military into the bad guys," said Deb. "Wait and film them attacking the sirens. Show innocent creatures being captured or killed. If people had seen the vampires screaming and dying in the tunnels back in Detroit . . ."

I checked the in-dash GPS and switched lanes to make the next exit. "Meaning there's a good chance we're going to be heading into a war zone tonight."

"The war's already here, hon," Deb said airily. "While you're off messing around in your lab or testifying and looking for 'compromise,' people like me are getting killed in the streets. Nobody should have to compromise their right to exist."

Two hours later, we were heading out in a rented thirty-four-foot fishing boat called the *Nemo*. The owner had been hesitant about letting three strangers take one of his boats, but a mental nudge from Deb and a large cash deposit from me persuaded him.

"When did you learn to drive a boat?" asked Lena.

"My dad taught me on our pontoon boat when I was eleven years old. We used to spend a few weeks each summer camping by the lake. I learned to sail, too."

It had been a while though, and the *Nemo* was significantly bigger than I was used to. Its twin outboard motors made the old pontoon boat look like a child's bathtub toy.

The weather was good: clear skies and gentle winds. The waves were topping out at about two feet, and the *Nemo* cut through them with hardly a bump. We moved quickly enough to keep the spray behind us, making for a surprisingly dry ride. On another night, I'd have been happy to just cut the engines and drift beneath the stars with Lena.

Deb stood at the port rail, working on a bucket of KFC she'd insisted on picking up on our way to the docks.

I leaned out from the small cockpit. "I thought Renfields had to eat living bugs and birds, not dead ones."

"Hon, nobody eats fried chicken because it's good for them." She tossed a bone into the waves and grinned.

Whereas Deb was acting like this was nothing more than a late-night ocean joyride, Smudge was visibly anxious. I'd kept him in his cage in the cockpit, shielded by the clear acrylic windscreen. He'd spent the whole time crouched flat, with threads of smoke rising from his back.

I flipped on a small overhead light and checked my books. I'd sealed some of them in plastic bags as a precaution in case things went badly. I used C. S. Lewis to create an additional vial of healing magic for Lena, then ran my finger along the inner edges of the page. The book was beginning to char. I'd have to update the Porter catalog with a note to leave this one alone for a couple of years.

"How much farther?" called Deb.

I checked the screen. The *Nemo* was fitted with a radar and satellite positioning, overlaid with an electronic chart of the waters off the coast. "About two miles."

The owner had also mentioned the state-of-the-art radar, which he used to pick up flocks of seabirds that led him to the best fishing locations. Unfortunately, the Coast Guard's radar was probably much better than our own. Between that and their radar detection systems, we needed another way of sneaking up on them. "Take the helm, love?"

Lena kissed my ear and slid past me to grab the wheel.

I traded the Lewis for another book. "Time to engage the cloaking device."

Lena glanced over her shoulder. "Stuart Little?"

"In the book, Stuart had a mouse-sized car." I hadn't read this one in years, but it had been a favorite when I was in kindergarten. I reached into chapter eleven and pulled out the miniature automobile. It was just as I'd imagined it: half a foot long, bright yellow with black fenders. "You see that tiny button on the dashboard? That's the invisibility button."

"And a mouse's car has an invisibility button because ... ?"

"Because it's cool!" The nice thing about using children's books for libriomancy was that you tapped into a different kind of belief. Children had less skepticism about such things, fewer questions about how invisibility would or wouldn't work. If a button made a car invisible, then that's all there was to it. Press the button, and the car became impossible to see.

I drew that piece of the car's magic into myself, then pushed it into the *Nemo*. "Watch your step, Deb! We're about to disappear."

She tossed the remainder of the bucket overboard, wiped her hands on her pants, and grabbed the rail.

"Are you all set with your heading, Lena?"

She glanced at the stars and the moon. "I'm good."

I used the tip of a pencil to press the tiny button in the car. It vanished from normal sight, along with the rest of the boat. Lena, Deb, Smudge, and I disappeared as well.

"That's disconcerting," commented Lena.

We continued to cruise along the waves, appearing to fly just above an abnormally smooth V where the bottom of the *Nemo* flattened the water beneath us. I removed my glasses and focused not on the ocean, but on the magic flowing over the boat and ourselves. It was a bit like the final scene of *The Matrix*, only instead of seeing glowing green computer code, I saw the black-inked characters from the book.

"A thousand bucks to anyone who can explain why my glasses blur my magical vision even when they're invisible," I muttered. It had to be either a side effect of the charring on my retinas, or else something to do with the logic of young *Stuart Little* fans.

A loud thump vibrated the cockpit, followed by copious swearing.

"Mind the canopy," I said.

"Bite me." Deb rubbed her head. "How far until we reach the sirens?"

"Five minutes or so?" I put a hand on Lena's back and eased around her to take the wheel. "Lena, do you have the earplugs?"

I heard her unzipping a bag. "I picked up some noise-canceling headphones to go with them."

I shoved the foam earplugs into a pocket and hung the headphones around my neck. Having survived the weakened song of a scarred siren last year, I had no interest in suffering the full power of an entire group.

"Lights at eleven o'clock," said Deb.

Her vision was better than mine. I replaced my glasses and squinted into the darkness until I spotted the lights of the approaching ships. "How many?"

"Three."

I guided us closer, keeping the engines low and hoping nobody would hear us over the waves and the noise of their own vessels. By the time we were near enough to make out the individual ships, the frontmost cutter had come to a stop and was lowering equipment into the water. Uniformed men stood watch at the rails, assault rifles in hand.

"Any sign of Vanguard?" I kept my voice to a whisper, despite the fact that it would be impossible for anyone to overhear.

"Nothing yet," said Lena.

An explosion sent a shudder through our boat. I'd missed the source of the blast, but the ocean bubbled and burst like a geyser a short distance from the lead cutter. They hadn't even tried to communicate with the sirens, or to survey the ocean floor. They'd simply begun bombing.

"Shit!" I'd hoped to have more time to observe and plan. I snatched several books and carefully removed the magic keeping them invisible, like peeling fruit. Nobody was likely to notice a few books floating above the water. I flipped to the page I'd bookmarked during my flight, peered over the top of my glasses, and created a personal body shield that should stop any mundane bullet.

Next up was *Control Point*, a military fantasy with several potentially nasty new forms of magic. The power I wanted was called aeromancy. I absorbed the book's magic and seized control of the wind, turning it against the lead cutter. The waves grew taller and battered the ships from the side. Slowly, they began to veer away.

Three more explosions followed, the bright flashes muffled beneath the water. A body floated to the surface, her long, matted hair streaming like seaweed. I couldn't tell whether the siren was dead or simply stunned.

My grandfather had told us stories about fishing with dynamite, tossing lit sticks into the water and then rowing out to scoop up the concussed fish. The Coast Guard was using the same approach on a larger scale.

"Earplugs," Lena shouted.

I'd almost forgotten. I shoved the foam plugs into place, then cupped the headphones over my ears. The world fell silent.

I strengthened my assault, trying to push the lead cutter into its companions. A collision at sea should keep all three ships busy long enough for the sirens to escape, and for me to sneak on board and find out what the hell was going on.

I had just stepped out onto the deck when the sirens responded.

Despite our precautions, the sound rising from the ocean drilled into my marrow, making my bones buzz with desire. Lena found my arm and clasped it tight. The slightest edge of the sirens' song stirred memories and longing.

For me, it summoned the despair I'd struggled with a year ago. I felt like my chest had been hollowed out, rotted from the inside by everything I'd lost: friends who had died in the fighting back home; my brother's trust; my dreams for New Millennium; even Gutenberg, though that one was tempered by relief that he no longer ruled the Porters.

Lena kissed me, supplanting the sirens' magic with her own. I slipped my arms inside her jacket and pulled her tight. I don't know how long we stood there, frantically kissing and grasping at one another, until another explosion interrupted the sirens and our own desire.

I broke away and looked around for Deb. She'd moved to the bow and was staring out at the waves, but she hadn't flung herself into the ocean, which was the normal response to an unfiltered siren's song.

If the sirens had hit us that hard, I couldn't imagine what they'd done to the crews of those Coast Guard ships. Only they weren't leaping overboard or collapsing in despair.

Another round of explosions went off. In the flickering light, I saw that the crew were wearing hearing protection similar to our own. They'd known exactly what they were up against, and had come prepared.

I swore long and loud over the implications, but I'd have time to sort that out later. I clapped Lena twice on the shoulder to let her know I was moving out, then swapped books and reached deep into Rick Riordan's *The Lightning Thief*.

I was starting to push my limits. Characters cried out in my head, and my vision flickered with the imagination of countless readers. I seized one particular image, pulled it free, and donned its power. Wings peeled open from the sides of my sneakers.

I leaned over the rail long enough for the waves to spray my face. The cold water helped me focus on this world.

I tapped Deb's shoulder twice in the signal we'd agreed on. She caught my arm and stepped around behind me. I gripped the rail as she climbed onto my back and clung like a child. I was shocked to realize she weighed little more than my niece. Renfields tended toward the slender side, but Deb was a scarecrow.

She pounded my chest with one hand. I nodded and spread my arms for balance as my winged sneakers lifted us aloft. It was like walking on marshmallows. I leaned forward and tried not to think too hard about the physics.

I failed. With an unstable source of lift anchored to my feet, we were far too top-heavy. We should have toppled head over heels within seconds of leaving the deck, but the wings and their magic seemed determined to keep us upright. Even if they strained my ankles to the breaking point in the process.

I crouched until my knees touched my chest, which eased the stress somewhat, and gave me one more reason to be grateful for invisibility magic. We would have looked completely ridiculous flying over the waves in a deep squat.

We were a good thirty feet up now, high enough for a painful belly flop should things go wrong. Halfway to the nearest ship, I saw a group of men using some kind of rescue net to haul a siren on board. Another siren was sprawled on the deck. A group of people huddled over her body, securing her while a man knelt and did something to her mouth and throat, no doubt to mute her power.

Wind wasn't enough to stop this. I paused in our flight and grabbed *Control Point* again. Instead of aeromancy, I switched to portamancy, the magic Cole's protagonist used to open doorways to an alternate dimension. Cole's soldiers had found other uses for a two-dimensional rift in reality.

I didn't bother trying to anchor my gate to a real-world location. I simply sent the gate hurling through the air like a Frisbee.

It sliced the tip of the bow from the first cutter as neatly as a light saber through a vampire.

It was like throwing a lit firecracker into a wasp nest. Dozens of guardsmen swarmed over the deck. Some checked the damage while others searched the water for the source of the attack. I'd dissolved the gate, so there was nothing to find, but that didn't stop one of them from shooting into the waves.

I hovered in place and waited for the mental after-images to fade. Those gates were particularly challenging to work with, especially since I was trying not to hurt anyone. I simply needed to turn the ships away, or to distract the crew long enough for the sirens to escape and for us to find out exactly who had issued these ships' orders.

I started forward, then hurled myself to the side as three figures burst up from the water in front of us. Deb's grip tightened into a noose around my neck. The shift in weight dragged my body into a backward arch. I wind-milled my arms, but I couldn't right myself with Deb dangling from my neck. My head was pounding, and I struggled to breathe.

She began to swing back and forth, which increased the pressure on my throat. My vision clouded, and my spine popped like I'd gotten an adjustment from the world's most sadistic chiropractor.

With one last swing, Deb hurled a leg up around my

waist. The momentum helped me to roll over in midair, allowing her to resettle herself on my back. I carefully bent my knees and re-centered our weight, hissing in pain as strained back muscles made their unhappiness known.

Once we'd stabilized, I looked around to try to get a read on the new arrivals. Vampires, most likely. They could fly, and they didn't seem to have any trouble with water, which narrowed down the potential species. No wonder we hadn't spotted any Vanguard boats: they hadn't bothered to bring any.

Two more vampires rose up behind another ship. They touched down on deck, seized the closest crewman, and hauled him into the air before anyone could react.

If the vamps were of the bulletproof variety, this would turn into another slaughter, far worse than what I'd seen in Lansing. I couldn't let that happen. I reached for another book, but before I could use it, a floodlight on the farthest ship swiveled around to focus on one of the vampires.

In less than a second, the light burned him to nothingness.

Another vampire dove into the water, dragging a struggling guardsman down with him, but the light followed them. Moments later, the guardsman surfaced and began swimming back to his ship.

More floodlights chased the other vampires through the air. The Coast Guard had to be using ultraviolet bulbs, powerful enough to simulate the sun's rays. Not only had they been ready for the sirens' magic, they'd prepared for vampires as well. They'd known what Vanguard was sending to intercept them . . .

This was a test. A fucking research project. *That* was why every previous Vanguard attack had involved only a single species. Too many variables weakened your results.

Send werewolves to assassinate the governor and attorney general, and make sure the FBI is en route. Time how long it takes the werewolves to complete their mission, then measure their effectiveness against law enforcement. Anyone who got their hands on the surveillance footage would have a trove of data on speed and strength, as well as the effect of the mundane bullets that killed one of the werewolves.

Now they'd moved on to more advanced weapons, designed specifically to work against inhuman species.

Had the Porters helped them develop those weapons? UV was a known vampire weakness. It was possible the Coast Guard had developed those spotlights on their own. But they'd also known roughly where to search for the sirens.

Deb couldn't have known. She wouldn't have sent those werewolves out to die as lab rats. She and the rest of Vanguard were pawns.

Deb was pounding me on the hip, trying to get my attention. How long had I been floating here, seething? I nodded hard and knocked her fist away. Hands trembling, I grabbed Butcher's *Small Favor*, a book I'd brought along as a last resort. I ripped open the book's magic, focusing on a scene with Queen Mab. I channeled Mab's power into the water closest to the ships and drained the heat from the ocean.

Waves froze with a sound like giant bones snapping again and again. Frost spread over the hulls. The ice cracked and reformed as the *Kagan* came to a halt. The cold spread to touch the other two ships, locking them together in an expanding iceberg.

I closed the book. That much power had charred the pages enough to render it useless for at least a decade, but it had done the job. None of these ships were going anywhere until they freed themselves.

Already men were firing their weapons into the ice, trying to crack it away. I had to give them credit for professionalism. This couldn't have been a threat they'd trained for, but they hadn't hesitated to improvise, splitting their forces between vampires, sirens, and my own magic.

I flew toward the *Kagan*, keeping my distance from the disturbingly large front cannon. We landed on the aft deck behind a pair of men who were securing an unconscious siren to a rescue stretcher. Everyone wore ear protection, so I didn't worry about being quiet.

Deb hopped off my back, but gripped my hand in hers so we wouldn't get separated. Her skin was cool and damp, with a texture that reminded me of flaking paint.

I had no way of freeing the siren without being discovered, but I was able to place a tracking dot on her leg with the same book and magic I'd used on Deb a few days before. I clenched my fist as I watched the men quickly and efficiently pass their prisoner down a narrow set of stairs into the body of the ship.

I'd studied the ship's layout in Vegas. The bridge was near the front of the upper deck, directly below the radar. Windows provided a hundred-and-eighty-degree view. According to Charles' instructions, we needed to reach the Command Information Center.

He hadn't been optimistic about our chances.

"Good luck with that. The CIC is one of the most secure rooms on the whole damn ship. Invisibility won't get you through those doors or let you hack into the computers."

We approached the bridge and waited. The sirens' song would make radio communication difficult, meaning someone would have to relay orders directly. It wasn't long until one of the deck crew came running. He pounded three times on the door.

Through the window, I could see the bridge crew donning ear protection. Twenty seconds later, the door
swung inward. I used aeromancy to summon a gust of
wind strong enough to wrench it open and hold it while
Deb slipped inside.

This bridge was far more cramped than anything I'd
seen on *Star Trek*. I counted nine people crowded together, most of them working over somewhat outdated-
looking control panels. Thick cables were strung along
the ceiling.

Heavy foam panels had been added to every surface,
presumably for increased soundproofing. Additional
panes of glass were welded into place over the windows.

I'd have recognized the commanding officer even if
he hadn't been sitting in the captain's chair. The thick-
shouldered, balding man made me think of a gargoyle,
calm as stone as he observed everything happening
around him. According to the reports Talulah had dug
up, this was Commander Jeffrey Hill. He'd taken command of the *Kagan* two months ago.

Deb homed in on Commander Hill. I relaxed the
wind and allowed the struggling crewman to drag the
door shut.

Within three minutes, it opened again. Commander
Hill stepped out, followed closely by Deb. Her magic
tangled his thoughts, guiding him toward the CIC. Several people watched him leave, their expressions ranging
from concern to confusion, but none tried to intervene.

Why struggle to hack locks and computers when you
could hack the man in charge? Hill led us deeper into
the ship, down another flight of steps, and through a
heavy, narrow doorway. I barely noticed whatever it was
he did to gain access through the next door. My attention
had been caught by the sidearm secured to his hip.

That was no standard-issue military weapon. It was a

JG-367 handgun, invented by Johannes Gutenberg shortly before his death. The titanium "barrel" was a solid wand. In addition to firing blasts of deadly energy, it could put targets to sleep, transform them, petrify them either temporarily or permanently, and more. The grip used a built-in telepathic interface, allowing the owner to switch modes at will.

We had field agents around the globe working to keep weapons like this out of mundane hands. How the hell had the Coast Guard gotten hold of one? The only place you could get a JG-367 was from the pages of a book by Stuart Pan. Gutenberg and the Porters had slipped several paragraphs into the final manuscript of his last bestseller, meaning any libriomancer—and nobody *but* a libriomancer—could use the book to create the gun.

It was possible Commander Hill had gotten it through the magical black market. I'd gone that route once or twice myself in the past. But given their knowledge of siren migration routes and their preparation against the vampires, it was more and more likely they were working with someone from the Porters.

I was going to find that someone. From there, I would work my way outward until I'd found everyone who'd orchestrated these killings, everyone who'd signed off on using magic to spread terror and hate and death. And I would show them that magic could also bring justice.

Caught up in that thought, I almost got left outside when Deb and Commander Hill squeezed through the doorway into the CIC. I hurried after them, yanking my jacket behind me so it didn't get caught in the door.

Once inside, Hill tugged off his hearing protection and looked around. I followed suit. This was even more cramped than the bridge, with rows of computers and radar screens showing the status of various parts of the *Kagan*.

"Report," barked Hill. "Where'd that ice come from?"

"Nothing on radar, sir," said one of the crewmen.

A woman wearing a headset and microphone added, "The reports I'm getting suggest the ice hit us first, then spread to the *Czerneda* and the *Independence*. Tracing the path of the spread backward puts the source off our port bow."

"Order one of the gunners to rake that area. Probably too late, but we might get lucky and startle up whoever's hiding out there."

"What kind of vampire freezes the fucking ocean or chops the nose off a ship?" asked the man who'd spoken first.

"Belay that, Sitterson," snapped Hill. "Glue your eyes to that radar and find me the rest of those sirens."

"Aye-aye, sir!" Sitterson flushed and turned back to his screens.

"Lynch, any change in our orders?"

"No, sir," said the woman in the headset. She glanced at the man beside her, both of them clearly confused as to what their commander was doing here, and both of them just as clearly unwilling to ask.

"Get me the printout."

"Sir?" asked another man, this one squeezed into the far corner of the room.

"We're up against creatures who can mess with your thoughts, Lucas. Any one of us could be affected, and I want to be damn sure we complete our mission as ordered."

"Aye-aye, sir!" Lucas squeezed past his crewmates and handed over a folder.

A light flashed at Sitterson's station. He leaned closer. "Looks like electrical damage, sir."

He spun around too quickly for me to get out of the way. His chair struck my knee, making me stumble. Nobody else seemed to notice, but Sitterson scowled and reached out. His hand caught my sleeve. "Shit! We've got an intruder!"

Sitterson lunged out of his chair and crashed into me, knocking us both into the crewman at the next station. His hands found my shirt, then my throat, and he slammed me against the floor. My head struck the metal deck. My vision flashed.

Deb came up behind Sitterson and peeled him away, tossing him to the floor like he was a dirty outfit ready for the laundry.

"Secure the door," Hill shouted. "Whoever you are, you're not getting out of here. Surrender, or you *will* be killed."

He'd drawn his sidearm. That was a mistake. I knew the JG-367. I'd read the book it came from. Not only could I read its power, I could mess with it.

"Show yourself, and tell me what the hell you're doing on my ship." Hill kept the gun pointed to the floor in front of him, his finger off the trigger. "Lynch, radio the *Czerneda* and the *Independence*. Tell 'em they may have invisible vamps sneaking on board."

I tugged the JG-367's telepathic control text into myself, switched firing modes, and triggered the weapon. A silver beam of light touched the floor, transforming metal to stone.

"Fucking magic." Hill reached for a mundane sidearm on his other hip, while simultaneously trying to holster the JG-367. This was what I'd been waiting for. I fired it again, this time sending a sleep spell directly into his leg. He collapsed.

Deb snatched the folder from his hand.

"Right there!" One of the crewmen pointed my way. "There's two of them!"

I'd overextended myself. In setting off Hill's weapon,

I'd lost my invisibility spell. I could see the text crumbling around me. I only had a few seconds before Deb and I would be completely visible.

Two men blocked the door. Deb hurled them aside. I barely had time to jam my earplugs back into place before she wrenched open the door. The song of the surviving sirens outside slammed over me and the crew. I blinked hard, trying to focus. With shaking hands, I pulled my headphones into place, further quieting the sirens' magic.

A gunshot cracked behind me, little more than a quiet pop, but fire erupted through my forearm. I climbed up the stairs and out onto the deck. My head was spinning. Men with machine guns were running toward us.

Deb caught me around the waist, climbed the rail, and jumped. My winged sneakers slowed our fall, but that magic was dissolving as well. I dropped what was left of our invisibility and concentrated on holding on to those tiny wings.

A spotlight swept past me, but most of the lights were aimed elsewhere.

I stopped breathing when I realized my mistake. The invisibility spell that had protected the two of us had shielded Lena and the *Nemo* as well. When that spell failed, our little fishing boat had become visible.

The *Kagan*'s deck guns fired, ripping enormous holes through the *Nemo*. A second ship added its assault to the *Kagan*'s.

Between the two of them, they tore the *Nemo* apart.

JAPANESE VOTE BRINGS ASIA CLOSER TO WAR

The Japanese legislature narrowly voted to amend Article 9 of the Japanese Constitution today, in what many see as a serious threat to peace in the region.

Established in 1947, Article 9 prohibits Japan from maintaining an armed military, stating in part, "The Japanese people forever renounce war as a sovereign right of the nation and the threat or use of force as means of settling international disputes."

This historic vote follows weeks of increasing tension after China used a nuclear weapon against an alleged magical threat within its own borders. A statement from China's Ministry of Defense claimed the nuclear strike was only authorized as a last resort. "The threat posed by these magical rebels is equivalent to an active terrorist organization with nuclear capabilities. No nation would willingly allow such a threat within their borders."

Japan's Prime Minister rejected that explanation. "The world cannot tolerate a policy of nuclear aggression against potential magical threats. Nor do we believe the world could survive such a policy. We call upon all nations to condemn this attack, and we offer refuge and aid to those targeted by this act of war."

According to Article 96 of Japan's Constitution, an amendment to Article 9 requires a 2/3 supermajority vote by the legislature as well as an affirmative vote by the people. A special election has been scheduled for one week from today.

Chapter 10

"What are you?"

"I'll need you to be a little more specific, Isaac."

"Are you alive?"

"That's an interesting question. It's also a difficult one to answer with any accuracy. I'd say I'm as alive and self-aware as Smudge or Lena."

"Both of whom nearly lost their minds when they were brought from their books into the real world. Based on everything we know, shouldn't you be insane?"

"Where does such madness arise? Is it the shock of finding oneself in another world? I spent more than five centuries in your world. Is it the shortcoming of text, the inability to truly capture a complete mind in print? But then, a book written by a libriomancer is more than mere text. Particularly a book written by me, if I say so myself."

"Particularly if you're borrowing techniques from the Students of Bi Sheng."

"You noticed that, did you?"

"Are you a ghost?"

"The Porters have been shamefully sloppy with their

classification of 'ghosts.' When a vampire uses their power to speak with the dead, are they truly contacting a ghost? The mental and spiritual energy I used to guide my automatons, do those tattered remnants of humanity qualify as ghosts? Or Meridiana's so-called ghost army? Those poor souls had little in common with their living counterparts."

"You're avoiding the question."

"I have no answer for you, Isaac. I simply am."

I WIPED WATER FROM my eyes and searched for Lena among the wreckage of the *Nemo*. I couldn't see her, and there was no trace of her magic in the waves. I tried to fly in their direction, but my fading, waterlogged wings could barely keep us afloat. I switched tactics, looking around for any surviving sirens. If they knew we'd come to help them, they might be willing to return the favor.

Deb pounded my arm and pointed. I screamed in pain. A bullet had torn a line along my forearm. I clasped my other hand around the wound, trying to slow the bleeding. Old horror stories about sharks flashed through my head. Right now, I didn't have the strength to fight off an angry goldfish, let alone Jaws.

Once my eyes stopped watering, I looked to see what Deb was pointing at. A motorboat cut through the waves behind us. I counted eight people on board, most of them armed. One man scanned the water with a small but powerful spotlight. They paused to gather another unconscious siren, then circled toward us.

I wasn't sure I could stop them without killing myself in the process. Not with the amount of magic I'd burned through in the past hour. Nor did I want to hurt them.

Whatever was happening, it didn't make all of these people villains. Most were simply doing their jobs.

I took the printout of the *Kagan*'s orders and shoved it into one of the plastic bags I'd used to protect my books.

Deb pointed to the water and pantomimed swimming.

I shook my head. We had no boat. Even if we could evade the Coast Guard, neither of us were in any shape to swim to shore.

Nor was I willing to leave. Lena might have survived. I couldn't abandon her to drown, or to be rounded up with the sirens.

Deb's face twisted with anger and disgust. She shoved away from me and dove into the ocean.

The boat pulled alongside. One man fired a spray of bullets at the water where Deb had vanished. Rough hands hauled me in and tossed me down beside the unconscious siren, making me cry out again. I cradled my arm against my body. Three other guns pointed toward my chest.

"There was a woman on that boat," I shouted. They couldn't hear me. I gestured at the wreckage, searching for a way to make them understand. Given Lena's size and the wood growing along her skeleton, her body should float. If we reached her quickly enough, if I could get her back to her oak tree—

I got a kick to the side of the head for my trouble. They probably thought I was trying to do magic.

One man tugged off my shoes. Without my weight to worry about, they promptly flew off into the darkness.

I spat blood and tried to control my shivering. Lena knew how to swim, and she was tough enough to survive a gunshot or two, but those deck guns were a much higher caliber than anything she'd faced. I squinted up at the closest man. "My friend was on board." I exaggerated each word, willing him to understand. "We have to find her. Please."

Had Lena had time to grab Smudge's cage? He'd survived falling into a river back home, but that water had been far calmer and warmer than the Atlantic.

The boat turned about.

"No!" I tried to sit up. "She's still out there!"

A hand twisted into my hair and threw me back down. I rolled onto my side, trying not to vomit. The captive siren lay inches away. Blood dripped from her ears. The explosions could have easily burst her eardrums. Someone had fastened a thick strip of woven nylon around her neck, like a dog collar tugged so tight it dug into the skin. It had been ratcheted into place, and I saw no way to unlatch it.

I focused my attention on the siren's magic. It was faint, but legible. Unlike Deb or Lena, sirens weren't book-born creatures. They had evolved naturally, and that made it harder for me to parse their magic. Harder, but not impossible.

I blinked, trying to focus. Everyone on board was protected against the sirens' song. I'd have to manipulate the power of that song directly, to fashion the longing and despair into a weapon and thrust it through each and every one of my captors before they realized what I was doing.

It was a flip of a coin whether my mind would snap first, or if one of them would put a bullet through me. It was also the only way I could possibly get back to search for Lena.

The boat jolted like a car hitting a pothole. One man aimed the spotlight into the water beside us, while another covered the same spot with his weapon.

A second jolt followed, and a wooden spike punched through the side of the hull to stab the gunner's leg.

Lena. Thank God. I sagged backward in relief.

Bullets riddled the water. The motor sputtered and died. A man near the back grabbed what looked like an oversized smart phone and began tapping out a message, probably alerting the *Kagan* that they were under attack. I rolled along the floor and kicked the phone out of his hand, sending it overboard.

He kicked me in the ribs, but like the rest of the crew, he appeared to be more concerned with Lena's assault. The wooden spike continued to grow. Branches twined around legs, feet, anything they could reach. They ignored me and the siren. When this was over, I'd have to ask how she could see or sense who to entangle.

One man pulled a knife and sawed at the branches, which were now coming through both sides of the boat. Was Lena directly beneath us? It would protect her from gunshots, since they couldn't shoot her without sinking us, but how could she breathe?

Another branch took control of the wheel. That was enough for the crew. They turned their full attention to cutting and breaking themselves free. One jumped overboard. I slowly slid a hand into my jacket and pulled out an orange plastic squirt gun. While the others struggled with Lena's attack, I leaned out and shot the swimming man in the back of the head with a squirt of water from the river Lethe. It was a diluted dose, and should be just enough to wipe their memories of the past day. Maybe two.

Lena appeared inclined to let them go. The branches loosened, and people dove away almost too fast for me to tag them all with the squirt gun.

Soon, only a single man remained, bound like a wooden statue. I crawled to the wheel, restarted the engine, and did my best to steer us away from the cutters as Lena pulled herself on board.

"Smudge?" I shouted.

She pointed toward the remains of the *Nemo*.

I brought us around one-handed. Water was seeping through the holes she'd punched in the hull, though the branches mostly sealed them.

She brought her face to mine. "Are you all right?" she mouthed.

I shook my head. She reached into the pocket of her jeans and pulled out a glass vial encased in wood. She must have grown an oak shell to protect it. She removed the top and placed a single drop on my tongue. The burning and throbbing in my arm vanished, as did the other pains I'd acquired.

Lena turned away and reached into the water. A moment later, she was hauling Deb on board.

I spotted an angry red flare bobbing atop one of the larger chunks of the *Nemo*, a section of deck and hull about the size of a small car. Lena must have gotten Smudge out of his cage before swimming out to intercept us.

Lena pulled one of the branches free and extended it toward Smudge. The wood grew, stretching until it touched the wreckage. Smudge scrambled onto the end of the branch, a pillar of steam and flame and fury. He raced onto the top of Lena's head and clung there like a crown of fire. Lena grimaced, but Smudge's flames were mostly on the top of his body, and her hair was wet enough to keep it from igniting.

Another boat was closing in on us, but they held their fire. They wouldn't risk hitting one of their own. I opened up the engines and steered toward land. Lena untangled our imprisoned guardsman. Once she'd checked to make sure he was uninjured, she grabbed him by the waist and collar and lifted him over her head. I twisted around and squirted him just before Lena hurled him into the waves, directly in the path of the other boat.

They slowed down, more concerned with rescuing their colleague than with catching us.

I grabbed Deb and pointed to the wheel. She took over, allowing me to examine the siren. Lena crouched beside me. Smudge darted from Lena's head onto my shoulder.

Lena formed another branch into a thin, short-bladed knife, and used it to cut away the collar. The siren was awake now, her eyes round as she watched. Her face tightened in pain as Lena pulled the collar free.

I started to swear in five different languages. The inside of the collar was barbed. Each metal spike was a quarter of an inch long, and left bloody, pencil-sized holes in the siren's throat. Six were concentrated in the front, with four more spaced around the sides and back of the neck.

My own healing cordial had shattered during the fighting. Lena offered a drop from hers, but the siren refused, squirming away. Without a word, she pulled herself over the edge and vanished into the ocean.

Lena's mouth was a tight-pressed line. She moved over to relieve Deb. A moment later, the boat's lights switched off.

It didn't look like anyone was pursuing us. Between the sirens, the ice, and their own amnesiac crewmen, they had more than enough to worry about.

Which made this an ideal time for me to pass the hell out.

The next several hours were about as much fun as pulling out your own spleen. Through your urethra. Magic could heal physical injuries. It did nothing to help my mind and body recover from the amount of power I'd channeled tonight.

I remembered coming to on the boat, and Deb holding my collar while I leaned over the inflated rim and heaved everything I'd eaten in the past twenty-four hours into the ocean. When my consciousness finally managed a hard reboot, I found myself on my back in the sand, staring up at the cloudy night sky. I was wrapped in a damp blanket and shivering hard. Sweat covered my skin, and my muscles felt like melted rubber.

Smudge sat atop my chest, glowing like a tiny space heater. I brought my numb hands over his back.

"Oh, look. Mount St. Helens is awake," said Deb. "Please tell me you're done erupting."

I didn't have the strength to flip her off. "You look like you're feeling better," I croaked.

"I've been munching on minnows. And you look like hastily resurrected shit."

"Don't worry, I look better than I feel." I pushed myself up on my elbows. "Where's Lena?"

"She went back out to dispose of the boat, in case the Coast Guard had a way to track it. She'll be back soon with the car." She leaned over and grinned, displaying what I assumed was a bit of fin stuck between her teeth. "Still think Vanguard is overreacting?"

Someone had replaced my glasses on my face. The lenses were so badly streaked they made my vision worse, and the right hinge was bent. I tried to clean them, but my ocean-soaked clothes were useless. "What time is it?"

"About one in the morning."

"Great. Wake me up when the clock hits January."

"What happened to you back there?"

"Too much magic." Back when I'd been a traditional

libriomancer, magic used to make me lose my appetite. It hadn't made me lose the contents of my stomach.

Ponce de Leon once told me true sorcerers used wands and staves to channel their magic, allowing all that power to damage their tools rather than their bodies. Unfortunately, he'd disappeared again before explaining exactly *how* to perform magic with such tools. It was one more thing I intended to research, if I ever got the opportunity.

I looked around, trying to figure out where we were. Through the ink-like smears across my vision, I saw empty docks stretched out to either side. This time of year, people would be starting to bring their recreational boats in for the season, though I spotted a docked pontoon boat and a pair of sailboats a little ways off.

A car door slammed nearby. Lena hurried toward us through knee-high grass, a single wooden sword ready in one hand. "Isaac?"

"I'm alive. Mostly."

"Glad to hear it. Can you walk?"

"Have I mastered the skill? Yes. Can I demonstrate it at this particular moment? I'm not sure."

She scooped up Smudge and set him on her shoulder. His flames died down. Either Lena's presence made him feel safer—understandably so—or else he'd been burning entirely for my sake, trying to keep me warm.

She took hold of my arm and pulled me slowly to my feet. The ground wobbled a bit. "They're talking about this on the news. The radio called it a terrorist attack against Coast Guard vessels. There hasn't been an official statement yet."

"They'll need time to get their story straight." Deb paused to snatch something small from the sand, probably a crab or crawfish or some such. She popped it into her mouth before I could make out the details. "I don't think anyone got a good look at me, but Isaac here's another story. Once they hauled Mr. Bigshot Television Star into their rescue boat, it was all over."

"They shouldn't remember any of it. I hit them all with a shot of Lethe water."

"That's dangerous stuff to be carrying around," Deb said.

"So are you."

Lena helped me into the car. "Were you able to get what you needed?"

"I hope so." I reached into my jacket and retrieved the slightly damp and crumpled printout, turned on the interior light, and began to read. Half a minute later, I began to swear.

"The orders are straight from Thomas M. Hayes. The Commandant of the U. S. Coast Guard. They called it Operation Ocean Song."

"Where are they taking the sirens?" demanded Deb.

"The Virginia facility, whatever that is. I put a tracker on one of them." I kept reading. "There's an entire paragraph about assessing the effectiveness of the vampires' assault, and of the Coast Guard's anti-inhuman weaponry. They were told to expect resistance, and to use whatever means necessary to execute hostile vampires."

"And you let them," Deb said quietly. "You stood there and watched while they burned those vampires to ash. You could have sent all three of those ships to the bottom of the ocean."

I was too tired to be angry. "Yah, I could have killed a few hundred people and lost our shot at finding out what the hell is going on."

"So what now? Shall we sit around some more while those assholes dissect their prisoners to find out how sirens work? Just like the Porters used to do." Deb twisted around in her seat. "We saw *children* floating on those waves, Isaac. Every siren who died, every one who gets cut open, enslaved, or crippled by those monsters, that's on you. You and your damned Porters."

Lena frowned at that. "The Porters?"

"The commander of that ship had a JG-367," I said. "There's a good chance it came from one of us. A leak from the Porters would explain how they were so well equipped to deal with the vampires and the sirens."

"So what the fuck are you going to do about it?" Deb demanded.

I held up the stolen orders. "We're going to start by rescuing those sirens."

Lena started the car and pulled onto the road. "It's about five hundred miles to Virginia. We get on 95 heading north, and Isaac can catch up on his beauty rest. I'll wake him up when we reach the state border, and he can pinpoint exactly where they're going."

"Can't he track them now?"

I held up one hand, noting the faint ashen pallor of my fingertips. The more I manipulated so much raw magic, the more I'd char my own body in addition to the books. "Only if you want me to puke on you again. We know where they're going. I just need a little time to recover."

"And then what?" Deb's mental pressure made my temples throb. Was she doing it deliberately, or had this kind of mental manipulation become habit? "More sneaking around and doing nothing, like an impotent, helpless—"

"That's enough." Lena grabbed Deb's shoulder with one hand. Deb opened her mouth to protest, but Lena squeezed, eliciting a squawk of pain and protest. "We drive to Virginia and assess the situation. Then we figure out our next move."

"You mean Isaac figures it out," Deb muttered.

"While you go along with whatever your boy-toy decides."

"This would be an excellent time for you to shut up."

I turned to Lena. "To change the subject, how did you stay submerged for so long in the water out there?"

"I grew a hollowed wooden tube and used it like a snorkel."

"Nice."

Deb folded her arms and glared out the window, but she didn't say anything more.

I rubbed my forehead. The Commandant of the Coast Guard had ordered his people to seek out these sirens, to kidnap them and destroy their homes, killing who knew many in the process. He'd also sent them out to assess the vampires' strengths and weaknesses.

Someone was using Vanguard to supply them with expendable lab rats.

I watched Deb for a while. She had connections in Vanguard, and she was certainly capable of selling people out. But her fury felt genuine, and she'd been telling the truth back at the airport. She wanted whoever was behind this as much as I did.

Thomas Hayes had ordered the Coast Guard's assault, but who had infiltrated Vanguard? Who was passing along Porter information and equipment? Who coordinated the attacks in Lansing and elsewhere?

My thoughts kept circling toward Senator Alexander Keeler. In addition to chairing the Joint Committee on Magical Security, Keeler served on the Appropriations Subcommittee on Defense, reviewing and approving military spending. How many high-ranking contacts had he made in his years on that subcommittee?

He'd also summoned any number of Porters to testify in D.C. How many of his questions had been for the public record, and how many had been his way of probing our attitudes and beliefs, searching for someone who would be sympathetic to his goals?

Perhaps someone like Babs Palmer.

My jaw was clenched so tightly my teeth were starting to hurt. I forced myself to relax. "Wake me up when we reach Virginia."

I woke up four times: twice from nightmares, another time when Lena hit the brakes to keep from hitting a deer, and finally when my tooth beeped with an incoming call.

"Hitto soikoon!" I swore, repeating one of my grandfather's favorite Finnish exclamations. *"All right, I'm awake. Who's this?"*

"I've been asked to help investigate a possible Vanguard attack on three Coast Guard vessels earlier tonight."

"Hi, Nicola." I sat up and rubbed my neck, trying to work some of the stiffness out. *"How's life in D.C.?"*

"Aggravating. According to your staff, you left New Millennium for an unscheduled weekend in Michigan."

"Yah, that's right. After the week I've had, I figured I'd earned a little time back home. What time is it, anyway?"

"Five thirty-four in the morning. You say you're home right now?"

"Trying to get some rest."

"In that case, you might want to call your cell provider. According to this, your cellphone is currently on its way to Virginia."

Shit. I grabbed my cell from my pocket and powered it down. I had no easy way of removing the battery, and a determined libriomancer could probably track it even turned off. "Lena, could you do me a favor?"

She glanced at me in the rearview mirror. I pantomimed destroying the phone. She reached back to take it, and crushed it in her hand.

Nicola was humming to herself. Her magic spilled over the connection, sending a faint buzz of energy through my skull. It wasn't a cohesive spell; she probably didn't realize she was doing it. *"Why would Vanguard target Coast Guard ships, Isaac?"*

"Theoretically? I'd start by looking into where those ships were when the attack happened, and what their mission was."

Nicola sighed. *"I don't have time for this."*

She could have knocked me unconscious or dispatched a team of field agents to intercept us if she really wanted. *"They were bombing siren nests and taking prisoners."*

"I see."

"The ship's captain was carrying a JG-367."

"Are you working with Vanguard?"

"No. I think someone is using them. Nicola, I spoke with Babs Palmer before I left Vegas. She was spooked. Do you think she—"

"The council put Babs through a very strenuous . . . let's call it an interview process. Whatever differences we might have, she genuinely wants New Millennium and the Porters to succeed. I can't see her providing magical weapons to people who could turn them against us, whether that's Vanguard or the Coast Guard or anyone else."

That was a good point. *"She knows more than she was telling me. Something frightened her, Nicola."*

"I'll look into it. Don't do anything stupid, Isaac. Things are precarious. Derek tells me people are using this attack as one more lever to push additional antimagic legislation through, and to increase funding for magical and military defense."

"What do you want me to do? Sit around and wait for more people to die?"

"I didn't tell you to do nothing. I told you not to do anything stupid."

"You're not the boss of me," I muttered.

"I have the New Millennium org chart, and it turns out I am."

"Curses. Foiled by the org chart." I smothered a yawn. *"Thank you, Nicola."*

As soon as I hung up, Lena reached back to hand me a packet of Saltines, followed by a two-liter bottle of Sprite. "I know how you get after too much magic. We're in a hurry, and we don't have time to stop at Urgent Care to get you rehydrated."

I made a face, but untwisted the cap and forced myself to take a swallow. I washed down three crackers, then massaged my fingers. The numbness had faded a bit with sleep, and the flesh had regained some of its normal coloring. I grabbed *Flow My Tears, The Policeman Said*. I didn't need to create anything new; I simply had to tap into the tracking spells I'd created before.

The one I'd planted within Deb was easy to find, like a flashlight shining directly into my eyes. The siren was more like a firefly flickering at the edge of a field. "Head northwest. I'm not sure how to gauge distance, but it feels like we've got a few hours to go. If we keep driving . . ." I looked more closely at Deb. "Are those nightcrawlers?"

"I was hungry, and the gas station a few hours back had a bait store." She grinned and plucked a long, squirming worm from the Styrofoam container of dirt. "Want one?"

I looked away. *How to Eat Fried Worms* had been one of my favorite books as a kid, but the reality was about to cost me my three Saltines.

"Who were you talking to?" asked Lena.

"Nicola. For some reason, she thinks I might have been involved in an attack on Coast Guard ships earlier tonight. Which reminds me, if either of you have cellphones, you should probably destroy them."

Deb rolled her eyes. "Like I'm stupid enough to bring a cellphone along on a mission like this?"

"Mine died in the Atlantic," said Lena. "I meant who were you talking to before that. You were snoring like a chainsaw for a while, but then you started mumbling. You sounded upset. You were arguing with someone."

I froze. "What did I say?"

"You were talking about ghosts," said Deb.

I rubbed my arms for warmth. My clothes were completely dry, but my body couldn't let go of the chill from last night. "Just a dream."

"Really?" Lena pressed. "Because it sounded like half of a conversation. You kept stopping, like you were waiting for someone else to speak. A couple of times, you cut off in mid-sentence. If you're hearing voices, there's no way you're up for saving those sirens. Not with books potentially crawling around inside your head and setting up camp."

"It's not that. I'm familiar with libriomantic possession. I've had characters start talking to me, and I've seen what happens when you keep pushing."

My first mission with Lena had involved a former Porter who'd lost his mind to the characters in various books.

"This isn't the first time," Lena said softly. "You were mumbling in your sleep a week ago, too."

"How long since you saw your shrink?" asked Deb. "That's still standard procedure for Porters, right?"

"I canceled my last few sessions with Dr. Karim."

"Why?" Lena didn't bother to hide her anger.

I couldn't blame her. In addition to the normal mental and emotional dangers that came with my job, I'd also gone through a bout of serious depression the year before, hurting both Lena and Nidhi in the process. I had things more or less under control these days, but ignoring a condition like that was a good way to let it sneak back into your head and start wrecking the place. "I needed to sort something out, first."

"And you didn't say anything about this to me?"

I stared out the window, watching the grassy hills in the distance. "It's not possession," I repeated. "There's only one voice."

"What does it want from you?" asked Lena.

I snorted and banged my head lightly against the window. "I don't think he wants anything. It's what I want from him."

Deb whistled and shook her head. "You're running around searching for conspiracies and taking on the damn Coast Guard with another mind hitching a ride on your cerebellum?"

"I'm in control."

Lena didn't speak, but I could feel her frustration radiating through the car. As for Deb, she simply tossed back another chunk of worm like she was a kid munching popcorn at the movies.

"I've been talking to Gutenberg."

From: nkiruka89165091@disposimail.net
To: ivainio42@gmail.com
Subject: Second Star to the Right

Isaac,

Looks like we'll be on the run again soon. They're making up some bullshit about truancy and Dad being an unfit parent, but it's just an excuse. Dad wants to head north into Canada. I'd rather go somewhere warm. Mexico, maybe. It doesn't feel like there's anyplace that's really safe for people like us. People are getting snatched up all over the world to be recruited or studied or locked away where we won't scare anyone.

I'm sure the men in black suits will be showing up to ask if you know where I am. Tell them Dad and I ran away to Neverland.

Give Smudge an M&M for me!

-Jeneta

Chapter 11

"How long has it been since you read a book purely for pleasure? Without worrying about its magical potential, or because one of the Regional Masters asked you to update its entry in the Porter catalog?"

"What does that have to do with anything?"

"Shelley used to complain about it with writing. The more she learned of her craft, the harder it became for her to simply read for enjoyment. She worried that mastery would rob her of the joy she once found in stories."

"Shelley?"

"Mary Shelley, yes."

"YOU KNEW MARY SHELLEY?"

"I did."

"I hate you a lot right now."

"I bring it up because I'm concerned about you. You've grown more cynical."

"Have you seen the news lately? No, I suppose you haven't. Wars and riots and slaughter tend to tarnish things like hope and optimism."

"Not for a libriomancer."

"I seem to recall you being pretty damn cynical."

"Yes. And then I died. Am I the example you want to follow?"

"I THOUGHT WE WERE all in agreement that Johannes Gutenberg was dead," said Deb.

"Technically, so are you," I pointed out. "But yes. I was there. His magic had been peeled away, and he was impaled through the chest. He died pretty much instantly."

"You see where that could raise questions about you conversing with him." Lena kept her attention on the road. I didn't need to see her expression to hear her concern.

"You've got that phone in your tooth," Deb said, before I could respond. "What if someone's tapped into that? They could be talking to you in your sleep, trying to pry information out of you. Or maybe it's a crossed signal, and you're overhearing someone else's conversation."

"It's not the phone. I *wish* I could sleep through that thing. It jolts me awake every time someone calls, and I haven't figured out how to take it offline at night." I sat up straighter and leaned to the side, trying to catch Lena's eye in the rearview mirror. "I'm all right. Smudge would know if anyone tried to pull a Voldemort and return through my body or anything like that. This is something else."

"Another research project?"

"Not officially." I picked up my book and concentrated on tracking the siren. "I'll tell you more later. I promise."

"Go ahead and say it," Deb piped up. "You'll fill her

in once the dead woman's not around to overhear. I'm hurt by your lack of trust, Isaac."

"Uh huh. Go one week without pulling a gun on me or mentally manipulating werewolves into committing murder and working with terrorists, then we'll talk."

The siren's signal had grown significantly stronger. I leaned against the window, my attention split between the magic and the real world.

"Slow down." The signs on the side of the road said we were heading west on Route 58. Ten minutes later, I sat up and pointed to a narrow turnoff, blocked by a chain-link fence. "There."

Lena drove another mile before pulling off the side of the road. "You're sure they're here?"

"I'm sure." I grabbed my jacket and books and climbed out of the car. I wasn't fully recovered from last night's exertions yet, which meant I was better off sticking with traditional libriomancy. Creating physical objects from books tended to char the books. When I started manipulating that magic directly, that was when the charring was more likely to move into my own flesh.

I pulled out an old red-covered role-playing manual and skimmed the Treasure section. This was one of the earliest editions, and the first I'd used as a kid. Several other editions had already been charred from overuse, making their magic too dangerous and difficult to control. These manuals just had so many good toys to play with . . .

I double-checked the rules, then pulled out a trio of rings. "According to the rules, once you put these on, you'll be invisible until you remove it or attack something. If that happens, remove the ring and put it back on to redo the spell. We'll still be able to hear one another, and so will anyone else, so keep quiet."

"What counts as an attack?" asked Lena.

I snorted. "I once stayed up until three in the morning arguing that question with our dungeon master in college. I said tickling an ogre wasn't an attack because it didn't cause harm or damage. He said it required an attack roll, and therefore the ogre could see me, and therefore he could stuff my wizard headfirst into the privy."

My breath turned to fog in the cold morning air. I reached back into the car to retrieve Smudge from the dashboard. Since his cage was at the bottom of the Atlantic, I set him on my shoulder. He crouched down, seemingly content and comfortable.

I'd just started walking when a strong hand squeezed my backside. I jumped and spun. Lena had slipped on her ring, but I could see the shadow of magical text where she stood. "This could be fun," she said with a chuckle. "How about saving these for recreational use back home?"

She reached toward me again. I stepped to one side. When she turned away to try to find me, I snuck in for the counter-goose.

Lena spun. "Unfair. You can still see me."

"Prison break now," Deb snapped. "Sex play later."

I froze. "Shit."

"What's wrong?" asked Lena.

"The siren. I just lost her." I double-checked the book I'd used to track the siren. Its magic remained strong, and there was no evidence of charring or other damage that might interfere with my spell. I had no problem sensing Deb. Only the siren had vanished.

"You think they killed her?" asked Deb.

"It shouldn't matter. The spell doesn't rely on the subject being alive."

"Unless they destroyed the body. Would your spell work if they burned her to ash to destroy any evidence?"

"They wouldn't do that. Not yet. They wanted the

sirens alive and brought to Virginia for a reason. Even if they loaded her onto a helicopter or plane, they couldn't have gotten here more than a few hours ago."

"You hope," said Deb.

We ran until we reached the turnoff. An old road sign named it Prison Road. After about a mile, we learned why.

"They put the sirens in jail?" asked Deb.

A ten-foot chain link fence topped with razor wire surrounded a two-story brick fortress with narrow windows. Tall walls stretched out from the side to enclose what I guessed to be an open exercise yard. A sign alongside the road noted that the facility was closed, and trespassers would be prosecuted.

"Does that look closed to you?" I pointed toward the parking lot before remembering they couldn't see me.

I counted nine cars in the lot, which was fenced off with an ID scanner connected to the gate. Cameras watched the road, the sidewalk, and the grounds around the building.

"Any enchantments on the fence?" asked Lena.

"Nothing here, but there's plenty on the prison itself. The doors, the bricks, the windows, pretty much everything. The fence is just to stop outsiders from poking their noses in."

The magic of Lena's bokken stirred, sharpening in her hands. "Shall I make us an entrance? Or would that count as an attack and blow my invisibility?"

"I wouldn't risk it. Someone might see the hole in the fence, or they could be running an electrical current to monitor for breaks. Don't worry, I've got this." I set a book on the ground. When I removed my hands, it became visible. After a few minutes of turning pages and setting gravel in place to hold the book open, I was able to reach in and create a handful of sparkling dust. I sprinkled a pinch over each of us. "Think happy thoughts."

Lena found me by touch and wrapped her free arm around my waist. "Happy thoughts, coming up." She kissed me hard, and soon we were both floating over the top of the fence.

Deb followed a short time later. I refrained from asking what she considered a happy thought these days.

The fields around the building were unkempt and overgrown, but the prison itself looked well-maintained. Voices carried over the top of the wall, along with the buzz of machinery.

We followed the walkway from the parking lot to the main entrance. State and national flags flew to either side of glass doors. I waved to one of the cameras, then peered through the glass, careful not to touch anything. Invisible or not, the oils from my skin would still leave prints.

I squinted, trying to read the faint text of magic. The words darted about like crickets fleeing Smudge, wiggling and squirming too much for me to read, but they felt familiar. I stepped back a few paces. "It looks like the wards extend into the air over the yard, kind of like the setup at New Millennium. They probably cover the roof, too. I can't tell what exactly they do."

"There's no need to find out," Lena said hastily. "So don't go poking them."

"Where's your sense of adventure?"

"I must have misplaced it in the Atlantic, right around the time two military ships started shooting at me."

"Right." I turned my thoughts to happier memories. "I'm going to take a quick peek over that wall."

I flew up, careful to keep a safe distance from the wards. Inside the walls, a small group of men, women, and children were working to clean an overgrown and mostly barren yard. A girl ran a weed trimmer along the

base of the wall. An elderly man gathered broken concrete from the crumbling remnants of an old basketball
court. I spotted one guard standing in the shade of the
wall by a metal door leading back into the prison. He
had no gun; just a metal club or electrical prod of some
sort.

He also wore a gleaming badge with a familiar black
pearl worked into the center.

"Damn." That pearl was identical in both appearance
and function to the one Babs Palmer wore around her
neck. This could be trickier than I'd expected.

As prisons went, I'd seen worse. That didn't change
my growing desire to tear it apart brick by brick.

They'd attacked and kidnapped sirens without provo-
cation. Had the rest of these people been targeted the
same way? Locked up for the crime of being different?

I studied the prisoners magically, trying to identify
their species. They appeared *blurry*. I could make out
bits of their nature, but most of the text was faded, little
more than smears of ink. The effect was similar to the
magic-suppressing amulet the guard wore, but more dif-
fused. It appeared to have been implanted or injected
inside their bodies.

"What the hell did you do to them?" I whispered. I
was fairly certain three were vampires. Another looked
like a werewolf, as well as what might have been a selkie,
and a confused-looking woman who appeared to be a
pretty fresh zombie. I saw no sign of the sirens.

I drifted closer. The wards shifted in response, angry
words moving like a swarm of fish splashing to the surface to feed. I pulled away and dropped gently to the
ground. I found Deb peering through the glass of the
doors, while Lena sat with her hands merged into one of
the bushes beside the walk.

"I'm trying to grow the roots," she said as I approached. "I'm searching for underground cables and pipes, anything I can disrupt in case we need a distraction."

"How'd you know I was back?"

"Your coat. It's not quiet."

I filled them in on what I'd found. "The sirens could still be here. If someone dampened their magic the way they did with the other prisoners, it would explain why my tracking signal went dead."

I approached the doors, my attention drawn to the wards like Smudge chasing a laser pointer. I tugged the sleeve of my jacket over my hand and gently tested the handle. The door didn't budge. "Less than a year since the world discovered magic, and they've managed to renovate this whole facility. Wards over everything, armed guards with magical protection, and who knows how many inhuman prisoners snatched and locked up. Whoever's behind this, they're efficient."

The more I studied the eddies of text in the wards, the more the patterns began to make sense. There were currents . . . fixed points that seemed to anchor the magic in place. I concentrated on the closest, then swore.

"What is it?" asked Lena.

"Feist."

"English please, love."

"Raymond Feist. One piece of the magic here comes from his Riftwar series. It references a soul jar used to trap the life of a rather nasty necromancer." I pointed to pale lines of fresh mortar, where bricks had been carved out and replaced. "I think they created the jars, then physically sealed them into the wall. There are other spells working in parallel, but the soul jars are strongest."

Lena sucked her breath through her teeth.

"What does necromancy have to do with anything?" Deb asked.

"Watch." I couldn't remember the last time I'd wanted so badly to be wrong. I reached out, bringing my ring of invisibility toward one of the soul jars.

I recognized the attack the instant it began. That didn't stop me from nearly pissing myself as shadows converged on the spot I'd touched, then leaped toward me.

My invisibility flickered. Two incorporeal beings of shadow and madness ripped at my magic. I jumped back, but even that single touch was enough to freeze my veins. These creatures sought not merely to kill me, but to unmake me. To dissolve my thoughts and erase my memories and burn my component cells until nothing remained but raw, angry magic for them to feed on.

"Isaac?" Lena moved toward me, her swords raised.

"Stay back!" I reached for the spells in the wall and poured my own strength and will into the text, strengthening their magic to drag my attackers back into their metaphorical jars. Slowly, they quieted. I tugged my invisibility back into place like a torn coat.

"Who's going to tell me what the hell just happened?" asked Deb.

The first time Lena and I had fought these things was in Detroit. I'd reached deeper into a book than I'd ever tried before, reducing it to ash in the process. From that blackened ruin had come a thing of death and hunger and charred magic. It fed on my attacks and Lena's strength. We'd finally had to drop an entire warehouse on the damned thing, and even that hadn't been enough to destroy it.

Later, we'd discovered more of them, echoes of long-dead magic users, trapped and enslaved. A young libriomancer named Jeneta Aboderin dubbed them "devourers." They were also known as the ghost army. I'd destroyed hundreds of them the year before.

Babs Palmer had been assigned to round up and eliminate the rest.

"Basically, the walls are infested with incorporeal,
magic-munching piranha." Lena lowered her swords. "I
hate those things."

"A lot of the stories about piranha are exaggerated,"
I said. "They can kill, but the idea that they'll reduce you
to a skeleton in seconds is total myth. These, on the other
hand . . ."

There was no question of Babs' involvement anymore. The pearls, the devourers, even the wards over the
prison. They all carried her fingerprints. I tightened my
jaw to call Nicola, but her cellphone went straight to
voice mail.

"Can you get us inside?" asked Deb.

"Maybe." I studied the doors. "We could also head
back to New Millennium and confront Babs with what
we know. Bring in Nicola and the other masters."

"And leave those sirens here to die?" asked Deb.
"Abandon everyone inside those walls? As soon as whoever runs this place realizes they've been compromised,
they'll either move or kill the prisoners."

"I agree," Lena said quietly. "We can't leave them
here."

"All right. Let me fly up and scout around a bit more—"

Lena gasped. Her fingers merged with the wood of
her swords. She dropped to one knee and plunged both
weapons deep into the dirt.

"What's wrong?" I reached for her, but she flinched
away.

She raised her head, staring at something deep within
the prison. "We need to go in now."

"Now you're talking," said Deb.

"If we bust through those doors, we could bring the
whole place down on our heads," I warned.

"*Please*, Isaac."

I couldn't see Lena, but I recognized the magic crawling over her skin, armoring flesh in supernaturally strong oak and bark. Spikes of wood grew from her joints.

How had I ended up being the cautious one? "All right. Give me a minute to get the door open. I might be able to do this without setting off any alarms."

I unwrapped the compact mirror I'd been working on back at New Millennium and stepped up to the locked doors. Devourers shifted restlessly in the wall, like sharks sensing blood. I held the mirror perpendicular to the glass and hoped I'd strengthened the soul jars enough to hold the devourers back.

When I'd experimented with mirrors for the Gateway Project before, I'd tried to use the reflection to help me with targeting. This time, the glass was invisible, leaving nothing but a ring of text and magic. I peered through that small circle to the pushbar on the inside of the door. Treating the mirror as if it were a book, I pushed my fingers through the glass.

They emerged inside the prison. My fingertips touched cold metal. Very slowly, I eased my hand and the mirror forward. My fingers pushed the bar inward, unlatching the door and easing it open. Deb caught the edge.

That had worked better than I'd thought. Without the reflections, I'd been able to concentrate solely on the magic and my destination. I'd have to try adding an invisibility spell to the mix back at my lab.

Deb slipped inside, followed by Lena. I stepped through last and carefully pulled the door shut behind us.

Two men jogged toward the door. They wore dark blue uniforms and badges like the one I'd seen in the prison yard. I pulled my companions to one side of the hallway. With this being a prison, simply opening the door had probably tripped a signal or alarm.

Deb started toward the guards. I caught her arm and whispered, "Not yet."

Ever since I'd gotten my first close-up look at Babs Palmer's magic-dampening work, I'd been thinking about ways to bypass it. Not for any nefarious purpose; I just wanted to see if I could do it.

The flaw in such defenses was that they had to be magical themselves. I'd read the book Babs had used to create her magic-hating oysters. I knew the text bound up in the seeds of those pearls.

I handed Smudge to Lena and crept closer. The effect of the amulets spread outward in a vaguely human-shaped cloud, a shield with indistinct boundaries. I waited for the men to move past me, then stepped behind them until I touched that outer edge. Their amulets ate away at my invisibility like acid. As my hands became visible, I reached for the text of their protection.

It felt like grabbing an electromagnet after filling my veins with iron filings. Not only did the pearls physically repel my efforts, but every one of those imaginary filings shifted in response, tiny needles stabbing my hand from the inside.

My arms were visible to the elbow now. The pain in my fingertips faded. The resulting numbness was even more worrying.

I studied the carnivorous text crawling up my arm, twined it around my fingers, and pulled back, taking their protection with me. I dissolved the magic and tried to fix my invisibility. To Deb, I whispered, "Now."

I remembered the first time Deb had tried to manipulate my thoughts. She'd gotten much stronger since then, as more and more of her humanity slipped away. Her power touched both men and settled over their minds like gravy on a pasty.

Her invisibility flickered. Apparently influencing

someone's thoughts counted as an attack, even if no harm was inflicted. She yanked the ring from her finger and switched it to her other hand, vanishing just as the guards shrugged and turned around.

"It's probably nothing," said one. "Another electrical short."

His partner tested the door to make sure it was latched. "I'll put in a maintenance ticket to get an electrician out here."

"I'll do a loop through the halls. Think we better do another prisoner count to be safe?"

"Safe from what?" He shook his head. "Don't worry about it. Ain't nobody got time for all that paperwork."

We tailed the second guard toward the front office and followed him inside. Two more uniformed guards, a man and a woman, sat in front of a bank of screens. Unlike the other guards we'd seen, these carried Tasers and mundane firearms. I checked the video feeds from throughout the prison. Most displayed empty hallways and cells. I didn't see the sirens anywhere.

"Nothing," said the man we'd followed. "Log it as an electrical short. José's walking the rounds to make sure."

Lena and I moved toward an electronic map of the prison on the wall to the right of the video screens. According to the label at the top of the map, we'd broken into the Mecklenburg Correctional Center. LED lights marked the doors. Most were green. Others blinked yellow, including the front doors where we'd entered. I studied the map, trying to guess where they would have taken captive sirens.

I'd memorized about half the layout when Lena stepped past me, yanked a Taser from the holster of the nearest guard, and pulled the trigger.

He collapsed to the floor. Lena, now visible, caught the next guard's forearm as she reached for a button on the desk. Lena hauled her from the chair and slammed her to the floor hard enough to expel the air from her lungs.

Deb's fingers caught the throat of the third guard, the man who'd inspected the doors. She hauled him close and whispered something. His face lost its color, and he fainted.

I looked around the room. Two guards lay unconscious, with the third gasping for breath. "Lena, what the hell?"

"You were taking too long." Lena studied the map. Her bark skin strained against her shirt and jeans, and had torn several small holes at the knees and elbows. Her swords were tucked through her belt. Ridges of oak shadowed her eyes. "I'll meet you back here."

"What's going on?"

"It's something I have to do, love. We'll make better time if we split up. I'll call you if I find the sirens." She adjusted her ring, but its magic had been damaged from its proximity to the guards and their badges. I reached to try to repair it, but she simply shook her head and ducked out the door.

"Huh." Deb leaned against the wall and folded her arms. "When did she develop an independent streak?"

I ignored her and crouched beside the only guard who remained conscious. Her badge reached out to interfere with my magic, giving me a shimmering, ghostly appearance. I removed her weapons and slid them to the far side of the room. "A group of sirens was brought here earlier today. What happened to them?"

"I'd tell him, hon." Deb smiled. Her yellowed teeth and taut skin gave the impression of a living skull.

"I saw something about them on the books," the woman said warily. "They showed up before my shift."

"Where are they?"

"I don't know! All detainees are chipped, then sent through decontamination and cataloging. We haven't gotten any orders about new residents."

"Prisoners," said Deb. "That's the word you want. Or 'victims,' if you prefer."

"Deb, would you please ask her to take a seat at the computer and pull up everything she can find about the sirens?"

"I can't." The guard pointed to the map. Many of the lights had turned red, and a larger light on the bottom left blinked red. "Command knows you're here. They'll have locked the terminals by now. Probably the doors too. You're trapped in here."

Deb tested the door. It didn't budge.

I dragged the desk away from the wall. These weren't computers, just dummy terminals whose cables led out of the room, presumably to a server somewhere. I climbed over the desk and studied one of the cables more closely.

"What is it?" asked Deb.

Each cable was as thick as my little finger. From the stiffness, they probably had a layer of metal shielding beneath the black outer coating. I yanked one from its socket. There was a spark of electricity and magic. "I'm not a network tech, but this is weird."

"We don't have a lot of time, hon."

"Hold on." I tightened my jaw and called Talulah. *"I need help hacking a computer system at an illegal secret prison, and I don't have much time."*

"I'm off-site. Hold on." I heard her whispering to someone. Music swelled in the background, followed by explosions.

"What was that?"

"It's nothing. We're at the movies."

"We?"

She hesitated. *"Vince asked me out. I know he's a little young for me, but—"*

"You can date Smudge for all I care. I'm sorry for interrupting, but I really need to get into this system. Given what we've seen in the past twelve hours, it's probably protected with firewalls and magic both."

"What kind of operating system?"

I twisted around and glanced at one of the monitors. "Um . . . it's a split screen. Graphic interface on the right, command text on the left."

"Can you be more specific?"

"The text is green."

She sighed loudly.

"Isn't there something I could just stick to the keyboard to take control?"

"The keyboard?" Talulah laughed. *"Do you know how computers work?"*

"Can you help me or not?"

"That depends on what they've set up. Charles Stross' work might have something, or maybe Kelly McCullough. They've both written about magic-infused computing. There's a bookstore in the mall. Let me see what they've got on the shelves. It would be easier if you could get to the servers."

"That I can probably do. I'll call you back shortly." I hung up and checked the map again. Both wings of the building were lined with small, regularly sized rooms I assumed were individual cells. A larger enclosure could have been a cafeteria.

I turned to the guard. "Where are your network servers?"

She pointed to a nearby room on the map. "You'll never get to them. They're the most secure part of the whole facility."

"Ten bucks says you're wrong."

Deb had pulled a packet of thick plastic zip ties from one of the guards' belts, and was securing their ankles and wrists. "Hon, are you seriously making bets here?"

I stepped back and studied my hand. The guards' badges had eroded a bit of the ring's power. I was visible, but faint enough it would be almost impossible for anyone to identify me. "Can you do your brain whammy thing to make them forget about us?"

"I'll give it a shot."

I checked the camera screens again, but saw no sign of Lena. Several teams of guards were running down the hallways, but I couldn't tell whether they were coming after us or trying to capture Lena.

Given the nature of Lena's powers, I had a sick feeling I knew what she'd sensed. I grabbed one of the pistols we'd taken from the guards and handed it to Deb. "Would you care to unlock the door?"

She finished whispering to the guards, took the gun, and emptied it into the door by the handle. A quick kick finished the job, busting the door open.

I led us deeper into the building and took the second hallway on the right. This part of the prison appeared to be for the staff. We passed locker rooms and a small break room, turned left, and came to a riveted steel door that made me think of a bank vault, not a server room. Through a small vent in the bottom of the door came the humming of some sort of fans.

There was no knob or visible lock. An electronic keypad was mounted to the wall next to the door.

"I don't think we're going to be able to shoot your way through this one," said Deb.

"No problem." I grabbed Alan Dean Foster's re-released novelization of *Alien*. I'd marked several scenes with sticky tabs. I skimmed the one I wanted and pressed the open book to the door by the keypad. Yellow-green alien blood oozed onto the metal and began to sizzle.

The acidic blood ate through the book within seconds, nearly taking my hand with it. Scraps of paper fell away, eating pits into the floor where they landed. The metal bubbled and smoked, filling the air with a sharp, toxic scent.

"Who's out there?" someone yelled. New alarms buzzed throughout the prison.

Chunks of dissolving steel dripped and sagged, creating a hole the size of my fist. The titanium barrel of a JG-367 poked out through the opening.

Deb grabbed the end of the barrel and pushed it against the edge of the hole, so the titanium touched the acid. The gun hissed and smoked. She pressed harder, until half the barrel came off in her hand. "How long will that keep burning?"

"You don't want to know." The hole was almost as big as a Frisbee now, and had eaten through part of the wall as well as the door.

Deb shoved the door open. The guard inside had tossed away his magical pistol and was clutching a Glock 22 in both hands.

"Shooting her will just piss her off." I stepped into the doorway, little more than a translucent afterimage.

The man turned toward me, his eyes wide. Deb snatched the gun and hammered her fist into the bridge of his nose, quick as a snake. She adjusted her grip on the gun and pistol-whipped him, leaving him bloody and groaning on the floor.

His badge lacked the magic-damper his colleagues had worn. I relieved him of his other weapons while Deb zip-tied his hands and feet. Only then did I look around. There were no servers humming away. No tangled cables or racks of routers lit up like Christmas trees. Only a floor-to-ceiling curtain cutting the room in half. I tugged the curtain aside.

Four narrow steel-framed beds were stacked tightly atop one another like a bunk bed from a claustrophobic's nightmare. Small fans circulated air over the occupants. The faces of all four sleepers were physically identical to Babs Palmer's secretary, Kiyoko Itô.

The women's shaven heads were covered in electrodes, all flowing together into black cables like thicker versions of the ones I'd seen in the guardroom.

I called Talulah back. *"I've got interesting news about those servers ..."*

New Fighting in Ukraine

Renewed military action between Russia and Ukraine is being blamed on a mythological creature known as the vodyanyk.

Described as malevolent, slime-covered water spirits, vodyanoi are said to live in rivers and other bodies of water. According to folklore, they would destroy dams and bridges when angered, and often drowned unsuspecting passersby.

Reports claim Russian supporters near the town of Luhansk began dying sixteen days ago. Each morning, three new bodies have been found washed up on the banks of the Siverskyi Donets River. At first, these deaths were blamed on pro-Ukraine militants. Multiple eyewitnesses now describe an elderly-looking man, covered in scales and seaweed, roaming the streets at night.

Russia has made no official statement, but Luhansk has seen an influx of armed soldiers, as well as tanker trucks said to be carrying poisons that could be used to kill all life within the Siverskyi Donets.

Government officials at a Ukrainian cabinet meeting disavowed any influence or control of the vodyanyk, but warned that Russia's actions would only increase the creature's anger.

Chapter 12

"If you could go back and do it over again — libriomancy, the Porters, and everything else — what would you change?"

"For one thing, I'd stay the hell away from the book that killed me."

"You know what I mean."

"You want to know if it was worth it. I can't answer that, Isaac. We can know what was, but not what might have been. I oversaw five hundred years of magical history. The Porters spread throughout the world. The knowledge we amassed is beyond anything I could have imagined. We stopped countless threats. Was it the best possible outcome? Perhaps not, but I'm proud of what we accomplished."

"Those five hundred years of secrecy also set up the ignorance and fear that are triggering backlash and war against people like us."

"Human ignorance has never needed help. You think society would be more stable if magic had developed and evolved openly? Perhaps. Or perhaps kings and emperors *would have added magic to their arsenal and committed atrocities to make the horrors of the past centuries look like schoolyard brawls. Perhaps they yet will."*

"Or maybe they'd have accomplished miracles."

"Exactly so. It's impossible to say. This is quite the gamble you've taken, Isaac. I hope the dice fall in your favor."

E ACH WOMAN—EACH COPY OF Kiyoko Itô—wore a simple black hospital gown. Unlike Babs' secretary, these Kiyokos weren't wearing the amulets that blocked me from reading their magic. I removed my glasses and sat down next to the bottom-most Kiyoko. "They're from a Japanese novel."

"Since when do you read Japanese?"

"I can't read the text, but I can understand the images, the ideas and belief and excitement of the readers."

"So what happened to not creating intelligent beings from books?" Deb whispered. "I thought Lena was the exception to that rule."

"I think these are clones," I said slowly. "Quick-grown in a laboratory, and written to be a blank slate. They probably created her as a batch of cells."

"Keep your voice down."

"I don't think she can wake up while she's plugged in." I grimaced as I tried to make sense of it all. "It looks like she's based on that old myth that humans only use ten percent of their brains. She was written to be a semi-autonomous multinode supercomputer."

"What the hell does that mean?"

"Every piece is part of a larger, smarter system."

"How smart?"

I didn't answer. *"Talulah, are you still there?"*

"Just made it to the bookstore. I've been listening in. Clones as a biologically networked computer? Very cool."

"I need you to hack into every camera you can, throughout the country, and run facial matches on Kiyoko Itô. But don't *use any New Millennium or Porter network."*

"How many do you think are out there?"

"I wish I knew."

"All right. I'll see if I can crack one of the customer service terminals here in the store and make this my base of operations, just as soon as I can figure out how to keep people's attention elsewhere."

"What about Vince? He should be able to conjure up a 'look-away' spell to keep people from noticing."

She sighed. *"He wanted to catch the end of the movie."*

"Tell him to get his ass over there, and that if he makes it in less than five minutes, I'll help him find the truth about his runaway crow."

I turned back to the Kiyokos. It looked like each one had a psychic link with all her sisters. I glimpsed combat scenes from her book, where a team of Kiyokos moved impossibly fast, relying on inhuman teamwork and precision to disable a larger force of armed soldiers. The book was called . . . it translated to *All of One*, by Shunrō Kuronuma.

I'd hoped to wipe the prison's servers and erase the evidence of our break-in. Lethe water would probably work to wipe these four, but if they were linked to Kiyoko in Vegas or any additional clones, we were in trouble.

"Can't you use one of those books to mind meld with them and find the sirens?" Deb asked.

"I don't think so. It would be my one mind against at least four of them, maybe more. They'd overwhelm me the second I touched their thoughts."

"Then maybe we should stop wasting time. Shoot them to bring the system down, and let's get back to searching."

I stared at Kiyoko's face. Faces. It was possible she was being used, a tool for Keeler and Hayes and whoever else was pulling the strings of this conspiracy. Or she could have been a willing participant. Assuming "willing" was a term that even applied to a programmed clone.

Was the Kiyoko in New Millennium Babs' prisoner, her accomplice, or her jailer?

The phone in my jaw beeped. *"Yah?"*

"Vince is here. I ran a program from Blackout 2020, *a dystopian thriller. I know you said to focus on the U.S., but I decided to go global. It's already tagged two matches. One in Taipei, China. The other in D.C. Both date-stamped within the past week."*

"Any recommendations on how to hack a biological computer?"

"We could try a direct neural hack from Neuromancer, *but cross-novel tech is risky as hell. The tech they're using, what book did it come from?"*

"All of One. Shunrō Kuronuma."

"Give me a minute to dig the details out of our catalog. Looks like Japanese cyberpunk. Published back in 2012. Oof. Neural hack is out unless you want your brain turned to pudding."

"How much longer?" asked Deb, her words tight.

"What if I just yank these electrodes off of her?" I asked.

"I'd have to read the whole book, but I wouldn't advise it. Too many writers go with the trope that a sudden disconnect from cyberspace can fry your brain."

"We're about to have company," Deb warned.

"Isaac, I'm not going to be able to get you in, but if the

clones are all connected, I might be able to use the one at New Millennium as an entry point."

"She's got that magic-blocking pearl."

"She's also wired into a physical network in Babs' office, which means I can tap the cables. We'll head back and see what we can find."

"Thanks. And Talulah, where exactly was the match in D.C.?"

"That Kiyoko was coming out of the Pentagon."

The sound of hard-soled boots on linoleum converged outside the door. I moved to one side of the beach ball-sized hole. Deb took the other.

"This is your one chance to surrender peacefully." The speaker sounded both angry and eager. "We know there are two of you in there, and we *will* kill you if necessary."

I glanced at the Kiyokos. Was she communicating our actions to her team? I hadn't had time to read more than a fraction of her abilities.

"Any ideas?" asked Deb.

I remained mostly invisible, which gave me an advantage, but they were probably wearing more of those magic-damping badges. I could hit the environment around them, turn the floor to quicksand or fill the air with fireworks to blind them. The alternative was to use magic on Deb and myself. If we shrank ourselves to ant size and snuck into the walls, the guards would have a hard time—

"Drop your weapons!" The command was followed by a burst of gunfire. I flattened myself against the wall, but they weren't shooting into the server room.

There was a noise like a baseball bat hitting a coconut. I heard one body drop, and the gunfire died. Someone else started to swear, a sound that cut off abruptly with the crack of oak against flesh.

"Your girlfriend's back," Deb commented.

I glanced through the hole in the door. Two men were

down, one unconscious and the other likely wishing he
was, judging from the obviously broken legs and his
pained whimpering. Lena hurled a third guard into the
wall like he weighed nothing.

The cold efficiency with which she tore through the
guards frightened even me. I searched for any magic that
might be influencing her emotions, fueling her rage, but
there was nothing. She backfisted another guard. The
jagged, fresh-cracked stubs of broken branches protruding from her knuckles cut deep gashes along the side of
his face.

Bullets had torn at least three holes in Lena's shirt
and jacket. Judging from her bulk, she'd grown her
wooden skin at least an inch thick. It slowed her move-
ments, preventing her from reaching one of the remaining guards as he raised his pistol. Two more bullets
thudded into her side.

She strode toward him and struck the side of his head
with her bokken. She'd blunted the edges, thankfully.
Gun and guard both fell.

Lena spun in a quick circle, making sure everyone was
down, then approached the door. "The cell block's sealed
off. If you're finished here, I could use a hand getting
through."

Lena marched us into the north wing of the prison. We
passed three more unconscious guards, as well as a supply room that had been sealed shut. It looked like Lena
had stabbed a branch into the doorframe and broken
it off, leaving it to grow and grip both door and wall.
Someone pounded the door from the inside, but the oak
bulged more than an inch to either side of the crack.
They'd need a chainsaw to cut their way out.

The door blocking Lena's progress wasn't quite as heavy-duty as the one into the server room, but it was a close second. Lena had grown additional saplings here, probably trying to pry the door free of its hinges, but the steel hadn't budged.

"Are the sirens back here?" I asked.

She picked a bullet fragment out of her wooden stomach. "I don't know."

"Lena—"

"I can't worry about the sirens until I deal with this, Isaac. With him." She slammed a fist into the wall hard enough to splinter the stubs on her knuckles. She grimaced and shook her hand.

"All right." I used an older fantasy to create what the Porter catalog referred to as Excalibur #29. This was a simpler take on the mythical blade: Roman in style, with a golden hilt. I brought the scabbard along as well. In this version, the scabbard had certain healing and defensive magic. Lena had her healing cordial, but I'd lost mine the night before. I drew the sword and pressed it into Lena's hands. It turned visible, escaping the magic that still concealed me.

Lena plunged the blade into the crack at the edge of the door. She hauled down, muscles flexing beneath wood. I grimaced at the metallic squeal as she cut through the hinges. She yanked Excalibur free. Power flowed through her saplings. They flexed and bulged, twisting the door from its frame to reveal the prisoners beyond.

"Déjà vu," I whispered. This corridor looked like it had come straight from the pages of my report describing the vampires' dungeons in the Detroit salt mines. Each cell was airtight, with small steel doors for passing food and other objects in and out. A layer of thick Plexiglas stood just beyond the steel bars that had probably been here since the prison was built. The cells were furnished with narrow beds, a steel toilet and sink, and little else. The prisoners I'd seen in the yard pressed against the Plexiglas, watching Deb and Lena.

Lena handed Excalibur to me. "Get them out of there."

"Where are you going?"

She strode down the hall without answering. I thought about trying to stop her. I didn't think she'd kill anyone if she didn't have to, but I'd never seen her like this. She disappeared around a bend.

I either trusted her or I didn't. I turned to the nearest cell and stabbed Excalibur between the bars, through the Plexiglas.

My invisibility wavered. I tried to force the sword down to cut a doorway. Excalibur wouldn't move. Clearly, stabbing wasn't the right approach here. I should have created a damned lightsaber.

A devourer in the wall stretched out to envelop the blade. I yanked it free and stepped away until the spells trapping the devourer in place tugged it back like a dog at the end of its leash. After taking a moment to repair the sword's magic, I moved in and slashed a quick X. Enchanted steel cut through the bars and the door beyond. I completed one more swing, this one low and horizontal, before Excalibur crumbled to black, gritty dust in my hands.

Broken bars clanged to the floor. A kick from Deb knocked a triangular chunk of three-inch thick Plexiglas loose. That only left the devourer.

"You're gonna need more swords," Deb commented.

I stepped carefully through the hole into the cell. Shadow reached for me, even as I strengthened the spells in the wall, tightening the thing's leash and choking it back, inch by inch, until it was pinned in place and helpless.

A young werebear crouched in the far corner. She was thirteen years old at most, and looked to be in good health. Her loose-fitting red jumpsuit was dirty, and her ragged hair had been cut short. She sniffed the air. She might not be able to see me very well, but she could smell my presence just fine.

"It's all right. We're going to get you out of here. Where are your parents?"

"No entiendo."

"Me llamo Isaac. Soy de los Porteros."

She cocked her head. Either I'd bungled the Spanish or else she didn't know what the Porters were. Possibly both.

I sat down a short distance away and examined the magic they'd forced into her body to prevent her from changing forms. The text was identical to that of the pearls in the guards' badges, but it was concentrated in the throat. They'd inserted or injected it beneath the skin, tagging her like an animal.

I reached out, and she flinched away, one hand jerking up to cover a dark scab on her neck.

They'd probably put a tracking chip in there, too. I considered trying to use my enchanted mirror to pluck it out, but trying to open a portal into a child's throat was dangerous enough. When you added that damned pearl to the equation, I'd almost certainly end up killing her.

"Deb, we've got to find another way of opening these doors. Any suggestions?"

"Ask him." Lena hurled a large, muscular man to the floor in front of the cell. She held a second guard by the collar. He struggled like a kitten in his mother's jaws, with the same lack of success.

The girl's flinch told me everything I didn't want to know. "¿Te hizo daño?" I asked, as gently as I could.

"A mí, no. A mi hermano."

I stepped out of the cell. "Where is this girl's brother?"

The man on the floor groaned. "Three cells down, on the left."

Lena brought her bokken to the throat of the guard struggling in her grip. The wood was needle-sharp, and had drawn a visible trickle of blood. "I know what you did to him. What I do to you depends on the choices you make in the next few minutes. Open these doors."

"What's she talking about, Franklin?" The second man started to rise. Deb drove her heel into the middle of his back, pressing him against the tile.

Lena shoved Franklin toward the door. He pulled a metal baton, spun, and swung hard.

Lena blocked the blow with her forearm. Metal hit oak. Franklin grimaced from the impact, which had probably sent vibrations all the way to his shoulder. She moved forward and struck his wrist. I heard bone snap.

Franklin cried out. His partner tried to roll free. Deb bent down, and he caught her in the nose with a wild punch. Blood poured down her face, but she simply bared her teeth and grabbed the back of his neck.

"Don't kill him!" I wasn't sure which of them I was talking to.

Lena raised her bokken. "I won't ask again, Franklin. You're going to open these cells, and then you're going to help us find the sirens who arrived here last night."

"Look around, freak," he spat. "I hope you liked the tour, because you and your friends are going to spend the rest of your lives in a prison just like it."

"This isn't a prison," Lena said quietly. "It's a laboratory. You think I didn't see the tools in the exam room where you and your partner were cowering? Scalpels made of steel, silver, gold, titanium . . . for testing our weaknesses, right? Dental tools for extracting vampiric fangs. Electrical probes. Neatly labeled test tubes of everything from holy water and colloidal silver to various types of acid. Then there's the locked refrigerator with the biohazard warning. Blood and tissue samples? Or are you testing bioweapons on your captives?"

"If they're experimenting on inhuman subjects, where are the researchers?" I asked.

"Four doctors oversee the testing," said Franklin's partner. "They come in a couple times a week."

"Shut your face, Johnson," snapped Franklin.

"Fuck you, man. This place is messed up and you know it."

"Oh, Franklin doesn't care about that," Lena continued. "He has other interests."

"What's that supposed to mean?" Johnson spun. "What the hell did you do, man?"

"Nothing. I didn't—"

"You think you can hide your desires from a nymph?" Lena examined the edge of her bokken. "I could feel your filth from beyond these walls. What you wanted to do. What you'd done."

"You sick fuck," snapped Johnson. "What's wrong with you?"

"My friends want to find those sirens," said Lena. "I want that too, but I can't concentrate on sirens when your twisted lust permeates the air. It's an oily smoke that clings to the skin, polluting everything it touches. I mean to end that pollution."

"I'll open the cell doors," Franklin whimpered. "They're computer controlled, but there's an override code in case of emergency. Fire, computer failure, that sort of thing. It's how I . . ." He flushed and stared at the floor.

"How you took this girl's brother from his cell," Lena finished. She hauled him to his feet. "Use it."

They moved to a control panel at the far end of the

hallway. Moments later, bars began to swing open with a series of loud clunks, and Plexiglas doors slid to the side.

The prisoners stepped uncertainly into the hall. Their subcutaneous magic-dampers played havoc with my tattered invisibility spell. "My name is Isaac Vainio. We're going to get you out of here. There are other prisoners, a group of sirens. Have any of you seen them?"

A few of the prisoners shook their heads. The rest were silent.

"They're gone." That was the other guard, Johnson. "Left about two hours ago. We're not equipped to hold marine species long-term."

Deb swore and hammered her fist against the wall. "Why bring them here at all, then?"

"Tagging, scanning, and cataloging. The computer equipment is state of the art. Examinations that would normally take hours are automated, and—um, why is that ghost dude on fire?"

Heat seared my ear. I craned my head away from Smudge as well as I could, but I was pretty sure he'd blistered the lobe. "We're about to have trouble."

"There." One of the prisoners pointed to the broken door behind us. I saw movement beyond, and then a shotgun barrel poked through.

Deb was already shoving the closest prisoners back into their cells. She threw herself to the floor as the first gunshots rang out. I followed suit and rolled up against the wall, being careful not to squash Smudge in the process.

Lena strode past me, one arm outstretched toward the oaks she had grown in the doorway during her initial attempt to break through. They creaked and twisted to life. Branches twined around the gun. Lead shot thudded into Lena, but none penetrated her oak skin.

Several branches cracked and broke, weakened by the

guards' badges. The tree continued to grow, weaving new branches through the doorway in a thick wooden web. Leaves sprouted from the branches, further obscuring us from view.

"Hold fire," someone yelled from the end of the hall. "You've got no way out. This is your only chance to surrender."

"I can't hold them very long," Lena said quietly.

I could hear the guards pulling and snapping the branches of her makeshift barrier. With their badges siphoning Lena's magic, her tree was little more than mundane wood. She gasped in pain at every broken branch.

I looked around, trying to orient myself. If this was the north cell block, the walled yard I'd seen was on the opposite side of the facility. My enchanted compact mirror wasn't big enough for anyone except maybe Smudge to escape through, even if I'd been confident in my ability to set a destination I couldn't see. The devourers would stop any magical attempt to break through the outer walls.

That left making my own door as the only option.

"What about him?" Another prisoner, a vampire, hauled Franklin out of the control room where he'd been hiding.

Lena strode toward him. "You opened the cells. That's a point in your favor." She paused just long enough for him to open his mouth, then cut him off. "It's not enough. Not even close. So if there's anything you want to tell us, anything about the sirens or the researchers or the people running things here that might make me decide *not* to hand you over to the werebears, this is your chance."

"Hurry up," Deb shouted.

Franklin looked at the prisoners, then at Lena, and swallowed hard. "I don't know much about the researchers, but one of the big shots was through here a couple of days ago for a surprise inspection. Some senator. Keebler, or something."

My jaw clenched so hard I was surprised I didn't set off my implanted phone. "Keeler."

"Yeah, that's the guy. I saw him at the end of my shift. He didn't look happy. Whatever they're doing here, I guess they're not doing it fast enough for him."

I was going to check out a copy of Kafka's *Metamorphosis* and turn the bastard into a giant cockroach. "Anything else?"

He shook his head and blinked back tears. "What are you going to do to me?"

"Do you know what a geis is, Mister Franklin? It's a kind of curse. A magical command with consequences if you try to disobey."

"What kind of consequences?"

"Whatever I want." I pressed my thumb to his forehead. "When you leave here today, you're going to drive to the closest news station. You're going to tell them all about your magical prison here, and then you're going to confess to everything you've done to these prisoners."

His tears broke free.

"If you lie, your tongue will transform into a leech and crawl into your throat. I've never tried this particular curse, but I'd give you fifty-fifty odds of survival, assuming someone's fast enough to trach you and kill the leech before it goes too deep."

"I can't," he whimpered.

"You'd better. Because if you haven't confessed within the next twenty-four hours, let's just say it won't be your tongue that develops a mind of its own and starts burrowing inward."

His eyes went to the rip on his shirt where his badge had been. Lena must have torn it away.

"Those badges protect you from external magic," I said. "They won't protect you from me. This curse is written onto your skull. Just like Gutenberg used to do." I shoved him away and turned my back. "Deb, can you erase us from their thoughts? Leave Franklin's geis and terror in place, though. It's time to get the hell out of here."

Loading Pinti6.4.

Hello, Talulah.
Shall we play a game?

Pinti:> bd 192.142.82.1:80

Location: http://www.newmillennium-intra.org
Server: Ito4
Connection blocked

Pinti:> Run PW-scan 192.142.82.1:80

PW-scan 192.142.82.1:80 loaded
PW-scan 192.142.82.1:80 terminated
0 results

Pinti:> Run PW-dump 192.142.82.1:80 -palmerb /s

PS-dump 192.142.82.1:80 loaded

Pinti:> bd 192.142.82.1:80 -u/palmerb -p/PS-dump

Location: http://www.newmillennium-intra.org

Server: Ito4
Connection loading

Pinti:> Run McCullough.TP2 -palmerb

Loading . . .

McCullough.TP2 installed

Pinti:> Load webgoblin

Webgoblin installed

Pinti:> servertrace

Server: Ito2
Location blocked

Server: Ito3
Location blocked

Server: Ito5
Location blocked

Server: Ito8
Location blocked

Server: Ito9
Location blocked

Server: Ito10
Location blocked

Server: Ito12
Location blocked

Server: Ito13
Location blocked

Press any key to continue . . .

Chapter 13

"How frightened were you when you founded the Porters? When you publicly broke away from the old master-
apprentice model of sorcery and challenged a system that
had existed for centuries?"

"It was one of the most terrifying things I ever did, and
one of the most exhilarating. Once you make a choice like
that, you commit the rest of your life to dealing with the
consequences."

"Damn. I wish you'd said that a year ago before I
wrote that letter to the world."

"Cheer up, Isaac. If you survive, you'll have plenty of
time to learn to live with the aftermath. If not, there's nothing to worry about."

"You're still an asshole, you know that?"

"I do, yes."

A METAL CANISTER STRUCK the wall at
the end of the hallway and began to spew thick
smoke. A second followed.

Instantly, my eyes started to burn. Tears streamed down my face. I backed away, coughing and cursing.

Some forms of tear gas were flammable, and Smudge was still burning. If he ignited the gas, it would quickly kill us all.

"In here." I pulled the closest prisoners into a nearby cell. Lena gathered the rest. "Give me as much space as you can!"

I dropped my invisibility and grabbed *Control Point*. Through dripping eyes, I conjured up a wind to keep the worst of the gas in the hallway.

It was only a partial reprieve, and short-lived as well. Ashen shadows reached from the walls, drawn to the scent of active magic. The wind sputtered. Between the devourers and the prisoners' implants damping my efforts—

Those implants attacked magic. Devourers were magical chaos.

"Everyone form a circle around me." I coughed harder. Mucus flowed freely from my nose, and I could barely see anymore. The younger prisoners were crying and screaming. The older ones were doing their best to help, ripping off their sleeves to form makeshift masks. The werebear I'd spoken to earlier doubled over and vomited in the corner.

The wind from my book weakened further, but that didn't matter. I was watching the devourer.

As the prisoners closed ranks around me, it pulled back as if burned. The magic-dampers and the devourer reacted like potassium and water, each seeking to destroy and consume the other.

The devourer lunged again, tearing at the prisoners' enchantments as it tried to reach me. At the same time, those enchantments ate away at the devourer, dissolving its outer edges into smoke.

I wiped the worst of the tears and snot from my face. The devourer wasn't strong enough to counter so many spells at once. It struggled like a hooked fish.

I reached toward the closest of the prisoners and did something I never would have imagined: I tried to help the devourer. I joined its assault on the magic-dampers. Just as I'd destroyed the guards' badges when we broke in, I worked to unravel the text poisoning the prisoners.

It was easier this time. Don't get me wrong, it hurt like hell, and the gagging and coughing didn't help, nor did the sensation of acid eating my throat and lungs from the inside. I retrieved Excalibur's scabbard. "Everyone grab hold."

The scabbard countered the worst of the physical damage, easing the burning sensation.

By the time the devourer faded into nothingness, I'd helped it to completely strip the magic-dampeners from nine of the prisoners, and weakened the rest. It would have to be good enough. Half of us were curled up on the floor, coughing and crying. Smudge was an angry ball on my shoulder, the bristles of his body glowing like matchsticks.

I traded *Control Point* for *Neverwhere.* "Who's ready to get the hell out of here?"

I was the last one through. The prisoners had gone first, beginning with the nine who could escape without damaging the gateway I'd created. For the rest, I had to maintain and repair the portal as their weakened magic-dampers eroded it from within.

I sent Smudge through with Lena, waited for her and Deb to disappear, and then hurled myself out of the cell.

I fell facefirst onto a linoleum floor. I shut the book

and destroyed the portal behind us. Some of the tear gas had followed us through, but the air here was much better. Most of our escapees were crowding around a drinking fountain, gulping and rinsing their eyes.

"Didn't you say that book connects doorways that are similar in nature?" Lena asked hoarsely.

I nodded.

She glanced around at laminated posters and narrow, orange-painted lockers. "And you teleported us from a prison into a high school?"

"Looks that way." We'd emerged through a pair of metal fire doors. It was the weekend, so the building should be relatively empty.

Relatively, but not completely. A teenaged boy emerged from the bathroom and stared at us. At Lena, mostly. She still looked more tree than human. Then there were the prisoners, dressed in their jumpsuits and looking as conspicuous and out of place as a moose on a motorcycle. He coughed and backed away. "Jesus. What have you guys been smoking out here?"

"Which way to the nearest exit?" asked Lena.

The kid pointed down the hall. "Are you here for the yearbook planning meeting?" he asked dubiously.

"Book club," I said, which triggered another coughing fit. When I could speak again, I added, "I think we got the date wrong."

"Right." He backed away.

As soon as he was out of sight, I wrapped both hands around Excalibur's healing scabbard. Lena doled out healing potion to the rest of our company. Tear gas still permeated our clothes and hair, but this should help the worst of the damage.

I twisted to get one of the books I kept on hand for emergencies. We'd dealt with most of the magic-dampening, but the prisoners could still be carrying active tracking chips. Between the devourer and creating our escape, I'd redlined my magic, but I needed to create one more spell before I could rest. Thankfully, this one was basic libriomancy.

"This way." Lena had begun to shed her armor. Chunks of wood and bark fell away, while the rest reabsorbed into her skin. Behind her, she left a path of woodchips leading to the double doors at the end of the hall.

We emerged into a small staff parking lot. I waited until we reached the sidewalk and got a few blocks away before activating the book's magic.

The electromagnetic pulse was invisible to the eye, but it should have fried every piece of advanced electronics within five hundred yards, including those tracking chips. Hopefully I hadn't blacked out the school or cooked the circuitry in the cars in the process, but I didn't have the time or energy to worry about that.

"Where are we?" asked Lena.

"Washington D.C. More or less. We should probably call a cab." I counted our new companions. "Several cabs."

"No cab's going to let us in," said a slender man whose rough, bumpy skin gave the impression of scales. "Not looking and smelling like this. They'll either shoot us on the spot or call the cops."

Deb pointed to a convenience store on the corner. "Let me make a call."

"Vanguard?" I guessed.

She didn't answer.

I tested the communicator in my jaw as we walked, hoping the magic had survived the EMP. I was able to dial Nidhi, but she didn't answer. Neither did Nicola.

Lena and two of the older prisoners herded the group to the parking lot behind the store, where we wouldn't be quite so conspicuous. A stack of plastic milk crates stood next to the door. Two of the younger escapees had stripped off their jumpsuits and tossed them into a dumpster. Clad in nothing but plain white underwear and undershirts, they looked utterly miserable.

"What did they do to you?" I asked.

A mixed-blood vampire pushed up his sleeve to show me a grid of tiny pinprick scars. "Day one was the allergy test from hell."

"They studied our abilities before they doped us with whatever that black shit was," added the older werebear, a heavyset teenager with black bangs masking his eyes and nose. "How strong we were, what kind of stimulus triggered our change, whether or not wounds suffered in one form carried over to the other. They do, by the way."

"They were looking for potential soldiers." That was the fellow with the scales. "They kept talking about different functions we could perform. Infiltration. Reconnaissance. Infantry. Assassination."

"If the fuckers had offered a decent paycheck, I'd have enlisted," muttered the werebear.

"That would require them to treat us like people." Deb emerged from the store carrying several gallon jugs of milk. "We're weapons. Tools. They want to use what we can do, but only if they can control us."

She handed out all the jugs save one. That one, she twisted off the top and poured the milk directly over her eyes and face. "It helps neutralize the tear gas." She blinked and looked around. "Who's next?"

I waited for the others, then used what was left in one of the jugs to bathe my eyes. The milk helped more than I thought, and the burning eased. I dribbled a bit over Smudge as well. He jumped back and scowled at me, then went back to grooming himself with his forelegs. From the smoke rising off his body, he'd burnt off the worst of the tear gas residue once we escaped the prison.

Deb wiped her face and turned to me. "So you can carve curses into people's heads now? Giving Franklin a hungry leech-dick is hard core. Where'd you learn that bit of nastiness?"

"I didn't. But Franklin didn't know that."

Her face hardened. "You mean you just let him go?"

"What did you want me to do?" I snapped. "Castrate him on the spot? Execute him?"

"Both. Both is good."

"You saw how his partner reacted. If Franklin doesn't turn himself in, Johnson will do it for him. He's finished."

"You should have done more."

"I know that." I was so burned out I could hardly see straight.

"He said something to you before we left," Deb pressed. "Is that why you brought us to D.C.?"

"That's right." I took out a book at random and fanned the pages. It stunk of tear gas.

"You're not going to tell me."

"Right again."

A short time later, a gold full-sized van pulled into the parking lot.

"That's our ride." Deb waved to the driver and opened the sliding door.

I wasn't convinced everyone would fit, but we managed. Former prisoners balanced two or three to a seat, with others hunched and packed together on the floors. I sat with Lena in the back, wedged between a werebear and the zombie. Thankfully, the zombie was in good shape, with only the faintest smell of rot.

"Where are we going?" I asked.

"Somewhere safe." The driver was a Latina woman

with large sunglasses and small features. She rolled down the windows and turned up the air conditioning, trying to cycle as much fresh air through the vehicle as possible.

"One of your Vanguard safe houses?" I asked Deb.

"Something like that." She had ended up on the lap of a good-looking vampire who appeared to be in his twenties. Like several of the others, he'd ditched his prison jumpsuit in the parking lot. Knowing Deb, I doubted her choice of seatmate was an accident. "The day you announced our existence to the world, you painted a bull's-eye on everyone who isn't human. The way things are going, we may have to build a full-fledged underground railroad."

"It's not going to come to that," I said.

"Nobody ever believes it will," said the driver. "That's why it does."

After an hour or so, we arrived at a Jewish synagogue called Am HaTorah, a modest-looking brick structure with large wooden doors. A circular window with a Star of David was set into the front wall overhead. A narrow strip of grass ran between the sidewalk and the road. Well-trimmed bushes bordered the stairs. The sign out front announced that Am HaTorah was closed for roof repairs, though I saw no sign of workers.

Our driver led us up the steps and unlocked the front doors. "Let's get you cleaned up, shall we?"

Once everyone was inside the lobby area, she locked the doors behind us and disappeared into the temple proper. She returned a short time later and grabbed a handful of black yarmulkes from a bin against the wall, beneath a row of fringed prayer shawls. She handed the yarmulkes to the men and boys.

"Come with me," she said. To me and Lena, she added, "Not you. Not yet."

"You're not exactly welcome here," Deb explained.

"Lena would be, if they didn't know she was bound to a Porter."

I took a seat on a low wooden bench. Lena joined me a moment later. "What did Franklin tell you?" she murmured.

"Alexander Keeler was taking a guided tour of the prison a few days back."

Lena whistled softly. "Have you told Nicola?"

"I haven't been able to reach her yet." I tried Nicola's number again. This time, a male voice answered.

"Who is this?" I asked.

"My name is Brandon. I'm Ms. Pallas' secretary."

"Nicola doesn't have a secretary."

"She didn't, no. But with everything she's been dealing with lately, she finally agreed to take one on. What's this about, please?"

I hung up.

"What is it?" asked Lena.

"Nicola only gives her cell number out to a handful of people. The other council members, a couple of the New Millennium directors, Derek Vaughn. What are the chances that she'd route calls from her secret boyfriend through a secretary?"

Lena nibbled at her fingernail. Rather, at a bit of wood that had either grown or gotten embedded beneath the nail. "What about Nidhi?"

"I tried earlier. No luck."

"Isaac . . ."

"I know. I'll send someone to check on her." I clenched my teeth and subvocally dialed my former employer.

A male voice answered. *"Copper River Library."*

"I need to check out a book," I said. *"I can't remember the author or the title, but it was blue, and I think there was a woman's face on the cover."*

"Do you want *me to hurt you? What's going on, Isaac? Is everything all right?"*

"Not even close. I need a favor, Jennifer." I winced. *"Sorry. Jason."*

"Don't sweat it. How can I help?"

Jennifer Latona had been my boss at the Copper River Library for several years. I'd been working as a cataloger for the Porters, and my job at the library was the ideal cover, letting me requisition and review new titles for potential magic.

Back then, Jennifer hadn't been my favorite person in the world. To be fair, the feeling was quite mutual, and I'd probably earned her disdain. Being able to draw seventy different versions of Excalibur from various books gave one a jaded view of mundane authority.

Our relationship had changed eight months ago. By then, all of Copper River knew the truth about me. Some immediately stopped by asking for magical favors. Others treated me like a minor celebrity. A handful avoided me altogether, as if my mere existence would damn them to hell and transform their children into radical satanic lesbian role-playing gamers. But most folks treated me no differently than they had before, something I both needed and appreciated.

For that acceptance, among other reasons, I'd bent the rules from time to time in the beginning, before the police and the FBI started cracking down on illegal magic use.

I hadn't expected Jennifer Latona to show up at my door. I certainly hadn't expected her specific request. After talking with her for three and a half hours and seeing how much it meant to her, I couldn't turn her away. We ordered an old Dungeons and Dragons manual via Interlibrary Loan, which I used to create a magical item known as a "Girdle of Masculinity/Femininity."

Traditionally, this was a cursed item used by immature dungeon masters to torment their equally immature players. When Toby and I were kids, he'd tricked my ninth-level wizard into donning one, permanently transforming Salador the Blue into Saladina.

In this case, however, it had been a gift, one that Jennifer—now Jason—had dreamed about for much of his life. From what I'd seen, Jason seemed far more relaxed and content than Jennifer ever had.

I'm told that when a woman from the FBI Magical Crimes division stopped by a week later, Jason raised enough hell to bury half the U.P. in sulfur and brimstone. He shouted that what was under his clothes was none of the government's damn business, loud enough to draw the attention of everyone in the library and probably anyone in the neighboring buildings as well. He threatened to sue for everything from harassment to unreasonable search and seizure. He called up the ACLU and the National Center for Transgender Equality right then, using two different phones and putting both organizations on speaker so they could listen in.

He received an official apology from the FBI three days later.

"Lena and I have gotten ourselves into a bit of a mess," I said.

"Is this the part where I should pretend to be shocked?"

"We're trying to get in touch with Nidhi, but she's not answering her phone."

"I'll head over to her place and check on her."

"Thanks, Jason." I gave him my number. *"I owe you big-time."*

"No, you don't." He said it so firmly I didn't know how to respond. *"I'll be in touch soon."*

Lena touched my arm and pointed to an older man in a pastel blue shirt and dark tie standing in the inner doorway. He was five-foot-six, tops, and appeared human. Deb was with him.

"Isaac, Lena, this is Rabbi Miller," said Deb. "He's taking care of our friends."

"Thank you for that." I stood up and extended my hand. His palm was damp, the only sign of nervousness.

"Isaac Vainio." He looked me up and down. "You look younger in person than you do on the television." He wrinkled his nose. "We've got showers and clean clothes downstairs. Nothing new or stylish, but they won't make your eyes bleed."

He turned to Lena and shook her hand. His intonation softened. "You're safe here, my dear."

"Thank you." She stretched and rubbed her shoulders. "A shower and clean clothes sound divine."

"Through that door to your left and down the steps. Lupe will show you where the clean towels are stored."

I studied him for any sign of magical manipulation, but found none. Deb hadn't influenced his mind, and neither had anyone else. "You'll help these people find their way home?"

"We will, though it may not change much in the long run." He beckoned Deb and me into the inner temple. I donned a yarmulke from the bin and followed. Rows of pews led to a raised platform on the eastern end of the building. Heavy curtains hung on the wall behind the platform.

There was no sign of the prisoners we'd rescued, though I spotted several doors leading to other parts of the building. Rabbi Miller sat down on one of the pews and motioned for us to join him.

"You don't sound very optimistic," I said.

"Home should be a place of comfort and safety. For your friends downstairs, and for people like Deborah here, I'm not sure any such place exists."

Deb grimaced, but didn't correct him, which surprised me. I'd never seen her let anyone get away with calling her Deborah.

"If it's futile, why bother?" I asked.

"You'll never hear me say it's futile. Whether we succeed or fail, we've given these people one night of comfort and security. We've shown that not all humans fear them. And really, Isaac. You don't do what's right because you know it will work out. You do it because you know it's right."

"Are you part of Vanguard?"

He smiled. "Lupe and I are part of an informal network founded by a Quaker in Pennsylvania. 'The Society of Friends.' I've always admired the elegance of that phrase. We extend friendship to those who need it. Some of our more politically active members have taken to calling themselves Vanguard, yes."

"Does that friendship come with a price tag?"

His brow furrowed. "What do you mean?"

"You don't know?" I turned to Deb. "You haven't told him someone was using Vanguard to recruit soldiers and assassins, or how you brainwashed those werewolves into attacking the capitol?"

Rabbi Miller had gone very still. Deb's eyes were tight, and her lips peeled back from her teeth. Smudge shifted to watch her. The smell of smoke rose from his body.

"Is this true, Deborah?" Miller asked at last.

Deb was still glaring at me. "You son of a bitch."

"Just because we worked together over the past twenty-four hours doesn't erase what you did."

"Judge not, lest ye be punched in the face for being a self-righteous prick," Deb snapped. "I didn't have a choice. We don't all get to be the new Johannes Gutenberg, living in magical luxury, away from the blood and death and hate."

"You planted that hate in their minds! You sent them out to kill and to die!"

"Isaac, could you please head downstairs and leave the two of us alone?" asked Rabbi Miller. "You were right to tell me." Deb started to protest, but he silenced her with a look. "He was right, and you know it. Secrecy and lies only feed the darkness. I believe you and I need to have a private conversation."

I stood to go, then hesitated. "Will you be all right, Rabbi?"

Deb looked up at me. "Seriously? You think I'm gonna put the whammy on a rabbi in his own fucking temple?"

I said nothing.

"Oh, just go." Deb sagged back in the pew. "The good rabbi is trying to demonstrate that he still trusts me. He figures guilt and self-loathing will keep me in line."

The corners of Rabbi Miller's mouth tugged upward. "Am I wrong?"

Deb waved me away. "For the record, I hate you both."

We stayed at Am HaTorah until nightfall. I managed a brief nap, full of dreams about running through a maze of twisty passages, all alike. I was either chasing Guten-berg or running away from him. The dream wasn't clear on that point.

Dinner was canned tuna fish and crackers. Nothing fancy, but there was more than enough for everyone. Once we'd eaten, we thanked Rabbi Miller once more and set out to find a place to stay for the night. Neither he nor Deb said a word about their conversation. He'd arranged for Lupe, the woman with the van—and his wife, as it turned out—to drop the three of us off.

At my request, Lupe let us out in front of a small library, a two-story building with old wood siding that looked close to a century old. Once inside, Deb used her hypnostare to erase our arrival from the memory of the staff. After that, it was just a matter of letting her divert their attention while we settled down to wait for the place to close. I snagged a book from the shelves to pass the time.

"Calvin and Hobbes?" asked Deb. "Really?"

"You know, I'm still trying to figure out what to do with you," I said. "Bashing Calvin and Hobbes isn't helping your case."

I finished three of Watterson's collections before the lights finally went out. As soon as the doors were locked and the last car left the parking lot, I settled down at one of the computers to pull up the news.

Footage from our attack on the *Kagan* had already made it onto the Internet, though none of us had been identified. There was blurry video of vampires swooping down to attack the three ships, which had supposedly been on maneuvers as part of a training mission. Another shot showed the ice trapping the ships in place.

The next article included a close-up photo of the *Kagan*'s bow, highlighting where my magic had amputated the tip. That damage, combined with the ice, suggested the vampires hadn't been alone. The Joint Committee on Magical Security was demanding a full investigation into the Porters.

I pulled up another story and groaned. "The president is calling for all people to work toward the peaceful integration of nonhumans into our society, but it sounds like he's also putting the National Guard on standby, and he's indicated his willingness to sign the newly expanded RAMPART Act."

"We're not going to let him round us up into his

fucking camps." Deb snarled and kicked a chair hard enough to crack one of the wooden legs.

"Don't take it out on the library," I said without looking up.

"Integration my undead ass. Did they teach you about the Great American Melting Pot in grade school?" she asked. "Some of us don't like the idea of being melted down and blended into stew for the rest of you to devour."

Lena sat down beside me. "You brought us to D.C. to stop this, right?"

"We need proof." If we could tie Keeler to the attacks in Lansing and elsewhere, prove that he'd orchestrated terrorism and assassinations in order to manipulate public opinion, we'd be able to shut him down and turn the country's anger around.

"You know who's running things?" Deb leaned in, practically drooling in her eagerness.

"I think so, yah." I glanced at Lena.

"What we don't know is who's running you," she finished.

Deb tensed and pulled away. "What do you mean?"

"I've read *Renfield*," I said. "I know what you've become. You're powerful, sure. All those lives you consume, added to your own. But you were written to serve. Whether you were running around doing Alice Granach's bidding in Detroit or serving Gutenberg as liaison between Porters and vampires. It's your nature."

Deb snorted and jerked her head toward Lena. "Hers too, but weren't you telling me how she'd become more?"

"She's become more." I didn't bother to keep the anger from my voice. "You've become less. I saw your bookshelves in Detroit. You want to pretend you're still the same person, but there was a month's worth of dust on those covers. You once told me immortality meant the chance to read everything, to learn everything. When's the last time you opened a book?"

"I've been a little busy preparing for war, hon."

"You didn't even know who you were working for when you betrayed Vanguard," I snapped. "Then Lena and I showed up at your door and trashed your pet vampires. At that point, you started following our lead. How the hell am I supposed to trust you when you'll happily turn on us as soon as you find the next potential Dracula to your Renfield?"

"I knew exactly who I was working for," Deb said calmly. "I have no intention of betraying her."

Lena connected the pieces before I did. "Granach."

Alice Granach had helped rule the Detroit nest for more than sixty years. She was a century and a half old, born and turned long before the urban fantasy surge brought a new wave of sexy, angsty vampires into the world. "Granach ordered you to brainwash those werewolves?"

"Alice Granach died in the firebombing of Detroit, trapped a thousand feet belowground."

"I'm sorry." I meant it. I'd met Granach once. She was in many ways unique.

"She ordered me to send a message to humanity. To make it clear you couldn't murder us with impunity. Killing Governor Sullivan and Attorney General Duncan sounded like a good first step."

"What else have you done?" asked Lena.

"Not much." Deb sighed. "I didn't know about the other attacks that night. I helped kill two very bad people, but in the process, I played into the hands of whoever's running this conspiracy. I tried to find who was behind it, but my anonymous contact was a dead end. They were too careful. The only other lead I had was the *USCGC Kagan*. Then the two of you came along and busted through my front door. It sounded like we were after the same thing, more or less. I figured you had a better chance of tracking them down. And I was right. You know who's been pulling everyone's strings."

I didn't answer.

"You can't shut me out now. Sure, I screwed up. Give me a chance to make it right."

"By killing more people?"

She shrugged. "Sounds good to me."

"This isn't about revenge. We're not going to escalate the fighting if we can help it."

"That's a big if, hon." Deb leaned closer, assaulting me with a scent like roadkill. "Remember, you wouldn't have gotten the *Kagan*'s orders without me. So ask yourself one question. Are you sure—are you one hundred percent positive you can take this person down without my help?"

Bi Wei,

Hǎo jiǔ bú jiàn! I hope you and your fellow Bì Shēng de dú zhě remain safe.

I'm writing to you from the road. By now, you've likely heard about the terrorist attacks here in the States. You'll be shocked to hear that Isaac and I have been in the middle of things, searching for answers.

We've found two high-level leads who may be responsible. We've also found evidence that this may go beyond the United States. One of the people involved is a book-born woman named Kiyoko Itô. According to Isaac, she's a living computer, a clone with a psychic connection to her fellow clones.

One of those clones has been spotted in China.

I don't know her role in all this. Our plan is to confront the man we believe is responsible, a senator named Alexander Keeler. I hope that by finding and exposing the truth about these attacks, it will help to set things on a better path.

We're not completely certain what we're up against. Our enemies have protected themselves from magic, and they have weapons specifically built for people like me. I know your people have tried to withdraw from the world, but I have to ask you for two favors.

If you don't hear from us, please find and protect Nidhi. Then, contact Nicola Pallas from the Porters, and Isaac's research team at New Millennium. They know most of what we've found. You're the only person I know and trust with the power to succeed if we fail.

I'm sorry for asking this of you after you've done so much for me.

Love,
Lena

Chapter 14

"You never trusted inhumans. You never allowed them to be a part of the Porters. Why?"

"The Porters was an organization of people who used magic. Inhumans are magic, but they can't use it the way we do."

"Neither can Nidhi Shah, but she's been with the Porters longer than I have."

"It's hard enough keeping the loyalty of people from different nations, different religious backgrounds, different philosophies about the world. How could I trust someone to put the Porters above his own species?"

"Some of them would have. Lena would have."

"Right now, she probably would. But she's evolved a great deal in recent years. Who's to say she'll remain loyal ten years from now?"

"You could make the same point about me. About anyone."

"Oh, I was keeping a very close eye on you, Isaac. Tell me, do you think you could have done a better job building and protecting the Porters? That's not a rhetorical question, by the way."

"I don't know. I'd like to think so."
"Mm ... so would I."

"**Y**OU ENCHANTED A LETTER opener?" asked Lena.

"I figured it was less conspicuous than carrying a full-sized sword." I'd borrowed the old letter opener from the library's circulation desk. It was essentially a dull plastic knife, nine inches long and bright red. The name of the library was stamped in faded black on the handle, along with a note to CELEBRATE READING: TAKE THE 2012 SUMMER BOOK CHALLENGE.

I'd copied the magic of a sword called Wayfinder into the letter opener, drawing on Fred Saberhagen's *The Complete Book of Swords*. When I looked closely, I could see the typeface from the book wavering within the plastic.

"Gutenberg used to do something similar with his sword. A Katzbalger. I never got the chance to study it, but it looked like he'd transferred the powers of dozens of tomes into that blade. Wayfinder had the power to lead its wielder to whatever he or she wanted. The downside is that it doesn't always choose the safest route."

We'd tried finding Senator Keeler's home the old-fashioned way, but every public database and directory had failed me. More significantly, several magical attempts had failed as well. Keeler was likely shielding himself with magic, just as we'd been doing.

"Why didn't you use that thing to begin with?" Deb demanded. "Whip it out and tell it to take us to whoever's in charge of this circus."

"All magic has limits, and that's a pretty abstract question. It's going to be tricky enough finding a specific individual. If all we had was a vague idea who or what we

were looking for, this thing could have led us around for
months. We might have come face-to-face with our bad
guy and never known if he was the one we wanted, or just
another quest ticket we had to collect along the way."

I clutched the letter opener. "Anyone need to use the
bathroom before we go?"

When nobody answered, I pushed open the library
doors and stepped onto the sidewalk. Keeler had hidden
himself and his home from magical detection, so I
couldn't target them directly. "Find us someone or something that can lead us to Senator Alexander Keeler."

It was the first time I'd spoken the name in front of
Deb. Her breath hissed through her teeth. "Keeler. That
weasel-faced ass-pustule. I should have guessed."

I turned in a slow circle until the plastic tip quivered
in my hand. "This way to the weasel-faced ass-pustule."

Four hours later, we were on the D.C. metro, heading
northwest. We'd stopped on the way so Deb could steal an
oversized hoodie from a Goodwill donations bin. It was
far too large, hanging down to her thighs, but the hood
helped to conceal her gaunt and jaundiced complexion.

I wore a Phillies baseball cap from the same bin, with
the brim pulled low to shield my eyes. Hiding Smudge
had been trickier. Keeping him on my shoulder would
attract too much attention. I ended up digging through a
recycling bin outside of an apartment building until I
found an old soup can. It was a bit cramped, but he'd be
safe in the can in my pocket for now. I'd dropped a
gummi worm in to keep him happy.

We were alone on the metro car, except for a police
officer standing at the far end. She'd been watching us
since we boarded. Sooner or later she was going to figure
out where she'd seen me, and the more I tried to hide,
the more suspicious I'd look.

I turned in a casual arc, keeping the letter opener

tucked into my sleeve. When it passed over the officer, it vibrated hard.

"You're sure?" whispered Lena.

"It keeps pointing to her."

Deb sniffed. "We're supposed to do what, exactly?"

"It doesn't work that way. The sword—letter opener—is like a compass, not an instruction manual."

Deb cracked her knuckles and stood. "Give me a few minutes to get inside her head. If she knows anything, she'll tell me."

I didn't like the idea of violating another innocent person's mind, but simply following an already-suspicious cop around wasn't a great plan either, and since I had no other ideas . . . "Be quick."

"Men never appreciate the pleasure of taking things slowly." Deb sniffed and walked toward the cop, who tensed. One hand moved casually to the gun at her hip. I could see the moment Deb reached out to touch the woman's mind and ease her alertness.

"Do you trust her?" Lena whispered in Gujarati.

I slipped an arm around her waist. "Nope. You?"

"How many times has Deb tried to kill you now?"

"To be fair, I'm not sure she was really trying that hard back in Detroit."

"How hard do you think she'll try with Keeler?"

I'd been worrying about the same thing. "Killing him would be too quick. She wants him to suffer. It would be much more satisfying to expose him, watch his life and career unravel. But we should be ready to grab her if we have to."

Deb returned a short time later, leaving the police officer slumped asleep on the seat. "Officer Sheldon over there responded to a call at Keeler's place two weeks ago. Graffiti complaint. Turned out to be an ex-boyfriend of Keeler's daughter. Sheldon couldn't remember the address, but she called dispatch and had them pull it up from her report. The Keelers live in the Spring Valley neighborhood, up in the northwest part of D.C."

I glared at the letter opener. Always the risky path. "Did the dispatcher ask why she wanted to know?"

"You worry too much, hon. Sure, they asked, but Sheldon said she was trying to catch up on paperwork. Nothing suspicious." She grinned and clapped me on the arm. "It's two more stops. We can either catch a taxi from there or walk the rest of the way."

"All right. Remember, once we get to the house, you follow our lead," I warned. "Nobody gets hurt."

"You know something, hon? You're a boring date."

We took a cab to the edge of Keeler's neighborhood and walked the last several miles over hills and around curving roads, several times setting off motion-detecting house lights or rousing dogs that barked like we were an army of evil mutant squirrels come to declare war on kibble and chew toys.

I blamed Wayfinder's magic. The damned letter opener wanted to make sure the whole neighborhood knew we were passing through. I was tempted to dissolve its magic altogether, but if things went wrong, we might need it for a quick escape.

Any one of these homes probably cost as much as an entire block back in Copper River. We circled through a roundabout, veered left, and finally stopped in front of a two-story brick colonial with black shutters. A brick wall circled the property, with a brass-trimmed iron gate across the driveway. Oak trees lined both sides of the road. We kept our distance from the gate and the cameras mounted to either side.

I checked for signs of magic. "The gate's clear. There's a spell over the doorway to protect the house, but it's a passive defense. I can pull it down without alerting anyone inside."

We moved just past the corner of the yard, out of the cameras' field of view. Lena scaled the wall and balanced on top. She pulled me up one-handed and pointed toward the front door. "Another camera."

Ivy covered the sloping ground to either side of the driveway. Neatly trimmed hedges guarded the porch.

I studied the black hemisphere mounted over the door, then retrieved the soup can from my pocket. Smudge was sleeping, curled into a ball with a half-eaten gummi worm clutched in his forelegs. As gently as I could, I pulled his magic free and sent it into the camera. "Come on."

By the time we reached the brick walk, the camera had filled with smoke and flickering red flame. I waited for the fire to die, then returned Smudge's powers. I hadn't been gentle enough. He glared at me, like he was silently vowing to inflict burnt, crispy vengeance on me at some point in the future.

The porch lights switched on automatically as we approached the white-painted arched doorway. My anger grew with every step.

Alexander Keeler had sat on his little throne, presiding over the Joint Magical Committee and telling the world how dangerous we were, how much damage we could do if we weren't "properly regulated and contained."

All that time, he'd been using us. Capturing and studying and torturing us. Turning public sentiment against magic.

How far did his ambitions go? The prisoners from Mecklenburg had been assessed as potential soldiers, and Keeler had come out in favor of a selective draft of libriomancers and inhumans, similar to the one implemented by Russia. What would he do with his magical army once he had it? He had the Coast Guard in his pocket. Had he corrupted other branches of the military as well?

I double-checked my books, ready to create a shield or knock out everyone within a hundred meters as needed. If they had a clone of Kiyoko on site, we'd need to incapacitate her as quickly as possible.

"Shall we?" I raised my hand to knock.

Deb caught my wrist. She sniffed the air. The mannerism reminded me of an animal.

"What is it?" I checked Smudge, but he was sulking in his can.

"I'm not sure." She let go and nodded, her attention on the door.

I hesitated, then knocked. When nothing happened, I tried the doorbell. A low chime echoed through the house.

"Maybe they're out?" suggested Deb. "Congress is always running off for breaks and vacations."

"Not with everything happening in D.C. right now. Keeler might be working late at his office, but his family should be here." I had no interest in terrorizing the man's wife and children, but they'd be able to tell us where to find him. I tried the door, but it was locked.

Lena pressed her fingertips to the door like Spider-Man getting ready to scale a building. Her hands sank into the wood, just as if she was joining with her oak tree back home, though the door was too thin to possibly contain her.

Or maybe it could. I'd never fully figured out what happened to Lena's body when she merged with her oak. The tree didn't visibly increase in size or mass. The wood within her flesh didn't change her human form, either. They simply coexisted in the same space.

I was still thinking when I heard her unlocking the door from the inside. It swung open, and Lena gestured us in.

Deb sniffed again. "Oh, shit."

Smudge shifted and looked around, but didn't ignite. "What is it?" I asked.

"Blood."

The interior of the house was dark, save for the glowing keypad of a security system by the door. Faint voices and flickering light came from deeper in the house.

"The alarm's turned off." Lena readied one of her bokken.

We entered the foyer. To the left, an open door led to a small music room. The streetlights through the front window illuminated a baby grand piano. A pair of electric guitars hung on the wall.

I kept checking on Smudge. He acted like we were in no danger, but my gut told me otherwise. I didn't see anything suppressing his senses.

On the other side of the foyer was a living room as big as my first apartment. A ridiculously oversized television hung on the wall, playing an infomercial about carpet stains. A middle-aged woman sat sprawled on the couch. It was possible she'd fallen asleep while watching TV, but her posture was stiff, her body weighed down by a heavy blanket of magic.

I crossed the room and touched her throat until I felt the slow bump of her pulse. "She's alive."

"Keeler's wife?" guessed Lena.

"Probably." I studied her more closely. "If I'm reading this right, someone used a copy of *Firestarter* on her."

"Wouldn't that, I dunno, set her on fire?" asked Deb.

"The title character is a magic pyromaniac, yah, but there's another who can force people to obey his voice. At one point, he commands someone to sleep, and they don't wake up for six months. All you'd have to do is reach into the book and bring the sound into our world. It's elegant, but damned dangerous."

"So whoever did this was a libriomancer," said Deb. "One of your team?"

I shook my head. "I didn't tell them where we were going."

"Keeler has three children," Lena said tightly. "Check the rest of the house."

We found the bedrooms near the back of the house. All three kids lay blanketed in their individual rooms by the same enchantment as their mother. I rejoined the others in the hallway. "I can wake them up, but they're safe for now. Deb, you said you smelled blood?"

"Upstairs."

An unconscious man sprawled at the top of the stairway, a gun in his hand. Blood from a cut cheek and split lip had stained the tan carpet. His dark suit and muscular build made me think bodyguard or private security. Was it normal for a senator to have armed security in his house, or had he been afraid someone would try to hurt him?

I stepped carefully over his wheezing form and looked about. A second bodyguard slumped against the wall opposite a large, opulently furnished bathroom. Smudge was alert but calm. Whoever had done this was already gone.

"In here." The coldness in Lena's words told me what she'd found. "Watch your step."

In the faint light coming through the windows, the blood on the desk and floor shone like black mercury. Lena switched on the overhead light, using her sleeve to avoid leaving fingerprints.

Senator Alexander Keeler's lifeless body lay against the wall behind his desk. His throat had been torn open.

I was no forensic detective, but it looked like Keeler had put up a fight. He clutched a broken desk lamp in one hand, like he'd tried to use it as a club. His knuckles were bloody. His left hand curled like a claw, as if he'd broken it. Perhaps by punching someone or something inhumanly solid.

I spun toward Deb. "Did you tell anyone from Vanguard about Keeler?"

Deb stared at the body, her head shaking in slow denial. "When exactly did I have the chance to do that without you and Lena breathing down my neck?"

"On the metro. The police officer. You could have told her to deliver a message—"

"Deb wasn't part of this." Lena knelt beside the body. "Look closer. He was dead before we set foot on the metro."

Keeler's hand and forearm were a dark raspberry color where the blood had pooled. I wrapped the bottom of my shirt around my thumb and pressed the back of his hand. The color didn't change. It had been a while since I read up on livor mortis, but I was pretty sure that meant he'd died between six and twelve hours ago. I checked the wall clock. That put the time of death no later than eight p.m.

"First they killed him, then they killed his computer." Deb pointed to the overturned desktop unit beneath the desk. The side of the computer case had been torn away, and judging from the bent metal brackets inside, Keeler's murderer had physically ripped the hard drive free.

The oak file cabinet in the corner was a mess as well. A cylindrical lock lay on the floor, leaving a matching hole behind in the upper drawer. Both drawers had been yanked open roughly enough to twist them off their tracks.

It would be just past eleven back in Vegas. I backed

away and called Talulah. *"Any chance you can hack into the security footage for Alexander Keeler's house?"*

"Hello to you, too. Look, I'm good, but even I need a little more information to work my magic. What's going on?"

"We need to know who else has visited the senator in the past twenty-four hours."

"Depends on who set their system up and how. Is the video hosted on site?"

I glanced at the computer. *"If so, I think it's gone now."*

"Of course it is. Can you at least tell me what company they're using?"

I thought back to the security panel inside the door. *"Nighthawk."* I gave her the street address as well.

"It's a start. I'll call you back if I find something."

I crossed Keeler's office to where a series of framed photographs sat on the bookshelves. There were the usual school photos of the kids in their private school uniforms, a family trip to Disney, a dusty wedding photo . . . I studied a shot of Alexander Keeler at the ribbon-cutting ceremony at New Millennium from almost a year earlier.

I spotted myself in the photo, standing toward the back in an ill-fitting suit and tie. I hadn't known much about Keeler back then. All I'd cared about was that New Millennium was opening, that we were finally going to show the world what we could do. The towers in the background had been under construction, but we'd been given the okay to begin work on a handful of research projects.

I turned back to the desk and picked up a relatively recent New Millennium brochure titled A MAGICAL FUTURE. The cover showed our facility in Vegas. Inside were all the ways we hoped magic would benefit the world. The back listed future potential New Millennium sites in other countries.

"Can you talk to him?" asked Lena. "Or look into the past to see who did this?"

"Not with the books I've got on me. When I armed up at the library, I didn't expect to have to talk to the dead."

Keeler's family hadn't fought back. The sleep spell had struck them before they could react. Them, but not the security guards upstairs or the man himself. Either the libriomancer wasn't strong enough to knock out the entire household at once, or else they'd targeted only the people downstairs. Assuming it was deliberate . . . "They needed Keeler awake."

If his guards had time to draw their weapons, they'd had time to shout a warning. How much time had that given him?

"To question him," guessed Lena. "Find out how much he knew and who he'd shared it with."

"How much he knew about *what*?" Deb glared at the body.

They'd destroyed his computer and ransacked his files. I found a cellphone with a broken screen on the floor beside the wall. An empty slot on the side showed where the SIM card had been removed.

He hadn't called 911. Otherwise the police would have discovered the bodies long before we arrived.

Alexander Keeler had been a bigoted, manipulative, obsessively narrow-minded man, but he wasn't stupid. So what had he done in those seconds between realizing someone was in his house and the moment that intruder ended his life?

He might not have done anything. A lot of people froze in situations like this. I stepped around the desk and imagined myself in his place. The guards would have called out. We'd seen no evidence that either man had fired his weapon. They'd been overpowered quickly.

I examined the desk. He'd had a computer, but no

time to compose an email. He might have scrawled a note instead. I checked the notepads and a half-empty packet of printer paper, going so far as to rub a pencil over the top sheets of each in case it picked up indentations from a previous page, but found nothing.

Grimacing, I checked the senator's pockets next. I found his keys, eighty-three cents in change, a silver business card holder, and a leather wallet. They hadn't taken his money or credit cards. The business card holder held about twenty of Keeler's own cards on one side, and four more on the other.

I imagined my own office, mentally overlaying it with Keeler's. "There's no printer."

"Maybe there's a wireless printer somewhere else in the house," suggested Lena. "One the kids shared for homework and things like that?"

"The paper's here, and I can't imagine someone like Keeler bothering to walk downstairs every time he needed a printout. Especially given the sensitive nature of his work." I spread my arms and turned slowly to get a feel for what he could have reached from his desk. The file cabinet was just beyond arm's reach. Easy enough to push back in a rolling chair and grab whatever he needed, and there was a gap of about four inches between the side of the cabinet and the wall . . .

I leaned over and picked up a small black wireless printer that had either fallen down in that gap or been deliberately moved out of sight. A single LED blinked amber. My heart pounded. "I need a blank sheet of paper."

Deb handed one to me. I set the printer down as carefully as an armed bomb, fed the paper into the top, pressed the OK button, and hoped.

The printer hummed to life and tugged the paper through. "Keeler sent whatever he was working on to the printer. With no paper, the printer held it in memory.

His killers destroyed his hard drive and cellphone, but who's going to bother—"

The paper finished printing and fell into my hands. The light kept blinking. "There's more."

Deb fed more paper into the machine while I read the first lines of Alexander Keeler's final document. I read them a second time, then a third, trying to comprehend. Trying and failing to reconcile everything I'd thought, everything I'd assumed, with Keeler's words.

Lena touched my arm.

"I was wrong," I whispered numbly. "He didn't go to the prison to check on their work. He went to expose it."

Keeler had been drafting a press release about the Virginia facility. Phrases like "trampling Constitutional freedom" and "betrayal of American ideals" jumped out at me. He'd been working to expose them, the same as us.

This was the same man who'd championed the RAM-PART Act, seeking to register and detain inhumans as well as libriomancers and other magic-users. But Keeler had wanted these things done openly, in full view and with the approval of the American people. As I kept reading, I started to see that no matter how much the man had hated and feared those of us with magic, he hated government secrecy and overreach even more. "It says he was tipped off by a source within the Department of Homeland Security."

"The Coast Guard reports to DHS," Deb said quietly.

I grabbed the next page of Keeler's letter, which discussed "secret abductions and unethical experimentation" as well as the "deliberate fueling of tension and hostility in regards to magic" and "plans for a bigger, deadlier attack, intended to unite the world against inhumans and magic-users."

I hadn't liked the man, and he'd never bothered to

hide his hostility toward me, but he'd died trying to do the right thing. When this was over, I was going to make sure people knew it.

My jaw beeped. I jumped hard enough I pulled something in my back. I had to get Talulah to turn down the intensity on that damn communicator. Then maybe we could add a caller ID function. *"Hello?"*

"Isaac? It's Jason." I tensed. The last time I'd heard him so somber was when he'd been getting ready to fire me. *"Nidhi's gone."*

"What do you mean Nidhi's gone?" I spoke out loud for Lena's benefit.

"She's alive," said Lena. "I'd know if she wasn't."

"I've been searching all night. I called her apartment. When she didn't answer, I drove down and knocked. No answer, but her car was in the lot. I woke up some of her neighbors, asking when anyone had last seen her. She was taken away late last night."

"Who took her?"

"Two men from the FBI. It's too late for me to get through to anyone at the FBI office in Detroit. I'm talking to a reporter friend to see if they have any contacts who might be able to tell us what's going on."

I swore silently. Not silently enough. The implant decided I was subvocalizing, and passed my curses along to Jason.

"I'm doing everything I can."

"I know you are," I said tightly. "Thanks, Jason. Have your reporter friend put the spotlight on Nidhi and the FBI. There are people who might try to make her disappear. Don't let them."

"I'll try."

"And try calling an agent named Steinkamp. He met Nidhi in Lansing. He might be able to help." I recited

Steinkamp's number from memory, then hung up. How the hell could I have all this magic, all this power, and still feel so damned helpless?

"Nidhi might not be a libriomancer," said Lena, "but she's one of the smartest people I've ever met, and she's tough as hell. We'll get her back."

Nidhi had faced down people far more dangerous than FBI agents. I nodded.

"Look at this." Lena picked up a business card from Keeler's desk, one of the cards I'd pulled from his case. "You said Keeler got a tip from inside DHS."

The card was from a Darlene Jackson-Palmer in the DHS Public Affairs office. I clenched my jaw and called the number on the card. Nobody would be there at this time of night, but I could at least leave her a message.

A male voice began speaking after the first ring. *"Thank you for contacting the Department of Homeland Security Public Affairs Office. Darlene Jackson-Palmer is on indefinite administrative leave. If you need assistance, please contact—"*

I hung up. "She's gone."

"Jackson-Palmer," said Lena. "Any relation to a certain libriomancer?"

I stared at the card. "If someone high up at DHS is behind all of this, they might be using Darlene Jackson-Palmer as a hostage. That could explain why Babs was so upset. She got drawn into this to protect Darlene's life."

"We don't know that for certain," said Deb.

"It fits. It also answers another question." I looked at Lena. "During the hearing, Keeler asked why my niece got into our medical trials."

"You think someone brought them in as potential hostages too?"

I left the office and stepped carefully around Keeler's

unconscious bodyguards. "Not someone. Russell Potts. He's the DHS representative on the New Millennium board."

"You're sure he's involved?" asked Deb.

I'd been sure about Keeler, too. "I can't prove anything yet, but I'm not taking chances with my family. I'm going to get them the hell out of there, and then Potts and I are going to have a very unpleasant chat."

I called Talulah once we'd left Keeler's house. My throat was dry, and sweat dripped down my sides. *"I need to confirm whether Babs Palmer is any relation to a Darlene Jackson-Palmer at DHS. Make sure nobody at New Millennium knows you're running this search."*

"This isn't my first concert, Isaac. Hold on . . ." I heard the machine-gun clicking of her keyboard. *"Darlene is Babs' sister."*

"How long has she been working for Homeland Security?"

Another pause. *"According to her LinkedIn profile, just under a year."*

They'd hired her right around the time we started building New Millennium. *"Thanks, Talulah. Any luck with that security footage yet?"*

"Working on it." She paused. *"Vince texted me about a half hour ago. He's going over our research projects again. He noticed that Doctor Palmer has been poking around your Gateway files."*

Another piece fell into place like a sledgehammer to the sternum. *"Understood."*

"You look like you can't decide whether to puke or punch something," Deb said as I hung up.

"Keeler's press release mentioned a bigger attack, something that would unite the world against magic. The bastards intend to start a war. And I think they mean to use my research to do it."

The CHAIRMAN: Please tell us about the Gateway Project.

Mr. VAINIO: The goal is to create a safe, stable portal that can establish instantaneous transportation between two points. I got tired of losing half a day in airports and on cramped planes every time I got called to D.C., or needed to commute between Michigan and New Millennium.

Mr. HOFFMAN: How much could a portal like that move? What distances are you talking about?

Mr. VAINIO: I've seen a small, short-lived portal connect the Earth and Moon, so we know it can reach at least two hundred thousand miles. We'd have to run some tests to see how much magical energy was involved, and what kind of charring—

Mr. HAYS: Charring?

Mr. VAINIO: Magical damage. If you channel too much power through a book all at once, for example, the results look like you held a blowtorch to the pages. Human beings can suffer the same damage. I lost fifteen percent of my vision that way.

The CHAIRMAN: What applications do you see for this project?

Mr. VAINIO: Space exploration. Commercial trade and transportation. We could use Gateway to take samples from the Earth's core or drive a rover directly onto Uranus. If we're able to go large scale, we'd drastically reduce fossil fuel consumption.

The CHAIRMAN: Have you thought through the potential abuses of such technology? The privacy concerns? What's to stop one of you libriomancers from opening a portal into Fort Knox?

Mr. VAINIO: If I want gold, I can just pull it out of a book.

Mr. HOFFMAN: The point remains, this raises serious questions.

Mr. VAINIO: All of which are being considered by New Millennium, as well as the Department of Homeland Security oversight process. But you're right. Any new technology carries the potential for harm, and magic is no different. Does that mean we turn our back on progress?

Chapter 15

"What was the mission of the Porters?"

"What is this, pop quiz time with Professor Gutenberg?"

"Indulge me."

"You made us each swear an oath to preserve the secrecy of magic, protect the world from magical threats, and to expand our knowledge of magic's power and potential."

"I created the Porters. That made them—you—my responsibility. Part of that responsibility meant being prepared in case the Porters themselves ever became a threat."

"Why are you telling me this?"

"Because you helped create New Millennium."

"**D**O YOU TRUST DEB on her own?" asked Lena.

"Do we have a choice?" Of the three of

us, she was likeliest to have been captured on camera at the Virginia prison. I'd spent most of that mission more or less invisible, and Lena had looked more like a walking tree than a woman. I'd never seen her so heavily armored, and neither had anyone else.

We'd sent Deb back to Michigan with instructions to check in with Jason Latona and fill him in on what was coming next. If necessary, she could help break Nidhi out of whatever holding pen the FBI had tossed her into. "Granach ordered her to strike back. Right now, you and I are her best hope of doing that."

Lena rolled down the window and leaned into the desert sun. "I don't trust her either."

I listened to the rattle of my pickup as we crested the next hill, bringing the New Millennium complex into view. Talulah had confirmed there were no public warrants for me or Lena. Depending on how much was known about the attacks on the *Kagan* and Mecklenburg prison, Babs might suspect what we'd been up to. But if she was an unwilling accomplice in all this, maybe she'd keep those suspicions to herself. All I needed was a few hours.

The other possibility was that everyone knew damn well what we'd done, and were simply waiting for us to walk into their trap.

I pulled up to the security booth and rolled down my window. "Morning, Marion!"

The sparkler grinned at me. "It's a gorgeous one, Mr. Vainio. Hi there, Ms. Greenwood. How was your weekend?"

"Refreshing. Got through three books on my reading list." I passed over my ID and did my best to keep my thoughts calm. I had no hostile intentions toward New Millennium. Only toward a few select individuals.

"Only three? You're slacking."

Lena stretched past me and winked. "Believe me, he really wasn't."

Marion blushed and returned my badge, along with a temporary visitor's ID for Lena. "New rule from Dr. Palmer. Everyone has to display their ID at all times."

I checked the visitor's badge for magic before passing it over. It wasn't enchanted, but the plastic was thick enough to conceal a tracking chip, or possibly a listening device. Lena clipped it to the bottom of her T-shirt.

While I listed off the magic we were carrying, a human guard emerged from the booth to check the back of the truck. He also dropped flat and shone a flashlight beneath. "All clear."

"Is everything all right, sir?" That was the empath, a middle-aged vampire with the beard and build of Santa Claus. "You're pretty anxious."

"We were listening to the news on the drive," I said. "The whole world seems to be going to shit. I'm guessing the extra security measures here mean Babs is getting nervous too."

"It's ugly out there." He studied me a moment longer, then waved us through.

Lena tapped her badge and raised one eyebrow.

I brought one finger to my lips. It might be paranoia, but until we knew for certain, paranoia might keep us alive and free.

I parked the truck and climbed out. We walked hand-in-hand, making small talk as we crossed the grounds. "My team has a Monday morning check-in meeting. It shouldn't take too long. You're welcome to wander, or you can hang out in Franklin Tower until we're done. Vince was supposed to be getting a lion cub from Zimbabwe. I don't know if it's arrived yet."

"I definitely have to meet the cub," said Lena. "How's Lex doing?"

"She was great when I saw her last week. I need to stop by and see how she's progressing."

I smiled and waved to the people we passed, all the while trying to act normal without *acting* like I was acting. Don't stare at security personnel, but don't be too obvious about not staring. Don't look over my shoulder to see if anyone was following. Don't talk too much or too loudly. I was overthinking things, and I couldn't stop.

By the time we made it to the Franklin Research Tower, I'd acquired a whole new level of respect for James Bond and his real-life counterparts.

My team waited for us in the Wheeler conference room. Talulah's privacy toys were set out on the table, their magic securing the room. I sagged into a chair and wiped sweat from my forehead.

"There are at least thirty-nine clones of Kiyoko Itô," Talulah said without preamble. "I can't get a location on them, and I haven't found a way into their biological hard drives."

"What about the security footage at Keeler's place?" asked Lena.

"Two intruders. Looks like one male, one female. Both wore ski masks."

"I've been digging into Thomas Hayes," said Charles. "He's been with the Coast Guard twenty-three years. Joined up right after college. Took over as commandant two years ago. The Porters don't have a file on him and his family, so he probably didn't lose his wife to a selkie or anything else that would give him a personal grudge against magic."

"DHS could have told him the sirens were a threat," Talulah pointed out. "He might believe he's doing his job and protecting his country."

"Hopefully Mr. Potts will be able to answer that question, along with a long list of others."

"Potts." Vince all but spat the name. "He was bad enough before he was running things. Now—"

"What do you mean running things?" I interrupted.

They looked at one another. "You didn't hear?" asked Charles.

"Obviously."

"Nicola Pallas and Thérèse St. Pierre were both taken into FBI custody for questioning," he said. "They're trying to implicate the Porters in this Vanguard mess, particularly the attack on those Coast Guard ships."

That left only Russell Potts and Heather Neuman as active members of the New Millennium board, and while Neuman was a good doctor, she didn't have the strength of will to stand up to Potts.

Russell Potts I could handle. I was more worried about Kiyoko, having seen enough of her book to know the violence she was capable of. "Talulah, do you have any way of taking Kiyoko offline?"

She shook her head. "It's a distributed model. There's no 'queen' ruling over the hive mind. Breaking her psychic link is what causes her stuttering and physical difficulties, so if anyone has to go up against her, your best bet is to isolate her from her clones' thoughts."

"Any of those magic-eating pearls should do the trick," said Charles. "We figure the real reason she wore one was to make sure nobody realized what she was."

"What's the plan for taking Potts down?" asked Vince.

"First, I eliminate his leverage. Then we get proof." The pieces all fit, but I'd been sure about Keeler, too. "Vince, you said Babs had been snooping through my Gateway reports?"

"That's right."

"I need you to be my backup plan. If Lena and I get caught, your job is to destroy the Gateway Project."

I left my team in Franklin Tower, ostensibly carrying on with their individual research projects. We "forgot" our ID badges in my office, just to be safe.

I borrowed a rat carrier from Vince's work area and clipped the shoulder strap from an old laptop case to either side. It was like carrying a light, metal purse for Smudge. It would do for now.

We walked to the hospital tower without incident. Once there, we signed in at the front desk and took the elevator to the third floor.

A new sign had appeared on the door to room 318.

VISITORS: PLEASE REPORT TO THE NURSES' STATION
NO SICK VISITORS OR STAFF
WASH HANDS BEFORE DONNING MASK
MASKS MUST BE WORN BEYOND THIS POINT

Countless nightmares flickered through my thoughts in the time it took me to open the door and step inside. My attention went first to Lex, who was curled beneath several blankets in bed. A nurse was placing a blood pressure cuff around Lex's arm. At the foot of the bed, Russell Potts stood talking to Toby and Angie in low tones.

"Sir, you can't be in here without mask and gloves," said the nurse.

"Isaac?" Toby's eyes were shadowed. His surgical mask muffled his words. "She's right. You can't—"

"What's going on?"

He frowned. "You didn't hear?"

"Alexis has contracted an infection of some kind,"

said Potts. "It seems to resist libriomantic healing." He pointed to the black pearl strung around Lex's neck. "The doctors believe it's magical in nature, and were hoping this would suppress it."

"Will she be all right?" asked Lena.

Potts shrugged. "Unfortunately, it's too early to tell."

The nurse stepped toward me, keeping herself between me and Lex. "Both of you need to step through that door, use the hand sanitizer outside, then go directly to the nurses' station for mask and gloves. Otherwise, I *will* call security."

‹*Talulah, we may have a problem over here.*› There was no response. Either I was out of range, or else the damned pearl was blocking me.

I stared at Potts. "What have they tried so far? If I could see a copy of her chart—"

"Her doctors say the best thing for her right now is rest," Potts said firmly. "Give it time to see if the magic-damper helps."

"I'm surprised to see you here, Mr. Potts. Medical isn't really your area."

Toby frowned. He'd picked up on the edge in my voice.

"With Thérèse and Nicola unavailable, I have broader responsibilities now," said Potts. "The most important of which is the health and safety of our patients. Wouldn't you agree?"

A soft click told me Lena had shut the door behind us.

I'd left my jacket and most of my books behind, because I thought it would be too suspicious. I had only a single paperback tucked into the back pocket of my jeans. I'd brought it along in case I had trouble getting my family out of here.

"They're talking about moving us into quarantine." Angie sounded numb. To finally see her daughter healed, only to watch her succumb to an unknown illness . . . it was enough to break the strongest spirit.

The nurse started toward the phone. Lena moved to block her way.

"I'm sorry," I said. "Nobody told me. When did she start feeling ill?"

"Early this morning," said Angie.

Potts stepped closer to Lex and her pearl.

"What's going on?" demanded Toby.

Lena hadn't brought her bokken. Wooden swords were too conspicuous. Instead, she reached beneath the back of her T-shirt to unsheathe a wooden dagger the size of a Bowie knife. The edge sharpened in her hand.

"Are you threatening me?" Potts snapped.

"Are you threatening my niece?" I replied, my words deceptively calm and cold. "Take that damned pearl off of her so I can read what's happening to her."

Potts didn't move. Angie ripped the pearl necklace from Lex's neck and took it to the bathroom in the back of the room. I heard and felt its influence being flushed away.

"You've been working with Vanguard," Potts said. "We suspected as much. What do you hope to accomplish? Will you kill me the way you killed those people in Michigan?"

"You have a problem, Mr. Potts." I split my attention between him and the nurse. "I'm relatively certain everyone in this room cares more about the welfare of that little girl than they do about you or me. And now that the magic-damper is gone, I can see exactly what you had done to her."

To Toby and Angie, I said, "Magic couldn't heal her, because she's not sick. She's been cursed." The pearl would have suppressed the symptoms, but it couldn't destroy the underlying cause, any more than it could permanently change Lena's nature.

"You're insane." Potts started toward me.

A wooden knife thudded into the floor between his feet. Lena tightened her fist. Oak spikes grew from the knuckles.

I yanked off my glasses and studied Lex's leg. The curse was centered on her knee. Tendrils spread to the foot and up her thigh toward the hip, like a weed taking root.

Lex groaned and opened her eyes. "Uncle Isaac? I don't feel good."

"I know, kiddo. I'll fix it."

"Smudge is glowing. Is he hungry?"

"Not this time." I ripped the magical portion of Lex's curse aside and crushed it into nothingness. That didn't repair the physical damage it had done. "Lena, do you have that healing cordial?"

She handed me the crystal vial without a word. I placed a drop on Lex's tongue.

"What now?" Potts demanded. "Will you kill me, too? Murder me in front of your poor niece? It won't help. You can't hide what you've done."

"How does that feel, Lex?"

She made a face. "Better."

The nurse stepped closer. I nodded, and she began checking Lex's vitals.

"You suspected me, but you weren't certain." I needed to move, to pace, to do something to suppress the need to physically throw Russel Potts through the window. "You didn't know how much I'd uncovered. So you cursed my niece, just in case you needed leverage. That was a serious error in judgment."

I pulled the paperback from my pocket: an old copy of *Renfield*. "Tell me, Russell. How do you feel about eating bugs for the rest of your life?"

I didn't turn him, though it was damned tempting to let him live out his days as one of the inhuman creatures he'd helped to persecute. Instead, I turned to a passage describing the Renfield's ability to influence minds, and used that to put him into a more suggestive, agreeable mood. He sat on the floor and looked up at us, a relaxed, ridiculous smile on his face.

"Who killed Alexander Keeler?" I asked.

"Kiyoko thirteen, and a vampire we hired in D.C. I don't know the name."

That didn't make sense. "His wife and children were incapacitated by libriomancy."

"By a recording of libriomancy. One of your incident reports talked about Nicola's ability to incapacitate a man via cellphone, suggesting that magic could be recorded and duplicated electronically, albeit with some loss of power."

Clever. How many such recordings had they made, and how many times could one be used before it lost its potency? "The sirens. Where are they?"

"I don't know."

"Who does?" asked Lena.

"Kiyoko. Lawrence McGinley."

"Secretary of Homeland Security?" said Angie. "*That* Lawrence McGinley?"

Potts nodded happily. "The one and only!"

Throughout our questions, the nurse had been dutifully examining Lex. Now she turned to Toby and Angie. "Her heartbeat is steadier and stronger. It may be an hour or two for her fever to come down. That's normal after most magical healing. It takes time for the body to realize it's better."

"But she is better?" asked Angie.

"I think so, yes." She glanced at me. "Can I go? I have other patients ..."

"What's your name?" I asked.

"Tamika."

"I see two choices, Tamika. I can adjust your memory of what happened here. That would probably be safest for everyone, especially you. If Potts and the people he's working with think you're helping us—"

"What's the other choice?" She folded her arms and lifted her chin.

"Helping us. I need to get Lex and her parents out of here. That would be easier if she wasn't on quarantine."

Tamika nodded. "I'll update her records with a note that you cleared her 'infection.'"

"Doesn't a doctor need to sign off on that?" asked Toby.

"I've been working in hospitals for twenty years. I think I can forge a doctor's scrawl."

"Thank you," I said. "I'll make sure Potts doesn't remember anything that happened here."

"Give me ten minutes, then you get that little girl somewhere safe."

Once she'd left, I turned back to Potts. "Who else is involved?"

"McGinley has contacts with people in China, France, Britain, and Afghanistan. I don't know names."

"What does he want?" whispered Toby.

"To form an alliance of nations to control the use of magic throughout the world, with us on top," said Potts. "Once we bring the Porters down for working with terrorists, DHS will take over operations of New Millennium, using it as a central hub of magical research and intelligence."

"Keeler wrote about another attack, something big," I said. "What is it? Does it involve the sirens? The Gateway Project?"

Potts gave a clumsy, exaggerated shrug. "Nobody told

me the details. We were worried you might catch on and read my mind. What you're doing is illegal, by the way. I should arrest you."

"What's going on, Uncle Isaac?" Lex was sitting up. Her color was better, and her voice stronger.

"You were sick because of me," I explained. "Because this man wanted to use you against me."

"Are they going to take my leg away?"

"No way, kiddo. I promise." I turned back to Potts. "Where's Darlene Jackson-Palmer?"

He shrugged and chuckled. "Kiyoko thirteen picked her up after she went to Keeler. I don't know where they took her."

"What about Nidhi?"

He shook a finger at me. "That wasn't us. The FBI wanted to question the lead Porters. Doctor Shah was brought in because she'd worked with one of the other council masters. The one from Bangladesh, I think."

I blinked. "So she's safe?"

Potts shrugged. "Maybe. Maybe not. One phone call from McGinley, and she's rotting away in a secret prison for the rest of her life. Or maybe we'll just burn down your lover's oak instead. We have lots of ways to hurt you, Isaac."

"How many prisons do you have like the one in Virginia?" asked Lena.

"Four in the U.S. Several others overseas."

"Do you know when this big attack is supposed to happen?" I asked.

He shook his head. "I imagine it will be soon though, thanks to you. If McGinley thinks he's been compromised, the best play is to launch the attack and make sure you Porters take the blame. That way, whatever you say ends up sounding like a desperate attempt to blame someone else for your crimes."

I looked at Lena. "Anything else?"

"How did you infiltrate and manipulate Vanguard?"

"FBI informants. They've got plants in extremist groups across the country."

I shoved the book back into my pocket. "Time to forget about this conversation, Russell. You're going to sleep now. When you wake up, you won't remember anything that's happened today."

"That sounds nice." He closed his eyes and stretched out on the floor.

Lena sheathed her knife. "Gateway?"

The Gateway Project would give McGinley's people the ability to strike anywhere in the world. "First we use it to get my family out of here. Then I destroy the whole damn project."

Toby scooped Lex up in his arms. His face was pale, and he kept staring down at Potts. "They organized those Vanguard attacks. They sent terrorists to kill people on their own side."

"Bad guys are real assholes, eh?" I glanced around the room. "Did Lex ever get those books I sent over from the library? I may need them to get us back to Franklin Tower unseen."

We told the nurse at the desk we were taking Lex for a walk. Once we reached the elevator, I used the invisibility spell from Stuart Little's car. We made it across the grounds, but one of the guards outside Franklin Tower wore a magic damper. We stopped a short distance from the doors while I made a quick phone call.

Five minutes later, Vince Hambrecht burst through the front doors. He grabbed the closest guard by the arm. "Have you seen an acid-breathing cobra with three heads come through here? She answers to the name of Selma. You've gotta help me find her."

While the visibly unhappy guards helped Vince search, the five of us slipped inside and made our way to the elevator. I stopped at my office to grab my jacket and books, and then we headed for the fifth floor.

The door to the Gateway Project was locked and sealed. A notice pinned to the door prohibited anyone from entering without written permission from Babs Palmer. I saw no cameras, but the electronic ID scanner was probably rigged to sound an alarm. A second, magical barrier overlapped the first, creating a bubble around the entire room.

I pulled out a copy of Stephanie Burgis' *A Most Improper Magick*. I'd tucked a bookmark into the proper page. The protagonist could verbally disrupt magic. I handed Smudge to Lena and waited for them both to move down the hall, then used the book to pop the magical bubble. It took out our invisibility as well, though it didn't reach Lena.

I swapped it out for *Neverwhere* and headed down the hallway to the supply closet. I'd borrowed the mops and other cleaning materials on more than one occasion when my experiments went wrong.

I'd used *Neverwhere* too much recently. The energy flowing through the pages had begun to turn them the color of ash. I sighed and pulled its power into the supply door, then opened it and stepped through to the Gateway room. The others followed a moment later. I switched on the lights and looked around. Most of my work was where I'd left it. "They haven't gotten it working yet."

I gathered books from the floor and my worktable and sat down on the floor to work.

"You're sure you know what you're doing?" asked Toby.

"The theories are sound." I began by twining stories together, pulling passages from different books and braiding them into a doorway in the center of the room.

Story was magic. Magic was story. Memory was also story, disparate events linked together in our mind to create a narrative. I simply needed to bind magic and memory together. It was the same thing I'd done with *Neverwhere*, splicing the text with the imagined destination in my mind. This was simply bigger, more stable, and hopefully more precise over long distance. Assuming it worked.

Water rippled over the partially formed doorway, each wave taking on a silver sheen as story elements combined. I glimpsed other worlds: fantastical forests and twisting tunnels and alien skies sprinkled with strange stars and oversized moons: fragments of realities that lived only in the minds of the authors and their readers, but were no less real for not existing. They flooded my thoughts, each one trying to impose itself on my memories.

I pushed them aside, concentrating on my own memories of the Copper River Library. Of lounging on the beanbag chairs as a child, reading *Goosebumps* books and *Bunnicula* and *A Wrinkle in Time* and everything else I could get my hands on.

That place had been a second home long before I'd come back as an adult and begun working there. I'd kept my first library card, a battered old laminated thing with my careful eight-year-old's signature, up until last year when it was lost with everything else in a house fire. I'd read every book in the children's section and moved on to the adult books. I remembered the summer after fifth grade, when the whole place smelled of sawdust and paint from renovations.

Slowly, the ripples cleared and sagged, melting into a circle on the floor.

"What's happening?" asked Lex.

"Um ..." I'd hoped for a vertical doorway, but it looked like I'd created a hole instead. On the other side were the colorful shelves, carpeting, and toys in the children's section. The portal was horizontal on this end and vertical in Copper River, but it appeared to be working. "It's all right. I think."

The lights were on in the library. I grabbed one of my notebooks, tore out a page, and folded a quick paper airplane. I sighted past the shelves and threw.

A moment later, Jason Latona stepped into view. He picked up the airplane and looked around in confusion.

"Can he see the portal from his side?" asked Lena.

Jason jumped and spun. "Lena? Where are you?"

"Vegas."

"Hi, Jason!" I said. "Remind me, have you ever met my brother and his family? Would you like to?"

"Your friend Deb said you might be bringing company, but she neglected the details."

I helped Lex toward the portal. "Sit here. I'm going to lower you through. You're going to meet a friend of mine."

Jason stood with his head cocked to one side, studying the barefooted legs that seemed to protrude straight out of the air at his chest level. "You know, Isaac, one of the reasons I took a job up here was because the U.P. is supposed to be quiet and relaxing."

"Oh, bullshit. This was the only library that would take you as director."

"You shouldn't say that word," said Lex.

"You're right. It's much more grown-up to say 'bovine feces' or 'taurus excrement.'"

"Isaac, do you mind?" said Angie.

"Sorry." I lifted Lex by the arms. "This is going to feel weird, but Mr. Latona will catch you, okay?"

She bit her lip, but nodded.

I winked and lowered her through. Just as she disappeared, Smudge erupted in flame. Lena drew her bokken and whirled to face the door.

"Angie, Toby, get out of here." I grabbed books from my jacket. The instant Toby and Angie made it through to Copper River, I seized the text of the gateway and prepared to tear it apart.

The door shattered inward. Kiyoko Itô entered the room and promptly stumbled back from the punch Lena landed on the bridge of her nose. Blood spattered from Kiyoko's nostrils, but she didn't appear to care. Babs Palmer stood behind her, the magic of her rings and tattoos humming like electrical lines.

I couldn't tell whether this was the same Kiyoko I'd seen outside of Babs' office or another clone. She wore a skullcap of electrodes and copper wire. She cocked her head to one side, and the sprinkler system came on. Strobe lights flashed from the corners of the ceiling.

Lena lunged. Kiyoko twisted, but the wooden sword stabbed through her side. She reached out to catch Lena's wrist. Before Lena could twist free, Kiyoko snapped a kick to her chest. Lena fell, and Kiyoko staggered back.

The falling water outlined Lena's body.

That was all Kiyoko needed. Her right hand gripped the bokken protruding from her side. With her left, she pulled a black pistol from a holster in the small of her back and squeezed off four shots in quick succession.

I couldn't hear the impact, but Lena staggered. "Remove all magic," Kiyoko said calmly.

When I hesitated, she put another bullet into Lena, who gasped. "I've been instructed to capture Isaac Vainio alive. I have no such orders for your companion."

"Those bullets are enchanted." Babs sounded utterly drained of emotion. "Lena's armor won't protect her."

I raised my hands. Whatever Kiyoko might be, her body was human. She couldn't last long with a sword in her gut. I needed to stall her. "Let me help my friend."

"This is not a negotiation." She turned the gun toward me and fired again. There was a burst of heat from my hip, and the cage broke away. Another shot tore through the center of the cage.

I dropped to all fours. Smudge lay in his cage, blue flame shooting like a welding torch from the front of his body. Kiyoko's bullet had sheared off his right foreleg.

"Remove Lena Greenwood's invisibility," Kiyoko said calmly.

"All right!" Swallowing hard, I grabbed Smudge's cage, crawled over to Lena, and started to unravel her invisibility. I took my time. Nobody else performed this kind of libriomancy, so she couldn't know how long it was supposed to take. As Lena slowly faded into view, I looked past her to the portal.

Lena was bleeding, but the bullets didn't seem to have gone all the way through. I focused my concentration on the portal. All those stories strung together on the floor, powerful and fragile at the same time. Left to its own devices, it would dissolve on its own within the hour.

I wiped my hands on my jacket and felt the lump where I'd tucked the enchanted compact mirror away. I couldn't leave anything that might allow Babs and the rest to recreate my work.

"If you cooperate, they will survive," said Kiyoko. "Back away."

I mentally reached out to the portal, seizing its text in my mind and flipping it like a giant magical pancake. I grabbed the compact and tossed it and Smudge's cage to the floor next to Lena, just before the portal landed atop them. They disappeared, and the portal dissolved an instant later.

"There goes your leverage," I said quietly. "You really shouldn't have told me your bosses need me alive. Especially since I don't think I feel the same way about you."

Kiyoko's body was human, but she'd been born of magic. I seized that magic and pulled, ripping away the heart of what made her more. I turned my attention to Babs next, grabbing the power of her tattoos and her jewelry and turning it against her and Kiyoko both.

My vision blurred. I saw Babs collapse, and Kiyoko cried out in pain, obviously damaged. The cool precision with which she'd shot Lena and Smudge was utterly lacking when she dropped to one knee, raised her trembling arms, and put a bullet into my chest.

MEMO
To: All New Millennium Personnel
From: Babs Palmer, Director of Security
Subject: Internal Security Breach

Effective immediately, Isaac Vainio has been terminated from his position as Director of Research at New Millennium.

Several days ago, an internal investigation carried out in cooperation with the FBI and DHS discovered evidence that Isaac had been working with the group known as Vanguard, and had actively participated in at least two Vanguard attacks. He has been taken into custody for questioning.

Talulah Polk is also suspected to have ties with Vanguard, working through Isaac. She is currently a fugitive, having fled New Millennium at approximately 10:30 Monday morning. If you have any information on her whereabouts, please contact security immediately.

All research projects are to be placed on hold, and the remaining research staff will report directly to Russell Potts. Their only duty is to assist the FBI, DHS, and New Millennium security with the ongoing investigation into this matter.

I cannot overemphasize the damage this incident does to New Millennium's reputation and our ability to perform our mission. The future of New Millennium depends on your cooperation.

Chapter 16

"Hello? Gutenberg? Anyone?"

THE WORLD WAS A kind of technicolor static, spheres of yellow and red floating across an infinite canvas the color of a flooded river back home. It was a bit like the afterimages you get when you rub your eyes after staring at a bright light, but when I tried to blink to clear my vision, nothing happened.

‹*Isaac?*›

I could have been dreaming. Or possibly dead, though that seemed improbable. There was a familiarity to all of this, reminiscent of having my mind ripped from my body. It was annoying how many times that had happened to me. Separating mind from flesh was surprisingly easy, though reuniting the two could be a bit of a trick. But if my body was gone, why did the air smell like burnt popcorn?

‹*Sorry. Hold on . . . is that better?*›

The smell ended with the suddenness of a guillotine. My vision changed as well. I could see blurry points of blue and green and white, all sparkling like Christmas decorations through a frosted window.

‹Is that Christmas thing an actual memory, Isaac? Or are we just seeing random misfires from the visual centers of the brain?›

‹Talulah? What's going on? Are Lena and Smudge all right? Where are Lex and her parents?›

‹One question at a time. Lena's fine. Smudge is limping, but he seems to be getting along. I healed them both the best I could.›

Her words ripped open a maelstrom of emotion. I should have gotten everyone out more quickly. I should have found a way to escape with them, to heal them all myself. ‹You're with them? How?›

‹I hacked into the security feed from the Gateway room. I pieced together where they'd gone and got the hell out of there.›

‹If you figured out where they went—›

‹Relax. It took me three hours to figure out who you were talking to on the other side of that portal. Your friend isn't listed as Jason in any official records, which makes him much harder to identify, especially after someone fried that part of the video. Now that they've got you, I don't think they're as worried about the rest of us.›

‹Thank you. What did they do to me? Where the hell am I?›

‹Easy, Isaac. If you get too worked up, your readings will spike, and I'll have to pull out and try again later.›

The thought terrified me, though I wasn't sure why. ‹I remember the fight in my lab, and then you calling my name. There's nothing in between.›

‹You were sleeping. Nothing to worry about.›

‹Don't lie to me. I don't remember falling asleep or

waking up. I wasn't dreaming. It's like I didn't exist until you started talking to me.

The pause stretched out for what felt like several minutes, but I had no objective way to measure the time. Finally, Talulah said, *‹You existed, but you were on standby. Like a computer in sleep mode.›*

The terror grew. *‹You're holding back. I can feel it. Talulah, what happened to me?›*

‹As far as I can tell, they brought you to the server room and hooked you into the network. Direct neural linkup, probably similar to what Kiyoko wore on her scalp. It lets her get into your brain, copy and sort through your memories, and so on.›

‹Why?› There were far easier ways to read someone's mind.

‹Reading your mind is the easy part.›

Obviously, since Talulah seemed to know my thoughts whether I tried to "speak" them or not.

‹They want to know how your brain works,› she explained. *‹How you're able to do the kind of magic you do.›*

They thought they could do that by plugging me into a damn computer? *‹Wait, how much have they pulled from my memories?›*

‹Everything.›

‹Then they know about Jason. They know where—›

‹They know you sent Lena and your family to the library. They don't know where everyone went when they left the library. Like I said, I don't think they care about the rest of us anymore. We're safe. I've spent the past two days poking around, trying to activate your consciousness without tripping any alarms.›

Two days. I hoped someone was taking good care of my body. *‹How did you get in?›*

‹That magic phone in your jaw. I'm using it as a kind

of modem. I created a telepathic connection to a secure laptop, built a hard firewall and sent the signal through a series of encrypted Tor routers, and added a layer of magical programming just to be safe.›

‹*If they took my memories, they'd know about the communicator.*›

‹*I'm sure they know about it. That doesn't mean they know what I can do with it. You didn't.*›

‹*Or you're Kiyoko, trying to trick me into trusting you so you can access more of my mind.*›

‹*True enough. But you're as helpless as a brain in a pickle jar, so there's not much you can do about it either way. If I wanted your cooperation, all I'd have to do is stimulate the pleasure center of your brain. Or your pain center, if I was feeling unkind.*›

‹*Good enough for me. So how do we get me out of here?*›

‹*You're going to do magic.*›

‹*Cool. How the hell am I going to manage that?*›

‹*With help. I'm going to try to activate the parts of your brain that deal with reading and memory. In some ways, it will be similar to what Kiyoko is trying to do.*›

I felt trepidation and uncertainty in her words, along with something more. A moment later, I recognized it as guilt. ‹*What aren't you telling me?*›

‹*I need you to think about a book you've read, one that would do serious, targeted damage to a server room.*›

Firestarter was the first book that came to mind. It was fresh in my memory after encountering its magic at Alexander Keeler's home.

‹*That should work,*› said Talulah.

‹*I'm not doing anything until you tell me the truth.*›

Silence stretched between us. ‹*If I do, you'll wish I hadn't.*›

‹*If you were trying to make me trust you, you missed badly.*›

Another pause. ‹*You're not Isaac Vainio.*›

I felt like she'd tossed me off the Mackinac Bridge. ‹*I don't understand.*›

‹*The first thing Kiyoko did when she spliced your brain into her network was to make a backup.*›

‹*I'm . . . a backup?*›

‹*One of three, and taking up an obscene amount of server space. From what I've been able to map out, there's the original you, unconscious in your physical body. Then there's a dev and QA environment, along with a clean backup.*›

‹*That can't be right. I'm me. I mean, I'm not just memories. I'm conscious.*› Wasn't I? Life wasn't limited to the flesh. Libriomancy had proved that a thousand times over. ‹*Which one am I?*›

‹*You're the clean copy. Development is where Kiyoko messes with your head, poking and prodding to see what happens. If she breaks you, she can make a new copy. QA is where she pushes things through to a simulation for Russell Potts or Babs Palmer or whoever else to interact with.*›

‹*I don't suppose you can cut and paste me onto your laptop or something?*› She could probably sense the fear behind those words, but I didn't care. There was always a way out.

‹*I'm sorry, Isaac. My laptop couldn't hold a single day of your life. According to this, six Kiyoko clones are stacked up in cold sleep in the New Millennium server room, doing nothing but hosting your backups. When you add in all the software and security protocols, it takes two human brains to maintain a single mind. Though I'm sure I could improve that ratio with the right compression algorithms, especially if we prioritized—*›

⟨*Talulah.*⟩

Sorrow broke through our connection and washed over me. ⟨*I can't get you out, and we can't let Kiyoko keep a copy of your mind.*⟩

⟨*You're planning to kill me.*⟩ She didn't answer. She didn't have to. ⟨*There has to be another way. What about Kiyoko's physical body? If you woke me up in her body, I could cause all sorts of mischief here. Imagine four Isaacs running around. We'd have this mess sorted in a half-hour, tops.*⟩

⟨*It's not a simple matter of severing the control protocols. Your mind is striped across two physical brains, similar to a RAID 6 server array, with error-checking bits worked into—*⟩

⟨*And in English, that means?*⟩

⟨*Your backup minds are like pieces of a jigsaw puzzle in two separate boxes. I can't put you back together. The one time I attempted it, your mind died instantly. I managed to make it look like a software failure, but it was a close thing.*⟩

⟨*Oh. That . . . that sucks.*⟩

⟨*I know.*⟩

I wanted to stall. To joke and argue and squeeze every second of life out of this mess. From what Talulah was telling me, I'd existed for only two days, and I'd spent most of that time in stasis.

But was this existence worth it? Trapped in the emptiness with nothing but Talulah's voice and the random misfiring of my simulated visual neurons for company? I was alone. No matter how long I dragged things out, I'd never see Lena again. I'd never touch another human being. I'd never get the chance to punch Russell Potts in his damn face. I'd never get a rematch with Kiyoko to show her what happened to people who shot my friends. I'd never do magic.

No ... everything else might be lost to me, but Talulah thought there was a way I could touch magic one last time. ‹*Tell me what you need from me. And ... do me one favor?*›

‹*Of course. What is it?*›

‹*Take the bastards down. All of them.*›

The world was a kind of technicolor static, spheres of yellow and red floating across an infinite canvas the color of a flooded river back home. It was a bit like the afterimages you get when you rub your eyes after staring at a bright light, but when I tried to blink to clear my vision, nothing happened.

‹*Isaac?*›

I could have been dreaming. Or possibly dead, though that seemed improbable. There was a familiarity to all of this, reminiscent of having my mind ripped from my body. It was annoying how many times that had happened to me. Separating mind from flesh was surprisingly easy, though reuniting the two could be a bit of a trick.

‹*It's Talulah. Lena's with us. She's alive. So is Smudge. You're a prisoner at New Millennium. I'm hacking your brain, and I need you to remain calm. We're only going to get one shot at this.*›

‹*Slow down. What do you mean, hacking my brain?*›

‹*Kiyoko hooked you into her network. You've been there for two days. In a nutshell, they're reviewing your memories and trying to reverse engineer you and your magic.*›

‹*Oh.*›

‹*Once we start breaking you out, I think I can keep Kiyoko in the dark for about ninety seconds. After that, I have no idea what she'll do to you.*›

‹*How do I know—*›

‹That this isn't a trick? You don't. But if I wanted to make you do something—›

‹You could just trigger the pleasure center of my brain. Or the pain center. That makes sense. I suppose there's not much I can do either way, eh?›

The pause that followed stretched long enough to make me think something had gone wrong. ‹How . . . why did you say that, about the pleasure center of your brain?›

‹I don't know. It just made sense. Why? I can feel bits of your emotion, and they're freaking me out.›

I caught the edge of her thoughts. Something about psychic echoes and mental resonance, tied to tremendous guilt and sadness. ‹I'll explain later. We're going to create a distraction, but in order for you to get away, they'll need to think you're dead. Do you remember reading Debt of Bones when you were in college?›

‹Terry Goodkind, yah. How did you—right, you're in my brain.› I tried not to think about the implications and how much of my life had become a book for Talulah, Kiyoko, and anyone else to peruse. ‹The death spell?›

‹Exactly. Think back to that book. I'm going to try to amplify the memory from here, and you're going to cast the spell.›

‹How?›

‹I'll explain as we go. Where were you when you read it?›

I concentrated on the memory and found myself in my old dorm room at Michigan State University, camped out in the lower bunk of the metal-framed beds. A green carpet remnant covered most of the tile floor. The air smelled like the beef-flavored Ramen noodles I'd cooked the night before on the hot plate we weren't supposed to have.

I looked down at the book in my hands. I could feel

the roughness of the paper, the faint wrinkles in the worn spine. ‹*This is just a memory. Without the physical book to tap into*—›

A new voice intruded. ‹*So this is what old man brain looks like.*›

‹*Jeneta?*›

‹*She's here with us,*› said Talulah. ‹*I'm looping her into the conversation. Call it a telepathic group chat.*›

I laughed. ‹*How did you find her?*›

‹*I've lost some cred since word got out I could do magic, but I've still got close to a million subscribers on YouTube, along with six figures on Twitter and Instagram and so on. I put the word out that I needed to talk to Jeneta, and asked my followers to pass it along.*›

‹*It made the front page of Reddit,*› Jeneta added. ‹*Hold on, I'm downloading a copy of your book.*›

For an instant, I saw through Jeneta's eyes. She was in an unfinished basement. Talulah sat on a Papasan chair beside her, working over a pile of computer hardware I couldn't begin to identify or sort out. Lena rested on the floor, Smudge perched awkwardly on her hip. From this angle, you could barely see his missing leg.

‹*Can you see the book?*› asked Jeneta.

I was back in my dorm room. ‹*I see it.*›

‹*Talulah, we're ready. Hold on, Isaac. We're going to create a distraction.*›

Darkness flickered across my vision like an eyeblink, but in that fraction of a second, everything shifted. Talulah was suddenly turned away, her shoulders hunched like she was in pain. Jeneta's e-reader had moved as well, and Lena was sitting up. ‹*What was that?*›

‹*Seventy-four seconds before Kiyoko catches on,*› Talulah said flatly.

‹*Remember the book,*› said Jeneta. ‹*See it in your mind.*›

I focused on the pages. This particular book was one

I'd read not for magic, but for pure escapism. I'd gotten brutally dumped a few days earlier. Relationships were hard enough at that age without me constantly having to sneak off-campus for secret magic lessons.

I saw Jeneta reaching into the screen of her e-reader. I did the same with my book, touching the scene that described the death spell.

Nothing happened. I couldn't feel the belief, the power of the story. This was nothing but a memory, with no physical resonance—

‹Relax,› said Jeneta. ‹It worked before. It'll work again.›

Before I could ask what that meant, Talulah announced that we were down to fifty-five seconds.

‹I'm doing the best I can here.›

‹Hold·on.› Talulah reached out to touch Jeneta's forehead, and the connection between the three of us strengthened. I felt the magic of her e-reader and the story beneath that too-smooth screen. I clung to that scene, to a spell designed to make onlookers believe you had died. I siphoned the magic into my thoughts.

‹The damage is spreading faster than I expected,› said Talulah. ‹We're about to lose contact. You've got guards coming your way, Isaac. I'm going to fry your connection to the network and wake you up. Cast the spell and get the hell out of there.›

They vanished. The memories of my dorm room faded a moment later, though I could still feel the pages of the book, still see its magic crawling through my limbs. My eyes cracked open, dry and crusty. I was in a too-bright cubicle made of thick glass partitions, like an oversized museum display. Electrodes and needles porcupined my body. My limbs and torso were strapped to a chair that reminded me of the one in my dentist's office. I seemed to be naked save for a hospital gown.

I smelled smoke. Sparks and blue flame jumped from

an electrical outlet in the wall. Smoke curled out of a handful of tall, heavy-doored cabinets that resembled slender white refrigerators.

Goosebumps tightened my skin. I wiggled and tugged, trying to slide my arm free. I lost a layer of skin and torqued my shoulder, but managed to pull my right hand loose. I yanked the needles from my veins, then tugged the electrodes off my scalp.

My hair was gone. The stubble on my head felt like sandpaper. On the other hand, someone had healed the bullet wound in my chest. I suppose my hair was a fair trade for not dying.

Beyond the glass walls of my own personal containment unit, flames spread to a bank of computer equipment. Alarms blared from beyond the door, and I heard voices arguing outside. The metal door rattled in its frame. Talulah must have done something to lock it.

I unfastened the other straps, climbed from the chair, and immediately collapsed into the glass wall. After two days, my limbs were weak as softened wax. I braced myself against the chair and stumbled to the rubber-sealed door of my isolation cubicle.

As I forced the door open and stepped free, the outer door shook like it had been hit by a runaway Buick. Whatever was trying to get in here, they weren't human. Another hammer-blow dented the door inward. Gray mist flowed through the crack below. I squinted, trying to read the magic as it filled the room. This particular vampire appeared to be Sanguinarius Machalus.

The bastardized Latinization of D. J. MacHale's name made me wince to this day, but I pushed my linguistic annoyances aside and concentrated on the death spell. I could still feel the book in my hands, its magic in my blood, waiting to be triggered. I couldn't hold it for much longer, but I needed this to be believable.

The vampire reformed into a young man in a turquoise New Millennium shirt. He pulled a JG-367 and pointed it toward me. "Don't move!"

I studied the particular passages that had allowed him to transform into mist and back, and pulled those strings of text around myself.

He punched the keypad by the doorway. The door started to slide open, but jammed after three inches. All that pounding must have dented or damaged the track. Thick fingers wrapped around the edge of the door and pulled.

Metal squealed. I moved my attention to the weapon.

The door ripped free and slammed across the hallway, tearing chunks of plaster and drywall along with it. It was like someone had fired a cannon through the building. The floor shook, and the glass walls behind me shivered.

In that moment, I activated the death spell, dissolved my body into mist, and triggered the JG-367.

The gun shot fire and electricity through me. Even in gaseous form, it felt like I'd gone walking on hot coals after bathing in lighter fluid.

The second vampire stared from the doorway. He'd gotten through just in time to see me disintegrate in a blast of flame. "Holy shit, Darren. What the hell did you do?"

"I didn't—I was only trying to stun him." Darren stared at the JG-367 like it had twisted around and bitten his balls off. "The dude was trying to get free, and then you started smashing everything and the damn gun just went off."

A third figure appeared in the doorway. This one appeared human, though it was hard to be sure. My senses were rather dulled at the moment. I wasn't sure how a cloud of mist could see or hear at all, for that matter.

"What happened?" she shouted, standing a few paces back from the vampires. "Where'd he go?"

I flowed toward the doorway, blending in with the smoke pouring from the walls.

"Oh-shit-oh-shit-oh-shit," whimpered Darren. "It was an accident."

If he hadn't been working for the folks who'd shot me and tried to turn my brain into their own personal playground, I'd have felt sorry for him. As it was, I simply drifted out the door and left him to his fate. Passing the woman was like getting too close to a furnace. I shied away from the magic-dampener she was wearing before it could force me back into my normal form.

"Check the backups," she shouted.

"Everything's fried!" called the second vampire. "The backups are dead. Looks like the fire started in here."

Grief struck me with those words, though I wasn't sure why. If Talulah had found a way to fry the backup servers, so much the better.

"Why aren't the fucking sprinklers working?"

Presumably because Talulah had disabled those as well, to help cover my escape and destroy whatever information they'd gotten from my head.

"Dr. Palmer's gonna kill me," moaned Darren.

My movement seemed to be a matter of focusing my awareness on a particular part of the mist. The rest shifted to gather around that center point. I felt like a gaseous inchworm scooting down the hall.

I gradually learned to smooth out my motion. I slipped beneath a door and into the stairwell, where I allowed gravity to drag me to the ground floor. I'd been seven or eight stories up, but where? Had they kept me in Admin where Babs could keep an eye on me? Medical, in case something went wrong?

I thinned myself over the floor, striving for invisibility.

I extended a tendril of mist through the main doors and looked around outside. The light of the setting sun might as well have been the flame from an acetylene torch. I pulled back, but I'd seen enough to recognize the Franklin Research Tower. They'd locked me up in my own damn building!

I'd only meant to take Darren's ability to shapeshift into mist. How had I ended up with his vulnerability to sunlight, too? I filed that question away with a hundred others, all waiting their turn on my research whiteboard.

If I was stuck here until sundown, I might as well take advantage of the time. I wondered if Babs and Kiyoko had cleaned out my office yet . . .

United States Will Allow U.N. Inspections of New Millennium Facility

WASHINGTON—Following a contentious debate, the U.S. government has agreed to allow a United Nations team to inspect New Millennium in Las Vegas, Nevada.

Members of the U.N. Security Council have pushed for inspections since New Millennium was first opened, but until recently, all resolutions were vetoed by the U.S. and the United Kingdom.

That changed earlier this week, following revelations that a high-ranking researcher at New Millennium had been involved in terrorist attacks. The new resolution passed ten to five in favor.

Kristen DeCaro, the U.S. Ambassador to the United Nations, spoke at a press conference following the vote. "The United States recognizes that the potential dangers of magic, as well as the potential benefits, are not limited to any one nation. Let this serve as a model of openness and transparency for the world, in the hope that we can come together to regulate the use of magic and protect the lives and freedom of all people."

A bipartisan group of eighteen U.S. senators immediately published a letter of protest in the New York Times, demanding the removal of DeCaro.

U.N. inspectors are scheduled to arrive tomorrow.

Chapter 17

"How do you keep this kind of power out of the wrong hands?"

"That's the wrong question, Isaac. I managed to do it by suppressing magic altogether. But you can't go back to the way things were, even if you wanted to."

"Fine. How do you share magic with the world without risking—"

"You can't."

"There has to be a way to prevent the most dangerous—"

"There's not."

"You're even more annoying dead than you were alive. At least then you were doing things."

"Would you like to trade places?"

"I helped reveal magic to the world. People are dying because of what I did."

"Other people will live because of your choice."

"What am I supposed to do, add up both columns to decide whether or not I made the right choice?"

"There is no right choice. You chose. Your job now is to make the most of that choice."

B ABS AND THE REST would be suspicious as hell. A lone guard accidentally disintegrates their pet libriomancer, while a convenient fire wipes the servers? The death spell should help convince everyone I'd truly gone up in smoke, but no spell was foolproof, and too many folks were walking around with those damn magic-sucking pearls. If they were smart—and dammit, whatever else I might think of these people, they clearly were—they'd be searching for me, just in case.

The entire tower was now on lockdown. It had taken close to an hour just to make it up to my office while evading security. Twice, people had opened my office door and looked around. I'd managed to keep out of sight behind my desk, or by dissolving into mist and flowing into the bottom of the half-full garbage can with the old food wrappers.

I made a mental note to start storing a change of clothes in my office. It wasn't easy trying to plan an escape wearing nothing but a hospital gown. I had nowhere to carry my books, and the draftiness was distracting as hell.

Flying over the wall was out of the question. The wards over New Millennium allowed insects and birds to pass through, but would zap anything larger, or anything magical. I could try to hitch a ride out the main gates, but I lacked the books I'd need to counter the heightened security measures, and I wasn't sure I could make it to the Library Tower without being seen.

I'd come up with one option. I gave myself an hour to think of an alternative. When that hour passed, I added another thirty minutes, then fifteen more, like a kid hitting the snooze button on Monday morning before school. I *really* didn't want to do this.

Finally, hope and denial gave way to resignation. I turned back into mist, crept out of my office, and made my way toward the restroom.

New Millennium was designed to be as self-sufficient as possible, but there were limits. Nobody had put together a magical sewage treatment plant yet, and it was more economical to tap into the city's infrastructure than to try to build it all ourselves. The sink pipes in the bathroom should provide a way out.

I flowed beneath the door. Before I could do anything more, I heard footsteps in the hall behind me. I hurried into the closest stall. The bathroom door opened, and a man's voice called out, "Anybody in here? I saw smoke."

With one fire having broken out today, they'd be quick to respond to any hint of another. I remained silent, hoping he'd run off long enough for me to escape. Instead, he stepped in after me and pushed open the first stall, then the second.

Aw, crap. Today just kept getting better.

I pulled myself into the toilet. Water pressed around me, trying to break me into discrete bubbles of gas. I had to compress myself into a fraction of my usual size, which left me feeling both crushed and bloated.

Also, the water was really, really cold.

"What's going on?"

I froze. That was Babs Palmer's voice.

"Thought I saw smoke."

"In the bathroom?" Babs sniffed. "Get back to your rounds."

One set of footsteps left, and the bathroom door swung shut. I didn't move.

Eventually, I heard Babs' boots clopping like hoof-beats over the tile. If she used magic, I wasn't sure I'd be able to counter it in this form. Or she could simply toss one of those pearls into the toilet, and I'd . . . I wasn't sure what would happen if I was forced back into my normal form while submerged in the toilet water, but it wouldn't be pleasant.

"Six, five, three," Babs whispered.

A short time later, she walked away. The door opened again, and the bathroom fell silent. Had she left, or was she trying to trick me into revealing myself?

What the hell was six five three supposed to mean? It didn't sound like any spell I'd come across. In the Dewey Decimal system, 653 referred to books on shorthand. It could also be a code word or command keyed to her jewelry. Maybe she was trying to tell me something, and didn't want anyone else to overhear or understand. Or maybe she'd set a trap to petrify me the moment I emerged.

I couldn't risk it. The water burbled behind me as I burrowed down the pipes.

Three very long, very cramped hours later, I was walking along the side of a road, barefoot and dripping and smelling of water purification chemicals and worse. I managed to flag down a passing car. The passenger window lowered, and the driver grimaced.

"I know," I said. "It's been a long day."

He snorted. "Looks like a hell of a night, too. Sorry, man. I don't know what you've been into, but I can't let you in my car. You need me to call someone for you or anything?"

"I don't think so." I looked around. "But do you think you could tell me where to find the nearest bookstore or library? What I really need is a book of fairy tales."

He didn't miss a beat. "Let me pull it up on the GPS."

"Thanks." I looked down at myself, then back at him. "You're not going to ask about the hospital gown or anything?"

He flashed a broad grin. "Buddy, I've lived in Vegas for twenty years. If there's one thing I know, it's when not to ask questions."

I arrived in Michigan wearing a brown wool tunic and a pair of seven-league boots, with an old library book tucked under one arm.

I'd gone to the Copper River Library first, but it was locked and empty. I checked Lena's oak tree next. She wasn't there, but when I touched the tree, the roots shifted to reveal a folded square of paper with a Grand Rapids address on it.

A short time later, I was back in the Lower Peninsula, double-checking the note against the blue-gray ranch house in front of me. A flat ceramic bumblebee hung beside the door, the word WELCOME arching over its wings. I stepped onto the porch and knocked.

Jason opened the door and immediately covered his mouth, trying to hide his laughter. "You look like you just climbed down from a beanstalk." His nose wrinkled. "And you smell like—"

"I know what I smell like." I held up the book. "Don't let me forget to send a check to Sunrise Library in Las Vegas for the book and the broken window."

"Isaac!" Lena nudged Jason out of the way and grabbed my arms. She was moving a bit stiffly, and I could see the edge of a bandage peeking out from the neck of her T-shirt, but she was alive. The mere sight of her lightened the tension and anger I'd been carrying since I woke up.

"Damn, I'm glad to see you." I pulled her into a hug, careful to keep my arms low and away from where she'd been shot. "I'm sorry. I didn't realize how fast Kiyoko was. I didn't—"

"Shut up. I'm all right." She ran a hand over my scalp. "I'm not sure you can pull this ruggedly bald look off. You're cute, but you're no Vin Diesel."

Smudge crawled from her shoulder to mine. The slight irregularity of his gait broke my heart. "I'll fix you up, buddy. I promise. I'll regenerate that leg as good as new, and if that fails, I'll make Charles build you a new one. A bionic leg. What do you think? Is the world ready for a bionic fire-spider?"

Jason reached past me and shut the door.

I forced myself to stop babbling long enough to ask, "Where's everyone else?"

"Sleeping," said Lena. "Talulah and Jeneta were both exhausted after hacking into your head. Especially Talulah. She spent more than a day lost in her laptop, and none of us knew what was happening until they were ready to break you out. Nidhi finally raided the medicine cabinet and started handing out melatonin and Nyquil to make people sleep, but I couldn't."

"Wait, Nidhi's here? She's okay?"

"She's fine," said Jason. "I talked to Agent Steinkamp, and he confirmed that Nidhi was only supposed to be brought in to be interviewed. It sounds like there was a mix-up in the system, and she was put into detention by mistake."

His face wrinkled. He didn't buy the "mistake" bit any more than I did. "Thank you, Jason. You may have saved her life."

Jason blushed and turned away. "Shower is down the hall on your left. First door. I'll get you a towel and some real clothes."

Lena traced the curve of my ear with her right hand. "Grab two towels, please."

I shook my head. "I need to talk to everyone before—"

"Let them sleep," said Jason. "You've been gone almost three days. Another hour won't hurt anything."

With that, Lena was dragging me down the hallway and into a bathroom decorated with fish and other sea creatures from *Finding Nemo*. Any awkwardness I felt about showering with Lena in a strange home faded quickly as Lena yanked my tunic over my head and tossed it into the plastic garbage can next to the toilet. I turned on the water, then helped Lena peel off her shirt. I ran my fingers gently over the skin at the edge of her bandages. "Are you sure . . . ?"

"You'll need to be gentle." She tugged the bandages loose. The bullet holes underneath were dark and scabbed: one on her stomach, the other on the inner curve of her left breast. Two other bullets had struck her left shoulder. Tiny lines bulged around the edges of the wounds, like the roots of a plant. "Not *too* gentle, mind you."

I unbuckled her jeans and slid them over her hips, kissing my way down her body and carefully detouring around her injuries.

Her hands tightened around the back of my head. She groaned, then pulled me up and kissed me hard, her tongue seeking mine, our hips pressing together.

"I've missed you," she whispered when we broke away.

"I missed you, too."

She flashed a mischievous grin. "I can see that."

I stepped into the shower. "Give me a few minutes to wash up, and I'll show you just how much I missed you."

I woke up early the next morning. Between changing time zones and spending two days in a coma, my schedule was utterly wrecked. I tiptoed past the lumpy sleeping bags in the living room where my brother was snoring away next to Lex and Angie. Talulah was on the couch.

Lena had explained that this was the home of Jason's ex-husband, a revelation that made me realize how much I didn't know about my former boss, while simultaneously adding an additional layer of awkwardness to the whole shower sex thing.

Once people began materializing in his library, Jason had gotten on the phone to search for a safer location. When he learned Rich was on a business trip for the week, Jason had loaded everyone up and taken a road trip downstate. I wasn't clear about whether he'd asked permission, first.

I entered the kitchen to find Smudge and another firespider playing in a large frying pan in the middle of the kitchen. Jeneta was watching over them. She'd lined the pan with a layer of cooking oil and popcorn kernels.

"Popcorn for breakfast?" I asked.

Jeneta jumped, then beamed up at me in a rare, unguarded show of emotion. "Nkiruka's been teaching Smudge how to pop corn. He didn't like the oil at first, but as soon as he ate his first piece, he was hooked."

Nkiruka was Jeneta's fire-spider, a gift from me a year ago. Nkiruka and Smudge were currently chasing each other in circles around the pan.

As for Jeneta, a year had done wonders for her. She looked *whole* again, healthy and . . . not necessarily relaxed, but she no longer had that hunched-over, shadowed look, like she was constantly preparing for an assault.

I sat down across from her. Smudge skidded to a halt, finally noticing me. He scrambled out of the pan and raced over to climb up my leg, leaving tiny oil spots on my borrowed khakis. He perched on my knee, either inspecting me to make sure I was all right or else waiting to see if I'd brought him a snack.

"Thanks for helping me get out of there, Jeneta," I said.

She shrugged. "You did the same for me."

I brought Smudge to eye level and studied the quarter-inch stub of his foreleg. The stump had healed over. Fire-spider wounds were self-cauterizing, and I could see the remnants of someone's magic—either Talulah or Jeneta, probably—where they'd tried to heal him. A second layer of text ran deeper. This was the curse from Kiyoko's enchanted bullets. I brought a finger toward Smudge, trying to separate the curse from his innate magic.

Red waves of flame rushed over his back. I yanked my hand away.

"Can you help him?" Jeneta asked, her eyes on Nkiruka.

I lowered Smudge back into the frying pan, just as the first kernel popped. I felt sick to my stomach. "I could use his original book to restore his body. It would essentially reset his physical form."

"But . . . ?"

"I can't do it selectively. It would reset his mind, too. He wouldn't be my Smudge. He'd be the Smudge I created back in high school, confused and frightened. He wouldn't know me. He wouldn't remember anything."

She pursed her lips and exhaled softly. "He's got seven legs left. The missing one doesn't seem to slow him down much."

I watched him pounce on a fresh-popped kernel. "I thought I'd be able to fix this."

"That's how I felt when my mom and dad split up."

Paige and Mmadukaaku Aboderin had never forgiven me for the months their daughter had gone miss-

ing, possessed by a thousand-year-old necromancer.
We'd saved Jeneta, but the strain of those months, combined with the stress of their daughter's libriomancy and
the revelation of magic, had broken their marriage. Last
I'd heard, they were in the midst of a trial separation,
with Paige on sabbatical back in England. "Is your father
here?"

"Guest room in the basement."

"How's he doing?"

She shrugged one shoulder. "Depends on the day. He
doesn't like you very much."

"Yah, he can join the club. I don't imagine that'll
change soon." I listened to the sizzle of the oil in the pan
as the two spiders danced around, dodging exploding
kernels. "It's good to see you again."

She shrugged again and watched the spiders play.
"You too."

"What's been happening out there while I was sleeping?"

"Violence. Death. War. The usual." That was Talulah.
She smiled at Jeneta before taking a seat at the small
table in the corner of the kitchen. "Glad to see you made
it out of there."

"Thanks to you and Jeneta."

"Does this mean I can get a raise?"

I snorted. "I'll see what I can do. Any word from Mc-
Ginley or Vanguard?"

They looked at one another. Jeneta's face went blank.

"Vanguard, or someone speaking in their name, issued an ultimatum last night," said Talulah. "If the world
doesn't grant full legal equality and protection to magic-
users and inhumans, they'll make the atom bomb look
like a cap gun."

"Not any time soon, they won't," I said. "I shredded
the Gateway Project's magic before Kiyoko shot me.

Even if she siphoned the knowledge from my head, they don't have the ability to put it back together."

Jeneta's eyes were wide. "You got shot?"

"I got better. I'm assuming Babs fixed me back up, or maybe Kiyoko swiped some healing magic from the hospital. I guess it's harder to scan someone's brain if he's dead."

"So you think the threat is a bluff?" asked Talulah.

"A bluff doesn't make sense. Assuming McGinley and his crew are behind this, they know damn well nobody's going to give in to their demands. The only reason to put this out there is as the groundwork for their next move, to make sure Vanguard takes the blame." McGinley and Potts didn't *want* equality. They wanted an attack so horrific it would unite most of the world against people like us. "We've missed something. *I've* missed something."

I stood up and rubbed my eyes. I'd lost my glasses, and the charred spots floating across my vision like tiny stormclouds were both distracting and destined to give me a headache before too long. "Talulah, can you run a search to see if the numbers six, five, and three mean anything?"

"It's one of my project numbers. The International Alert System. Why?"

I closed my eyes and gently thumped my head against the wall. My chest felt as if I'd been put through an industrial press. My body wanted to laugh and cry at the same time. "Because I'm a damn fool. A blind, arrogant fool."

Talulah moved closer. "Isaac?"

"I thought they meant to use Gateway." My words sounded distant. My pulse drummed in my ears. "We need to wake everyone up right now."

Talulah closed her eyes. I heard only the edge of her telepathic wake-up call, but it was enough to shock my nervous system. "They're awake."

Minutes later, we'd gathered everyone in the living room. I sat on the old loveseat next to Lena, while Nidhi perched on the end. Talulah and Jason were on the floor. Jeneta plopped herself down on an old beanbag chair, while her father stood beside her, his arms crossed. Lex, Toby, and Angie sat on the couch, where Lex munched sleepily on a strawberry Pop Tart. Deb sat in the corner, chewing her thumbnail.

I was tempted to send Lex away. To send all three of them to another room. Jason, too. This wasn't their fight.

"I know what you're thinking," said Toby. "These people threatened my daughter. We're not leaving."

I nodded. "Talulah, can you please explain the IAS Project?"

She stood up and began to pace. "The International Alert System was a proposal for sending emergency warnings via TV, radio, cellphone . . . pretty much anything with a speaker. Charles and I had been working on a way to predict natural disasters. We were hoping to tie the two projects together. It would let us warn people sooner, giving them more time to reach shelter."

"How far did you get with that proposal?" I pressed.

"It was ready to go. I had a list of texts to use, and a plan for compiling their tech into a single program."

"Enough of a plan for another libriomancer to complete your work?"

"Possibly . . ."

None of her answers came as a surprise, but each one was an additional weight, crushing any remaining hope that I was mistaken.

‹*What are they doing with my work, Isaac?*›

Lena swore under her breath. "The sirens."

Talulah paled.

"Lawrence McGinley sent the *USCGC Kagan* and two other ships to capture a group of sirens," I said.

"They were transported to a facility in Virginia to be tagged and cataloged. Lena, Deb, and I tried and failed to rescue them. If McGinley were to broadcast the sirens' song through the IAS, he could kill thousands of people."

"Hundreds of thousands," Talulah said. "Millions, if they calibrate the broadcast just right."

Jason raised a hand like a student in class. "Are you talking about sirens like Odysseus-tied-to-the-mast, songs-luring-sailors-to-their-death, and all that?"

"That's right," I said. "Their song creates a sense of longing and emptiness nothing can fill. It's like reliving every loss and disappointment in your life all at once, and only the siren offers any hope of relief. That despair is what caused sailors to throw themselves overboard."

I wiped my hands on my pants. "I've heard it," I continued. "A broken version a year ago, as well as the muted song when we tried to stop the *Kagan*. I can still hear it. I spent months working with my therapist, trying to learn how *not* to hear it, how to keep it from dragging me back down."

"What good would it do to broadcast a siren song?" asked Jeneta. "It's not like most people can just hop overboard and drown themselves."

"No, they can't." I closed my eyes, remembering the desperation reaching through me. "Sailors sought out the sirens because they thought they could reach the source and stop the pain. There are other ways to end your pain."

"You're talking about suicide," said Nidhi.

I nodded again. "Hundreds of thousands of suicides. Millions."

"They can target anyone they like," said Talulah. "Worried about China's magical program? Angry at North Korea? You could probably reach ninety-five percent of both countries with a single broadcast. This isn't just a weapon of mass destruction. We're talking about potential genocide."

"Aren't there other Porters at New Millennium who would recognize Talulah's project?" asked Angie. "They'd be able to stop it, or at least trace who stole her work."

"Charles and Vince both would, yah. Along with anyone from DHS or the board who's been reviewing our research."

"So they'll broadcast the song within New Millennium, too," said Lena. "Claim Vanguard infiltrated the facility and launched the attack from there as a suicide mission. Once everyone's dead, who's to say someone from New Millennium wasn't an extremist? Especially if Potts and his people are in charge of the investigation."

"As long as his people have those magic-dampening amulets, they'll survive," I said. "While everyone else dies in despair and hopelessness."

"When do the U.N. inspectors arrive at New Millennium?" asked Angie. "If McGinley is going for international outrage, wouldn't it make sense to kill them too?"

Talulah swore. "They're supposed to begin this afternoon."

"Can we warn people?" Jason was as frightened as I'd ever seen him, his eyes big and his hands trembling in his lap. "Tell them to turn off their electronics, invest in earplugs, something like that?"

"The spell will power things up remotely." Talulah punched the floor. "We didn't want to risk people sleeping through a warning, or missing it because they'd switched everything off. I never imagined . . ." She hit the floor again, then slashed her sleeve over her face, wiping away tears of rage.

"Then we go public," Jason pressed. "Tell the world

McGinley is behind it. If we expose what he plans to do, he'll have to call it off, right?"

I shook my head. "He'd say it's Vanguard trying to set him up. He's spent months fueling people's fear of magic. You've seen the poll numbers. Who do you think the people will believe?"

"What about an electromagnetic pulse?" asked Lena.

"All of New Millennium's hardware servers are protected by nested faraday cages," said Talulah. "EMP wouldn't touch them, and Kiyoko is all wetware, not circuitry and hard drives."

"Does siren magic affect animals?" Jeneta was cradling her fire-spider in her lap.

"Nothing in *The Odyssey* talked about gulls drowning themselves or fish flopping to their deaths," said Jason.

"He won't limit the U.S. strike to New Millennium." Nidhi looked around the room. "If the goal is to solidify alliances with the United States, we have to suffer as much or more than any other nation. McGinley needs that horror and sympathy for when he seizes control of New Millennium and starts talking about making the world safe again."

"There are close to two million people living in and around Las Vegas alone," I said.

"This is insane." Jeneta sounded angry, but her eyes were damp. "They're going to murder millions of people, and for what?"

"For power and control." I thought back to my exchanges with Gutenberg. "And because people are afraid. McGinley sees that fear as an opportunity."

"What's going to happen?" asked Lex.

I smiled for her sake. "That's simple, kiddo. We're going to stop them."

Summary: The National Terrorism Advisory System (NTAS) has issued an Imminent Threat Alert. The Department of Homeland Security (DHS) has received credible warning of a terrorist attack against United States targets.

Duration: This alert will expire in one week. The alert may be extended if DHS acquires additional information.

Details:

- Members of the organization known as Vanguard are planning a large-scale magical attack against the United States, with possible coordinated attacks in other nations.
- The precise nature of the attack is unknown, but appears to involve one or more television, radio, or cellphone broadcasting stations.
- Vanguard traditionally targets nonmagical humans, particularly those who have spoken out publicly in support of regulation and security legislation regarding magic. Other targets may include magical humans and creatures who are perceived to sympathize with such efforts.
- This attack is believed to be planned for some time within the next forty-eight hours.

What To Do:

- Government facilities, national and historical landmarks, core infrastructure facilities, and other potential targets are advised to increase security for the duration of this alert.
- Avoid unnecessary travel, particularly to busy, crowded locations such as national parks, sports events, and major cities.
- Families and businesses should refer to the **DHS Emergency Preparedness Website** for guidance on creating an emergency plan.

- The fight against terror starts with you. If you see something suspicious, contact your local law enforcement office or call 911. Your vigilance could save lives.

Chapter 18

"I'm not ready for this."

"You never will be."

"Your faith is touching."

"It's nothing to do with faith, Isaac. No one is ever truly ready for times like this. We prepare ourselves the best we can, and we march out to face the enemy."

"I'm not much of a marcher."

"It was a metaphor."

"I thought the world would welcome us. Instead, they've spent the past year trying to crush us."

"Never discount hope, Isaac. Especially your own. Your fear is all too human. Accept it, but as you walk this path, let your hope guide you."

"And what if hope guides me off the edge of a cliff?"

"I said let hope guide you. I never said stop paying attention to where you're going."

"**Y**OU'RE OUT OF YOUR fucking mind," said Deb. "Derek Vaughn was on the committee that passed the RAMPART Act. He's part of the reason Nicola Pallas and who knows how many others have been rounded up like animals, and you want to ask him for help?"

"Vaughn voted against RAMPART," Jason pointed out.

"He's a politician. Isaac and Lena are wanted fugitives. Why the hell would you trust that weasel-dick?"

"Because Nicola has been dating that weasel-dick for the past two months," I said mildly.

The rest of the room went silent.

Talulah chuckled. "Good for her."

"Assuming he wasn't using her to get to the Porters," Deb said sullenly.

"It doesn't matter." I stood up and moved to the center of the living room. "We need Nicola's help, and he's the best lead we've got for reaching her. You're right, though. We have to be careful. The less Vaughn knows, the better. Talulah, can you secure a phone line?"

"In my sleep."

"I'll make the call," said Lena. "Derek knows me, and we don't want to give away that you're alive."

"Good." I checked the list I'd put together over breakfast. "Potts said they were working with people in China, France, Britain, and Afghanistan. Talulah, can you get a message to Shin-Tsu Chang? Give him a heads-up about Kiyoko and McGinley. Who do we know in France, Britain, and Afghanistan?"

"My mother is in Britain," Jeneta said quietly.

"Tell her to get out."

"You think McGinley will target his own allies?" asked Nidhi.

"I don't know! He might attack their enemies instead.

China and Japan have been rattling sabers at each other. Maybe he'll wipe out Tokyo as a favor." There were too many potential targets, too many possibilities.

"Let me talk to some friends," said Deb. "Put them on McGinley's trail. If we can get our claws on him, he'll tell us everything we need to know."

"Kiyoko will be protecting him, and he'll be shielded from magic," said Lena.

"Can he shield his scent? I know it's a long shot, but Vanguard has people on the East Coast."

"Do it." I picked up one of the disposable cellphones Talulah had bought. "Speaking of long shots . . ."

I wasn't surprised when a tinny voice said the number I was dialing had been disconnected. Getting Ponce de Leon's help would have been like bringing an Abrams tank to the Revolutionary War. But the old sorcerer had always valued his privacy, and he'd gone deeper into seclusion after Gutenberg's death. From what I knew, Ponce de Leon tended to sit back and let crises pass him by, like a squirrel hibernating through a harsh winter.

I hung up and handed the phone to Lena. "We could use some additional help."

She grinned. "I'm way ahead of you."

I'd testified to the Joint Committee on Magical Security that I didn't know the whereabouts of Bi Wei and her fellow students, and that much was true. I had no idea where they were currently located, nor did I have a reliable way of getting in touch with them.

They'd asked Lena the same questions. The only difference was that Lena had lied.

A half hour later, I sat with an untouched burger on my plate, watching as Talulah pulled up satellite imagery and military communications. She was working on a borrowed laptop, but had hooked the display up to the flat-screen television in the living room so everyone could see.

New Millennium was nothing but a pixelated blob. One of many steps Babs had taken to protect our privacy was to shield us from overhead photography, including drones, satellites, helicopters, and so on.

Jeneta plopped down beside me. Her smile held a hint of her old mischievousness. "I've been thinking. If this doesn't work, maybe we ought to we have a fallback plan."

My lips quirked, matching her grin. "I'm listening."

"How would you feel about colonizing Mars?"

"I'm listening very attentively."

"E-books aren't as limited as your dusty old paper books. I can do libriomancy on a cellphone, a tablet, anything that can display electronic books." She pointed to the television. "No more size limitations."

"I'd wondered about that," I admitted. "We never got the chance to really test what you can do ..." I trailed off, remembering why we'd been unable to finish exploring the possibilities of Jeneta's power. I noticed her father watching us from the corner. He rarely let his daughter out of his sight these days.

"When this is over, however it plays out, I want to break in—" She glanced at her father. "I mean, I want to rent an IMAX theater. Ms. Polk can work the projector. Put one of your science fiction books on the screen, and I'll pull out a ship capable of transporting the first group to Mars. Add some terraforming technology, and we could be living there within a year."

"You're talking about an awful lot of energy." I tapped the corner of my eye to remind her of the permanent scarring I'd suffered from trying to channel more magic than my body could handle. "No way. Think about what that would do to you."

"I'd need help," she admitted grudgingly. "But you've been working on that, right? Combining books for your Gateway Project. Why not combine libriomancers the same way, let them work together to reduce the strain on any one person?"

In the old days, before libriomancy, sorcerers had occasionally done exactly that. It wasn't something the Porters had ever really tried, in part because most libriomancers didn't work directly with magical energy. We needed our books as an intermediary. You'd have to have multiple libriomancers reaching into the same book, and there wasn't much benefit in having two people pull a magic sword from a story when one could do the same.

But a screen the size of a movie theater . . . I sat back, mentally cataloging the books we'd need to create a viable colony on Mars. If things went to hell, Mars might be safer than remaining on Earth. If we retreated to another planet, it would take decades for the rest of humanity to catch us. By then, we could have moved on to other worlds. "I wonder if there'd be any degradation in magical resonance from the hundred and forty million miles between Mars and all the readers and books back on Earth."

It was tempting as hell, both for the relative safety— and what did it say when trying to terraform and survive on another planet was the *safer* option?—and for the sheer awesomeness of going to Mars. I'd used magic to visit the moon, and that had been one of the most thrilling experiences of my life.

It had been immediately followed by one of the most terrifying experiences of my life, but still . . .

I shook my head. "I'm not ready to give up on this planet yet."

"Fine." She rolled her eyes. "So when do we leave for Vegas?"

"*We* don't," I said firmly, before her father could answer. "You're staying here with Jason."

She didn't argue. That, more than anything else, told me she hadn't fully recovered from everything she'd been through. A year ago, she would have argued with me on principle, secure in her teenage sense of immortality and invulnerability.

Instead, she asked, "How old do you have to be to start working at New Millennium?"

The question took me off guard. "I'm not sure."

"Well, check into it, will you? It would be nice to have a place where Dad and I didn't always have to watch our backs. After you kick McGinley's goons out of there, I mean."

I looked past her to Mmadukaaku. He'd never been comfortable with magic, and from the stiffness in his posture and the way he muttered to himself whenever he passed Deb, that hadn't changed.

"My daughter deserves security." He broke eye contact. "I've been trying to provide that for her."

"You've done great, Dad," said Jeneta. "I don't mean—"

He shook his head. "You shouldn't have to hide."

"Neither should you," she answered.

"You're both right." I stood to go, feeling far wearier than when I'd sat down. "I'll do what I can."

Nidhi found me out back a short time later. I sat on a squeaky wooden porch swing, an unopened book in my lap, looking out at a collection of bird feeders. They all bore metal shields to protect them from squirrels.

She sat down beside me without saying a word. After a while, she sighed and put an arm around my shoulders.

There was nothing romantic about it. Nidhi and I generally landed between friends and siblings on the relationship spectrum. But I found myself relaxing. Nidhi wasn't here to ask questions or press me for miracles. She was here to remind me we were in this together.

I handed her the book I'd been reading.

She opened the cover one-handed and flipped through the first pages. "There's no title."

"That's one of three copies of Johannes Gutenberg's autobiography. Would you make sure it's safe?"

"Of course."

There were plenty of biographies of Gutenberg out there, and most were woefully incomplete. You could hardly blame the authors. Gutenberg had done an excellent job faking his death back in 1468. He'd even gone back later to destroy his alleged gravesite as well.

Recent months had seen a surge in more "speculative" material on Gutenberg's life, some of it little more than tabloid nonsense slapped together to cash in on current interest. One edition went so far as to speculate that Gutenberg and Elvis Presley were one and the same. Another claimed he was the second coming of Christ. My favorite was a paranormal romance describing in lurid detail Gutenberg's affair with a vampiric Marilyn Monroe.

A man of Gutenberg's power, knowledge, and self-importance would never risk his story being lost to history and rumor. Nicola had discovered his autobiography a month after his death. She'd printed two copies for the Porters, then loaned me the original as part of an off-the-books research project.

Three copies weren't enough for traditional libriomancy, but there were other forms of book magic. I'd said once that all stories were magic. And all magic was story. This was Gutenberg's story, in his own words.

A million readers could imbue books with a great deal of power. A single reader . . . or writer . . . with enough power of their own might do the same.

Gutenberg had poured himself into this book. I'd read and reread it, adding my own magic. Five months later, Johannes Gutenberg had stirred from within the pages.

"Lena mentioned you'd been talking with him," said Nidhi.

"Sort of. It's not really *him*, you know? It's the collection of his experiences and impressions and emotions, as interpreted by the man himself. I think he tried to be as honest as he could, but he was also putting his best self forward for posterity. The end result . . . it might not be him, but it sounds like him. The same arrogance and experience. The same sadness. I'd left the book in my office in New Millennium. Babs or Kiyoko or whoever searched it must not have realized what it was."

"Could they have done anything with it if they had?"

"Probably not. I just don't want them to have it, you know?"

She watched a squirrel try to scramble up one of the birdfeeders, only to fall when it reached the metal cylinder halfway up the post. "What were you and Johannes talking about out here before I interrupted?"

"Choices. Consequences." Gutenberg had made mistakes over five hundred years, and people had died because of them. It had made him cautious. It had made him afraid.

How many people died as a result of my choice to help reveal magic to the world? How many would survive as a result of that same choice? How the hell was anyone supposed to solve that kind of equation?

"I changed the world," Gutenberg whispered. There was pride in his words, and fatigue as well. He had changed the world, and spent the rest of his life—half a millennium—managing the fallout from that change.

"You're not him," said Nidhi.

I was simultaneously reassured and annoyed by her words. "Not yet."

"Do you want to be?"

"I wanted to be a researcher. Look how that's turned out."

"Blaming yourself for all the evils of the world?" She clucked her tongue. "That kind of arrogance does sound like Gutenberg, I admit."

"Bite me."

She chuckled. "Your niece is adorable, by the way. Angie was helping her learn to ride a bike yesterday afternoon."

I smiled. "I wish I'd seen that."

"Johannes Gutenberg looked at the world as a whole. What was best for humanity? What was best for the Porters? Time and again, he chose safety and security over action and risk. The Chinese famine of 1958. The Holodomor in the Ukraine. Countless wars."

"He intervened in World War II," I pointed out.

"As I understand it, that was because of his fear of the atom bomb. He looked at events on a global scale, and he lost sight of individuals."

I reached up to take Smudge from the canopy over the swing. He'd been perched upside-down, warding off the mosquitoes. I carefully set him inside his cage. The snapped bar from Kiyoko's bullet had been soldered back into place, courtesy of Jason. "When we leave for New Millennium, will you keep an eye on things here?"

"Don't I always?"

"Jason's great, but he's in over his head. Toby doesn't

understand what's going on, and Jeneta understands too much."

She started to hand Gutenberg's autobiography back to me.

"I've read it too many times already." Whatever happened, she would keep the book safe.

Nidhi stood and grasped my forearm. "Before you go, make sure you go outside with Lex. Watch her on the bike. I've found that people fight better when we're reminded what we're fighting for."

RESEARCH PROPOSAL FOR MARTIAN COLONIZATION

By Jeneta Aboderin

Summary: I believe we can use libriomancy to build a human settlement on Mars.

Benefits: There are numerous benefits to building a human settlement on Mars.

1. Overpopulation. Earth has more than seven billion people. If we colonize other planets, we will reduce the population pressure on Earth.
2. Resources. According to Wikipedia, Mars has many valuable resources, including nickel, iron, and even gold. (https://en.wikipedia.org/wiki/Ore_resources_on_Mars)
3. Species Survival. 66 million years ago, an asteroid wiped out the dinosaurs. Humanity has to be prepared for another such event. We have technology and magic to protect our planet, but if that fails, colonizing other planets will make sure human beings survive.
4. Safety. The first group of colonists would be libriomancers and Porters and magical inhumans, who are best equipped to survive the hostile environment of Mars. This would let these people escape persecution on Earth.

Requirements: The following technology and equipment would need to be created using libriomancy.

1. A spacecraft small enough to be made from a projected e-book. The spacecraft should have

simple controls, a good fuel supply, enough room for a crew of at least 30 people, and enough speed to get to Mars quickly.

2. Right now, it takes ten minutes to send a signal to or from Mars. (https://mars.jpl.nasa.gov/MPF/imp/faq.html) An ansible device from the works of Ursula Le Guin or another SF author would allow reliable, instantaneous communication between Earth and Mars.

3. Terraforming. Books should be reviewed to find the best terraforming technology that's safe, efficient, and effective, with no damaging side effects.

4. Investigate the possibility of nanotech fabricators or other miniature construction robots to assist with the building process.

Once the colony is established, we could use a portal from Isaac Vainio's Gateway Project to transport food, water, books, and other supplies.

<u>It's very important that a full electronic library be included with the initial shipment!</u>

Proposed Colonists:

1. At least ten libriomancers, including one who can perform magic with e-books.

2. Vampires who can survive without oxygen, and who won't go blood-crazy and kill everyone.

3. Trained astronauts and scientists. (Magic users, if possible!)

4. At least two doctors.

5. One poet or writer (for sending stories back to Earth).

Chapter 19

I ASKED JENETA TO equip us before we left, so Talulah and I could preserve as much of our strength and magic as possible.

She began by replacing one of Lena's bokken with the same version of Excalibur we'd used before. Lena kept the healing scabbard, and I took the healing cordial for myself. Everyone else was also equipped with healing magic of one form or another.

Jeneta then conjured up potions from *The Complete Short Stories of H. G. Wells*. The story in question was "The New Accelerator," and the potion would essentially give us the ability to stop time while we retook New Millennium.

She also supplied us with a set of ballistic vests. Kevlar with ceramic plate inserts should slow down Kiyoko's enchanted ammo. There were a handful of other goodies, including my compact mirror gateway, which Lena had returned to me. I tucked everything into an old messenger bag I'd borrowed from Jason.

Talulah had a Bluetooth earpiece in her right ear, and

a large keyboard-looking thing made of plastic, chrome, and LED lights strapped across her shoulder like an electric guitar.

"Hacker's best friend," she said, noticing my gaze. "Cyberpunk has the best toys. This should help me pinpoint the system hosting the IAS software and keep Kiyoko occupied."

We gathered in the backyard to say good-bye, where we found Bi Wei standing in the shade of a weeping willow tree, watching the birds. Before anyone could react, Lena was bounding across the yard to greet her with a hug. She dragged Bi Wei over by the hand to introduce her to the rest of our group.

"I'm glad your people are safe," I said. "And doubly glad for your help, thank you."

Bi Wei smiled. "Given what Lena told me, this sounded like it could be as educational as our last collaboration."

"Educational." I snorted. "That's one word for it."

Physically, Bi Wei was much the same as I remembered. Young and physically slight, she wore a sleeveless purple dress with gold and blue lines curling about in fractal designs. Large designer sunglasses covered her eyes.

Magically, she was all but unrecognizable as the woman Lena had helped to draw forth from her thousand-year imprisonment. After so many years in isolation, the Students of Bi Sheng had chosen to establish a permanent telepathic connection, ensuring that they would never again be alone. If one were to die, their memories and experiences would be preserved.

Bi Wei was a spiderweb of magic. Threads of energy my mind interpreted as text were woven through her body and stretched into the distance. It reminded me of Kiyoko. I was relying on that similarity, hoping Bi Wei would be able to nullify her in a way the rest of us couldn't.

I turned to Jeneta. "Keep Nkiruka close. If she gets twitchy, round everyone up and get the hell out of here."

"No problem. Deb gave me a number to call. She said they'd help us disappear."

Nidhi stepped into Lena's embrace and whispered something before giving her a long, deep kiss. She finally broke away, then hugged me as well. "Keep each other safe."

"We will." I turned to Jason next. "Thank you for this." I gestured toward the yard and his ex-husband's house. "Tell your ex I'm going to pay to replace that frying pan."

Jeneta rolled her eyes. "How was I supposed to know fire-spiders would burn through the non-stick coating? I'm used to cast iron."

Toby grabbed my hand and squeezed. His lips tightened, and his eyes shifted to the side like he was searching for words.

"I know," I said, returning the handshake. "Toby, if things go south, talk to Mom and Dad for me. Tell them what really happened."

"Hell, no," he said gruffly. "Fix this mess, then explain it yourself."

"Toby . . ."

He nodded and looked away. "Yah, I'll tell 'em."

I hugged Lex, shook hands with Angie, then walked over to where Deb was sitting on the porch swing, dipping crickets into a small tub of ketchup. "You ready?"

She flicked another cricket into her mouth and chewed noisily. "I've been ready, hon. It's not like I've got anyone to say good-bye to."

Jeneta reached into her e-reader and withdrew a glass bottle from *Through the Looking Glass*, which she handed to Lena. Lena raised it in a toast and took several deep swallows, then passed it to Talulah. By the time it was Deb's turn, Lena had shrunk down to six inches tall.

I sat down to change shoes, lacing my sneakers around my neck and pulling on the seven-league boots I'd used to flee Las Vegas. I held very still as Lena climbed up onto my shoulder. It would be awkward as hell if my feet twitched and propelled me a half-mile away.

Talulah climbed into my shirt pocket, while a miniature Bi Wei floated on a gust of air to land lightly on my other shoulder. Deb climbed up next to Lena.

"Everybody hold on tight," I said, and started walking.

With each step devouring roughly twenty miles, we covered the 1900 miles from Grand Rapids to New Millennium in minutes.

Removing the boots and backtracking the two miles I'd overshot took a half hour. It was much simpler to stride at magically relativistic speeds across the continent, letting the boots worry about things like rocks and hills and rivers, not to mention wind resistance that should have stripped the flesh from my bones after the first step.

We circled around and settled in a hundred yards from the gate. New graffiti marred the walls, and the lights illuminated blackened patches of earth. The security measures I remembered were still in place, and there were devourers in the wall, just as we'd seen at the prison. One of the guards carried some sort of handheld scanner that reminded me of a Geiger counter.

"They've tightened things up," Lena said.

‹Testing,› said Talulah. ‹Can you all hear me?›

We each checked in, joining Talulah's mental conference call in a confusing jumble of overlapping voices.

"They're scanning for magic, right?" asked Deb.

"Among other things." The empath working security would pick up on our emotions as well.

I set my passengers on the ground and took what remained of the second *Through the Looking Glass* potion from my bag. Moments later, Smudge and I had joined the others as Smurf-scale miniatures of ourselves.

We jogged past enormous white bursage and creosote bushes, making our way toward the gate. The desert shrubs were the size of houses, and the gray cactus mouse we startled probably weighed as much as I did in this form.

"Keep an eye out for snakes," I said. "Shrikes too. Also scorpions and burrowing owls."

Lena punched my shoulder, just hard enough to shut me up.

At this size, it took another twenty minutes just to reach the side of the road. Every time I looked at New Millennium, I imagined a countdown clock, the digital numbers ticking down one by one like a Hollywood bomb.

"Over, under, or through?" asked Lena.

"I am *not* going in the way I came out," I said with a mock shudder. "The wards will stop us from flying in. I'm sure they're wise to the tunnel approach, too."

"Waltzing through the front door it is, then."

"I was thinking about hitching a ride." A line of dust in the distance heralded our way in. We crept as close to the gates as we dared and waited beneath a blue-green bush with thorns the size of claymores. "Bi Wei, will you be safe here?"

She'd brought out a velvet pouch of dominos, and was arranging them carefully in the dirt for a game I didn't recognize. "I'll be waiting."

"Wait, she's not coming with us?" asked Deb.

"That's not why I asked her here, no." To Bi Wei, I said, "If you don't hear from us in two hours, do whatever it takes to tear this place to the ground. If the siren assault begins before that and we can't stop it—"

"I'll do what I can. And I'll be waiting to try to help Kiyoko."

A National Guard truck approached, painted in desert camouflage. Potts was bringing in military reinforcements. "Angels and ministers of grace, defend us," I muttered.

"Hamlet, right?" said Talulah.

"Yah. Also McCoy from *Star Trek IV*." We waited for the truck to stop at the gate, then sprinted onto the road. I boosted Lena onto the right rear tire. She gripped the cracks in the tread to climb higher, then stabbed one of her bokken into the wheel well, hooked her knees over the handle, and dropped upside down to grab my hands.

Her bokken was already sending out branches. Lena pulled me up beside her, then did the same for Talulah and Deb. We pressed flat as the wood grew into a large, curved cage. From the outside, if anyone spotted us, it should look like a bit of tumbleweed stuck in the well.

That was the easy part.

One of the guards circled the truck and opened the back. Another was talking to the driver, checking paperwork and asking about their orders, what equipment they'd brought, how long they intended to be on-site, and so on.

"Anything magical?"

"No, ma'am," said the driver.

As boots crunched along the pavement, I retrieved a book from my borrowed messenger bag.

"Captain Underpants?" Lena whispered.

I plucked a ring from the pages. "The books straddle the line between comic books and novels. That makes them harder to use, but the popularity of the series means there's a stronger pool of belief, which balances it out."

"Hold on. I'm sensing something near the back." A woman dropped to one knee and peered around. She was better equipped than I expected, with both a mundane semiautomatic and a JG-367, currently set to disintegration mode. In addition to her own inherent empathy, she wore an amulet from Tamora Pierce's *In the Hand of the Goddess*, allowing her to see magic. She clicked a flashlight on and shone it beneath the truck.

As quickly as I could, I pointed the Hypno-Ring from *The Adventures of Captain Underpants*. "You were mistaken. There's nothing here. You can go about your business. Move along."

The woman straightened. "Looks like I was mistaken. There's nothing here."

"You know the drill," said a bored-sounding man from the other side of the truck. "Let me take a look, too. Back up a bit?"

Lena grimaced in pain as a second set of boots approached. Smudge scampered from my body, retreating to the back of the cage. The magic of my ring started to fade.

It was a logical setup, but annoying as hell. One guard wore the magic-dampener, while the other carried the magic-sensing amulet, enchanted pistol, and other goodies. As long as they kept their distance from one another, they could cover the other's vulnerabilities.

I'd broken one of those pearls before, back in Virginia. I did it faster this time, though it was no less painful. Once I'd torn the magic-suppressing field aside, I repeated the same hypnotrick I'd used on his partner.

Someone would eventually realize the amulet had gone dead, but I intended to be finished before that happened.

After what felt like hours, the truck pulled forward into New Millennium and drove slowly around curved roads until we reached Scot Tower, the admin building. The instant we stopped, Lena pushed the branches aside, opening a door from our cage. She lowered us to the ground and jumped after us, broken branches showering around her. We waited in the shadows beneath the truck as uniformed soldiers climbed from the back.

"Welcome to New Millennium, gentlemen." The voice belonged to Russell Potts. I fought the urge to vaporize the man right then. "You're here to bolster our own security staff. We want to be certain nothing happens to our guests from the United Nations. We've been advised of a potential insider attack."

Well, he wasn't wrong. I gritted my teeth and gathered up pebble-sized grains of sand while we listened.

"You should have been briefed on our facility and the abilities of our various enemies," Potts continued. "You'll be outfitted with additional equipment before beginning your rounds. On behalf of the Department of Homeland Security, I want to personally thank you for your service."

He led the men away, probably to receive their black pearls and enchanted handguns and whatever else Potts had decided they needed. Or more likely, he'd keep the pearls for himself and his chosen collaborators. If anger and outrage were what he was after, the murder of our National Guardsmen would be a bonus.

I crept to the edge of the truck to look around. Armed guards stood at the entrance of Scot Tower, one human and one sparkler. Barriers blocked several intersections. Soldiers patrolled in small groups along the edge of the roads. They'd turned New Millennium into a military base on lockdown.

‹I've made contact with Vince and Charles,› said Talulah. ⟨*They're in research. They've got a security escort, and their access to New Millennium systems has been restricted to almost nothing.*⟩

⟨*Give me a direct link to them?*⟩

⟨*Done.*⟩

⟨*Vince, Charles, this is Isaac. Has Talulah filled you in on the plan?*⟩

⟨*Hell, yeah!*⟩ exclaimed Vince. ⟨*Nice to know you're not dead, Boss!*⟩

⟨*I'm rather happy about it myself. Before we go any further, I need to make something clear. I'm not your boss anymore, and I won't order you to do this. You're free to say no, and you'll probably be a lot safer if you do.*⟩

⟨*The hell with that,*⟩ spat Charles.

⟨*What he said,*⟩ Vince added a half-second later.

⟨*We don't know exactly where they're working to bring the IAS project online. The code has to be pulled out of several books, then compiled through a program Talulah wrote. Kiyoko can't run it herself; she needs additional hardware, probably a group of high-speed servers. Talulah's going to work on finding those servers. Once she does, Lena and Deb will try to physically destroy them. Talulah will do what she can to fry them remotely.*⟩

⟨*Where are the sirens?*⟩ asked Vince.

⟨*That's one of several potential flaws with our plan. We don't know yet. I'm hoping to get to Babs so I can use her security cameras and other Big Brother tech to find them. Talulah should be joining you in research shortly. She'll help take out your babysitters. Your job is to keep her safe and give her time to get into the network.*⟩

I took out the potions Jeneta had created from H. G. Wells. "Don't try to run or move too quickly. Magic gives us some leeway from friction, but this potion isn't as forgiving as some. If you push it, you'll burn your clothes and skin right off."

"How long do those last?" asked Deb.

"Maybe twenty minutes, subjectively speaking. Only a second or two will have passed in real time."

"Stay away from any guards wearing those magic dampers," said Talulah. "Minimum safe distance is about three feet before they interfere with your mojo."

"Invisibility?" suggested Deb.

Talulah answered before I could. "It would block us from cameras and mundane vision, but it won't screen our thoughts and emotions, and it wouldn't surprise me if they've set up infrared scanners at the doors."

"We'll be moving too fast to see anyway," I said.

Lena unsheathed Excalibur. "Ready when you are."

"Everybody remember Newton's second law." I handed out the potions. ‹On my count. One . . . two . . . three.›

We walked out from beneath the truck. I put the few remaining drops of potion onto Smudge's mandibles to bring him into synch with me. I stripped away the magic of Wonderland, restoring all of us to normal size. The guards stood like statues frozen in time.

Talulah set off in a slow jog toward research while I headed for the front doors of Scot Tower. I circled around the guards and applied a gentle kick to the edge of the door. The metal hinges shattered.

Newton's second law: force equals mass times acceleration. Our mass was unchanged, but our velocity and acceleration had increased enough to inflict unimaginable damage to others, and to ourselves if we weren't careful.

I slowly pulled the door out of its frame and slipped inside. I circled past armed guards and other New Millennium personnel, being careful to stay out of range of those with magic-dampers. I reached the stairwell and destroyed that door as well.

Moving at this speed was the next best thing to having

superpowers. I wondered if you could really run across water like speedsters did in the comics, but that experiment would have to wait. ‹*I'm inside Admin. How are you doing, Talulah?*›

‹*Just got to Franklin Tower. Once I get to my office and jack in, I'll have to wait for this potion to wear off. I can't interface with the system at this speed.*›

‹*Understood.*›

I reached the fourth floor, where two men in military uniforms stood outside the outer door to Babs' office. Both wore magic-dampeners.

I pulled a straw from my back pocket, along with one of the sand-pebbles I'd gathered outside. It had expanded along with me and my clothes, caught up in the wake when I stripped away my shrinking magic.

I approached the first guard and dropped to one knee, careful to stay out of range of those damn pearls. After tucking the pebble into the straw, I lined the end up with the M4 assault rifle gripped in his hands.

This was going to be so cool.

A puff of breath launched the pebble. It shot out, struck the center of the rifle . . . and stopped, suspended in relativistically slow time.

Friction had melted half the straw. I trimmed off the end with a pocketknife and repeated the shot on the next guard's rifle. I used a second straw to fire pebbles at their holstered sidearms. Once time sped up, the kinetic energy in those tiny pebbles should make a wreck of their weapons. I could already see cracks starting to spread through the metal of the first M4.

As for getting in, I picked a spot on the wall about four feet to the left of the door, away from the guards and their magic-dampers, and kicked.

Cinder blocks crumbled inward. I continued to kick, widening the hole until it was large enough for me to squeeze through. I had to shift a little to the left to avoid one of the steel studs.

I pushed broken cinder blocks and drywall out of the way and crawled through the wall. The outer office—Kiyoko's office—was empty. The inner door was cracked open.

‹*Isaac, I'm in position, ready to plug in and raise hell. Would it be wrong to draw a Sharpie doodle on Charles while I'm waiting for this to wear off?*›

‹*Yes, it would. Wait, what kind of doodle?*› Smudge squirmed in his cage, anxious and glowing red. ‹*I'm at Babs' office. My fire-spider has a bad feeling about this.*› I peeked through the doorway. ‹*Aw, crap.*›

‹*What is it?*›

Babs was seated at her desk. Russell Potts stood looking over her shoulder at something on the computer screen. Behind them, toward the corner of the room, Kiyoko held a pistol to a seated, handcuffed woman I guessed was Darlene Jackson-Palmer. Her eyes were red, and she wore a magic-damping amulet.

Darlene's left eye was puffed like a pair of leeches. Blood dripped from her split lower lip. The knuckles of Kiyoko's left hand were swollen and bloody.

‹*Kiyoko's here. She's been torturing Darlene Jackson-Palmer to force Babs to cooperate. Darlene's wearing a magic-damper. I can't reach them without losing my speed, and I don't think I could take Kiyoko in a fair fight.*› I considered shooting a pebble at Kiyoko's gun, or at Kiyoko herself, but in either case I risked the gun discharging and killing Darlene. I studied the effects of the pearl more closely. ‹*They've modified the magic-damper. The effects aren't radiating out from the pearl. It's generating a spherical shield. Anything passing through gets nullified, but inside the sphere, Kiyoko's still hooked up to her clones.*›

‹Can you tear it down?›

‹I think—wait, no. Damn, that's clever. If I'm reading this right, the pearl is held in some kind of stasis. It's in the process of exploding. That shield is the magical shock wave. If I break it, the physical shock wave kills Darlene, Kiyoko, and possibly everyone else in the room.›

‹Who the hell came up with that?›

‹Babs, probably.› I edged around the desk to see what she'd been working on. ‹Double-crap. They know we're here.›

‹How?›

‹It looks like they set up a wider perimeter outside New Millennium, an invisible infrared fence or some such, and we tripped it. As soon as you're back to normal operating speed, let Bi Wei know she might be getting company.›

Heavy-duty headphones hung around Babs' neck. Potts clutched a matching pair in one hand. I studied the other windows on Babs' computer. ‹She's got a sound-editing program running and a microphone plugged into her system.›

‹Is it IAS?›

‹Doesn't look like it.›

The audio clip was a jagged graph on the screen, one minute and four seconds long. I sorted through the notes on her desk until I found what looked like a script. ‹It's voice masking software. They're prepping a speech, claiming this is retribution from Vanguard, the Porters, and all oppressed creatures who feel it's time to rise up against humanity.›

‹What are you going to do?›

‹It's Vegas. I'm going to gamble.› I grabbed a pen and paper from Babs' desk. The ballpoint immediately tore through the paper. The pencil I tried next simply broke. I found a fine-tip Sharpie that functioned, more or less, at superspeed. It went dry after a single sentence.

"Seriously?" Moving at superspeed, the wicking action couldn't draw ink to the pen's tip fast enough. I scrounged through Babs' desk, then Kiyoko's in the outer office, gathering more Sharpies. I tucked the finished note into Babs' hand and turned my attention back to Kiyoko.

Anything within that shield was unaffected. It would only nullify magic passing through the barrier.

I pulled out the compact mirror. Time to try some nonlinear thinking. If the glass had been larger, I could have tried to reach through to take the gun from her hand, but I didn't have the books I'd need to create another portal.

On the other hand, I might be able to make this one effectively *smaller*.

I grabbed the Sharpie from Babs' desk and started blacking out the outer edge of the mirror.

MAGICAL BLAZE IN THE WEST BANK CONTINUES TO SPREAD

In the past twenty-four hours, a fast-growing blaze has destroyed approximately two hundred square miles in the West Bank. Efforts to combat the flames have been ineffective, leading many to believe the fire is magical in nature.

Spokesmen for both the Israeli and Palestinian governments deny responsibility for the blaze, which has destroyed several Israeli settlements and driven more than fifty thousand Palestinians from their homes. Both governments blame the other for igniting a magical war using weapons they couldn't control.

The flames are centered in the northern part of the West Bank, and have thus far not crossed the Jordan River.

At approximately one a.m. local time, fourteen hours after the start of the fire, Palestinian militants began launching rockets into Israel. The Israeli military has gathered near the border, but appear to be holding back until the path of the flames can be determined.

One Israeli official threatened to refuse to allow Palestinian refugees to cross the border if the attacks continue, saying, "For every rocket that lands on our soil, a hundred Palestinians will die by fire."

Israel's Prime Minister was quick to disavow that threat, but did go on to say that the need for increased security would hinder their efforts to help Israeli settlers and Palestinian refugees fleeing the flames.

Many nations are offering aid, equipment, and personnel to assist in fighting the blaze and helping refugees. The Porters have dispatched a libriomancer from Denmark who will attempt to use magic against the fire.

Exact casualty figures are unknown, but official estimates put the death toll as high as five thousand.

Chapter 20

BY THE TIME I finished working, the speed potion was beginning to wear off. I stood up, wiped
my palms on my vest, locked the door connecting
Babs' office to Kiyoko's, and waited.

I heard a low click from Babs' desk. A second followed, then a third as her fingers slowly struck the keys.

Kiyoko turned her head toward me. Out in the hallway, two guards swore as their weapons exploded. I also
had the satisfaction of seeing Russell Potts jump so hard
he fell on his ass. The desk blocked me from seeing
whether my sudden appearance had managed to make
him piss himself.

"Hi," I said brightly. "I'm here to give you the chance
to surrender. I figure it's what the Doctor would do."

"What doctor?" Potts snapped as he recovered. "Who
are you talking about?"

"Doctor Who?" I threw up my hands in exaggerated
disgust. "Never mind."

The gun at Darlene's head never moved. Kiyoko
cocked her head to one side. "I'm sensing an attempted

intrusion into our systems. I presume that's Talulah Polk's doing? Order her to cease her efforts and surrender herself."

"So you can kill millions of people? I'm not going to—"

"You can't bluff me, Isaac Vainio. I've been inside your brain. I've seen your memories, the way you think, the lines you can and can't cross. I know you've snuck more of your friends in to help cause mischief, and that you're probably planning another clever quip right now to mask your fear and anger about losing New Millennium."

"I didn't lose it," I muttered. "It was right where I left it."

She smiled. "I know you more intimately than Lena. I know you've touched death before, and that the threat of death won't make you cooperate. Not your death, at least. But you have a chauvinistic protective streak toward women, one that was compounded by your failures with Jeneta Aboderin."

‹*Found it!*› Talulah exclaimed. ‹*The IAS is running on a server bank in admin. Lena, Deb, you're up.*›

‹*Be careful,*› I said. Sweat trickled down the center of my back. My heart was pounding like I'd just run a marathon. I did my best to match Kiyoko's smile. "When they pulled you out of that book and programmed you, whose idea was it to make you talk so much?"

"You can't stop this, Isaac," said Potts.

I pretended to stifle a yawn, then jerked a thumb at Kiyoko. "She's scary. You're just embarrassing yourself. You're strong and tough and evil, sure, but Kiyoko could snap every bone in your body without breaking a sweat. So why don't you shut up and let the grown-ups talk?"

He scowled and started to respond.

"Isaac's verbal barbs are how he masks his helplessness," Kiyoko said. "Engaging him is counterproductive. He won't assist us until I've demonstrated the consequences of refusing, just as I did before."

I took a step toward her and Darlene.

The gun swung around toward me, and I froze. Kiyoko nodded once, then aimed the barrel back at Darlene.

"Isaac, *please*," whispered Babs.

"All right, stop! You win." I raised my hands and inched closer. To Darlene, I said, "I won't let her hurt you."

"I wish it were that easy." Kiyoko sounded genuinely regretful. "The problem is, you've gotten out of similar situations before. It's given you a sense of invulnerability, an irrational refusal to accept that you might lose. Unfortunately for Ms. Jackson-Palmer, there's one effective way to shatter that overconfidence."

She pointed the gun at Darlene's leg.

Darlene closed her eyes. Potts clenched his teeth.

"No!" Babs stood and reached toward Kiyoko. Electricity surged from one of her rings, only to dissolve when it struck the magic-absorbing field surrounding them.

Kiyoko pulled the trigger. The walls amplified the thunderous crack of the gunshot. Darlene screamed.

Blood darkened Kiyoko's shirt. She staggered against the wall. The gun slipped from her hand.

"Isaac?" Babs stared at the bullet hole in my vest.

"I'm all right." I tugged open one of the Velcro pouches on the front of my vest and carefully removed the compact mirror. "The bullet was coming out of my vest, not going in."

Russell Potts launched himself toward the gun. I started to reach for the magic of Babs' enchanted rings, but she was quicker. She caught him by the wrist and collar and spun, smacking him face-first into her desk.

Power crackled down her arms. Potts doubled over and collapsed to the floor, his body twitching and spasming.

I stripped away the magic binding Kiyoko's weapon and my mirror. I'd blackened everything but a small circle at the center, roughly the size of the gun barrel. I kept part of my attention on Kiyoko as she slid down the wall. "I opened a portal into the pistol. The bullet went into that portal and came out through this mirror."

"How?" asked Babs. "Her shield . . ."

"Blocked incoming magic, like your lightning bolt. Gateway doesn't work like that. It's not a linear journey. Have you ever read *A Wrinkle in Time*? It's like that, just two points bypassing the space in between. The bullet left my mirror and passed through the shield. That would have stripped off any enchantments, but the bullet itself kept going."

One of the guards pounded the door. They had free run of Kiyoko's office, thanks to the hole I'd kicked through the outer wall, but I trusted Babs' security to keep them out of here.

Babs held up the note I'd written. "You're sure about this?"

"I'm sure, and thank you. There's no way I could have taken you, Potts, and Kiyoko together."

Kiyoko was no longer breathing.

Babs freed her sister and carefully removed the shielding pearl from around Darlene's neck. She dropped it into a padded metal box. The effects disappeared. Babs immediately activated another of her tattoos and used it to heal the worst of Darlene's injuries.

I crouched next to Potts. "I need to talk to him."

Babs waved a hand, and his seizures eased. Blood bubbled from his nose. He sat up, his back against the desk, and glared at me. "You're monsters."

I stepped to the side, staying out of his reach. "The

thing is, I've been trying really hard *not* to be a monster. But if you don't call this thing off right now? Then yah, I may have to get monstrous."

"He can't," said Babs. "Kiyoko is coordinating things. She's got one clone with the sirens. I don't know where they're being kept. Four others are calibrating the software for the broadcast. She'll have sent more to find out what happened here, and to deal with us."

"The IAS project?" I asked.

"I finished Talulah's work." Babs slumped. "It's loaded and ready to launch."

‹Deb and Lena, did you catch that? You're going to be outnumbered four to two.›

‹Maybe we should wait for Kiyoko to gather a few more clones to make it fair?› Deb quipped.

‹Don't get cocky.› To Babs, I asked, "Do you know who they're targeting?"

"China. Iraq. Palestine. Saudi Arabia. Denmark. Russia."

"Jesus," I whispered.

"You're both traitors," Potts spat. The pounding outside had grown louder. It sounded like they were smashing furniture against the door. "Today's attack will kill between one and two million people in the short term. In the long run, it will *save* tens of millions. It will put America at the head of an international power bloc, one that will keep creatures like you in their place."

I was trembling with the effort to stop myself from physically attacking the man. I jammed my fists beneath my arms to control it. "Creatures like us?"

"You're not human. Neither of you." He looked past me to Babs.

There was no hesitation in his answer. Nothing I could say or do was going to change his mind. I reached for a book. "Where are the sirens?"

He spat. A glob of spittle and blood struck my pant leg.

"All right." I touched the book's magic and prepared to rip the truth from his thoughts.

Smudge burst into flame.

Something hit the window hard enough to rattle the glass. Another impact followed less than a second later. The third strike punched a small hole through the window and the closed blinds.

Potts jerked and collapsed.

"Get down!" Babs dragged her sister to the floor. A second series of gunshots struck the window. I dropped flat just as the next bullet broke through. It buried itself in the wall, directly behind where I'd been standing.

"Kiyoko?" I guessed.

"It has to be. The windows are bulletproof. From the angle she'd need to hit Potts, she must be firing from another tower, hitting the exact same spot with each bullet until she breaks through. Nobody else could pull that off. She must have another camera in here, helping her aim. I thought I'd found them all."

I dragged my bookbag off the desk and hastily crafted a shield that would protect me from gunfire. I crawled over to check on Potts. Despite the blinds and the distance, Kiyoko's bullet had struck him in the center of the forehead. His dead eyes were frozen in anger.

The guards outside must have heard the shots, because they'd stopped trying to break in. "Babs, how much trouble can you cause for Kiyoko from here?"

A staccato burst of gunfire destroyed the monitor on her desk. Babs yanked open the bottom drawer and pulled out several hardcover books. She used the first to create a tablet computer, and the second for a pair of silver revolvers, one of which she handed to her sister.

"Let's find out." She raised the gun and closed her

eyes. Magic crept over the barrel, guiding her aim up and to the right. She squeezed the trigger, blowing a four-inch hole through the wall. She raised her head and waited, but there were no more gunshots from outside. "Guess that was the last camera."

I pointed to the tablet. "Does that thing have a USB port?" When she nodded, I handed her a black flash drive. "You had an audio file queued up and ready to go. If Kiyoko starts to broadcast, play this instead."

Babs held up the crumpled note I'd written. "Thank you, Isaac."

"What did he write?" asked Darlene.

"I told her I understood why she'd helped Potts and McGinley, and that I needed her help to retake control of our home." I approached the door. The outer office was quiet. Babs pressed a button beneath her desk, and the lock clicked. I cracked open the door and peeked into Kiyoko's office. The room was empty. "Lock it behind me."

I headed toward the closest stairwell. ⟨*Talulah, I need a status update.*⟩

⟨*Charles is at the Library Tower. He had the bright idea to create a dowsing rod to search for the sirens.*⟩

If he made the rod sensitive enough, it would pick up even small bodies of water, including any tanks for holding captive sirens. ⟨*Good thinking, but they've probably shielded the sirens against magical detection.*⟩

⟨*That's what I told him,*⟩ said Vince.

Charles cut in. ⟨*Better than sitting around doing nothing. In my day, we didn't wait for someone else to get the job done.*⟩

⟨*Both of you focus on your work,*⟩ said Talulah. ⟨*You're giving me a headache. Vince is prepping a surprise to keep everyone out of Research. Lena and Deb have reached the server room. They're in a standoff with*⟩

the Kiyokos. I've been able to get intermittent images out of the security cameras. I think Kiyoko has reinforcements heading that way.

⟨*What's the shortest route to the server room?*⟩

I spun and started to run, following Talulah's mental directions. Alarms rang out around me. Kiyoko began speaking over the PA system, her steady, reassuring voice filling the building. "New Millennium is on secure lockdown. Security personnel should report to emergency stations. All others, please remain where you are. Lock your doors and remain calm."

I swung open a door and took a bullet in the throat. Without magic, Kiyoko's shot would have gone straight through.

"Sorry, I'm in a hurry." I reached for the text that controlled her psychic connection to the other clones.

Her foot hit my jaw like a wrecking ball. By the time my vision cleared, Kiyoko stood over me with a knife in one hand.

"I have access to all Porter catalogs and databases," she said as she brought the tip of the blade to my chest. "This appears to be a personal shield unit from *Dune*. Such shields are vulnerable to slower attacks."

I grabbed her wrist, but she was stronger than she had any right to be. The tip gradually slid through the shield, then punctured my skin.

I abandoned finesse and tore viciously through the Japanese characters of her magic. She screamed. I levered the knife away and punched her in the nose.

Kiyoko didn't move. Whatever I'd done to her was the equivalent of running an eggbeater inside her skull. It wouldn't affect the other clones, but this one was nothing but an empty shell.

I tossed the knife away. I'd be hearing that scream in my nightmares for years.

She'd probably seen me coming on another of the security cameras. I took out *Small Favor* and poked a finger into the text like a kid sneaking frosting from a cake. The character of Harry Dresden was a wizard, and in Jim Butcher's universe, being a wizard meant nearby technology tended to fail. Tapping into that effect should take out nearby cameras.

‹*Talulah, we know the targets. Any chance you could run a separate instance of the IAS software?*›

‹*Working on it, but it would be a lot easier if Kiyoko would stop trying to fry my systems.*›

Gunfire all but deafened me. I heard Lena cry out, followed by the thump of wood against flesh. A woman screamed. I couldn't tell who.

I grabbed two paperbacks from my bag and hurried around the corner. Deb and Lena stood in the hallway, battling to reach the server room.

Lena must have created another sapling to try to breach the door. She'd gone all out this time. The tree was eight inches thick and continued to grow, roots crumpling the floor while branches tore the ceiling. The thick metal door was bowed inward. Another cluster of branches held a clone two feet off the ground, her limbs twined in wood.

Bullets spat from behind the door. Dark blood soaked Deb's thigh. Lena gripped Excalibur in one hand and the scabbard in the other. A bullet struck her shoulder, but even as it tore through wood and flesh, the scabbard's healing magic flowed over the wound, pulling muscle and skin back into place.

‹*Kiyoko and a group of at least ten armed soldiers are trying to break into Research,*› said Talulah. ‹*She knows where we are. I'm not sure how long we can keep them out. I'm going to try—*›

‹*You keep working,*› said Vince. ‹*I've got this.*›

‹*What are you—ooh, nice. Quarantine override. We've got doors slamming and locking all through the tower. That should slow them down.*›

Another Kiyoko stepped through a broken door at the end of the hall. I hurled a gateway from Myke Cole's *Control Point* past Lena and Deb. Three gunshots rang out, but the bullets vanished through the portal. Instead of using it to slice Kiyoko in half like I'd done with the *Kagan* days earlier, I forced the gateway around her like a blanket, sending her through to the other side.

As the "other side" was a nonexistent fictional world, it effectively erased her from existence.

"What took you so long?" Deb shouted. "Did you stop for lunch on the way?"

I stopped before reaching the doorway. Having failed to kill me in the stairwell, Kiyoko would almost certainly have switched to those enchanted bullets to make sure she penetrated my shield. "Call off the attack, Kiyoko. This can't work. Too many people know the truth. We can help you, but you have to end this."

The gunfire stopped. I blinked and turned to Lena, who shrugged. I wished I'd been able to read *All of One*, the book Kiyoko had come from. Was she independent enough to recognize a losing battle and surrender, or would her orders force her to fight to her own death?

I cast a quick spell on Smudge and opened his cage. He scurried down my leg, now invisible. "Go find someplace warm to hide, buddy."

The oak creaked and bowed, further crumpling the door. Lena risked a quick glance through the opening, then beckoned me over. I saw Kiyoko—one of them— tossing a semiautomatic handgun to the floor. I yanked on her psychic connection to her clones, tying myself into that mental network.

I saw through their eyes. I saw myself standing in the

hallway. Another Kiyoko worked in a darkened room by several large tanks, each one containing a living siren. I saw unfamiliar faces and locations, scenes from this country and others.

Three clones waited in the server room, hidden from sight. I saw their plan to kill us, retake Babs Palmer's office, and lock Talulah out of the network. They had deliberately stalled Lena and Deb, knowing I would join them. Knowing they would have the opportunity to kill us all at once.

My mind went numb, as if someone had poured liquid helium into my skull. Kiyoko collapsed in front of me. She had voluntarily ended her life, trying to take me with her. I barely pulled free. Before I could shout a warning, the clone trapped in the young oak tree turned her head and said, *"Sleep."*

A magically created being shouldn't be able to perform libriomancy. Everyone knew that, but I watched the power of that word, drawn from Stephen King's *Firestarter* by another libriomancer and stored in Kiyoko's memory, slam into Lena, Deb, and myself.

I did my best to claw through Kiyoko's magical assault, to rip the power of that story apart before it could drag me into slumber. This wasn't true libriomancy; it was a recording, a copy of the sound. Like any reproduction, it was weaker than the original. Slowly, I freed myself and reached out to help my companions.

Lena had dropped Excalibur and the scabbard when she fell. A Kiyoko stepped from the server room to pick up the sword. She pointed the tip at Lena's throat. The other two clones joined her, guns aimed at Deb and myself.

I ripped Excalibur's magic away, dissolving the blade into silver dust. I did the same to the enchantment on the bullets. When the Kiyoko standing over me pulled the trigger, her shots struck my shield and fell to the floor.

Lena kicked the legs out from beneath her Kiyoko, rolled to the side, and punched both fists into the clone standing over me. Wooden spikes punctured Kiyoko's side, and she fell.

Bullets thudded into Lena's back, but without their magical boost, none of them penetrated. Lena spun, slashing wooden claws.

Kiyoko ducked. The third clone launched a kick over the head of the second, catching Lena square on the bridge of the nose. The second clone bounced to her feet with an uppercut to Lena's jaw, allowing the third to snap a follow-up kick to the side of my head.

Both clones stiffened and spun to look into the server room.

"You had access to the Porter database and all of my reports." I spat blood and wiped my chin. "You should have known better than to piss off the fire-spider."

I'd sent Smudge into the server room to hide. Fire-spiders liked warm, enclosed spaces. Like server cabinets. By now, he would be making a merry, melted mess of whatever cables and circuits he found.

Lena grabbed a Kiyoko by the waist and throat and threw her into the oak tree. Branches snaked around her limbs, pinning her in place. Additional branches grew out to gag both captive clones.

Only one Kiyoko remained free. She knocked Lena aside and seized my throat. Her thumbs crushed my larynx, and she spun me around so my body was between her and Lena. I tried to peel her thumbs away. When that failed, I punched her in the nose and throat. Her grip only tightened.

My blood was pounding so hard I barely heard the gunshot. Kiyoko blinked, and her hands fell away.

"You dropped your gun, asshole," said Deb. She fired again, and Kiyoko fell.

I crawled toward Deb. Kiyoko had shot her three times through the chest, and had probably assumed she was dead.

"Thanks, Isaac. This has been the most fun I've had in years." Deb dropped the gun. Her head thudded to the floor. "Finish this, would you? For all of us."

"Hold on." I searched for Excalibur's scabbard, but it had vanished when I destroyed the sword. I reached into my bag. The healing cordial was in the outer pocket.

Deb wasn't breathing.

I found the potion. I could see her magic beginning to unravel, like insects fleeing the light. I forced her mouth open and poured a mouthful down her throat. "Swallow, dammit."

I plugged her nose and pressed her mouth shut. Nothing happened. I set the potion aside and reached for the fading text of *Renfield*, trying to force it back into Deb's flesh.

Lena picked up the potion and brought a droplet to her tongue. Then she gently pulled me to my feet.

"I couldn't stop all three of them," I said. "Destroying the sword, stripping the magic from the bullets ..."

The two surviving Kiyoko clones watched impassively from Lena's newgrown oak. I stepped past them into the server room. Smudge had turned the server towers into chimneys. I squinted until I found him, and returned him to his cage. "Nice work, partner."

Lena had done some damage as well. Oak roots cracked through the tiled floor and tangled into the electrical and cables. What little equipment hadn't been destroyed in the fighting sparked and died as I approached, fried by the tech-phobic magic of Harry Dresden.

‹Talulah, we're in the server room, and the electronics are dead. Can you confirm IAS is offline?›

‹Looks that way to me. The other clones probably have

*a copy of the software, but they'd need magical assistance
to reconfigure and start again. We've got good news over
here, too.›*

Charles' mental voice broke in to say, ‹*I found the sirens. They're in a subbasement beneath Metrodora
Tower.*›

It fit the mindset we'd seen from Potts and others. Put
the sirens beneath the hospital, using the patients as human shields. ‹*I'll head over there next. Good work with
the dowsing rod. I'd expected Kiyoko to have magic-
dampers blocking your efforts.*›

‹*She did,*› said Vince. ‹*That's how we found them. You
can't just take a marine creature out of the Atlantic and
drop her in a bathtub. Sirens can survive away from the
ocean, but they need time to adjust. If McGinley wants
his sirens healthy enough to sing, that means salt water, a
filtration system, pipes to circulate and oxygenate the
water—*›

‹*I couldn't find the tanks,*› Charles cut in. ‹*Vince suggested dowsing for pipes. We found several water pipes
that weren't on the plans. I traced them beneath Metrodora, where they all vanished. That empty area has to be
the shielded room where they're holding the sirens.*›

‹*What we haven't figured out yet is how to reach that
room safely,*› said Talulah.

‹*I've got an idea about that. Keep the research tower
locked down. Babs should have called security off by
now, but we don't know who else is loyal to McGinley. I'm
on my way.*› I turned to Lena. "Will she be secure here?"

"They're not going anywhere."

"Good." I looked down. Even in death, Deb smirked
like she'd just eaten someone's canary. "Then let's finish
this."

I hurled another gate through the wall in front of us,
sending a diamond-shaped chunk of steel and cinder-

blocks into nonexistence. I stopped only long enough to use another book to conjure wings onto my shoes, and to grab Lena. Then we were flying toward Franklin Tower.

Halfway there, with the two of us twenty feet above the ground, the sirens began to sing.

Transcript of a Call from U.N. Weapons Inspector Peter Malik to Special Commission Director Aamna Bercha

Malik: Aamna? This is Peter Malik. Approximately fifteen minutes ago, our security team moved us into the Metrodora Hospital Tower. They're saying we're under attack by an as-yet-unidentified enemy.

Bercha: Is your team safe and accounted for?

Malik: We're all here, and nobody has been hurt. Security's telling us we're confined to this room, a cafeteria near the center of the tower, until they receive the all-clear.

Bercha: What's the nature of the attack?

Malik: We don't know yet. There was a commotion at the administration building, and we heard a series of gunshots. I saw what may have been a sniper firing at the admin building from another tower. Our escorts are muttering about another Vanguard attack. One mentioned a rogue libriomancer named Isaac Vainio, believed to be working with Vanguard.

Bercha: I'm calling Washington. We're pulling your team out of there.

Malik: Understood. I recommend—

[Transmission interrupted by singing in an unknown language. Screams are heard in the background. Transmission ends 36 seconds later.]

Chapter 21

THE POWER OF THAT unfiltered song stripped away rational thought, leaving me a void. I barely felt us slamming onto the rocks. I tried to fend off the magic, but it was like trying to deflect raindrops in a thunderstorm.

We'd been so close—freeing Babs and her sister, disabling the IAS before it could be deployed, stopping most of the clones on site—and it wasn't enough. In the end, I'd been little more than an annoyance, a mosquito Lawrence McGinley would swat and forget about.

My friends would die in a terrorist attack. I'd be blamed as the "magical suicide bomber" who killed them. Sure, we'd stopped Kiyoko from spreading the broadcast to other nations, but it wouldn't take long for McGinley to devise another way of upping the body count.

Only that wasn't all he'd do. He'd hunt down and destroy my brother. Lex. Nidhi. Jason. Everyone who knew the truth, dead because of my mistakes. When I closed my eyes, I saw Deb staring up at me, silently accusing. I'd gotten her killed for nothing. I ground my palms against my eyes. Deb became Lena, dead on the ground, her oak rotting behind her. Lena became Toby. Toby, who had trusted me with his daughter's life and safety.

I crawled over the rocks. I'd twisted my ankle, or possibly broken it, I didn't know. I didn't care. The pain helped distract me from the ghosts of everyone I'd killed, and the music offered a thread of hope. The promise of redemption, if I could reach the source.

Pain seared my right ear, delivered by what felt like a burning pipe cleaner. I rolled away, momentarily distracted. Smudge clung to my ear, until I thought he'd burn the lobe clean off. I started to pluck him free, but his whole body was on fire. I reached for his magic instead, tearing the text away and killing his flames in the process.

The little bastard bit me again. He wasn't burning anymore, but he dug his mandibles right into the blistered cartilage of my ear. "Perkele!" My father would have smacked me for that bit of profanity. "What the everburning hell, Smudge?"

The throbbing practically deafened me . . . and in that moment, my thoughts cleared enough to dig the earplugs from my bag and cram them into place. I screamed as the earplug brushed my burnt, blistered ear, but they muffled the song enough for me to concentrate.

I saw others stumbling, searching for the source of the music. Lena was staggering toward the hospital tower. "Lena, stop!"

A second song joined the first. Nicola Pallas' voice flowed from the PA system, filling the air with The Beatles' "Yellow Submarine," sung in her own operatic style. Lena hesitated. All around me, people collapsed to the ground, caught between two competing magics.

"Thank you, Babs," I whispered. Nicola's song was a

recording of human magic, and wasn't powerful enough to fully overcome the sirens' song. It was a Band-Aid, not a cure, and I didn't know how much time it would buy us.

Lena shoved her own earplugs into place, then pointed to Franklin Tower, a quizzical look on her face. ‹*That's new.*›

A matte black wall twenty feet high surrounded my building.

‹*Vince's doing, probably. Using one of Talulah's projects.*› Talulah had been studying the feasibility of space elevator technology. The sheer volume of material we'd need to create a working tether into Earth orbit would char any book to ash long before we'd climbed a fraction of the distance. Talulah thought the key was to find a way of using mundane materials for the elevator, with a minimum of magic to act as a catalyst for self-replication.

I hadn't read all the books she was using, several of which were in Spanish, but the principle was sound, drawing in part on research into carbon aerogel from the California Institute of Technology.

Thankfully, Vince hadn't blocked off the other towers. Only a trio of National Guardsmen stood watch at the hospital, the magic-dampers shielding them from the songs.

Their weapons snapped up to point at us. One guard shouted something I couldn't hear.

I raised my hands and loosened one of the earplugs. "You hear those songs? If you don't let me stop them, they'll kill every unprotected person within these walls."

"New Millennium is under attack, and there's a warrant for your arrest. You need to set down your books and lie facedown on the floor right now."

I shrugged. "Did I mention I'm bulletproof?"

He pulled the trigger. Bullets sparked and fell as they

struck my shield. The instant they stopped shooting, Lena darted in, striking their guns aside and following up with the flat of her swords.

All three guards were human. Even with their dampers weakening Lena and her weapons, they didn't have a chance.

I crammed the earplugs in tighter and stepped past the guards. Inside the lobby, patients and staff stumbled about like zombies. One woman struck her head repeatedly against a wall. Blood painted her face and the front of her shirt. A man at the front desk bled from both ears where he'd gouged them with his fingernails.

I grabbed the first of the guards by the feet, and dragged him over to the woman. The moment the magic-damper's field touched her, she sank to the floor and began to weep.

Lena hauled the other two inside. We positioned the three of them in a loose triangle and herded everyone together where they'd be safe.

I moved out of range. ‹*Talulah, how do we reach that subbasement?*›

‹*Over here.*› Charles Brice pushed open the stairwell door from the inside and waved us over.

‹*What are you doing here?*›

‹*You were taking your sweet time, so I decided to get started myself.*›

I let that pass and followed him to the bottom of the basement steps, where a four-foot crater in the floor smoked and sizzled. It looked like Charles had used his eye laser to slice through the tile, but I had no idea how he'd blown up the foundation and rebar below.

‹*The sirens are almost directly below us.*› Charles' hand folded back on itself to reveal a small blaster cannon. He fired again, widening the hole into the basement.

‹*When the hell did you give yourself a hand cannon,*

and who signed off on it?› I snapped. *‹Wait, don't answer that. Just put it away. We're not going to need it.›*

‹Oh, really?›

‹How far down to reach the sirens?›

‹About twenty-five feet.› The barrel of his weapon collapsed into his wrist, and his hand clicked back into place.

‹There has to be another way in,› said Lena.

Charles shrugged. *‹Not that we've been able to find.›*

Lena touched my bookbag. *‹Do you have Wayfinder in there?›*

‹Don't need it. Vince, Bi Wei, can you both hear me?›

‹What's up, Boss?›

‹I can, yes.›

I smiled. *‹I'm going to need your help with this part.›*

A low *caw* alerted us to Kerling's arrival. The crow perched on the railing halfway up the stairs.

Vince hadn't stopped mentally railing at me for keeping Kerling's abilities secret. I did my best to shut him out, and extended one arm. Kerling hopped from the rail and glided down to land on my forearm. Her claws dug through my sleeve. She had quite the grip.

Charles stared. *‹You uplifted a crow's intelligence and taught her to teleport?›*

‹She taught herself.› I smoothed the feathers by Kerling's neck. *‹Don't ask me how.›*

‹Welcome to Rise of the Planet of the Corvidae.*›*

I ignored that, too. My attention was on Bi Wei as she descended the stairs to join us.

‹Who's that?› demanded Charles.

‹A friend. She's here to help us save Kiyoko.›

‹To do what?*›*

I turned my attention to Kerling. "Vince told you where we need to go. Can you get us there?"

‹You're trusting a bird to teleport us through solid rock?› Charles backed away. ‹You're out of your mind.›

Kerling spread her wings and shivered. Magic spread like dust from her feathers. I pulled that power around myself, then extended it to Lena, Bi Wei, and Charles. Kerling nipped my hand, as if annoyed by my interference.

The stairwell vanished, replaced by a large, cool room that smelled of seawater and smoke. The overhead lights flickered.

The PA system was muffled in here, weakening the protection of Nicola's music. I could feel the sirens' song vibrating through me.

A trio of what looked like modified hot water heaters sat in the center of the room. Copper pipes and white PVC tubes fed in and out of the tanks. There were no computers, nothing but a bank of switches and lights nearby, none of which were labeled.

Kiyoko stood in front of the controls, a futuristic-looking little pistol in one hand.

Lena and Charles spread out to either side of me. Kerling flew away to perch on one of the pipes in the shadows. Bi Wei simply looked around, taking everything in.

Kiyoko reached behind without looking and pulled a lever. Several seconds later, the song died down. I loosened one earplug.

"Order Babs Palmer to cease her interference," Kiyoko said.

I forced a laugh. "Yah, Babs doesn't take orders from me." I stepped closer to the three chambers and touched the pipes. One was hot enough to burn. Frost covered another. "You're torturing them."

She pointed her weapon at me. "You're still wearing your personal shield unit from *Dune*. In addition to their vulnerability to slower-moving objects, this technology has another canonical flaw. Shooting one with a laser weapon triggers an explosion equivalent to a nuclear blast. The destruction of New Millennium and much of Las Vegas isn't the attack we were planning, but the effect would be more than adequate."

"Damn," I whispered. "I hate well-read bad guys."

"If you're thinking of deactivating your shield's magic, please keep in mind that I've watched you dissolve such spells several times, and I believe my reflexes are fast enough to shoot you before you complete your attempt."

"Why aren't you affected by the sirens?" asked Lena.

"This clone was surgically deafened. I communicate by reading lips. As long as the sirens are quiet, I can also use the audio pickups in this room to broadcast your voices to me." She glared at me. "Each time you fought me, I learned," she said. "You've lost one friend today. How many more will you sacrifice?"

"Maybe it's time to learn a different lesson."

Lena tossed her swords aside, following my lead. "Your master is a madman. Why obey him?"

Kiyoko cocked her head. "Your lover is a nerd. Why would you sleep with him? It's because that's who and what you are."

"Hey!" A twitch of the laser made me swallow my retort.

"I *chose* Isaac. What have you ever chosen?" Lena stepped closer. "Don't let Lawrence McGinley tell you what you are. Don't let someone else define you."

"We are what we were written to be. Tools. Toys. Would you try to persuade a sword to become a ploughshare?"

"What will you do when your master dies?" asked

Lena. "You can't even conceive of it, can you? You can't imagine the possibility of a different life, but there are people who can help you evolve."

"Evolution is for the living." Kiyoko's laser pistol twitched, sending a beam of light through Lena's shoulder. Blood oozed from the pencil-sized wound. The gun snapped back to me before I could take advantage of the momentary distraction. "You and I are very much alike. We're both things. The difference is that you've run from that truth."

Bi Wei stepped past us. "Do you know why Isaac invited me here?"

"To stop me. I know who and what you are. Your magic isn't fast enough to keep me from pulling this trigger."

"You're wrong, but that's beside the point. He asked me to *help* you." She held up a book, an original Japanese edition of *All of One*. "This story created you, but it doesn't define you. I look at you through these words, and I see a being much like the Students of Bi Sheng. I see a web of magic connecting you to your sisters, making you greater."

Kiyoko reached back with her free hand to flip several switches, then pushed another lever. The sirens began to sing again. The sound knocked me backward, a wave of pain passing right through the walls of the three tanks. I clapped my hands over my ears, but it wasn't enough.

"The longer you delay," shouted Kiyoko, "the more people will suffer. Contact Babs Palmer."

Charles raised his arm. His hand hinged open.

Kiyoko moved too fast to see, snapping off two shots that punctured Charles' hand and the partially protruding weapon. He shouted and clutched his arm to his chest.

"We're not here to fight you," said Bi Wei. Her words carved a path through the song, strong and clear. "We're here to bring you home."

She moved so slowly and smoothly I didn't see her magic until it touched Kiyoko's. A single strand of text and power pulsed between them. Kiyoko stiffened and closed her eyes.

Lena stumbled past them to reverse the levers on the control panel. Slowly, the sirens quieted.

Bi Wei stepped back a moment later, but Kiyoko didn't move.

"What's happening?" I asked.

"I've freed her to choose for herself."

"Great. How long will that take?"

Bi Wei lifted one hand in a gesture that reminded me of a shrug. "She has tremendous knowledge, but little experience or wisdom. She's frightened, like any child suddenly finding herself alone. I believe she's reviewing what she knows about the world, particularly New Millennium, Secretary McGinley, even yourself. She may yet decide McGinley's plan is best in the long term, depending on which variables she considers most important."

"In which case she'll go ahead and destroy this place?" demanded Charles. He started toward Kiyoko, only to freeze again when the laser twitched toward him.

"She can see you." I pointed to one of the cameras. And if she read lips, that meant I could talk to her. "Kiyoko, you have a home here, if you want it."

The clone opened her eyes. "After my part in what has occurred, the authorities would never allow—"

"I'm not planning to ask permission." I looked at Lena. "I'm not going back to Copper River. From the beginning, they've treated New Millennium like a political pawn. I intend to turn it into a sanctuary. A home."

I'd made my choice back in Michigan, but speaking

the words made them real. They also brought a sense of relief. It was amazing how much mental and emotional weight could be sloughed away with a single decision.

"That won't stop their fear," said Kiyoko. "It won't end the wars."

"No, it won't. But it will give people a choice. It will give us a place where we don't have to be afraid."

"What of those who aren't interested in sanctuary?" she asked. "Those who choose to fight?"

"We help to stop them."

She tilted her head to one side. "John Dalberg-Acton stated that power tends to corrupt, and absolute power corrupts absolutely. It's true of Secretary McGinley. It was true of Russell Potts. It was true of Johannes Gutenberg. What will make you and New Millennium any less corrupt?"

"People like Nidhi Shah. People like Jeneta Aboderin, who are more interested in knowledge and exploration and possibility. People like my brother, who'll drive over and tear me down to size if I ever get too full of myself. People like Nicola and Babs and Charles and Vince and Talulah. People like Lena, and like you."

Bi Wei handed *All of One* to Kiyoko. "We will also be watching."

"You've seen inside my head," I said. "You know I'm serious about this."

"Yes. I also believe you're frightened of the responsibility, and of the consequences of this choice."

"Oh, yah. Terrified." I grinned. "Exhilarating, isn't it? So many possibilities . . . speaking of which, what's the transmission rate for your psychic connection?"

She blinked. "Nearly instantaneous."

"Jeneta's going to want to talk to you about her Mars idea. You might solve the communication lag she was talking about. Before that, though, I want to sit down and talk about the magic you did up in admin, when you threw that sleep spell at me. We've always believed intrinsically magical beings like you and Lena were incapable of using extrinsic magic, but that's exactly what you did!"

"I recreated a recording. That's not the same thing."

Was it my imagination, or had her cheeks darkened slightly? Was she flustered? "Imitation is one method of learning, and you haven't exactly had time to study or practice. Who knows what else you might be able to do."

Slowly, Kiyoko lowered the laser pistol.

"Thank you. Don't go anywhere." While Lena took the gun, I dissolved my shield generator, just to be safe. I hurried to the tanks next. Simple padlocks held the lids in place. "Do you have the keys?"

"There's an emergency release." Kiyoko turned to the control panel. Charles started after her, but I waved him back.

The side of the first tank cracked open. Water sprayed out in a thin, scalding sheet. It smelled like salt and blood and worse. Kiyoko turned a metal wheel, triggering a squealing sound from the tank, and then a curved, rectangular section was flung open.

I did my best to catch the siren as she slid onto the floor. She was naked, her skin scalded red. Abrasions on her wrists and ankles showed where she'd been restrained. Medical sensors—the same patches I'd created, the ones I'd seen on Lex after her procedure—were secured to her scalp and throat.

She was thinner than she should have been. Healthy sirens kept a thick layer of fat to help them survive the cold water, but this one's skin sagged loosely, and I could see the curved lines of her ribs. I grabbed the healing cordial.

Her eyes widened, and she tried to squirm free.

"You're safe," said Lena through clenched teeth. "This is to heal your injuries."

A flailing fist struck the side of my face. I almost dropped the potion.

Lena caught the siren's wrist. She screamed in pain, screams that only grew louder as Kiyoko crouched and whispered into her ear.

The siren sagged, blanketed by magical sleep. I maneuvered a drop of the potion into her mouth. Blisters melted back into her skin, and the redness faded.

"Thanks." Once the siren's body was restored, I offered the potion to Lena for the wounds from Kiyoko's laser. While Lena healed herself, I pulled Kiyoko's sleep spell from the siren, like clearing cobwebs.

The siren gasped, then looked down at herself. Kiyoko had already moved back to the controls to free the second. The first crawled over and scooped the second into her arms, holding her and crooning softly while I healed her injuries. Soon, all three sirens were huddled together on the floor, trembling.

I looked around for blankets or spare clothing, but found nothing. The sirens didn't appear to care. The first one stood, completely unselfconscious. "Where are we?"

"The New Millennium complex outside of Las Vegas," I said. "The middle of Nevada."

She shuddered, though I suspect it was mostly at the idea of being stuck in the middle of a desert. "Are there others?"

"I don't think so. Not here."

‹Isaac, it's Talulah. We may have another problem.›

‹Of course we do.› Lena moved in as I stepped away. Bi Wei had vanished. I hadn't even gotten the chance to thank her. ‹What happened?›

‹We have bombers incoming. I'm tapping into military

communications. It sounds like they've been ordered to level New Millennium.

I turned to the others. "McGinley can't afford witnesses. He's called in a bombing run."

"The wards on this place ought to keep any bombs out," said Charles.

"He's ordering me to open the main gate," said Kiyoko.

I stared at her. "How is he—right, one of your clones is with him. Charles, is our military good enough to put a rocket through our front door? I'm going to take your uncharacteristic silence as a yes. They set off that first bomb, bust open our walls from the inside—"

"He has determined I'm no longer enslaved by his programming." Kiyoko jerked back as if she'd been slapped. "He has now terminated my clone."

"Are you all right?" Lena asked, moving toward Kiyoko.

"It's disconcerting."

"I'm sorry," I said. I'd killed several of her clones, at least one in a particularly painful way.

The centermost siren cleared her throat. "Would someone explain what the salty fuck is going on?"

"We're going to get you home," I said. "Give me a day or two to reconstruct the Gateway Project, and I'll deliver you directly into the Atlantic or anywhere else you'd like to go. But before I can do that, I have to stop McGinley."

"I believe I can help with that," said Kiyoko. "I am, in most respects, a living computer. I have video files of his murder of me just now, along with many other incriminating actions and conversations, including his orders to assassinate Senator Alexander Keeler."

"Magically recorded evidence won't hold up in court," said Charles.

"It doesn't have to!" I whooped.

‹Isaac, are you one hundred percent sure we can trust her?› asked Charles.

‹Nope. That's part of how freedom works. Talulah, how long until the bombers get here?›

‹Ten minutes? Maybe less?›

‹Thanks. Stand by.› I clenched my jaw and dialed a number from memory.

"This is Agent Steinkamp."

"Hello, Agent. This is Isaac Vainio. We met in Lansing."

"I remember. Where are you, Vainio? You're wanted for—"

"In nine minutes, the U.S. military is going to drop a lot of bombs on New Millennium. I'm hoping our wards will protect us, but I'd rather not take that chance, so I wanted to offer you a trade. You get in touch with someone who can call off that attack, and in return, I'll send you a data dump of video files showing DHS Secretary Lawrence McGinley conspiring to commit murder, terrorism, and other war crimes, along with information on his coconspirators."

There was a long pause. "That's quite the accusation. If you could come by the Detroit office—"

"Eight minutes, thirty seconds. Keep an eye on your email." I hung up and smiled grimly. "Kiyoko, would you please email one of those clips to jarrod.steinkamp@fbi.gov? Something short and incriminating, if possible. We're on a tight schedule."

"What if Steinkamp's involved?" asked Charles.

"Not everyone is out to get us." ‹Talulah, how long would it take you to find out who's in charge of the bombing operation and get their contact number to Agent Steinkamp?›

‹On it.›

"The email has been sent," said Kiyoko.

"Thank you. Can you override the gate controls and make sure nobody else tries to open our front door?"

"I've been relaying our conversation to Babs Palmer. She and I will ensure that New Millennium remains protected."

"Excellent." I sagged against a support pillar and took Lena's hand. "Now we wait."

CONSPIRACY IN THE CAPITAL: SECRETARY OF HOMELAND SECURITY ARRESTED

The FBI arrested Secretary of Homeland Security Lawrence McGinley yesterday at 2:45 p.m. McGinley is accused of orchestrating a series of murders earlier this month in California, Oklahoma, Michigan, and New York. He allegedly ordered the assassination of Senator Alexander Keeler, chairman of the Joint Committee on Magical Security, as well as a prison guard named Oscar Franklin, Jr.

This comes immediately following the resignation of Thomas M. Hayes, Commandant of the U. S. Coast Guard. Hayes has confessed to ordering an attack on a group of sirens off the Atlantic Coast. He claims McGinley blackmailed him, but says he was unaware of the full extent of the Secretary's plans.

Details of those plans remain unknown at this time, though McGinley is believed by many to have had a role in an attempted terrorist attack at the New Millennium site in Las Vegas, Nevada.

At least one of McGinley's would-be terrorists remains at large. Kiyoko Itô, who previously served as one of McGinley's assistants, is said to have taken refuge within New Millennium. This contradicts earlier accounts that Itô had been murdered in Washington, D.C.

A spokesperson for the FBI says they are continuing to review the evidence, and to question those in custody. They expect to issue a more detailed statement within the hour. An anonymous source within the FBI suggests this statement will implicate high-ranking figures from several other countries in what looks to have been an international conspiracy.

Chapter 22

I KNOCKED ON THE door and waited. This was a run-down neighborhood, and the small house was in dire need of repair. The shingles were rotting away, one of the windows was boarded over, and the lawn was an overgrown mess. How long had it been since this family could afford the upkeep on their home?

"They might not be home." Nidhi stood behind me.

Technically, I shouldn't have been here at all. I was still wanted for any number of things, including destruction of Coast Guard property and however they wanted to classify my break-in to an illegal secret prison.

"If they're not home, we'll wait." I knocked again.

The door opened. The man in the doorway flinched when he recognized me.

"Mister Blackburn. Are your wife and son home this morning?"

He didn't answer right away. I didn't need Nidhi's insight to recognize the conflict on his face. The last time he'd seen me was after the Joint Committee hearing, when I'd refused to help his son Caleb.

He'd probably heard the news about me and New Millennium. He kept looking past me, checking up and down the street like he was searching for the police. "What do you want?"

Beneath his exhaustion and pain, I heard hope. Hope, and the fear of letting himself hope. "I'm here to help your boy. Hypoplastic left heart syndrome, wasn't it?"

"Yeah. Yeah, that's right." He nodded hard, then stepped to one side. "Come in."

A corpulent corgi waddled up to sniff us both. The dog barked once, then trotted off, its duty as a watchdog done.

"Louise?" Mr. Blackburn called out. "Get Caleb and get out here!"

Paper jack-o'-lanterns decorated the walls. A family photo above the couch showed Mr. Blackburn and his wife, along with their son Caleb and a second boy, this one a few years older. I guessed he was the artist who'd created the Halloween decorations.

Mrs. Blackburn emerged from the hallway, Caleb following close behind. She froze when she saw me.

"He says he's here to fix Caleb," her husband said.

She put a hand down to keep Caleb behind her. "Is it safe?"

I sat down on the old carpet and pulled out a polished wooden pen. "This used to be a sword named Wound-healer. Its power comes from a book by a man named Fred Saberhagen. It will heal his heart, and any other injuries. That's all. No side effects, no follow-up. Nothing but a healthy boy with a long life ahead of him."

"How did you find us?" she asked.

I cocked my head. "Magic librarian, remember?"

They looked at one another, communicating as effectively without words as Talulah did with her telepathy. The father nodded and said, "Do it. What do you need? Will it hurt?"

"It shouldn't hurt at all. Could you take Caleb's shirt off for me?" I winked at Caleb. "It might tickle, though."

A scar down the center of Caleb's chest showed where surgeons had tried to fix his heart. Caleb clung to his mother's hand with one of his own and sucked the knuckles of his other. He seemed not so much anxious as resigned. How many times had this kid been poked and prodded and examined in his short life?

I twirled the pen through my fingers. "We want your heart to be happy, right?"

He nodded warily.

"Great. I'm gonna draw a smiley face right over your heart." I frowned and rubbed my chin. "Can you remind me where your heart is?"

He shook his head.

I poked his foot. "Is it in here?"

He shook his head again, but I saw a trace of a smile.

"What about your armpit? Is that where you keep your heart?"

He shook his head again, pulled his hand out of his mouth, and touched his chest.

"Oh, right. That's a good place for it. Very traditional." I brought the pen to his chest and drew two quick circles for eyes, then a larger arc for the smile. The eyes ended up lopsided, and the smile was too wide, more like the Joker from Batman than a traditional happy face, but it didn't matter.

I capped the pen, tucked it away, and studied Caleb over the top of my new glasses to make sure the magic was active. "All set."

"That . . . that's it?" asked Louise. "That's all it takes?"

"How do we know he's really better?" asked her husband.

"Take him for a checkup," said Nidhi. "They'll want to run a number of tests. Let them do as many as it takes for you to be sure, and then take Caleb and his brother out to celebrate."

"I recommend ice cream," I added.

Caleb's father was crying silently. His mother just stared, like it hadn't sunk in yet. As for Caleb, he'd pulled away and run back down the hall to play.

"You said it was illegal," Louise whispered. "The other week, when we asked you for help. Will you get into trouble? Will we? Will they try to take Caleb away from us?"

"I'm already in trouble." I stood and stretched. "I've decided I don't give a— I've decided I don't care. When the doctors ask, tell them I broke into your house and healed him without your permission. Everyone saw that video clip after the hearing. They saw how frustrated I was. You had nothing to do with it."

"If you have any trouble, call us," said Nidhi.

"Anywhere, any time. I'll be able to get to you." I grinned. "I've almost got my teleporter back up and running again."

Mr. Blackburn grabbed my hand and squeezed. "Thank you. Thank you so much."

"I'm sorry I couldn't—didn't do this before." I watched him and his wife step back, their arms slipping around one another. "And thank *you*."

"What for?" asked Mrs. Blackburn.

I smiled. "For letting me know I made the right decision."

I waved to Marion as we drove through the front gates. I'd left Babs in charge of security while I was away. We'd given Darlene Jackson-Palmer a permanent apartment on site for as long as she wanted. I still had to talk to Babs about the ghosts in the walls, but that was one of many conversations Babs and I needed to hash out, and I wanted at least one day to recover before diving into my new job running New Millennium.

Lena was waiting for us at the parking lot. She kissed us both, slipped between us, and hooked her arms through ours. "Well?"

"We met with Nicola," said Nidhi. "She'll be staying in D.C. She believes the Porters have an important role to play in the world. But she and Vaughn are going to try to legalize this place."

"Normally, there's no way anyone would even consider it," I said. "But between the black eye the country's sporting thanks to McGinley's crimes and the fact that they don't have the physical ability to force us out, he thinks we might have a shot. He's going to write a bill that would treat New Millennium like a reservation."

In the past three days, we'd had close to three hundred people ask to make New Millennium their home, with more requests coming in every day.

Off to the right, two harpies played Frisbee sixty feet in the air. A group of young werewolves were tearing along the inner edge of the wall, dust and gravel spraying from their paws. A vampire and a libriomancer sat on a bench outside the newly converted DeGeorge Orientation Center, arguing over a book.

I'd offered Rabbi Miller a position in the DeGeorge Center, helping new arrivals, but he'd turned me down. For now, one of the Kiyokos was overseeing things. Twenty-three clones had come to live at New Millennium. If my math was right, that left at least half a dozen scattered across the world. When I asked Kiyoko if the rest of her sisters would be joining us, she simply smiled and said she wanted to see the world.

"How long before the two of you fly back to Michigan?" I asked.

"Tomorrow evening," said Nidhi. "I have clients scheduled for the day after."

I tried to keep my disappointment from showing. "Makes sense. And Lena needs to get back to her oak. The one she grew in the old server room isn't the same, I know."

"It kind of is," said Lena. "I grew it from the wood inside my body, and that wood comes from my oak in Michigan. It's a young clone. You're right, though. It's too young and small to sustain me, and we've *got* to get it transplanted somewhere with sun and soil."

"I'll see what we can do. Maybe when it's grown, you'll be able to stay longer."

They looked at one another. Lena kissed Nidhi's hand and said, "You could try one of those shrinking potions. It would be a lot easier to remove a tree the size of a bonsai. Then you'd just remove the magic and restore it to its proper size."

"Makes sense. I'll have to figure out how best to get an oak tree to drink a magic potion."

"Once you've done that," Lena continued, "it should be easy enough to do the same with my oak back in Michigan."

I stopped walking. "What do you mean?"

"I'm not about to trust some commercial service to transport my tree from Michigan to Nevada." She grinned and stepped off the sidewalk. "What would you think of a greenhouse over past the western residential building? The crops would help feed your expanding population."

I hadn't moved. "You're talking about moving here?"

"For someone so smart, you can be slow on the uptake sometimes." She blew me a kiss.

"What about Nidhi?"

"I'll need a few weeks to close out my cases in Michigan," said Nidhi. "But I think I could make this work.

With all the different cultures and backgrounds you're bringing into these walls, you'll need a mental health professional on staff. Especially with the fellow who's running things."

"Hey, now," I said, but she just chuckled. "Yah, you're right. If you have other therapists you'd recommend, I'll take all the help I can get. We've got members from three different werewolf packs squabbling about status. There's the proposed 'exchange program' between us and the Students of Bi Sheng. Any number of people here have lost friends or loved ones in all the fighting over the past year. I can talk to Kiyoko about living quarters. I'm not sure where the best place for Lena's oak would be. We should probably bring in some healthier soil, and we'll need to irrigate—"

"You're babbling," Lena said, laughing.

"You're damn right!" I walked over and threw my arms around her. "How long have you two been talking about this?"

"Since you gave me Gutenberg's book," said Nidhi.

I swallowed. "Thank you. Thank you both."

"It's not just about you." Lena turned away. "I've been going out these past few nights, while the two of you were in D.C."

"We should do that more often," I agreed. "I can't stand the crowds at the casinos, and traffic's a nightmare, but there are some great shows—"

"That's not what I meant. I kept thinking about Oscar Franklin in Virginia. The *wrongness* I felt from what he'd been doing." She shuddered. "I've been walking the streets at night or wandering through the hotels. Vegas is quite the sexually active city. Twice so far, I've sensed that same wrongness, that utter perversion of what should be a beautiful thing. Once was a man beating a prostitute. The other was a drunk boyfriend."

I glanced at Nidhi, who shook her head ever so slightly. This was news to her as well.

"What did you do?" asked Nidhi.

"I stopped them. I made sure the victims were all right, and then I offered to help them get home, or to go with them to the police if they wanted. Neither of them did." She shook her head. "I know having a vigilante running loose isn't the publicity New Millennium needs, but I feel like this is something I have to do."

"Well," I said slowly, "we should probably get you a mask."

"No capes," added Nidhi.

"You'll want to switch weapons. You're not exactly unknown, and there aren't many dryads running around with wooden swords."

"I'll get you cards with information about rape crisis hotlines," said Nidhi. "People sometimes change their minds about talking a day or two after the assault."

"What if we got you a light saber?" I asked. "A green one, naturally."

"Have you thought of a name?"

Lena pulled away from us both. "You're not angry?"

Nidhi smiled. "I get to bed a superhero. What I'm feeling is not anger."

"I trust you," I said. "We both do. You could have killed Franklin, but you didn't. As the administrator of this facility, I can't officially acknowledge or condone what you're doing. As your lover, I'm nothing but proud."

"Thank you." She kissed us both.

"Uncle Isaac!" Lex, Toby, and Angie had emerged from the Metrodora Tower. Lex was running toward me.

"I may have let them know you were back," Lena whispered.

"Thanks." I grinned and hugged Lex. "I take it the follow-up check went well? Look how fast you can run!

Are you sure we didn't accidentally give you bionic legs?"

"Dad says we can't stay here forever," she pouted.

"You're welcome to stay a while, but your parents have friends and family and work back home, and what about you? You've got school to catch up on, and friends to see, right?"

"I have friends here, too," she protested. "One of them made me this tiara. She pulled it out of her cell-phone!"

That would be Jeneta. Given all they had been through, they were one of the first families I'd invited to join us. Only Jeneta and her father had accepted so far.

Toby clapped me on the shoulder. "I half expected them to throw you in jail and toss away the key."

"I'm sure they'll try."

"My brother, declaring independence from the world." He shook his head. "Are you sure you know what you're doing?"

"Is he ever?" asked Lena.

"You have no idea." I rubbed my forehead, thinking of the various reports and emails waiting on my desk. "I've got three different proposals for starting a school. The vampires are negotiating with local cattle farmers for a steady blood supply. Vegas jacked up water and sewage prices. My research team is squabbling over office space again. Now that I've kicked out most of the DHS and NIH folks, we need to completely revamp our oversight process. Then there's negotiating with different countries about setting up additional New Millennium sites around the world. I'm tempted to drop Smudge on top of the paperwork and let him deal with it."

Lex tugged her mother's hand. "Can I go play tag with the werewolves?"

Angie paled. Toby winced. They both looked at me.

"She'll be fine," I assured them. "Those two are from the pack in the U.P. They know me, and they know what will happen if they hurt anyone. Especially my niece. They'll be as gentle with her as they would a newborn pup."

"Thanks!" Lex took off before her parents could speak. Toby and Angie both started running after her.

"Have fun," I yelled.

Toby turned long enough to shout, "Mom and Dad said to call them!"

"I will!"

I wished they could stay longer, but we needed the room. The Metrodora Medical Tower was ninety percent full, with more patients arriving daily. I had a team poring through our catalogs, searching for the most efficient healing magic and technologies for the influx of disease and injury. We only accepted patients who couldn't be helped by mundane medicine, but their numbers were in the millions.

It was overwhelming, but we'd figure it out. This was magic, after all. The possibilities were limitless.

My name is Isaac Vainio. Until a week ago, I was the Director of Research for New Millennium.

Johannes Gutenberg never believed humanity could accept magic and those of us who use it. He feared humanity would use magic as a weapon of war. That you would work to enslave or destroy us. Looking at the events of the past few months, I can hear his "I told you so" as if he were standing right beside me.

Gutenberg was right. He was also wrong.

One year ago, I wrote a letter to the world, a revelation of magic. Today, I write a declaration.

We've been here for millennia. We're not your enemies. We're your friends and family. Your neighbors, whether you knew we were there or not. And we're not going anywhere.

It's going to take time for the world to adjust. Change is confusing and frightening and at times violent. This isn't going to be pretty, folks. But we're not here to get in the middle of a war.

I'm declaring New Millennium a place of peace, a home and refuge for those of us who need one. Anyone with magic is welcome here, so long as you harm no one. We've also opened up our medical facilities to anyone in need. Don't worry about cost or transportation. Contact us with your situation, and we'll do what we can to help.

There's no such thing as a utopia. The world has problems, and so will we. To that end, we will work with the world to help you bring magical criminals to justice. New Millennium will not be a haven for any who want death or violence.

This is our home. I intend to make it a place of hope. A place you can bring your loved ones for medical treatment. A place where we can look forward, where we can show you exactly how awesome magic can be.

New Millennium can't stop your wars. What we can do is set our sights higher. We mean to build a path to the stars, and to the future.

I hope you'll join us.

Bibliography

Titles marked with an asterisk (*) were made up for this book.

Adams, Douglas. *The Hitchhiker's Guide to the Galaxy*.
Bell, Hilari. *The Goblin Wood*.
Brice, Charles L. *Dark Wanderer*.*
Burgis, Stephanie. *A Most Improper Magick*.
Butcher, Jim. *Small Favor*.
Carroll, Lewis. *Through the Looking Glass*.
Cole, Myke. *Control Point*.
Crichton, Michael. *Jurassic Park*.
Dick, Philip K. *Flow My Tears, The Policeman Said*.
Donaldson, Stephen. *The Mirror of Her Dreams*.
Foster, Alan Dean. *Alien*.
Gabaldon, Diana. *Outlander*.
Gaiman, Neil. *Neverwhere*.
Gibson, William. *Neuromancer*.
Goodkind, Terry. *Debt of Bones*.
Herbert, Frank. *Dune*.
Homer. *The Odyssey*.

Howe, Deborah and James. *Bunnicula*.

Kafka, Franz. *The Metamorphosis*.

King, Stephen. *Firestarter*.

Kuronuma, Shunrō. *All of One*.*

Lackey, Mercedes. *Tales of the Five Hundred Kingdoms*.

L'Engle, Madeline. *A Wrinkle in Time*.

Lewis, C. S. *The Lion, The Witch, and the Wardrobe*.

Lofting, Hugh. *The Story of Doctor Dolittle*.

McIntosh, Darren. *Blackout 2020*.*

Meyer, Stephenie. *Twilight*.

Neureither, Marion. *Sea Change*.*

Okorafor, Nnedi. *Zahrah the Windseeker*.

Page, Shannon and Lake, Jay. *Our Lady of the Islands*.

Pierce, Tamora. *In the Hand of the Goddess*.

Pilkey, Dav. *The Adventures of Captain Underpants*.

Riordan, Rick. *The Lightning Thief*.

Rockwell, Thomas. *How to Eat Fried Worms*.

Rowling, J. K. *Harry Potter and the Prisoner of Azkaban*.

Saberhagen, Fred. *The Complete Book of Swords*.

Stern, Roger. *The Death and Life of Superman*.

Stevenson, Robert Louis. *Treasure Island*.

Stroud, Jonathan. *The Golem's Eye*.

Tolkien, J. R. R. *The Fellowship of the Ring*.

Valente, Catherynne. *Palimpsest*.

Wallace, Samantha. *Renfield*.*

Wells, H. G. *The Complete Short Stories of H. G. Wells*.

White, E. B. *Stuart Little*.

Wright, James. *Nymphs of Neptune*.*

Once upon a time...

Cinderella, whose real name is Danielle
Whiteshore, did marry Prince Armand.
And their wedding was a dream come true.

But not long after the "happily ever after,"
Danielle is attacked by her stepsister Charlotte,
who suddenly has all sorts of magic to call upon.
And though Talia the martial arts master—
otherwise known as Sleeping Beauty—
comes to the rescue, Charlotte gets away.

That's when Danielle discovers a number of disturbing facts: Armand has been kidnapped; Danielle is
pregnant; and the Queen has her own Secret Service
that consists of Talia and Snow (White, of course).
Snow is an expert at mirror magic and heavy-duty
flirting. Can the princesses track down Armand and
rescue him from the clutches of some of
Fantasyland's most nefarious villains?

The Stepsister Scheme
by Jim C. Hines
978-0-7564-0532-8

"Do we look like we need to be rescued?"